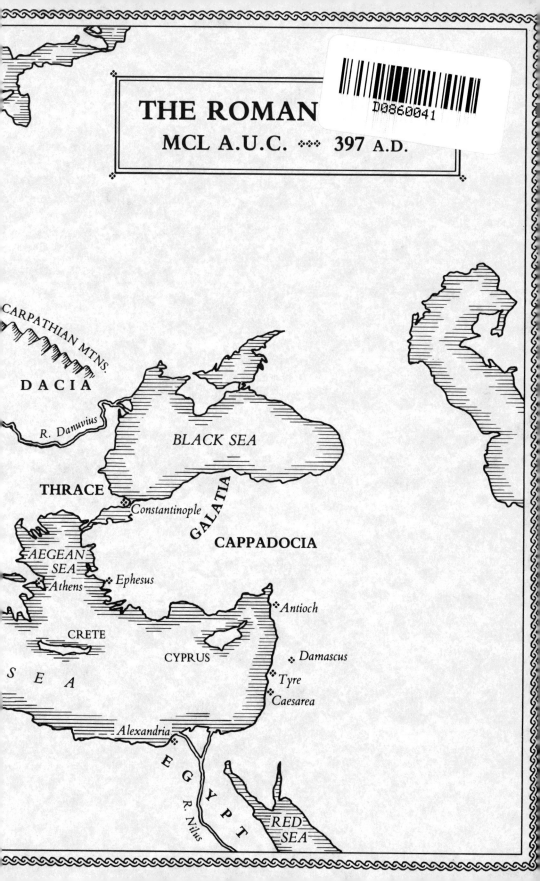

THE ROMAN

MCL A.U.C. ❖❖❖ 397 A.D.

CARPATHIAN MTNS.

DACIA

R. Danuvius

THRACE

BLACK SEA

GALATIA

Constantinople

CAPPADOCIA

AEGEAN
SEA

Athens

Ephesus

Antioch

CRETE

CYPRUS

Damascus

S E A

Tyre

Caesarea

Alexandria

E G Y P T

R. Nilus

RED
SEA

DOMINIC

DOMINIC

KATHLEEN
ROBINSON

St. Martin's Press   New York

Production Editor: David Stanford Burr

Library of Congress Cataloging-in-Publication Data

Robinson, Kathleen.
  Dominic / Kathleen Robinson.
      p.   cm.
    ISBN 0-312-06340-7
    I. Title.
  PS3568.O28919D6   1991
  813'.54—dc20   91-21547
                                        CIP

First Edition: October 1991

10 9 8 7 6 5 4 3 2 1

DESIGN BY JUDITH A. STAGNITTO

For
Mom and Dad
with Love.
Thanks for
believing in me.

Special thanks to Richard Curtis, Sandra McCormack, and Jordan Pavlin, for loving *Dominic* as much as I do.

PART I

I

Had my father been a Roman aristocrat, or a philosopher, he might have abandoned me to the wolves at my birth, for I was from the first dwarfed and odd-shapen, of little use to a poor Gallic goatherder. Fortunately, he was a simple man, and a good-hearted man in the bargain. Therefore, when I was laid at his feet by old Elgge the midwife for the acceptance ritual, my father lifted me up and cradled me in his arms, taking me, his only child, into his heart —loving me none the less for my stunted form. Neither did my mother lament over the short, stubby limbs I aimlessly waved, nor over the large, ungainly head I could scarcely move. Instead, she took me to her breast and heart.

I was christened Dominicus Dio, meaning "belonging to the Lord God," though I remained always uncommonly small to carry a six syllable name and can only remember being called simply "Dominic." The village priest baptized me into his Arian-Christian flock, the tenants who lived, worked, and died on the estate of Lucius Scipio Marcianus, province of Germania Superior, diocese of Gaul, in the western domain of the Roman Empire. The year was 375 from the Birth of Our Lord and, as Pagans reckon it, 1128 from the Founding of Rome.

I learned to crawl on the cool earth-packed floor of a round, wooden hut. In the beginning, that one dim circular room, with its mingled odors of soil, straw, sweat, wood, smoke, frying bread, warm goat's milk, and pungent goat-hide, was my universe. Once I had climbed upon and tumbled off every stool, bench, tabletop, bed, and barrel, once I had repeatedly pulled everything upon my head that could be pulled and eagerly burned my fingers on the coals and gravely tasted the charred wood-chips, once I had explored it all to my satisfaction, I then learned to step my bare feet up from the dirt floor to the huge (in my estimation) flat stone just inside the door, from there out onto the wooden threshold where I tottered elatedly on stumpy legs to take in my new domain. Assuredly I had crossed that threshold before on my mother's hip or my father's shoulders, but now I had come to it myself. Having conquered the hut, I could now set my ambitions on the forest-ringed clearing.

Trailing after Mama, I discovered the goat pens and the clay milking jars. After dutifully sampling the manure and the milk and the goat-hair, I went about making friends with the goats, somehow surviving their jumpy hooves, their nipping teeth, and their testy rebuttals. I learned which ones to chase and which ones to leave alone and how to milk the nannies. I watched Papa load the capped jars into the cart, saving always one jar for us, and lead the donkey away along the rutted track that wound into the forest. I lived through both successful and unsuccessful attempts at scrambling onto the donkey's back after luring him with salt to where I perched atop the fence. Sometimes I rode on the milk cart with Papa, following that mysterious road beneath the shadowy trees into the village, where I stared at the folk just as curiously as they stared at me. And I noticed with secret delight that yet another road, no wider than the cart track but much more trampled, wound away from the village into as yet unknown territory.

But to satisfy my exploring spirit I had the beckoning forest paths that led from the clearing around our little hut and goat-shed, paths that tunnelled deep into the woods where I could chase sunlight and shadow beneath gnarled oaks and shimmering maples, colonnades of stiff-needled pines, tall ash and white birch and scratchy, scented cedar. Mama and Papa let me roam, and more than once (but not so often as to vex them *too* much) one or the other had to come looking for me when I forgot the time or lost my path; then I would get a scolding and yet another patient lesson in landmarking and backtracking.

Still, I would not be kept from the forest. I loved its moist, fragrant earth, lush green bracken, and springy floor of brown needles full of crawling things and scurrying creatures which moved along the ground unseen except for an occasional trembling leaf or stalk that betrayed their passage. And the creatures I did see! Chattering squirrels and quarrelsome birds shattered the hushed stillness; small red foxes slipped shyly into the brush at my approach; deer stepped softly to a woodland pond and then startled away, sensing my stealthy presence. Ah, there were owls and hawks and bats and mice and weasels and rabbits, yet I was always reminded there were dangerous things, too, should I stray too far—wild boar and bear and wolves—but I only heard the hunting wolves howl from afar, and I spied down on fishing brown bear but once from high atop a ridge.

The meadows were my playground in spring and summer. When I could keep up (at least most of the way) Papa let me follow him as he drove the goats to the high grazing on mountain pastures. There we whiled the day together, wandering the hills and keeping a watchful eye on the goats. Then, toward evensong, Papa would let me blow the goat-horn, and the big billy would come trotting with billies and nannies and kids trailing behind him. On days when Papa must cut wood and cart it down-mountain to the Imperial Inn and Post, Mama and I herded the goats ourselves. We played and sang together and told each other tales. Mama's voice was high and clear and trilling; she sang ballads and lovers' tales with endings both happy and sad. She was slim and wispy and had a merry smile; she called me her little "elfkin" and playfully tugged at my headful of auburn-curled "elflocks" as we walked the gentle swells of green grasses or picked the wildflowers that flourished the high meadows like fallen bits of rainbow.

Mama knew tales, too, of heroes with swords who battled foul giants and wooed fair maidens and died tragic, noble deaths. I told my own stories—incoherent collages of odd bits and snitches I collected here and there—and Mama feigned surprise or terror or tears and led me on with nods and sighs.

"Dominic, my elfkin, you tell lovely tales. And you always give them happy endings."

"I like the tales that end happy the best, Mama. Why do they make the sad ones?"

Mama smiled. "Because life is like that—true tales don't always have happy endings either."

"Why not?"

"Because they don't, elfkin. Sad things happen and wonderful things happen and they all mix up together and then at the end . . . why, I suppose the end is a little of both. Aye, true tales are merry-go-sorry tales, so you cry and laugh at the same time. Living is like that."

"But we never cry, do we, Mama?"

"Be sure we do."

"But not for really *sad*!"

"That's because we have a happy tale, love." Playfully she shoved me backwards into the sweet-smelling grass. "So let me hear you laugh!" She leapt to the attack with tickling fingers. I shrieked in gleeful torment and rolled across the meadow, and Mama tickled me all the way down the hill until we both collapsed in a breathless, giggling heap.

Most times I stayed home with Mama when Papa took the goats. We worked the little vegetable garden, though I am certain at first I trampled more vegetables than I tended, but Mama patiently set me to pulling weeds and shooing crows. She kept me busy with little chores like feeding the hens and gathering eggs while she boiled goat's-milk and stirred it, squeezed it, and set it up into cheese; or she crushed barley, mixed and kneaded it, and baked barley bread; or she scrubbed and brushed goat's-wool which she carried to old Elgge who then spun it and wove it on her loom into thick cloth for warm winter clothing.

As I grew older Papa took me more and more often up the wooded trails with the goats to the high pastures. I still remember the day I first strode to the grassy top of the highest meadow. I was no more than five years old when I stood proudly beside my papa on that windswept mountain; the sun's late afternoon rays lit the dancing grass with streaks of gold while we gazed eastward to the blue-grey horizon. The mottled green forest below us dived steeply to a wide, wooded valley and ascended the hills again on the farther side.

"Look there, Dominic," pointed Papa, "there at the bottom of the valley. Do you see the river?"

I followed his finger and found a glinting blue-white thread amid the trees. "I see it now!" I exclaimed excitedly. "Why, I thought 'twas a *big* river!"

"Be sure, the River Rhine is big enough, but we're far from it here. That river marks the edge of the Empire. All on this bank of the Rhine belongs to Rome and all on that bank—"

"To barbarians!" I finished for him, pleased that I knew so much already. My eyes searched the far ridges. "But I can't see any."

6

"No more than they can see us, boy," he chuckled. "We're much too far away. Burgundians live in those woods. They're going through a quiet spell now—keeping mostly to their side of the river—but I hear down at the inn that up north Franks are raiding across river again. They've taken to rafting the current, too, and settling down with their near kin in the provinces." He shook his head in bafflement. "*Something* draws them into the Empire, though I can't think what. Seems to me life would be *free* over there, out from under Rome."

"Then why don't we live there, Papa?"

Papa looked to the eastern hills, his hand resting lightly on my head. "I have thought . . . but I doubt the barbarians would welcome us kindly. Besides, 'twould mean leaving so much behind—the house, the garden, and the goats, and the stipends of course, and the talk at the inn, and friends—no, we're Gauls, Dominic. Our folk have lived here since the raising of the mountains, long before the Romans, before Caesar, and we'll stay. Romans may take their tributes and call it theirs, but the land is ours. We will not run to the wilds."

On impulse I turned and looked to the western horizon where the sun tinted clouds pink and gold. Seeing only patches of woods and plains, I frowned.

"But where's the other side of the Empire, Papa?"

"The other side?" he smiled. "Son, you might travel for months and not see an end to the Roman Empire, and when you did, you'd be stopped by the sea. And at that you've seen only the west; there's still the eastern half. Look carefully. Do you see that bright streak gleaming at the edge of the wood?"

I nodded.

"That little river there flows west to the town of Treverorum. But look quickly before the clouds shadow it—can you see the highway that runs south to meet the river?"

I finally detected a tiny broken line I took to be a section of road; I nodded again.

"Now *that* road, Dominic, will go through more towns than you ever heard of and then eventually to Rome."

"Have you been there? To Rome?"

"Not likely," he answered, gazing at the bit of distant highway. "We're thousands of miles from Rome. I've not even been as far as Treverorum, nor am I likely to. Neither are you, son, unless. . . ." His gaze dropped thoughtfully to me.

"Unless what, Papa?"

"Unless, mayhap, God had something different in mind when He made you. But, Dominic, though we are bound to this land that Rome says belongs to Lucius Scipio Marcianus, and we may not lawfully leave it, remember: We are coloni; we are not slaves; here we have our own kind of freedom. In Rome, and in the towns, 'twould be worse, maybe especially for one like you, lad. Here our lives are our own until tax time, and as long as we give them what they consider their due, they leave us alone. Aye, we belong to this land as much as it belongs to us. Gaul is in our blood, son."

I looked down studiously at a scraped knee, trying to grasp some sense to his last statement. Ah, I thought, I likely had gotten enough Gallic dirt in that cut to have some of Gaul in my blood, too.

Papa swept his vision across the forested hills, where the sun ignited the tallest trees with brilliant green fire and cast others into deepening shadows. A sudden coolness in the air and the evensong of a mourning dove betokened the beginnings of twilight.

"Let's be off home, elfkin, before the wood grows too dark to see the path."

We hurried down the mountainside, my short-legged trot barely keeping pace with my father's stride. Papa lifted me onto his broad shoulders and let me blow the goat-horn's mournful note across the meadows, but the impatient goats were already gathered, awaiting us beside the path. Though darkness closed swiftly, both we and the goats well knew the way home. I rode all the way on Papa's shoulders, a position which always delighted me, for I could view the world from a giant's perspective and sit so high that overhanging leaves brushed my head. But tonight I was not looking; I was thinking.

For the first time I began putting together two facts. First, the road from our home connected in the village to another road which eventually reached the country estate of Lucius Scipio Marcianus, and from there it must somewhere connect to the highway for Treverorum, from which yet another highway ran, I had no doubt, straight to Rome. Second, I would likely never set foot upon those highways because I was bound to the land. A colonus belongs to the estate; he cannot leave by law. That, I realized, meant me—and my papa. Certainly he had never been anywhere off the estate. He could not.

But then Papa had said mayhap God had something different in mind when He made me. Now I began to struggle with that inexplicable difference. On the foregoing Sun's Day I had heard hard words from an older cousin's lips. Playing "catch me if you can" with the village children behind the basilica after Mass while the grownups gathered in front for news and gossip, I stumbled and fell just in time to trip my cousin and get him caught.

"You dumb *dwarf!*" he yelled in a fury. "Why don't you go back to the goblins where you belong?"

I stared at him, perplexed.

"I *never* belonged to goblins."

"Oh yes you did! My papa said you're a changeling! He said goblins came in the night and took the real babe away and left *you* instead, 'cause he knows you're no blood-kin of ours!"

"They did not!"

"They did so! And Papa said someday the goblins will come back for you and take you away to their caves and make you one of them!"

"They won't!" I wailed, terrified.

"They'll come creeping in one night and snatch you up and—"

"They never will!"

"—carry you deep underground and put awful magic spells on you—"

"No!"

"—and send you back to put nasty curses on all of us!"

"I'm not—I'm not what you said!"

"Changeling! Changeling!" He pointed his finger and jeered.

"Stop it!"

"Papa says there's no dwarf blood in *our* family and he never heard of any dwarf blood in *your* papa's family, so the hobgoblins must've brought you."

"You lie!" I screamed, charging at him and swinging my fists. But he was bigger and faster and dodged easily out of my way.

"Hobgoblin! Hobgoblin!" he taunted. "Can't catch me!"

Then his brother and the others—children I had been playing with happily just moments before—took up the chant.

"*Hobgoblin! Hobgoblin! Can't catch me!*"

"Shut up!"

"*Hobgoblin! Hobgoblin! Can't catch me!*"

"Who wants to!" I shouted, burning with rage. I fled them then, taking refuge at the front of the basilica where the grownups milled. Banished from their play, I sat forlornly on the portico steps and reviled their words. *It isn't true,* I muttered vehemently. *I don't belong to goblins.*

I wrestled with their taunts once again as I rode my papa's shoulders through the darkling wood, though I spoke nought of them until we were at last home, the goats penned, and we sat at table for supper.

"Have we dwarf blood in our family?" I ventured cautiously as I tore a piece of crusted, dark bread from the round loaf and watched for my parents' reactions from beneath a tangle of red curls.

Mama paused in pouring milk into my cup for just an instant and met Papa's glance across the table. She shook back her dark brown hair, filled the cup, and set the clay pitcher down deliberately.

"I suppose we do, love, somewhere," she told me matter-of-factly, "else we wouldn't have you, would we now?" She ladled boiled turnips and broth into my bowl.

"I'm not a changeling, then?"

"A *what?*" Papa exclaimed sharply in disbelief.

"A changeling."

"Where did you ever get a fool notion like that, Dominic?"

I breathed relief. It must not be true. "Sivor said his papa said the goblins came and changed me for the real babe because I'm no blood-kin of his so I must be a hobgoblin and they're going to take me away underground—the goblins won't take me, will they, Papa?" I stared at him round-eyed.

Papa had gone red in the face. "By God, be sure no goblins will take you, boy! You're no changeling!" He spoke grimly to Mama. "I'm going to have words with your brother, Rhihanna."

"And I!" she blazed. "Dominic, you're our own child, and there are no goblins. That's just silly tales to frighten children."

"How do you know I'm not a changeling?"

She laughed, a short burst of merriment. "Why, wasn't I there at your birthing? You came from my womb, my own little elfkin, just as you are now, only so much tinier. Be sure, you were never changed on me."

Ah, my mother would never lie.

"What *is* a dwarf, Mama? What does it mean?"

"It means, love," she began, brushing back my elflocks with affection, "one who is smaller than other people."

"Won't I grow taller?"

"Some."

"How some?"

"Never very tall, dear." She glanced at Papa in the glimmering lamplight. "And it means you are built sturdier, too, with shorter arms and legs, but fine strong hands and a noble head."

I shook the noble head vigorously. "I don't want to be a dwarf."

Now my parents looked at each other helplessly across the table. Papa cleared his throat.

"'Tisn't your choice, Dominic. 'Twas God's choice. He made you special—not like ordinary folk. He must have some purpose of His own for you, lad."

"So we are blessed with a dwarf child," Mama added. "'Tis why we named you Dominicus Dio, for you must be as special to the Lord as you are to us. Just have faith in the Lord's wisdom, and you'll never go wrong. He'll take care of you, love."

I looked from one to the other. They seemed so eager for me to understand, and I wanted not to disappoint them. Besides, I had full faith in my parents' wisdom, if not God's. I heaved my shoulders and dropped them with a long sigh.

"All right," I nodded and bent to my soup, privately resolving to fool them all and grow up just the same as everybody else. But I did not miss Papa's and Mama's eyes meeting, full of relief and worry.

Papa did indeed have words with my uncle, because my cousins never taunted me outright after that. But they laughed and whispered to the other children in a vicious campaign against me. I could see no reason for their cruel games, other than to deliberately hurt, and they did a good job of that.

Come late fall we drove the goats down for the tax collector and estate master to take their due. Then we returned home with the remaining goats and enough barley and oat fodder to last them the winter. Though Papa no longer had to take the herd to pasture, his quota of firewood for the inn was much increased in winter.

Roman law required that Lucius Scipio Marcianus maintain on the main road that bordered his estate an inn-and-post for the convenience of imperial agents, post messengers, tax assessors, military police, and other officials on imperial business. Papa chopped wood daily and took it down to the inn by the cartload, where the amount would be tallied to determine his monthly stipend of salt pork, barley, beans, olive oil, and vinegar wine. Papa was not the only man doing this same labor, for it took many wagonloads of wood to board the soldiers and travelers the inn hosted. Papa enjoyed his trips to the inn; he heard news from all over the Empire from the innkeeper and servants. On a winter's

11

evening he would prop his feet up by the fire after supper and tell Mama and me what official news or officially denied rumor he heard that day, or what mishap occurred on the estate, or the latest jest the stablehand rambled off. Our little hut seemed to me the cozy center of a turbulent world, snug against raving emperors and rampaging weather alike.

Papa knew tales, too, of the ancient gods—not just the Roman gods with their high-sounding names and questionable moralities, but also the Gallic gods, terrible to look upon and savage. The old folk in the village ofttimes sat together and told marvelous tales of the ancestral gods, and I made a rapt audience, even on Mass days when I should have had nought to do with such Pagan talk.

Yet when I heard tales of lame Volund the Smith and his magical swords, of brave Taranis slaying the hideous dragon, or of horrible Teutates and his thirst for human sacrifice, I believed with a child's unabashed wonder. Moreover, evidence in favor of these old tales lurked everywhere. Whilst walking in deep, quiet woods I would come upon a square, stone column, green with moss, and carved thereon would be a dragon, or a bear, or a boar, and the god to whom each beast was sacred; each scene told some story known to folk of Gaulish blood. I might imagine these ancient gods slept contentedly in the past, except for an encircling path of footprints freshly imprinted since a recent rain, proof of the barefoot worshippers who still danced and chanted in secret around the timeless column, invoking the god within. Sometimes an offering lay atop an altar rock. The gift to the god might be fruit, flowers, grain, or acorns, but again it might be the head, feet, and entrails of some small animal, adding its dried blood to the sacrificial stains of centuries.

The most feared and revered god of all Gauldom was Cernunnos, king of the forest, lord of all wild things. Carved columns depicted him taller than mortal men, thickly bearded, and as regally antlered as the grandest deer. Ofttimes his image sat cross-legged, surrounded by his woodland creatures. Cernunnos, the tales said, roamed the forests, master of the wilderness; the deer were his own herd, and when one was killed the forest king must be acknowledged and thanked, else he would stalk the hunter himself for retribution. As most children, I believed the tales and mused upon them, and sometimes shivered in a lonely, hushed grove, glancing quickly over my shoulder, half expecting to find an ancient god watching.

II

The autumn afternoon passed crisp and clear, and now evening whisked an early chill upon the Earth. Colored leaves swirled along the forest floor, then scattered aloft again in sudden whirlwinds. Along the path I kicked more leaves into the air, watching them catch the wind and fly away like flocks of red and yellow sparrows.

I would have chased them any other time, but night closed quickly this time of year—already the goats grazed far down in the lowlands—and I descended the mountain trail alone, my thick woolen cloak clasped close and the hood pulled well forward to shield me from the wind. My feet were warm, wrapped and wound in yards of goat-hide strips with the wooly side turned inward and the leather side outward, so I rattled the leaves with impunity, giving no thought to the cold.

Mama kept to home with a babe growing inside her belly, and Papa had gone carting wood to the inn, so I had begged and badgered to take a cheese and round of bread all on my own to an old hermit who lived up-mountain. Mama finally gave in. I took my time on the path, lingering to chuck rocks into a stream or at an angry squirrel or two before arriving at the isolated shrine of the hermit. The old man then kept me long with his holy talk and complaints of how the cold ached his ancient bones, persuading me to gather him an extra store of firewood, which I did not mind, figuring God would be pleased if he was looking.

And now, scurrying home, I heard a disconcerting tramping

and shuffling overtaking me along the path I had just come. Too many tales of things that lurked in the wood at night clamored in my mind. I froze rigid in my tracks, scarcely daring to turn around.

Yet I did turn, and all the while the sound of many somethings coming through the leaves drew nearer. Over a rise appeared dusky shadows moving among the half-bare trees. I felt I could not breathe my heart pounded so painfully; terror gripped my childish imagination, and I waited in dread for the Wild Huntsmen and Dark Elves rising from underground caverns.

As the shapes came closer, I saw with infinite relief that they were men—neither monsters nor ghouls—solid and earthly, garbed in skins and armed with mortal spears and shields. At first they were unaware of my presence even though they walked within a stone's throw, for I was small and was standing in fickle shadows that gusted with the wind.

When the lead man sighted me he stopped short and pointed wordlessly, his arm hanging in midair, eyes almost as round as his open mouth. They all halted, gaping, shifting uneasily, huddled together in one body.

It never occurred to me at the time just how I must have looked—a tiny hooded form in a twilight-shadowed forest—or that I might have caused them as much fright as they gave me. Instead, I only noted fearfully that they were neither Romans nor Gauls.

Burgundians, from the look of them, for I had heard that Burgundians smeared rank butter in their hair, and these men wore their yellow hair twisted and plaited in long greasy strands. Now I realized the danger I was in. The Burgundians could only be on a raid, striking at night to fade back over the river before dawn. I spun about to run.

At once they were all around me, hemming me in with stomping boots and shifting hands, so I could only stand still, entrapped in their circle. A man spoke, his voice hoarse and grating, in a language I did not comprehend; another, then another, repeated his words. Fingers pointed towards me.

Being not over a half-dozen years old and possessing no other defense than that naturally given to children, I began to cry. Tears seeped from my tightly squinched eyes and dribbled down my face. Unsuccessfully I tried to squelch a sob. A hand shot out and flipped my hood back, baring my head to the wind.

Still, no one touched me.

I heard them whispering among themselves—discussing me,

I had no doubt. While I tried to control the sniffles and tears that reappeared as quickly as I wiped them with my sleeve, the barbarians worked themselves into an argument. Certain words came up over and over, but I had no inkling of their meaning, only that I was the object in question. How the debate might have ended, I never knew, for a new voice boomed full and resonant over the others. All heads turned and instantly the circle parted.

On the trail stood a tall, wild-bearded man with tangled, windblown hair. He was clad completely in deerskin, even to his cloak and breeches, and from his head protruded the most magnificent set of antlers I had ever seen, worthy of the grandest buck in the mountains. Here, in our very presence, stood the fabled King of Wild Things, Cernunnos!

Even the Burgundians seemed in awe of him. As he shook his long spear angrily and berated them with menacing words, which still I could not understand, the barbarians faded hastily into the blackening forest, their retreating footfalls dimming in the distance.

I forgot them utterly. I saw only the horned god before me. He laughed and spoke in the ancient Gallic.

"So, little one," Cernunnos hailed me, "you thought to take on the Burgundian bandits alone, did you?"

I shook my head disbelievingly.

"Sooth, they will not raid in this direction tonight. We thoroughly frightened them, you and I."

To take in the whole height of him I had to stare almost straight up, for his antlers seemed to snare the very moon in their branches. I found my tongue and answered.

"I never frightened them at all, Lord Cernunnos. 'Twas you."

"*Lord* Cernunnos, is it? I need no such title. Cernunnos will do." He smiled and knelt, settling nearer to my height. "Do you not know who the Burgundians thought you to be? Nor the cause of their confusion?"

I did not.

"They thought you to be the son of Sindre, he who fashioned the golden ring Draupner and the thunder-hammer wielded by Thor."

"Who?"

"Sindre the Dwarf. His magic powers are feared among barbarians, especially Burgundians. Some of this drunken party counseled to leave you be, rather than incur the wrath of Sindre's folk, but the more besotted of them thought to hold you ransom. The mountain dwarves are known to have fabulous treasures buried away underground."

"The dark elves?" I whispered incredulously. "They took me for one of *them!*" I glanced right and left into the woods.

The forest king chuckled and laid a hand on my shoulder. "There's nought to fear. I've walked these mountains many years; never yet have I seen sign of elf or troll or goblin. And I've found but one dwarf, and that one is you, boy. Even so, I might now believe the old tales if I didn't already know who you are, Dominic, and where you belong."

I stared in astonishment! The Lord of the Wilds knew *me!*

"How . . . how do you know? . . ." I stammered.

"I could scarcely pass this way so often as I do without knowledge of you and your family. Why, sometimes on the meadows I hear your father call your name. Tonight, though, I never thought to run across you; I followed the Burgundians, hoping to divert them from their raid. Happily you half did it for me."

"How did you frighten them? What did you say?"

"I but threatened to bring the dwarf-folk down upon them and to lead all the deer from their side of the Rhine to this—if they set even one finger on Sindre's son." He rose to his majestic height again. "Now, 'tis late. Your mama and papa are surely searching the wood for you by now, Dominic. I should see you safely home."

Clouds shredded the moon behind his head, so that all I could make out was a crown of antlers, silhouetted black against the luminous, shifting sky.

How proudly I tramped homeward in the company of Cernunnos, the forest king! How many folk could claim to have even seen him, much less walked with him? I felt grand! My triumphant march ended too quickly; we spied a torch-flame zigzagging up the slope, chased by its own bright streaking tail. Then I heard my name frantically shouted across the dark hills.

Cupping both hands around my mouth, I yelled in answer, "Papa! I'm coming!"

"Here I will leave you, Dominic," said Cernunnos.

"Oh, no!" I cried. "Please, wait for my papa, else how will he believe I've seen you? He says you're a fairy tale; we must show him you're real!"

The horned god chortled and stroked at his beard. "Real? I will wait, little one, but be forewarned—things are not always as they seem. Surely you've learned that already this night." We continued down the trail as the light rose to meet us. I could see my father holding aloft the flame.

"Papa! Here!" I encouraged him, running ahead.

Papa knelt and caught me in one burly arm. "Dominic! Where in Heaven's name have you been?" he demanded, half relieved, half angry. "What could you be thinking to stay out so . . . late. . . ."

Cernunnos had stepped into the torchlight. Papa stood abruptly, tucking me under his arm like a bundle of wood.

"See, Papa," I babbled, struggling vainly to get loose. "I met the King of the Wood and we frightened the Burgundians and stopped their raid because they thought I was the son of Sindre and tried to kidnap me but—" Papa's hand clamped over my mouth and cut off the rest of my excited tale.

"So 'tis *you*," my papa said to the god, setting me on my feet. "You're alive after all."

"Aye." The stately antlers dipped in agreement.

"You know him, Papa?"

Papa ignored me. "What've you been telling my boy?"

"Nothing. 'Tis he who has told me. So Cernunnos is a fairy tale?"

"And what of this tale of Burgundians?"

"Dominic will tell you. I've a long journey home tonight."

"My pardons!" Papa exclaimed suddenly. "You've brought my son through the wood and I give you no thanks! Come, 'tis but a short way to my house. Join us at our hearth."

Cernunnos smiled. "I'm surprised at you, Ceradoc—a Christian inviting a Pagan god to sup, even though he be an old friend. But I accept."

Papa grinned back. "We've wondered how you fared, Rhihanna and I. She'll be glad."

Papa snatched me up under his arm again and led the way home. When we arrived I survived unscathed a welcome from my mother, a tearful one and no hint of a scolding, for she blamed herself for allowing me to go off to the hermit alone. Finally she turned her attention to our companion, not in the least affected by the fact that he was a god.

"At least he's been in good company," she smiled. "We'd heard you were still about; 'tis fortunate for us the tales were true. Please come in; there's plenty at table." Mama stepped out of the cold into the warm hut, holding Papa's hand. She was less than two months away from her birthing time, and he was mindful of her step.

Cernunnos moved to stoop through the low door but pulled back sharply.

"I forget these betimes," he grinned, and then to my astonishment he reached up and lifted the antlers from his head. He cradled them in one arm and, winking at me, followed my parents. I tumbled in behind them and saw him set the antlers gently on the earthen floor and lean his spear beside them.

"I told you, Dominic," chided Cernunnos, noticing how doubtfully I examined the antlers, "things may not be as they seem. Handle them carefully," he cautioned as I touched a finger to one of the points. "I'd be hard pressed to find another buck as impressive as the one that wore these."

The antlers set firmly fastened in a skull cap of hardened leather which was covered with soft deerskin. Nicks cut in the cap left slots for the ears. It must have fitted his head perfectly for the heavy horns to stay in place. They made a magnificent crown for a forest king. In the dark I had believed that the horns grew out of his own head.

I studied Cernunnos by lamplight. Without the crown he stood no taller than my own father; he appeared perfectly human, perfectly at home in our tiny hut. I approached him as he sat on a low stool.

"Then you're not real?" I demanded accusingly. "You're not the god?"

"Yes and no," he said good-naturedly. "Yes, I am real. No, I'm not the god."

I frowned. "You're *pretending* to be Cernunnos?"

"To be honest, I am. Still, I *am* the king of the forest," he chuckled, glancing at the antlers, "self-crowned though I may be."

My indignation must have shown. Mama shushed my next comment, suspecting that it might be rude, and shooed me to my own tall stool at the end of the table. I climbed to my seat and silently watched her lay cold goat's-meat, black bread, cheese, dried figs, and vinegar wine before us. Meanwhile, the imposter told how he had been following the Burgundian raiding party, intending to somehow scare them back over the river, when they stumbled upon me and afforded him the perfect opportunity. My father roared appreciatively; he always loved a good tale. Then

Mama joined us; we said grace (even the self-crowned god) and commenced our feast.

"Well, Girrik," smiled Papa (What now? My father knew his human name!) "you are not dead, as the imperial agents would have us believe."

"Not only not dead, my friend, but keeping alive the rebellion."

"Madness!" Mama blurted. "Why would you do such a thing? We are at peace! Leave the Romans be!"

"Rhihanna!" exclaimed Papa. "Girrik is our guest!"

Girrik regarded my mother gravely. "I understand your fears, woman, but this peace you protect is the Pax Romana. 'Tis a slavery to Gauls. We were once a free and proud people; look how we bow under the imperial whip."

Mama held her ground. "'Tis better than having troops slaughter us in our homes! None will be spared if Rome smells an uprising: neither my husband, my son, nor my unborn child! You, Girrik, you know it well; would you yet bring death upon us?"

"We will soon have a force to meet them."

"Ah!" My mother's eyes blazed. "Where is this force? Hiding in the forest? Where are your weapons? King Vercingetorix had all of Gaul rallied against Caesar, and he lost! Men were slaughtered, women raped, children taken into slavery!"

"But that was Caesar," argued Girrik. "Now the legions are lax; there's no discipline. And how many soldiers in the army are Gauls? On whose side will they fight? And the barbarian mercenaries! They'd like to see Gaul in rebellion, the Rhine frontier falling, Gaul allied with Germania!"

"Now you're talking nonsense," Papa growled. "We'd but trade one master for another. If the Empire fails to hold the river, the barbarians will overrun us as they please. How would we stop them? For three hundred years we've been bound to Rome. There is no king in Gaul anymore; there's only the Emperor—*two* emperors, Girrik. Rome can call troops from Iberia, from Britannia, even Constantinople and Africa. You're living in a dream world. The Roman Empire would swat the likes of us like flies."

"Go back to your forest, Girrik," Mama told him gently. "Be Cernunnos. Reign there as king. Forget Rome."

Girrik frowned thoughtfully, unconvinced.

"And be careful, friend," said Papa. "Emperor Theodosius has set his seal to an edict: The Church holds authority to deal as it sees fit with all things Pagan. There can be no worship at the shrines of the old gods, not even in Rome itself."

"That can never happen!" cried Girrik. "Even Romans still sacrifice to their gods! To Jupiter and Minerva! Theodosius cannot enforce such a law!"

"He'll not have to—the Church will do it for him."

Girrik snorted. "Which one?"

"The Roman Church."

Mama rose abruptly, despite her heavy womb, her mouth set in a tight line, and flung more logs on the fire.

"We're losing our priest," Papa said quietly. "Theodosius decreed the Arian Church heretical and unlawful. Our priest is stepping down; a new one is coming from Treverorum, appointed by the Bishop." Papa sighed. "Knowing how Bishop Felix feels about Arians, ours is lucky to bow out with his life."

Mama came back to the table. "We're not traitors!" she said in anger. "We're Christians! The Church in Rome can call us heretics, but it cannot simply murder anyone who doesn't profess the faith according to the Roman creed!"

"Ah, Rome!" exclaimed Girrik sardonically. "First *no one* can be Christian on pain of death. Then *everyone* must be Christian on pain of death. Now they must be the *right kind* of Christian, likely on said pain of death."

Mama shook her head. "I cannot believe the Emperor would allow the bishops to go that far."

By now I was drifting off to sleep. The voices began to fade and I nodded dangerously upon the high stool. Papa carried me off to bed and I heard no more that night.

Next morning when I woke our guest had gone. A few days later we discovered on our doorstep a freshly killed and blooded doe; we feasted on deer-meat well into winter.

III

Late January, on a cold, bitter dawn, my mother began her labor. Papa sent me off to fetch midwife Elgge and her daughter; by the time the three of us returned Mama was abed, looking deathly pale and wringing with sweat. She smiled weakly and told me to wait outside with Papa while the women did their work, so we built ourselves a fire of dried manure and sticks in the empty goat-shed and waited.

Morning crept by. Every so often Papa went into the hut to see how Mama fared, and each time he emerged grim and worried. Once he brought me yesterday's bread for breakfast but ate none himself.

Each time I asked, "How's Mama?"

Each time he answered, "Still trying. 'Twill be soon."

"Was I so long in coming?" I wondered.

Papa smiled. "You were in a hurry, boy. Elgge barely got here in time to catch you." Then his brow creased. "This babe is big. Maybe bigger than your mama can bear."

"What if she can't?" I felt a stab of panic in my stomach.

Papa shook his head. "I don't know, son," he said tightly.

We waited.

Far into the afternoon, Mama screamed. Not just once, but over and over, hardly taking a breath in between. Papa, half-dazed by the fire, leapt up and ran to the hut. I followed after, but no further than the goat-yard I stopped, terrified, as Mama's shrieks grew more horrible and frantic.

Cowardly, I retreated into a corner of the shed and pressed the heels of my hands over my ears. Still I heard. My lovely, gentle mama—I didn't want to hear her screaming like that. Mercifully, my own wretched sobs drowned out the sound.

When I could catch my breath again, all was quiet. I took my hands from my ears. How long had the air been so silent? I had cried a long time, I knew. The coals faded untended in the dark shed. I huddled next to them, numbed by something much worse than the cold.

A little later Papa stood in the doorway.

"Dominic." His voice was hoarse.

I sat frozen, praying not to hear what I feared to hear. Papa sat next to me silently, wanting not to say what he had to say. He reached over to lay his hand on my head, but instead he grabbed me close in his arms where I buried my face against his chest.

"Your mama is gone to her Lord."

Stillness.

"She took the babe to Heaven with her."

I trembled in his arms. *No, no, no!*

He sighed. "Now there's only you and me, boy. She won't be back. Understand?"

I understood. I had seen death before—animals and people. *But not my mama!* And what was Heaven that she went screaming? And who was this Lord who took her in agony? My despair turned to anger—anger at God—and then to fear, lest I be punished for my anger. Suppose in revenge God took my papa, too? I closed my mind and forcefully locked away those thoughts and the terrors they conjured. I felt Papa holding me and thought, *it isn't true—she isn't dead.*

When next I entered the house, Mama lay serenely sleeping, arrayed in her blue dress. A small bundle rested in the crook of her arm, its face covered. Elgge's girl cried; Elgge hugged me tearfully and kissed my forehead, then they left. Papa and I sat vigil by the oil lamp. Though I fell asleep with my head on Papa's knee, I know he did not rest. And I knew Mama was dead because she never looked at me or smiled at me or spoke to me, though I silently begged her to until weariness and grief wore me down.

Early next morning, Papa made a bed of straw in the cart and laid Mama and the baby in it. I looked back from the cart seat while Papa led the donkey. She no longer looked real—not like a living person. Neither did the little form that would have been my brother. I turned and stared forward intently, feeling a frightful jealousy for that dead babe. That he should be in Heaven with *my* mama, while I was left behind without her!

We took her to the basilica in the village; half the village waited for us—Elgge, her daughter, my uncle and aunt. The new priest said he could not say Mass for her, nor could she rest on holy ground, for she had been baptized by an Arian priest, never a Roman priest, and Bishop Felix expressly forbade. . . .

"Then baptize her," Papa interrupted gruffly.

"What? Now?"

"Aye, now. Baptize her and the babe."

The priest looked as if he was going to object. Then the Roman priest studied the faces of his reluctant Arian flock. He looked at Papa, stricken and grim. He looked at me—a long time he looked at me—then he smiled gently and nodded.

"I think the Lord will understand this once. Bring them inside."

The priest baptized my mama (I wondered if she knew) and the baby boy together.

"Now me and my son," said Papa, "so when our time comes we can lie beside her."

The priest hesitated only half an instant before he agreed. "The Lord would not wish me to stand between you and Heaven."

He baptized us both and said Mass, and then we filed out to the churchyard to bury Mama and the baby wrapped together in Elgge's finest blanket.

"Don't look," said Elgge, turning my face aside as they lowered the white bundle, but I had to see where they were putting my mama. Papa pulled me close and held me tight when they began shovelling dirt into the grave.

"Papa!" I sobbed in confusion, "how will Mama get to Heaven if she's way underground? She can't get out!"

Papa took my face in his two trembling hands. "She's already there, Dominic. She doesn't need her body in Heaven. She's spirit now—she's with our Brother Jesus—no harm can come to her anymore."

"Is she an angel?"

"Aye, she is, Dominic; she is. More beautiful than ever. And she'll be watching over us and waiting for us, so we musn't despair."

He raised his eyes to the overcast sky for a few moments in silent prayer, unmindful of the tears that streamed his face.

After the last prayer, people came to weep and embrace, and

half the village embraced the priest and said they, now, were ready to be baptized into the Roman Church, for they felt he was a good man and had done the right thing. Papa and I tramped home, and Elgge brought us supper.

That night a freezing rain fell, and I thought of the little mound of dirt in the churchyard and wondered if Mama could feel the rain and if she was cold down there. And I could not help it; I wept in despair. And Papa came and held me in his arms all night.

Our lives changed from that day onward. Papa was grim in a way I had never known him, and he kept me by him always. We tramped the lower forest and cut wood all winter. We boarded the goats with a friend of Papa's, entering the village only to exchange firewood for meager supplies of salt-pork and barley and to visit the lonely little grave. We never went again to Mass.

Papa's winter quota of firewood for the inn-and-post meant he must bring in a wagonload almost daily. More often than not, we dined at the inn, for home seemed desolate and empty, and we more and more frequently stayed the night rather than climb the slushy roads at dusk. Papa liked to sit at the table, sip at a goblet of wine, and listen to the talk. I liked to curl up near the fire and listen, too, especially if there happened to be a minstrel stopping by. Better than the talk, the innkeeper's wife made sure we got hot bread and broth, and she always saved something honey-sweet for me, like fig pie or raisin cakes.

Officially, the inn provided free lodgings for frontier soldiers and imperial messengers, but other folk stopped there, too, lured by the sign over the door: Mercury in winged cap and sandals, holding aloft the wand and serpent, a welcome sight to travelers throughout the Empire. Merchants and well-to-do journeymen could buy board and bed for a few coppers; a minstrel might pay his way with a few songs or tales. Of course, senators and patricians and such never stayed at the inn, preferring their sleeping coaches or guesting arrangements on private estates.

This allowed the talk to flow free and loose in the dining hall when no imperial agents happened to be about. Even the soldiers posted at the adjoining station-house were easy with their words, so Papa and I often found ourselves in interesting company indeed.

Four long tables with benches stood in two rows between the wide fireplaces at either end of the room. In winter, the choice seats were situated at the ends nearest the roaring fires, provided the guest had no objection to roasting on one side. The coldest seats were on the middle isle opposite the front door, which was apt to fly open violently and fling chilled blasts of wind across the midsection of the hall. At the back wall were stairs to the sleeping loft and a door to the kitchen and innkeeper's quarters.

Papa liked to sit halfway twixt the fire and the center of the room, so anyone sharing the table must either talk around him or directly to him. Papa would take his leisurely supper and listen— and talk. Folk passing through found that he had accumulated a wide assortment of gossip from all over the Empire, and sometimes he would become embroiled in some heated differences of opinion.

I would sit beside him, perched atop a wooden bowl over-turned on the bench, and even then I could just barely reach to dunk bread into the broth. Soon after I drained my mug, however, I would clamber down and settle against the warm hearthstones near a corner of the fireplace, where I was close enough to enjoy the heat without suffering its blast.

Drowsy though I might be, I managed to stay awake long enough to eat the honeyed morsel the goodwife always slipped me. Then, wrapped snug in my cloak, I would fall asleep to a drone of voices and the crackle of burning wood, scarcely aware when Papa at last carried me upstairs to the loft and tucked me into a bed of straw.

Talk that first winter was mostly of imperial edicts, rising taxes, heretic hunting, and the faraway war with the Visigoths. One frosty evening, just as Papa and I had unloaded the wood and settled down to supper, the inn door burst open and revealed a fur-cloaked, hoar-headed, steel-eyed figure on the threshold. He surveyed the room in one glance and stormed inside, dropping himself boldly amongst the soldiers.

"Salute, mates!" he rumbled gaily. "Make room for an old field trooper who's coppered his time! 'Tis twenty-five years since Die Kendic could call the Rhineland home!"

"Discharged?" cried one of the frontier soldiers in mock disbe-lief. "A live one?"

Another chimed in. "Faith, I heard 'twas no way out of this army but to die out, and even then they fine the corpse. Coppered, you say? Let's see."

With a parade-ground flourish the old veteran reached into his belt and presented a thin square of new copper. The soldiers passed it around, studying the impressive announcement of discharge imprinted in metal.

"Stationed in Dacia?" queried one, passing it back.

"Stationed!" hooted the old soldier, quaffing an offered goblet of wine. "I weren't stationed—I was fighting! Fighting the bloody Visigoths!"

"Ah!" The soldiers' eyes lit up. "How goes it?"

"We beat them clear out of Thrace and Macedonia, but 'tain't likely they'll be surrendering, if that's what you mean."

"Why don't Theodosius run those worthless barbarians back over the Danuvius where they belong?"

The coppered trooper eyed the speaker curiously. "Where're you from, boy?"

"Iberia, sir."

"That might excuse your ignorance on the matter of barbarians, Visigoths in particular. Those Goths are a thorn in the Emperor's side. With I figure at the most forty thousand fighting men—that's a wildly high estimate, mind you—and carting twice that many women and children, Fritigern and Athanaric managed to fend off Theodosius's crack field troops for nigh on six years. And with Gratian's troops holding the cursed Huns and Quadi on the Upper Danuvius, Theo's got no more legions to pull in without leaving Constantinople wide open or letting Africa go up in civil war."

The old warrior drained another goblet, belched, called loudly for supper, and smiled grimly at his audience, which by now included every soul in the room. A spellbound servant suddenly remembered his job and hurried off to fetch the meal.

"I'll tell you this, though," confided the veteran in a dramatic tone. "The Visigoth war won't go on much longer. Old Theo is ready to come to terms."

"The devil!" a soldier protested. "Terms with those Germanni dogs, after they raided and murdered the very people who gave them sanctuary when they came whining at the border with their tails between their legs! I say he won't!"

The hush in the room was thick enough to slice with a dagger.

Spreading both hands on the table with great deliberation, the old warrior slowly rose halfway to his feet, and for one heart-stopping moment he looked as though he might draw sword on the ashen-faced frontiersman. Then he eased back down, and everyone let out their breath at once. He was enjoying himself immensely.

"You say, do you?" he said sarcastically. "Lucky for you, I take you for a fool, and a fool can't be held responsible for his tongue. Instead of cutting it out, I'll just educate you as to exactly what happened when the Visigoths crossed over into the Empire."

I detected a tale in his voice and wriggled closer to better see the storyteller, all the more intrigued because this was to be a true story. Papa lifted me onto his shoulder, where I clung excitedly to his hair. The veteran's meal was served, and he began his account between mouthfuls.

"I was a frontier trooper at the time, just six years ago—seems longer somehow—on the border, same as you lads, guarding the River Danuvius, when we begun to get reports of barbarians gathering on the opposite bank. Visigoths, they were, and they sent a lone man across with a petition. They wanted to come over into the Empire; seems the Huns—Satan's own legions, I call them—were sweeping behind them and closing fast. The Visigoths figured they hadn't a chance, so they took the one choice they had: hightail it to the Roman Empire and ask for protection.

"While we waited for word from the Emperor, more and more of them appeared across the river. By the time orders came down there must've been a hundred thousand of 'em. Orders were to let 'em in!

"Unarmed, mind you! Why, there'd already been skirmishes when some tried to sneak over on their own, but we frontiersmen held them. And do you believe it? Them troops that held the border got slapped with a fine! And our officers lost rank! Aye, that was a sorry business, so we weren't too kindly disposed toward the Goths from the beginning.

"Anyway, conditions the Emperor made was the Visigoths cross over after they give up their arms and surrender the cream of their sons and daughters as hostage. Well, to a barbarian, surrendering his children is one thing—but his weapons!—that's something he's not going to lay down so easily. Aye, the river was up, we were having a hell of a time with the crossing, 'twas all pandemonium, and, naturally, some of the troops started looking the other way on the arms when the barbarians went to bargaining their goods in exchange for their own weapons—even the officers didn't shun a bribe, mind you! And they got to sampling some of the yellow-haired women, who were downright anxious to please when it came to keeping their men armed.

"Of course, *I* knew they was headed for trouble right off. Any damned fool could see what folly 'twould be to let that many Visigoths into the Empire with the most of them *armed!* 'Twern't no use in taking it up with my superiors, though. Why, even the generals, *they* went in on it, so I just held my tongue and loaded the rafts—men, women, kids, and cattle—and cursed the fate that put idiots in command instead of them with common sense in their heads."

Here some of the soldiers grinned and winked at each other knowingly.

"When 'twas said and done, we had a bleedin' armed camp of hungry barbarians this side of the river. And *we* had orders to keep *them* content as sheep. Nobody took to account the Military Governor in Thrace, though. Lupicinus, *curse him,* disobeyed *imperial orders,* mind you, from the *Emperor* himself, and gave the barbarians hell! First he strikes a quarter-tax on their goods, only we get orders to cart away a far sight more than just one quarter. Then he charges 'em ten times over market for food, and sells 'em *dog meat* at that—*diseased* meat, too. Why, the barbarians start getting sick, and they sink to selling what's left of their sons and daughters just so they don't all starve! By now you can be sure their mood is just this side of vicious.

"Whilst all this is going on, the *Ostrogoths* show up across the river, looking for refuge from the Huns. By now Emperor Valens sees his mistake and wants no part of any more Goths. But when we pull back from the border to relocate the Visigoths, naturally the Ostrogoths come right on over the river and set up their own fortified camp. Any idiot would know 'twould happen!

"Then that Janus-faced pig Lupicinus decides to feast Fritigern's Visigoths at Marciaopolis—just the generals, you understand, while the rest of the barbarians sit locked outside the city gates. Now you've got a tribe of angry, hungry Goths guarded by a legion of disgruntled Roman frontiersmen. Fighting's bound to start somewhere! And it did—why, 'twas raging and spreading faster than a fire in Rome! Suddenly Lupicinus orders the palace guards to dispatch the guesting Visigoths just as smooth as if 'twas all planned—which I wouldn't doubt—but Fritigern doesn't dispatch so easily. He and his men force their way out of the palace, slice through the city, and escape the gates like they did it every day.

"Now Lupicinus runs us after 'em, but the barbarians are ready for us. That treacherous dog Lupicinus flees the field and leaves us to cover his slimy, yellow back. 'Twas enough to make a soldier puke.

"Course, the Visigoths go on a rampage, working out their

vengeance on innocent folk who had nought to do with their treatment. They go thieving, raping, murdering, and burning all over Thrace. And every man of you here knows what happened when Valens marched his legions out to meet the Goths without waiting for Gratian's army to join him from the west. Wanted all the glory for himself, Valens did. Well, he got *glory* all right! Burned alive in a farmhouse where he lay wounded!

"I tell you, it never would've happened if Theodosius had been Emperor then. He'd have made sure the Visigoths was treated square in the first place. And he sure as hell never would've lost his whole field army to a lot of runaway barbarians! By the time Theodosius took command he had to pull troops from Gratian, who could ill afford the loss, and muster the frontier regiments for the field." The old man gazed at his audience proudly. "That's how I got into Theodosius's army. We chased those Goths all over the Balkans, but the mountains hid them too well and gave them safe advantage for an ambush.

"And now that the Huns grow bolder, raiding all up and down the Danuvius, well, Theo's no fool—he knows he can't wage two wars at once. The Goths now, they're a considerable army in themselves, and they're tired of living off the lean of the land. Now with Fritigern and Athanaric both dead, the *Visigoths* at least are talking truce. Theodosius needs them and they need him. They'll come to terms alright—and soon!"

Saluting his own speech, the veteran drained another goblet and leaned back from the table. His audience murmured and nodded ready agreement, satisfied with a tale well told.

Spellbound, I marveled at the power of the storyteller to hold folks so entranced with mere words, and I thirsted then and there to learn with equal skill the art of telling tales.

IV

In due season, spring melted the snows on the heights and time had come to herd the goats to the high meadows. This meant moving to the little hut which seemed so empty now without Mama, yet Papa and I were both pleased to be home in our beloved wilderness.

Home was where we spent most of the spring and summer. We herded goats, cut wood, and roamed the mountains as we pleased, except that each morning we hauled a cartload of milk to the village. When I was younger, the village had seemed far away and the trip was an adventure. Now that I was all of seven and had lived a winter at the inn, the half-morning ride to the little hamlet and back became only a daily chore, a chore we must be done with before the real business of the day began, for Papa and I both loved the forests and pastures.

Besides, the village was often a trial to me. Children I once played with after Mass now stared and pointed insolent fingers when Papa's attention was elsewhere. Then they would imitate my peculiar walk and run away giggling when Papa turned about.

"Pay them no mind, Dominic," Papa said. "They're ignorant and foolish, and they learn it from their even more ignorant and foolish parents. Everywhere are a few folk to be found with no heart, and these always the loudest and most outspoken, it seems. If there is a God, He'll call on them to account for themselves one day."

Then he held my gaze and said with deliberate emphasis, "Remember, there are plenty of good folk, too. We will not let these few harden our hearts." But I could see the children's cruelty made him angry, too.

Privately, I felt someone ought to call on God to account for *Himself*. My short arms and legs served only to divide everything in the world into two categories: things difficult to carry and things impossible to reach. And the taunts *hurt*—hurt terribly! I could not help my futile anger at being so unjustly singled out. But I pretended to ignore the snickers and stares, and I strove hard not to wonder if God had grown forgetful and made a mistake of me.

Yet God's own handiwork nurtured me. The fresh air and clear streams, the windblown paths and peaceful forests—all served to make me happy and hardy. My legs were strong from hiking, my arms strong from lugging wood; I feared nothing. Not the goats, which I herded about with impunity, not the donkey, which I rode about boldly. And I grew. Not dramatically, but steadily, a half inch or so a year. And I hoped always that God would change His mind and make me as tall as my papa.

That summer Papa and I visited the inn once weekly. We stayed for supper and conversation, and then began the long, pleasant climb home just before dusk. This time of year the company was varied and high-spirited, and rumors from the ends of the Empire arrived in all manner of garb and accent.

Here we heard from a minor envoy en route to Britannia that Theodosius had indeed come to terms with the Visigoths. The Emperor caused considerable uproar when he enrolled the entire Visigoth force into the Roman army under the leadership of one of their own chieftains, one Alaric. Theodosius granted the Goths lands of their own and charged them to hold marauding Huns and Quadi north of the River Danuvius—a bargain the Visigoths accepted eagerly.

Emperor Gratian, here in Gaul, had his own troubles, for we heard rumor of a far more menacing force moving across Gaul. No mere rude barbaric invaders, there approached an army of trained, seasoned Roman troops straight out of Britannia. At their head marched Magnus Maximus, captain of the Britannic regiments. His destination was Rome, his ambition: the Emperor's throne. Gratian quickly amassed his troops northward to do battle with Maximus.

By now winter was swift upon us, and Germanni barbarians raided virtually unchecked in the south. News of fierce battles, burning villages, and sudden deadly attacks buzzed about the inn daily. Travel came to a standstill as folk feared to be out on the roads.

A lone traveler, however, arrived afoot, carrying a hoard of bronze trinkets on his shoulders. A trader to the barbarian wilds, he had barely eluded the Burgundians and escaped across the River Rhine with his life. His news was not encouraging.

"General uprising," the trader informed us cheerfully. "The Germanni gather against the Empire."

"Nonsense," scoffed the innkeeper nervously. "They war more among themselves than they do with Romans. They aren't civilized enough to stand together."

The trader grinned knowingly. "Heard of the Alamanni, have you? Know what Alamanni means? It means 'all-peoples' in the Germanni tongue. They're a confederacy of tribes, all fired up to invade the Empire. As far as warring among themselves goes, where are your so called 'civilized' Roman legions while the barbarians are massing? Preparing to do battle with each other halfway across Gaul—that's where."

We looked from one to another in silence. The trader snorted disdainfully.

"Aye, I've heard. So have the barbarians, and they are no fools. Most of them hate Romans something fierce, and with just a skeleton force left along the Rhine. . . ."

"But we're Gauls!" protested the goodwife. "Not Romans! 'Tis we who suffer for it!"

The man shrugged. "We're all the same to the Germanni. The tribes are hungry, madam."

"We are hungry, too," Papa said quietly.

Now the trader fell silent. The others sighed and grumbled agreement. Papa put his hand on my head and smiled at me wearily.

"But we'll manage, son. Gaul will survive, and so will we."

I nodded.

As it happened, Emperor Gratian lost the battle to Maximus and was killed. Maximus now declared himself Emperor of the west. He seated his reign at Treverorum on the Rhine, not so very many miles from my home. Quickly our lives changed.

Maximus's troops seized the estate of Lucius Scipio Marcianus (who, by his own good fortune, was not in residence at the time) and arrogated its modest staples for their own. They conscripted every able-bodied youth they could lay hold of into their ranks. They ravaged every comely-bodied woman they likewise could lay hold of. Maximus's army treated Gauls as a conquered people.

The wayside inn was seized and converted into a fully occupied military post. Papa no longer let me go with him down to the inn with his load of wood.

Many Gauls took to the heights. Maximus could scarcely spare the men or the time to hunt them down, for the Germanni, ever watchful for weakness along the borders, plundered across the river.

Papa's old friend Girrik, in the guise of the Forest King, seized this golden moment to rally Gauls to rebellion in earnest. He gathered the runaway coloni to him and went about at night from village to village encouraging folk to follow him into the forested hills.

Our isolated little woodcutter's hut became a way station for Girrik's rebels. A knock on the door in the night would bring a message of troop movement or whereabouts of a supply shipment. When an attack was planned, Papa would go down and give the word to certain villagers who would pass by our hut—knives, swords, spears, and axes in hand—and Papa would take his broad axe and disappear with them into the night.

The rebels knew where to strike, partly because Papa always picked up an earful of information at the inn-turned-post. Rustic Gauls would converge suddenly from the woods upon tribute wagons laden with confiscated grain or attack a military agent's troops trying to collect the conscription and tax. Maximus retaliated; his troops combed the hills and forests; his agents arrested anyone whose movements looked suspicious.

Now more often the rebels who came through our hut were wounded or on the run. Most were fleeing for the wilds, and Papa knew just where to guide them—an unguarded bend in the river. We made our journeys by night; I trodded out with them, too, for Papa kept me by him these unsettling days. I was only ten—maybe eleven—then.

Theodosius did not take kindly to Maximus grabbing up half the Empire. He left off warring with the Persians and advanced swiftly westward. Before the summer was done we heard Maximus had been defeated and beheaded. Valentinian, a boy in his teens, was enthroned as Emperor in the west.

Theodosius sent a new general to restore order along the Rhine. General Arbogast rode in might across Gaul, relentlessly exterminating any lurking elements of unrest in the diocese.

Gallic rebels lay low and watchful.

The imperial treasury paid Lucius Scipio Marcianus a generous recompense for the losses his estate suffered during the five-year upheaval; the Gallic coloni who bore the brunt of the suffering received nothing—nothing but a power-mad general who exercised exorbitant discipline to grind them into subjugation.

I was twelve that chilly autumn. A few of Girrik's diehard rebels had taken the inn after Maximus's bestraggled troops deserted. Against all reason, they prepared to hold out until the end. Girrik and Papa and some others went down to persuade them to give it up and take to the hills. The diehards retorted that they were sick of running. Meanwhile a contingent of Arbogast's army rode hard upon the road. Girrik and Papa saw little choice but to gather a ragged force in an attempt to break the coming siege by surprise attack from the outside. Papa did not allow me with him, for despite my age I yet stood less than a yardstick in height, but I heard the sad news when he and another staggered into our hut in the night. Papa limped from a slash in his leg and breathed uneasily with a wound in the side. The other could scarcely hobble, even with Papa's help, his knee shattered horribly.

I fetched water and cloth for bandaging.

"I'm all right. . . ." Papa gasped, seeing my ashen face. "We had to run . . . the inn . . . burned to the ground . . . the men inside . . ." Papa shook his head, anguished. "We were not enough. . . ." He swallowed mouthfuls of water distractedly. "Gather some victuals, Dominic . . . we're leaving before first light . . . over the river. . . ."

But before dawn another rebel passed by with more tragic news. "Girrik is captured. Caught wounded near the village. Come morning, Ceradoc, he'll be executed—slowly—for all the village to witness."

Papa stared long into the paling night sky. He gripped his axe. "Dominic, take the pack and wait for me at the river crossing."

"Papa, no!"

"You heard me, boy. Hide yourself behind the hollow tree. If I've not come by evensong . . . take to the wilds without me."

"Papa, please, let me go with you!"

He gripped my shoulder with one hand, his axe with the other. "Dominic, the last thing I want is you to come with me. I cannot have you there! Understand, son, I have no choice but to do what I can for Girrik."

I nodded jerkily. "But—"

34

"But *no,* Dominic! I want you well away, lad. You'll be free at least."

"*Not without you!*" I wailed.

Papa hugged me to him longingly. I sobbed aching tears into his shirt. He sighed. "No, Dominic, no." His voice was sadly gentle. "I cannot take you into such danger; neither can I leave Girrik to their mercies. Go and wait at the river. The others will be there with the boat. At dusk go over if I'm not back. Go on. Find the others. Promise me."

"No. Only let me be with you."

He pulled me away from him and locked eyes with me. "I cannot. They are not adverse to executing children. I have to know you are safe, elfkin. Promise me!"

I swallowed hard against rising sobs.

"I promise, Papa."

"Good boy." He grabbed me close again, then pushed me away. "Go. Take your pack and get you to the river. I must leave; Girrik has no more time."

We parted hastily: I toward the darkled woods, he down-mountain. But soon I was blinded by my tears and turned back. For the first time in my memory I disobeyed my papa and followed after him down the rutted road to the village. I trailed him unseen into the hamlet just after sunrise. All the villagers stood together under guard in front of the basilica. I could barely see above their heads. Girrik hung by his wrists from a great oak tree—a tree sacred to the Forest King—and I heard his awful screams plainly across the morning mist.

I lingered behind for a moment, horrified by the agonizing cries that wrenched from Girrik's throat, but then a stronger instinct pushed me forward.

As the crowd parted for Papa, I saw just enough to make me wish I had not. Black-robed monks were gathered there, sanctioning by their presence what Arbogast's soldiers did to my papa's friend. Two held his feet; one dragged a sharp-pronged harrowing-rake down his naked skin. With excrutiatingly deliberate slow torture the executioner gouged deep, bloody furrows along the shrieking, writhing, captive flesh. I had never in my worst nightmares imagined that one human being could do such a thing to another.

Papa strode forward despite his wounded leg, despite the crowd, despite the ring of armed soldiers. He raised his heavy axe; simultaneously the nearest guard startled and drew back his sword.

Papa flung the axe out with skilled force; within the same movement the guard lunged out with his sword. The sharp axehead buried itself deep in Girrik's throat in the very instant the guard's sword plunged deep into Papa's breast.

"*Papa!*"

He spun and stared at me wistfully; then blood spilled from everywhere and he fell.

"*Papa!*" I heard an anguished cry that I scarcely knew was my own. I leapt forward. I watched the soldier raise the red sword to meet me. Then I felt firm arms wrap about me and hold me back.

"He's just a child!" snapped a woman's voice. "Isn't it enough you've killed his father!"

Elgge's girl, for it was she who held me, glared up at the man. I saw only my papa, lying on his face, soaking the earth with his blood. All was deadly silence—Girrik's cries had died forever—all eyes fixed on the soldier, the girl, and me.

Slowly the man bent, wiped his sword on Papa's back, and put it away. The woman straightened and faced him. I wrenched free and buried my arms around Papa's neck.

After a while, after the sound of departing soldiers faded, gentle hands patted at me. "Poor little lad. Come, Dominic, come with me."

I clung tighter to Papa's neck. In a colorless, lifeless fog I heard the voices.

Elgge's girl: "Let go, Dominic. Your papa's dead."

The priest: "The boy needs looking after. Are there not kin who will claim him?"

"I can give him a good home."

"You? A soldiers' whore? 'Tis no way to raise a child."

Elgge: "My girl and me can look after him all right, Father. She makes good pay."

The priest: "He wants a moral upbringing, not wantonness."

His relentless hands pried me loose from Papa and turned me to face him. "Your papa's gone to Heaven, lad, to be with your mother."

Not without me!

He smiled. "He was baptized with her, and you, too. This parting is hard, I know, but 'tis not forever."

He stood and confronted the villagers. "He's a ward of the estate if no living kin claims him. You know the law. Do you want that for this innocent lad? Whose father just valiantly sacrificed his life for one of your own?"

Folk glanced at each other murmuring, then all heads turned towards one man. I twisted to bring Papa back into my clouded vision.

The priest: "Are you not his uncle?"

My uncle: "His mother was my sister, Father."

"Then you acknowledge kinship. The boy is your ward."

"But, Father, I can scarce afford. . . ."

"If the estate takes him, he'll likely be sold to the mines; he's a good size for toiling underground. No, he's your nephew. You'll take the boy under your roof and raise him with your own two sons. Are you a Christian man or not?"

"Aye, Father, I am."

"Will you refuse this child of your sister Christian charity?"

"No, Father."

The hands forced my eyes to tear away from Papa.

"You've still a family, Dominic; be thankful of that. I know you loved your papa, but, lad, he'd be glad to see you with your blood-kin."

I saw only my tears, heard only the roar of my own blood in my head. And it was a long, long time before I ever stopped turning suddenly at the imagined sound of Papa's voice speaking my name, or startling to the familiar sensation of his hand resting atop my curly head, or watching for his broad smile somewhere in the twilight—only to remember anew that I would never know his voice nor hand nor face again.

And still, somehow, I lived.

PART II

V

My uncle dragged me roughly through the dark wood, his iron grip squeezing the scruff of my neck in a painful vise. My struggles served only to stumble me more clumsily over the rough trail dimly lit by cloud-mottled moonlight. Each time I faltered, the hand jerked me abruptly forward again.

If only I could free myself of his grasp, I thought desperately. Then I would easily lose him in the woods, for I was small enough to scramble through underbrush that he could never enter. My uncle knew this well, for he never eased the pressure of his hard fingers nor slowed the pace enough to allow me steady footing.

Why we were hastening into the chill, damp forest in the dead of night I had no inkling. That my uncle would be pleased to be rid of me I knew for certain. When he had roused me from sleep, kicked me from the straw bed in the barn, and bound my hands tightly in front of me with leather strips, I truly feared he had come to kill me. I still feared so. I could think of no other explanation for this night's outing.

For two years my uncle had complained that he had no use for a dwarf half the size of his own sons and twice as hungry. For two years he had rationed and tallied every morsel I swallowed and had seen to it that I paid back every bite tenfold in labor. For two years I had known well the sharp edge of his voice and the back of his hand. And now—I renewed his wrath by futile resistance, digging my rag-wrapped heels into the dirt and pulling away with all my strength. My uncle angrily hurled me backwards against a tree-trunk, knocking the breath from my throat and setting my head to ringing. With curses and cuffs he yanked me forward along the dark path again.

Terrified, I could only stumble miserably beside him. Surely he would not murder me! What if the priest found out? Or the estate masters? Legally I was the landowner's property, not my uncle's. He would have to tell them I was a runaway, and that would set the agents searching for me. These bewildering thoughts tumbled in my mind, but I could only believe that I was about to get my throat cut in some lonely thicket. Yet I was too familiar with my guardian's wrath to try and slip out of his grasp again.

After an eternity of staggering about in the black forest, we stopped abruptly at the edge of a road, shining greyishly under the gloomy sky. My uncle shoved me against something hard and cold that loomed beneath the shifting shadows of the trees. I recognized it as a shrine to the Lar, sentinel of the crossroads, worn smooth by the hands of countless travelers who touched the stone in reverence to the god who watched the road. I leaned my hot forehead against the cold stone column and fought to catch my breath and keep my knees from buckling. I took no comfort from the shrine, for the Lares of the roads are Pagan gods, and even if I believed in them, little help would they be to a Christian.

As my uncle's heavy breathing slowed beside me, I heard crackling steps in the wood. With a merciless hand clamped on my shoulder, he turned me around to face two black shapes materializing out of the gloom.

"So you showed after all," spoke one of the shapes. "Let's see what you've got there."

My uncle stood me against the white stone as much in moonlight as the clouds would afford.

"As promised," he said. "A dwarf. A young one."

A blurry face with foul breath came close and peered into mine. My heart pounded so hard it made my head spin.

"Strike a light, there, Bilky, and let's have a look at the little bug."

The strike of flint against iron and a flash set an oily rag-lamp aflame, and I blinked in the glare as it was shoved toward me. The face I met was hard, dirty, and grinning through yellow teeth. I flinched and flattened against the column as a quick hand flicked back one side of my cloak. The man eyed me critically.

I knew what he saw—a frightened fourteen-year-old boy,

barely three feet tall, with disheveled auburn curls straggling into his eyes. He examined my hands bound together, hands overlarge for stubby arms clothed in the rolled-up sleeves of a ragged shirt; nor did he overlook the stumpy legs so skimpily wrapped in threadbare rags that the windings gapped open in places, baring outsized feet to the chill wind. I shivered under his greedy scrutiny, sick at heart, understanding only too clearly my uncle's purpose.

"Aye," appraised the man. "'Tis a dwarf for certain. Shut the light, Bilky."

"I told you," my uncle's voice sounded in the sudden darkness. "Well worth your trouble, is he not? I believe the price we agreed on. . . ."

"We never agreed. You suggested. Twenty denarii. That's my price."

"Denarii!" protested my uncle. "I won't take bronze; I'll have silver. *Argent*—fifty argenti."

The man laughed hoarsely. "Five argenti. No more."

"This is robbery!" my uncle whined. "He's my own blood. My dead sister's only child." How desperate he must be to admit that, I thought resentfully. "I can barely force myself to sell him, but times being hard as they. . . ."

"Shove the muck!" snapped the other. "Will you take the five or no?"

"Argenti?"

"Aye."

My uncle sighed. "All right. He's yours."

Five silver coins changed hands. It was all over unnervingly quickly. My uncle disappeared into the night without a word or glance in my direction.

I stood frozen to the stone in shock. Before I could recover to slip away, another hand closed on my collar and hauled me forward. The two men struck off straight into the wood, following a narrow path, dragging me with them. After a long, exhausting tramp we came to a crude camp, where they let me drop beside a circle of fading coals. By now, I could not have run if I had the chance.

The one called Bilky added wood to the coals and stirred them into flame. He was small and weasely, with an unhealthy color on his skin. I watched him warily. The other one picked up a roll of sacking and a rope.

Bilky nudged me with his toe and grinned. "Better wrap him up tight, Luge, so's he don't run off in the night."

Luge bent over me. "Keep still," he growled unnecessarily, for I dared not move. He tied my feet together tightly with the rope and brought it up to lash my arms close against my chest, leaving my hands just as my uncle had bound them. Then he shook open the bundle of sacking; it fell in one long strip. I was ungraciously heaved onto one end, rolled up in it, and then tied fast in the middle. I could move nothing but my head.

"That'll hold you," Luge assured me before rejoining Bilky at the fire, where they conversed in low tones.

Now I began to perspire, partly from being wrapped so close, but mostly from dread. My wrists burned where the leather cut them; my fingers ached. I felt sick, but I held my churning stomach in check, not caring to lie in its meager contents all night. But I could not hold back the tears. They trickled down my face into my hair, leaving icy trails in their wake. The shrouded moon blurred in my vision as I thought of my papa, similarly wrapped and lowered into a hasty grave beside Mama. If only he were alive, this would not be happening! I remembered him run through with the sword before my eyes; I remembered the yearning look he gave me before he fell; I remembered only cavernous pain and vorant emptiness afterward. Two years gone—and still I could not think of him without despair.

I doubt I slept any that night, but I lay there in a nightmarish stupor until dawn. The sun was yet a pearly haze behind the trees when I was roused and unwound. Not until then did Luge think to untie my hands, which by now were swollen blue. I flinched as he unwrapped my wrists, revealing raw lines in the skin, and attempted unsuccessfully to move my stiff fingers. Later, as blood rushed back into my hands, I clamped my teeth shut to keep from crying out in pain.

We breakfasted on sour wine and dried figs, which I welcomed heartily, before packing up camp. In all it condensed into two knapsacks the men wore on their backs. Any hope I had of escaping was crushed when Luge knotted the rope snug around my neck. It was scratchy, not dangerously tight, but there was no way of getting it off without working long at that fast knot.

I felt like a dog on a leash. And Bilky led me along as if I were no more than a dog, tugging me forward when my pace slowed or pulling me up short if I scurried ahead too far. He laughed, too, at the way I walked, calling me "bandy-legs" and imitating me with a droll, rollicking gait. Luge, poor fellow, had no sense of humor at all and so was in a foul mood all day, especially since the grey heavens poured a steady torrent of rain on us throughout the afternoon.

Three days we traveled in procession: Luge leading, Bilky following, and me struggling to keep up so as not to feel the rope jerk at my chaffed and tender neck. In all this time I learned only that my owners were rogues and thieves and that they expected to turn a nice profit off me from someone named Ronaldo. They conversed between themselves, rarely spoke to me but to order me to sit or stand or walk or eat or—always—hurry, until at last the miserable journey ended. Luge knotted the free end of the rope to a tree limb—out of my reach, as most tree limbs are—and left Bilky to watch me while he ferreted on ahead.

We waited a long time. Bilky finished half a wineskin and snored against a tree, so I idly set to working at the knot under my chin. It was hopeless after three days of soaking and drying and soaking again. Next I tried slipping the rope over my head, which proved to be an excellent method of strangling myself. I tugged at the other end of the tether ferociously. At this point I no longer cared that I was being towed about by owners to whom I was just a piece of merchandise, nor did I care who Ronaldo was or what his uses for me might be; I cared only that I was tied to this damnable rope. I had tolerated it as long as I sanely could.

Since the tree limb was out of reach, I would have to climb to it, and the rope, I found, provided a ready access. I braced my feet against the tree-trunk and walked up, pulling myself hand over hand on the rope. Once I found myself securely astride the limb, I went at the knot furiously. This one was less carefully tied and unraveled more easily under my fingers.

Near victory shone in my eyes until Luge stomped into view, closely followed by another man. Desperately I tugged at the knot, my fingers fumbling in their haste. With a bellow and a bound, Luge reached the tree, grasped the rope, and jerked me savagely off the limb. I hit hard; my shoulder and head took the worst of the blow. Dazed, I could only lie there while tears of pain and frustration mingled with the dirt.

Luge's laughter rang in my ears. A soft voice interrupted him. "Quite a little monkey you have there, Luge."

I had no idea what a monkey might be, but I misliked the sound of it. By now Bilky was kicked conscious and heard himself called all manner of vile names. Luge then swiftly turned his attention on me.

"Get up," he growled, prodding me ungently with his foot.

I did so, slowly and carefully. My neck burned unbearably. A hand upturned my mud-streaked face, and I was looking into blazing black eyes.

"How old are you, boy?"

"Fourteen," I told him in a quavering voice.

"See now," bragged Luge. "Young enough to last a while and old enough so's he don't grow no more'n a couple of inches. What more could you ask, mate? When I seen him, I thought right off of my old friend Ronaldo."

Ronaldo's gaze traveled up the rope to the tree limb and back down to me. He looked unamused, but spoke genially.

"Can't be too sure about dwarves," he said. "A lot of them grow up feeble in the head. This one looks dull-witted to me."

Indignation found my voice for me. "I am *not either* dull-witted!" I cried. "Nor am I feeble-minded! And I'm sick of being tied on a leash!" This last outburst fizzled into a weary sob.

"There now," Luge grinned at Ronaldo, "ain't he a feisty one? Nothing wrong with *his* mind. What say you to twenty-five solidi?"

Ronaldo laughed heartily. "Luge, you *are* a greedy haggler! Why, where would I ever get my hands on so much gold? You ask a soldier's ransom. So much for an underfed dwarf? I'll give you three solidi."

I seemed to have suffered through a similar conversation once before.

"*Three?* He's worth twenty at least."

"Five. He'll need fattening up."

"Strong enough to climb, ain't he? Fifteen solidi."

"Ah, but does he have talent?"

"Twelve, and you're stealing him."

"Five."

Luge wagged his head from side to side. "Being's what he is," he said craftily, "I figure I can get ten easy from gamers. Nah, think I'll hang on to him awhile, mate." Luge jerked the rope on my neck; I gasped and staggered backward against him.

The dark eyes narrowed. "You don't know any gamers, Luge."

"So you think!" snorted Luge. "I come to you first, Ronaldo, being's how we've done business before and all. But a spunky little climber like this—a dwarf and all—I know what he's worth. There's them'll pay plenty to game him."

Luge jerked the rope again, and I cut short a whimper of pain. Ronaldo's black eyes flashed anger.

"I'll go ten," he said sharply. "Not a solidus more."

"Now that's more like my old friend Ronaldo," grinned Luge. "Done. Ten solidi." He gloated in satisfaction as the dark-eyed man nearly emptied his purse with ten gold coins. He tossed the end of the rope to Ronaldo.

"He's all yours." Then he guffawed loudly. "I knew you'd go soft-hearted over the little tyke—him and them big brown eyes!"

Ignoring him, Ronaldo knelt before me, pulled a glinting dagger from his belt, and slipped it carefully between my throat and the rope. I stood like stone and tried not to wince as he cut through the fibers with the sharp-edged blade. At last the hated rope fell away and I could turn my head without its fiery irritation.

I stared at my new owner uncertainly. He looked to be not yet past his thirties; his wavy locks were still raven black, and his sun-dark skin was little creased with age. From one ear dangled a gold earring, half hidden beneath his hair.

"Well, lad," he said kindly, "you've cost me a fair copper or two, haven't you?" His Latin was strangely accented, like none I had heard before. He twirled the severed noose in his hand. "Like as not you're thinking of running off as soon as you get the chance."

My eyes widened—proof he read my thoughts.

"Luge claims he bought you off your uncle. True?" He smiled gently at my reluctant nod. "Tell me, boy, where do you think to run to?"

I had no answer. I stared at his boots miserably. Even had I known where I was now, which I did not, I had nowhere to go, no means of getting along.

"I'll make a deal with you, lad," Ronaldo was saying. "You don't run away, and I won't tie you to any trees."

I raised my head in surprise, meeting his dark eyes.

"Come home with me," he continued, "and you'll find food and fire, a bed, and good company. 'Twill be no hard task, I'd wager, to feed you better than your uncle did. In return you'll learn my trade. Put your heart into it, lad, and you'll do well." He glanced darkly over toward Luge rudely berating Bilky as they shouldered their belongings, then his warm eyes engaged mine soberly. "None of my folk will lay a hand on you, boy. I can promise you that. Agreed?"

It was the fairest offer I had heard from anyone, so I nodded in agreement. Ronaldo clapped me on the shoulder with a grin.

"Ah, you've learned the first lesson already," he said, looking pleased. "When in trouble—strike a bargain." He stood and beamed down at me. "By the way, I am Ronaldo. What's your name, lad?"

"Dominic."

"Come, Dominico. Let's go home."

VI

Home proved to be a vagabond camp, well hidden in the vast forest. Such a merry mixture of sights, sounds, and smells met us as we emerged from the trees that an involuntary smile crept onto my face.

A smattering of wagons, seven in all, sat scattered at odd angles about a well-trampled clearing. And what colorful wagons they were! Though the paint was faded and peeling, the garish designs on the wood caught my attention. Bordered pictures of animals, skies, and fantastic beings decorated the nearest wagon. The only part not covered with painted scenes was a stitched oxhide top stretched over the lattice-work of poles that formed the skeleton of the wagon, resembling horizontal and vertical ribs. One side of the leather canopy was rolled and lashed partway up, but I was in no wise tall enough to see the contents within.

Besides, I found plenty to see outside. Such a strange collection of foreigners they were! Some were dark and some were fair, yet not one was Roman or Gallic, which in itself was an unusual sight in Gaul.

Now, Gauls—and I speak of true Gauls, whose ancestors owned this land long before the Romans came, whose stubborn strain still runs pure in my veins—Gauls pride themselves on their colorful hooded cloaks, finely tooled and decorated belts, and intricately worked brooches and clasps; in this wise we are akin to the Germanni barbarians east of the River Rhine. Even so, I was unprepared for the wildly-dyed, assorted attire of these outlandish vagabonds. Capes, skirts, caps, shirts, and vests of every possible hue swirled around us as the inhabitants surrounded me and my escort. Not even one drab Roman tunic fraternized among them. A jingle-jangle of jewelry accompanied this dancing carnival, joined by voices babbling in a sing-song language I did not understand.

Ronaldo held up both hands, rings gleaming in the evening sun, and called a halt to the chaos. Then he spoke grandly in his odd Latin, waving a hand dramatically at me.

"Dominico, the dwarf!"

The small crowd exclaimed and applauded its approval.

"May he bring us good fortune!" Ronaldo cried.

Someone laughed and chided him in equally odd Latin. "What will you make of this little rag-tag, Ronaldo? A beggar?"

Suddenly I was abashedly aware of my tattered, ill-fitted, cast-off clothes. Though I possessed a Gallic pride in appearance, my aunt and uncle wasted no such sentiments on me. They considered it a foolish endeavor to clothe me in the fashion of a respectable human being, since I in no way resembled that hallowed creature—not by their standards anyway. Therefore, I stood before these gaily dressed folk and hung my head in embarrassment.

"A beggar?" Ronaldo was cheerfully bantering. "Indeed not! This little fellow has the makings of an acrobat. Make him welcome into the family!"

Hands reached out and tousled me, while voices chattered in broken Latin intermingled with that unknown tongue. I ducked my head, for though they were not unfriendly, they were rough. Ronaldo waved them back.

"He is not yet accustomed to so many friendly folk at once. Dominico, these are your cousins. Mikato!" he bellowed. "Mikato!"

A younger replica of Ronaldo leapt forward. He looked only a few years older than me—perhaps seventeen or so.

"Mikato, come and meet your little cousin Dominico. Where is Felicia?"

"Here, Father," answered a girl's voice.

Mikato squatted before me and eyed me with lively interest. "An acrobat, eh?" he grinned. "I see we have our work cut out for us."

I blinked at him uncertainly. Then he was joined by a beautiful raven-tressed young girl with merry dark eyes. She chattered at me in her musical tongue.

"Hold, Felicia," admonished Ronaldo. "Dominico knows no Greek; he speaks only Latin."

She looked disappointed. Her next words were halting. "Welcome, cousin. We have been keeping supper for you hot by the fire. Are you hungry?"

I was bone weary more than hungry, and a little frightened at being the center of attention of these strange folk, but it was nice attention, so I smiled gratefully and took her proffered hand. She said something to Ronaldo in Greek. He shook his head.

"Do not speak of him in a language he doesn't understand. While we are in the west, Felicia, you should learn your Latin so that it flows swiftly like a dance. Aye, he is little, but he is as old as you are."

She blushed, a rosy glow touching her earth-brown skin, hearing her words repeated. "I meant no . . . how do you say it? . . . no meanness, Dominico."

Shyly, I nodded.

She smiled and tugged at my hand. "Come with me."

Under curious scrutiny from the gathered folk, I followed Felicia as she shooed our way through a cluster of scavenging goats. The camp looked to be a temporary one, and it could not have numbered much over four dozen occupants. As I later discovered, this manner of grouping altogether was an infrequent occurrence, indulged now only because they judged this particular spot safe territory, deep enough in the forest to be of no interest to Roman officials.

Felicia led me to a cookfire, where the others were gathering to ward off the twilight chill. She thrust a gaily decorated ceramic bowl into my hands and ladled into it a strangely aromatic stew. A circle of logs made cozy benches around the fire. I sat on one of the logs between Felicia and Ronaldo. Mikato settled beside Felicia and curled his arm comfortably about her waist.

The stew, I discovered happily, was rabbit and cabbage with just a few young turnips, yet it was so sharply spiced with unfamiliar flavors that I, accustomed to nought but salt, nearly choked on the first ravenous mouthful. I gulped, blinked my watering eyes, and proceeded more cautiously. Later I developed a taste for these exotic spices, especially that tingling delight called pepper. A jug of wine also came around, not the watered-down, sour-vinegar wine I expected, but hearty, sweet grape wine that brought a hot flush to my skin and sent my head floating off my shoulders. Before the meal was done I was enjoying the company immensely.

I was introduced to a myriad of folk. One of them was a lean, sinewy older man named Brossos, introduced as Master of Acrobats. Ronaldo told him I had climbed onto a high tree-limb. Brossos asked me how I did so and I explained how I walked up the tree-trunk pulling myself hand over hand by the very rope I was tethered to. Brossos laughed.

"I'd like to have seen that," he told me. "Quite a feat for a little one. Think you'd like to be an acrobat, boy?"

I was at a loss. "I don't know what that is. . . ."

"You'll find out soon enough. We'll see if you've a talent for it."

Then Ronaldo told them how I got down from the tree. The company sobered, and Brossos looked at my raw neck where the rope had chaffed and at my bruised shoulder where I had struck the ground after being pulled from the tree.

"A fall like that—untrained!" he muttered. "Ah, Hagia, come see, his neck needs tending."

An ancient white-haired scarecrow of a woman bent over me and with gnarled, brown hands pulled the filthy shirt aside from my throat.

"More than his neck needs tending. Who's been taking care of you, boy?"

I looked into her wrinkled face and bright, black eyes. "No one."

"It shows. Have a few more mouthfuls of wine while I get my medicines."

Mikato passed me the wine jug. "You'll need it," he said half jokingly, but only half.

I had eaten my fill and drunk more than enough strong wine by the time the old woman Hagia returned. Still, the fiery liquid with which she washed my neck stung so fiercely as to bring tears to my eyes, despite the wine. I clenched my teeth and fists and eyes until she was done.

"Good, good," she murmured. "There's no infection. The rest will wait 'til tomorrow."

Ronaldo laid a hand on my shoulder and smiled. "'Tis a brave boy we've got here."

I did not feel very brave, but his words heartened me. I smiled up at Hagia. I heard the chattering around the fire, in quick words unknown to me, like a chanting in some strange dream. These strange folk, with their odd clothes and foreign tongue, in this isolated camp of painted wagons and oxen and goats—ah, this was like a world unto itself, having no place in the real world. And I was in their world now, for good or for ill. Fleetingly, the thought passed my mind, *I shall have to learn Greek.*

A plucking of lute strings swerved my attention. Someone began a song—a slow, mournful tune with eerily wavering notes—joined by tiny cymbals ringing from a child's quick fingers. The three sounds—the lute, the voice, the cymbals—wove and wound inside my head in a most deliciously benumbing dance. My eyelids drooped, my head nodded, and I slipped dreamily to the ground, though many hands caught my fall and leaned me gently against the log. My exhausted body, overcome by the weary, grueling, three-day tramp, melted into a little heap. Then my mind disentangled from the music and drifted away into darkness.

Sometime in the night I dreamed Papa lifted me in his arms and carried me upstairs to the inn loft.

Papa?

"Shh—'tis all right, lad. Time for bed."

Papa.

I awoke shivering, though I was wrapped in a thick woolen blanket and lay on a mattress in some kind of . . . wooden tent? The outside voices and chatterings were unfamiliar. I spent a few confused seconds wondering where I was.

"Good morning," sang a cheery voice.

I turned my head and saw the black-eyed girl sitting crosslegged, watching me. I remembered then. I must be in one of the wagons.

I sat up abruptly and wished I had not. I felt suddenly dizzy and shaky and not a little ill. The girl thrust a wooden cup filled with a woodsy-scented liquid into my hands.

"For you," she smiled. "For the wine. Hagia said."

I swallowed a tentative mouthful or two, then drank half the herb mixture in a few gulps as I realized how thirsty I was. It was strong, but not unpleasant.

"Thank you."

"Better, Dominico?"

"Not yet," I grinned weakly.

"Ronaldo said you must not wake up alone. So I wait. Now come for breakfast."

"Let me sit just a bit longer."

"Drink more," she urged, indicating the herb brew.

I drank slowly, barely managing to get it all down. I looked all around the wagon; it was painted on the inside, too, at least the parts that were of wood. Solid benches lined the sides, serving as beds and seating; they were covered with bright-patterned cushions. I looked up. The inner lattice-work of the wagon frame was hung with all sorts of colorful blankets, cloaks, trinkets, and sharp-smelling bags of herbs. And over all stretched the oxhide canopy.

"Home," smiled Felicia, following my gaze around the interior.

"Whose wagon?"

"Ronaldo's, Hagia's, Mikato's, mine, and now yours, cousin."

Mine? I looked again. It was so unfamiliar with its pungent smells and colorful closeness, yet I felt, too, a sense of having been here before, an intuitive hint of how familiar and comforting I would soon find it.

"Come," Felicia urged. "Breakfast." She dropped lightly out the back of the wagon then reached out to take my hands.

"Jump—I'll steady you, Dominico."

I looked down. It was not far—three or four feet—but my uncertain stomach told me that to jump would be folly. Besides, my whole body ached already, especially my shoulder and neck, and I did not wish to worsen them. I shook my head at her waiting hands and climbed down carefully, feet first, until I felt bare ground through the tattered windings.

"Ha! You'll never make an acrobat that way!" laughed a youthful voice good-naturedly. I turned and faced a boy perhaps younger than me, certainly taller. He had the same black hair and eyes, the same brown skin, as Felicia.

Felicia loosed a torrent of Greek at him. Slowly his smile sank to a contrite expression.

"I'm sorry, Dominico," he said to me earnestly. "I forgot you were hurt."

"Then we're even," I told him, "for I forgot your name." I vaguely remembered his face from the night before.

"Gorgi."

I cocked my head up at him and studied him carefully. There

was something I needed to know, but I did not wish to sound stupid in the asking.

"Show me, Gorgi," I said casually, and a little impishly, "just how is it that an acrobat gets down from a wagon?"

Gorgi grinned and glanced at Felicia. She tossed her head.

"He's a big show-off already," she told me. "Pay him no audience."

Ah, an answer was forthcoming.

Gorgi swung himself easily into the wagon.

"Backwards or forwards?" he goaded, winking at me when Felicia turned her head away.

"Backwards," I said with growing interest, having no notion what he might be about to do.

So he stepped up onto the narrow board that formed the wagon's end and stood there, his back to us, as surely as if he stood on solid earth instead of an inch width of plank. Then he sprang up and back and spun head over heels *twice* in the air and landed on his feet all in an instant.

I stared at him in amazement. And my heart sank. I was certain I would never be able to do *anything* like that. I would only make a beggar after all.

"Oh, come on, Dominico," insisted Felicia, not even faintly impressed with Gorgi's exit from the wagon. "Everyone's waiting."

Everyone? I let her lead me around another wagon. Gorgi followed us, doing cartwheels all the way.

Well, *everyone* was not seated around the cookfire, but a good many folk were, and I was abashed at the sudden attention turned toward me. If Felicia had not pulled me into their midst I would probably have hidden under a wagon. But I was soon put at ease. Their greetings were friendly and gladdening. They made room for me on a log and passed a cup of fresh goat's-milk my way. They wished only to bid me welcome this fair morning, and I *felt* welcome. I sat among these gaily dressed vagabonds in my dirty, worn, dun-grey garb and drank in shyly their smiles and kind words. They made room for me and called me "cousin," as they did each other.

Some of the talk around me was in Latin, but much of it was Greek, which I did not understand. Most of them were dark-eyed and brown of skin, though some were light complexioned and fair of hair. Their ancestry, I learned, was Syrian, Egyptian, Macedonian. All were Roman citizens, as was I, but they spoke mainly the language of the eastern Empire and I of the west.

Dominico they named me, finding it impossible to call me by a name that ended so abruptly as Dominic. I did not mind; the sound of it fell pleasantly on my ears.

After a breakfast of steamed bread and warm goat's-milk I felt much better. Hagia then led me back to the wagon, the most garishly painted of the lot. Now I noticed the decorated carving on the wagon's side. Its central figure was a seated Pagan goddess with a serpent clutched in one upraised hand and a sistrum in the other. A crown of cow's horns embracing a radiant moon adorned her head, and a haloed infant suckled at her breast.

Hagia noticed me staring at the picture.

"Isis," she told me. "Queen of Heaven. And Horus, her child, the Sun."

I shuddered inwardly, for if nothing else, these past two years of being taken to Mass each Sun's Day by my uncle (doing his Christian duty for all the village and the priest to take notice) meant that I had learned to fear all things Pagan. The pitiful sight of hapless Pagans publicly flailed to death with lead-tipped whips by solemn black-robed monks had heightened my horror. Thus, with soul-wrenching trepidation, I approached the unholy wagon.

"Now, Dominico, take off your tunic."

I stood wide-eyed and petrified.

"Come, child, that filthy thing is good for nothing but rags."

Now Mikato and two other youths came hauling steaming buckets and poured water hot from the fire into a wooden tub just large enough for me to sit in. Hagia sent them away, and I unwound the threadbare wrappings from my feet. Then, embarrassed, I pulled the dun shirt that served as tunic over my head.

"Don't be shy; I've seen hundreds of naked little boys in my lifetime, many of which were my own. Get in the tub and scrape that dirt off you so a body can see what you look like."

While I cautiously eased into the hot but rapidly cooling water, she climbed nimbly into the wagon and reappeared with a ceramic jar of sweet-scented oil which she poured generously over my hair and back and shoulders.

"Rub it all in and wash it off with this," she said, giving me a rough woolen cloth.

When I finished she was satisfied with all but my hair. She poured an extra bucket of water, which was quite cool by now, through my snarled hair and tugged until she could comb her fingers through the curls. Then she gave me a towel and helped me clamber up into the wagon.

"Now for clothes befitting a child of free folk." Hagia raised the lid of a carved wooden trunk and began pulling out folded articles of clothing.

My eyes widened when I saw her shake out a thick wool cloak of deep woad blue. It was secondhand, to be sure, and much too large, of course, but it was beautiful.

"This belonged to my youngest son. He died of the fever two summers gone."

She swirled the cloak about my shoulders in a cascade of blue, fastened its bronze clasp, pulled the hood over my head, and commenced to tug and tuck and fix with bronze pins so deftly that before I could properly admire it she had already whisked the garment away and snatched up another. All the while she mumbled a confusion of Greek and Latin. I interrupted her.

"Grandmother," I said, for I had been taught my manners, and, anyway, around here she was probably *everybody's* grandmother, "do you know Ronaldo paid *ten solidi* for me?" I was thoroughly impressed, having never before in my life laid eyes on even one solidus, much less ten of them at once. "Why would he pay so much?"

"Ah, you're our luck, Dominico."

I frowned in puzzlement.

"Sit, child. Give me your foot. Either one—it doesn't matter. There. Don't you know a dwarf is good luck?"

I shook my head in astonishment.

"By the Styx! What ignorant folk you are in the west! And you are twice lucky, my little red-haired one, for red hair is blessed. Aye, and we need your luck, Dominico, times being what they are, with the Empire drawing free folk into its web like a spider catching butterflies."

I could think of no one who ever got any luck off me. The two I loved most were dead—what kind of luck was that?

"Now the other foot."

"Is the Empire chasing you?"

"Theodosius!" The old woman hissed the Emperor's name as if it were poisonous. "He will not let us be! We of the old religion are no longer safe in the east."

"Is that why you came to Gaul?"

"Aye. The young one, the Valentinian, we hear he is not so hard, not so big a spider, eh? This Theodosius will not live forever.

And the stars said 'twas time we moved on. Our road is here, in the west.''

Hagia was finished with me now, the measuring and sizing done, and only the sewing to be completed. She waved me to stay seated. I watched her in silence awhile, but I needed to talk about something that worried at my mind.

"Grandmother. . . ." I began.

"The folk call me Hagia, or Mother Hagia." She snorted. "Or Old Hag, if I annoy them, which I do as often as I feel they need it. You must call me the same, Dominico."

I nodded. "Mother Hagia, suppose I do not make an acrobat? What if I cannot? I don't think I can . . . do what Gorgi does."

"Looks too difficult, does it?"

"Aye, very difficult."

"So it is. Yet that does not mean you cannot learn. Wait 'til you've tried, child, before giving up. Brossos is a good teacher—the best."

"But what if I cannot learn? What will I be then?"

"Hagia will tell you what you will be, Dominico," she said, setting to work altering a pair of brown woolen breeches. "If not an acrobat, then you'll be a dancer or musician. You'll be whatever it takes to survive, be it gambler, charlatan, thief. There is a place for you here; we bring diversion and amusement and, aye, magic, to folk who see none of the world except what comes to their doorsteps. We follow the festivals, whatever gods they may honor, and we bring with us magic and mystery—we *are* the magic and mystery, my little red-haired wonder, and so will you be, too."

"No!" I stared at her, horrified. My voice dropped to a whisper. "I cannot! For my very soul, I cannot!"

She glanced at me sharply. "Why not?"

"I'm a Christian! I cannot join in Pagan festivals! 'Tis a mortal sin!"

Her bony hand shot out and grabbed my arm as swift as a hawk snatching a hare in its claws.

"*A Christian!*" she screeched angrily.

I shrank back in terror.

Instantly she relented; her face softened, her voice grew kindly.

"No, no, my Dominico, I would not hurt you, not at all. I never meant to frighten you, child."

I stared at her, speechless.

"Ah, but a *Christian?* My dear, what will we do with you?" She swept aside the wagon flap. "Ronaldo!" she shrilled, her old voice high and cracked, yet loud enough to be heard throughout the camp.

Ronaldo appeared shortly, and she let loose a stream of words as he swung into the wagon. He looked at me gravely.

"What's this? You're Christian?"

Timidly, I nodded.

"And why do you refuse the festivals?"

My words were faltering. "'Twould condemn my soul to burn in Hell for all eternity," I whispered.

Ronaldo smiled wanly and shook his head. "I'd be hard pressed to threaten you with a fate worse than that, lad. Still, we made a bargain."

"I never bargained my soul."

Ronaldo grinned. "A natural, is he not, Old Hag? We must bargain anew with our little dwarf." Then to me: "Keep your soul, Dominico. You need take part in no Pagan rites or rituals; you need worship no gods or goddesses. All you need do is entertain the crowds. Folk come to enjoy themselves and spend a little coin. They love surprise and skill, and you will give them both. I won't ask you to be Pagan, just enthralling. Now that doesn't sound so damning, does it?"

"I suppose not," I said hesitantly.

"Then we have a deal?"

"I can stay Christian?"

"If you must."

"We have a deal."

"Done. Old Hag, he's all yours." Ronaldo leapt down from the wagon, but I called after him.

"Ronaldo!"

"What, lad?" he asked, poking his head in through the flaps.

"Nor can I cheat or lie or steal."

Ronaldo raised his eyes Heavenward, but in appeal to which gods I dared not guess.

VII

 If I appeared to be getting cocky, I had reason if anyone did. My new wardrobe elated me. The woad-blue hooded cloak was without doubt the finest piece of clothing I had ever owned. It even clasped with a bronze pin cast in the likeness of the head and horns of a bearded goat. Under my cloak I wore a saffron-yellow shirt of fine, light wool, belted at the waist with a strip of tooled leather buckled with a bronze goat charging. My breeches—very un-Roman— tucked into oxhide boots (I'd never had *boots* before!) which were notched and turned down to form a cuff and fit my feet just perfectly. And were all this not enough, Hagia was fashioning me a shortsleeve, oxhide overtunic for the coming winter.

Hagia, I soon understood, was more than the old woman's name; it was both name and title. Indeed I learned it was a term of veneration. She was the oldest person among the vagabonds and therefore, by virtue of her years, the wisest and most respected. Hagia means something akin to "wise-woman" and is an hereditary title. Ronaldo, Hagia's eldest and only surviving son, was patriarch of the clan, honored as head of the family even by those not blood-related. Felicia was Ronaldo's daughter, and granddaughter to Hagia, therefore she was in line to be "wise-woman" one day. Felicia's mother had succumbed to the fever that swept the clan nearly two years ago and reduced their numbers to little more than fifty. Though her name, Felicia, was Latin, her ancestral language was Greek. No older than my fourteen years herself, Felicia was betrothed to Mikato, her second cousin. Mikato, as might be expected, looked to be clan patriarch himself someday, but meanwhile Ronaldo ruled surely as had he been Emperor. Such was the wandering caravan of exotics of whose company, to both my delight and dismay, I suddenly found myself a member.

Delighted I was because they were undoubtedly the gayest, most devil-may-care folk I had ever known. Ofttimes of an evening, when the mood struck, they would dance and sing, drink and tell tales—I learned some of my bawdiest songs and scariest stories around these campfires—until half the night was gone. And they were so full of love, these vagabonds, and gave it so freely and heartily that I never felt anything but one of them. They called me cousin—a favored term of endearment bestowed quite indiscriminately upon any member of the clan whether they be blood-kin or no.

Dismayed I was, too, because they were Pagan clear down to their toenails. I might have understood it had they stuck to one religion and believed it devoutly, but not them! They reveled in every outlandish religion on Earth and indulged in all manner of Pagan practices.

To be honest, in their hearts they belonged to the Egyptian cult of Isis. The horned lady painted on Hagia's wagon was the goddess holding the infant Horus on her lap, and on the other side was depicted Osiris, Lord of the Dead, a throned deity with a short shepherd's crook in one hand and an odd little whip in the other. At his feet lay an emaciated sort of dog and a set of pan-scales.

The story goes that Osiris was chopped into pieces by his wicked brother Set and scattered about the Earth, but Isis, his faithful wife, gathered up all his parts, reassembled them, and with her powerful enchantments brought him back to life. Isis and Osiris have an infant son, Horus. Isis is the Queen of Heaven, Osiris is the Lord of the Dead, and Horus is the Sun.

Osiris, Judge of the Dead though he may be, was not the principal deity invoked by the vagabond clan. It is Isis whose incantations possess the power to resurrect the dead into immortality, and it is the Ship of Isis, in the shape of the crescent moon, which carries souls to the blessed abode of Osiris. So it is to the goddess that incense smokes, sistrums jangle, wine flows in libation, and garlands adorn the cow's horns. For as Osiris is sometimes known as Serapis the Bull, Isis is in another guise called Hathor the Sacred Cow.

Their Paganism did not stop at incarnations of this triune family. A whole pantheon of lesser gods and goddesses made up the clan of Isis—adopted cousins, no doubt. The favored "cousin" of the whole lot was Dionysus, who was not Egyptian at all, but Greek. The rites of Dionysus called for much less serious celebration than those of Isis. It is no secret that the God of Wine and Revelry was by far the most popular Pagan deity in Gaul during those troubled times. Five Bacchanalia a year were celebrated throughout the province, unlawfully of course, and no wonder. No other cult excited so many drunken orgies at once—drinking bouts lasting days at a time, sexual passions indulged with indecorous abandon—and no other god enjoyed such devoted daily libation from his fervent worshippers as did Dionysus.

Always the festivities included much drinking, singing, and storytelling interspiced with gambling at dice or knucklebones, pickpocketing, and fortune-telling. To speak fairly, the vagabond troupe did provide legitimate entertainment; the musicians, dancers, jugglers, and acrobats excelled in their art. Excellence, however, did not guarantee a generous audience. I learned quickly that many folk responded much more readily to a clever swindle than a worthy performance.

But I count my take before I earn it, as the saying goes. First I had to learn my trade, and a difficult craft it was. I confessed my fears of failure to Brossos, and the master acrobat assured me they were only natural and that *he* would be the better judge of whether I had any talent at it. He talked to me quietly for a long time, not of acrobatics but on the strengthening of the inner self. Then he gave me my first exercise. He bade me stand barefoot in a small birch grove secluded enough that the sounds of camp seemed distant and unintruding. He instructed me to close my eyes and not to open them until I heard his voice.

"I'll not be far away," he assured me, "so nothing will befall you. I will not tell you how long you'll wait; it may be a short time or it may be all morning. While you are standing here with eyes closed, Dominico, you are not to think of acrobatics or worry whether you can do them; you are not to think of lunch or wonder what Felicia and Gorgi are doing, or what I am doing, for that matter. I'll tell you. I'll be engaged in an exercise of my own."

"Well, then, what shall I think about?"

62

"*Think* of nothing. *Experience* everything. Be aware. Be aware of every sense but sight. Sight is a wonderful sense, but it over-powers the others. Engage your sense of touch, of smell, of sound. Do not think about them, simply be aware of leaves rustling in the wind, birds singing, scurryings in the grass. Be aware of the smell of the trees, the earth," he took an audible sniff on the air, "even the cookfires. Be aware of the wind brushing by your skin and tangling in your hair, the sun warming your head and face and body, the clothes touching your skin. Think nothing about these things, only experience them.

"And finally—and this you will become better acquainted with each time we do the exercises—be aware of the breath flowing in and out of your body, of where you stand, of your feet in the grass and your toes and muscles shifting to keep you standing. Be aware of every muscle in every part of your body and how all move in harmony, tensing and relaxing to keep you upright. And lastly, be aware of your sense of balance, the sense that knows you are upright and steady. When your muscles become tired, be aware of that, too. Yet let all these experiences flow through you without thinking on them.

"Ready? Good. Stand here beneath this tree that dances so gaily with the wind. You will be aware of sun and shadow playing across your eyelids. Stand relaxed, feet a little further apart. Aye, that's good. Now close your eyes. Breathe deeply three or four times and loosen your body. Ease into the center of all your senses. Let them pass into and out of your mind. If your mind races off here and there after that thought and this, as it will try to do, simply bring it back to the center and continue to experience yourself here and now. Let yourself be aware.

"I will call you when the exercise is over. Begin now, starting with the outer senses, moving gradually to the inner."

I heard him tread the grass a little way, then all was still. A moment later I realized that nothing was truly still around me. I took a few deep breaths and began the first journey into my senses.

I was so taken with newly experiencing the outer senses that I had scarcely begun on the inner senses when I heard Brossos suddenly speak my name as though from another universe. I startled, having forgotten he was there. The time seemed too short, yet it seemed very long. Brossos told me it had only been a short while. When I told him I had not completed the exercise, he laughed and clapped a hand on my shoulder.

"My boy, that's wonderful! You've taken time to experience

fully. Most beginners try to rush through the outer to get to the inner, and that you cannot do, at least not at first. Tomorrow's exercise will be longer and the next day's longer still. You will soon find the outer senses not so engrossing and will move naturally toward the inner. And then . . . well, I'll not overburden your mind with too much the first day. Well done, Dominico, well done."

I glowed with pleasure and pride. Thereafter, each morning I looked forward to my session with Brossos, sessions which made each day, even a gloomy one, seem clear and alive and overflowing with promise.

But do not imagine there was no more to learning acrobatics than that. The inner exercises were only one facet of my training. Brossos taught me the simpler stunts and then set Gorgi to helping me practice them: handstands, cartwheels, somersaults, forward and backward flips in succession until I could do them in my sleep and frequently did so. The harder tricks I practiced with Gorgi, Mikato, and Ronaldo under Brossos's direction before trying them with the rest of the tumblers. I learned to stand balanced on one man's shoulders and use the next man's shoulders to support a forward flip over his head and land lightly on my feet. I learned to do a handstand in another's hands! I learned to make it look easy, too, yet the learning of it brought me to tears of fatigue and frustration many a night.

Of course, my first lesson had been not so dramatic. "Before you learn the stunts," Brossos had told me, "I will first teach you how to fall."

I retorted in all innocence, "I'd rather you'd teach me how *not* to fall."

My remark was received with hoots of laughter from my fellow acrobats. Soon I discovered that a smooth fall was indispensable. I practiced falling until my reactions became automatic, and they saved me many a time, for if ever there was a human pyramid or tower to be built, a sound wager was that I would be the one on top. I lost count of the many times I rolled to a standstill only slightly shaken after falling a score of feet. Within a few weeks, though, falls became rarer and rarer. I mastered each rigorous exercise and progressed to the next one. Almost without realizing it, I was becoming an acrobat.

And there were other lessons I learned with equal alacrity: dancing and Greek. Lovely Felicia, the dark-eyed dancing girl, the most captivating charmer I ever met, taught me both. I burned to learn Greek, the natural language of my new family, and Felicia loved to talk, so she enlisted Gorgi—who was just as charmed by Felicia as I, but he would never admit it—to help her.

I learned at a frustratingly slow pace at first, struggling to memorize the words for the objects they named for me over and over, striving to understand their day-to-day phrases and reply correctly, straining to catch the meaning of their conversations, until after a fashion I was able to communicate in Greek. Then Felicia had a brilliant idea—she always had a brilliant idea about something or other. She determined that no one should speak to me in any language but Greek, and I must answer in kind. She scolded anyone who reverted to Latin in my presence. Brossos, however, informed her mildly that if it took Latin to instruct me in acrobatics, then Latin he would use.

And then there was the dancing! If ever there was music playing, Felicia whirled into motion, and if ever there formed a circle of dancers, Felicia pulled me into it. Indeed she took me in hand, and in her irrepressible company I lost any lingering shyness of these strange folk. One bright and blustery afternoon, after a particularly energetic practice of stepping and spinning in time to the jing-jang of Felicia's finger cymbals, the two of us dropped against a wagonwheel and cooled our throats with deep draughts from a wineskin. Felicia swept at her disarrayed hair and tried without success to unravel one of her two bronze combs from the long strands.

"Dominico," she finally said fretfully, "I cannot see them. Will you do it for me?"

"Surely." I stood beside her and began to work at disentangling one of the combs. "This one looks to have nested for good. I believe I'll have to take the shears to it."

"Oh no you won't!" she admonished laughingly. "I should die of shame—or else disguise myself as a boy. But wouldn't that be fun! I could become an acrobat!"

"You'd never fool anyone, Felicia. You look nothing like a boy."

"You think I'm pretty, Dominico?"

Embarrassed, I stammered, "Why . . . yes . . . I think you're the prettiest girl I've ever seen."

She smiled. "Thank you, cousin. Tell no one this, but, secretly, I think I'm really very beautiful. Does that sound horrible of me?"

"Not at all," I grinned. "'Tis nought but the truth." I had worked one comb free. I handed it to her and started on the other.

65

"When my mother named me Felicia, she thought it meant 'beautiful.' She only discovered later that it means 'happy,' but she didn't mind. She only laughed and said that now I would be both.

"What means your name, Dominico?"

"It means 'belonging to the Lord.' "

"Oh. And do you? Belong to the Lord?"

"I don't know. My mother thought so."

Felicia smiled. "Well, if you do, I thank him for bringing you to us."

"You think he did?"

"But of course. If you belong to him, 'tis he who led you here. Your god must want you to be one of us."

I stopped toying with the bronze comb. I had never thought of it in quite that way before.

Felicia sat for a moment in silence, then spoke her new thoughts.

"You must learn the men's dances before festival. I'll get Mikato to teach you."

"Cannot you do it?"

"I *could*, I imagine; they're simple enough. But I'm not allowed. I can only show you the mixed dances."

"I don't think Mikato will want to," I said reluctantly.

"Why not? He teaches you tumbling."

"He complains I am clumsy and slow."

"Pooh!" She tossed her head violently, forgetting I held a combful of her hair. "*Ouch!*"

"Sorry. But you're not holding very still."

"Mikato forgets he has been an acrobat since he could walk. You've only just started, Dominico."

"I do stumble over my own feet sometimes. . . ."

She giggled. "And mine."

"And you are never impatient with me." I handed her the second comb. "Here. Done."

Felicia turned her luminous black eyes to mine. "Of course not, cousin, why? . . . Oh, pay Mikato no attention. He is *always* impatient—about *everything*. Really, I overheard Brossos tell Ronaldo that you're one of the quickest learning acrobats he ever taught; he thinks it's because you want so very much to do well."

"He said that? I'm the quickest?" A warm glow of pleasure flushed my face.

"He did. And come the next festival you'll be performing. Ah, it will be wonderful, Dominico! You'll see how it feels!"

"Truthfully, I'm a little frightened, Felicia. Suppose everyone should laugh and jeer and make fun of me?"

She caught my hand in hers. "They won't, cousin!"

"Some folk think 'tis funny I'm a dwarf. They make a jest of me."

"How can they, Dominico, when you're so delightful? Why, you're the loveliest person I've ever known!"

Taken completely by surprise, I dropped my head and peered aslant at her with an abashed grin, having no experience replying to compliments from lovely young ladies.

"Are you glad you came to us?"

"Aye, with all my heart," I answered, not until this moment realizing how true that to be.

Felicia smiled lightly. "I'm glad, too. And just for you I'm going to do it." She sprang to her feet and shook the many layers of her skirts into place.

"Do what?"

"Teach you the men's dances, of course," she whispered conspiritorially as she dragged me by the hand toward the wood. "Just never you tell how you learned them."

And I never did.

Encouraged beyond belief by Felicia's words, I leapt with renewed enthusiasm into my acrobatic training. Brossos's unusual methods did wonders for my well-being, for they involved a strengthening of the inner self as well as the muscles. He insisted that it was not enough to balance oneself. No, one must *become* balance. The acrobat must be capable of closing his eyes, locating his personal center of balance, and holding it indefinitely. I required hours, even months, of centering my awareness into my own point of equilibrium and staying with it even if I or the surface beneath my feet should move. I forget how many times I fell from a blindfolded stance on a free-rolling barrel, yet those do not begin to approach the number of times I balanced the barrel successfully. The day I could walk an empty wine cask forwards and backwards blindfolded—under the sharp eyes of Brossos—I had accomplished that inner balancing. Once I found I could pull myself into that calm center, I never lost it entirely. It held me in good stead the rest of my life, but all it meant to me then was that now I was truly one of the troupe.

How do I describe how it felt to be a valued member of the clan—to be a beloved cousin, a fellow acrobat—to know their stories and songs and dances, their faces and names and smiles—how do I contain the delirious feeling in words? After two years of wretched loneliness, now I was no longer the despised misfit. I belonged. I was one of their own. I was Dominico the acrobat. Dominico the vagabond. Dominico of the free folk.

VIII

Saturnalia!

My first Pagan festival!

Merry old Saturn ruled once again for seven riotous days! On a frosty December morn our little band of vagabonds entered the country estate of Cicero Plotinus, patrician from a venerable Pagan lineage, though entered is too mild a word to describe our spectacular arrival.

I led the procession, showing off a dizzying series of forward flips, back flips, and cartwheels. Behind me came the troupe of shouting and cavorting acrobats, and following them wove a chaotic swirl of musicians and dancers. Two of our gayest wagons, pulled by garland-bedecked oxen and accompanied by a colorful array of our oldest and youngest members, brought up the tail.

Our reception was fantastic, as we had hoped. On all sides folk dropped their work and ran to applaud our parade—to point and clap and laugh and exclaim excitedly. In a series of toppling, tumbling scenes, I saw a flock of children racing beside me, giggling and squealing with joy.

Upon gaining the steps of the estate house I turned and (dizzy now—steady, steady) leapt at Dreeko, whose waiting hands propelled me onto his shoulders, from which I climbed (quickly, quickly now—a slow climb looks clumsy) to the peak of a six-man pyramid. The dancers formed a circle around us, whirling and spinning in one direction, while our pyramid slowly rotated in a counter direction. As soon as I knew myself to be unshakably

69

balanced, I risked a few glances down at the spectacle. The effect was stupendous, *I* thought anyway. Of course, I occupied the best position to view our formation, directly from above, but it must have been nearly as effective from the ground, too, because the crowd proclaimed approval loudly. Then the circle of dancers expanded and the pyramid crumbled, beginning with me at its top. We bowed. After receiving formal welcome from the estate-master on behalf of Cicero Plotinus, we prepared our camp for the seven-day festivities.

Saturnalia is like no other Roman festival: all social rules are suspended for the duration. This is one tradition even Theodosius and his edicts could not interfere with in the West. From the seventeenth through the twenty-third of December business comes to a standstill, gambling is suddenly legal, and slaves are no longer subservient to their masters. On the contrary, slaves and servants become belligerent, outspoken, obnoxious tyrants, while masters smile, bow, and wait on them at table. Among the upper classes this is accomplished with much decorum, I am told, but in the lower strata and out here in the country, this incongruous state is made universally tolerable only because virtually everyone is blind drunk. All is forgotten and forgiven in the Grand Headache Rites which follow hard upon Saturnalia.

Merry old Saturn ruled during the Golden Age of Rome, when food and drink were plentiful, slavery and taxes nonexistent, freedom and peace more than empty rhetoric—in short, the good old days—and for one week a year the populace pretends all is well once again. The happiest celebrant is the man proclaimed Festival King by popular vote, for he plays the god throughout the proceedings. His every desire is numen—one nod from the crowned inebriate on the throne and it is done. The festival revolves around him: feasts, entertainments, and even people are at his disposal.

I witnessed this particular Festival King ordering an old enemy stripped naked, smeared with manure, and forced to crawl on his hands and knees, braying like an ass, while children goaded him with switches. The besotted celebrants roared and whistled and hooted at the poor man uproariously, but I turned away and refused to watch, too vividly reminded of my two blood-cousins' idea of fun.

"Come, Dominic, you be the captured Hun and we'll be the Roman generals."

"No!"

"Yes. We must tie your hands for the triumphal march into Rome."

"And we'll drive you before our chariots with whips."

I eyed the brambles my cousin carefully broke off—vines with wicked, inch-long thorns.

"No!"

"Ah," winked the other cousin, holding my shirtscruff in his grip, "the cowardly Hun begs for mercy."

I clenched my jaws shut and said no more.

"Stupid goblin rolled down the hill into the brambles," they explained to my aunt.

From experience I knew better than to contradict her sons, so I kept quiet while she scolded me soundly for having made shreds of my only tunic.

In olden times the Festival King would have paid dearly for his privileges; his life would have been sacrificed to Saturn at the end of seven days. Among Roman soldiers, the king, after being chosen by lottery and enjoying a month's revelry, would have dutifully cut his own throat in the end. I have heard of a soldier who once refused the honor on grounds that he was a Christian. I believe they executed him. However, those days are long gone. In these civilized times a mock sacrifice satisfied the revelers, and even that might be forfeit since Theodosius had forbidden Pagan sacrifice of *any* kind—human or animal.

Really, it scarcely mattered, for the worship of Saturn no longer played an essential part in the festivities anyway. Carousing and gambling dominated the activities. Hardly any event took place that someone did not lay a wager on it, from how many cups of wine a man might down to which horse could outrun the others. Indeed, no few of our vagabond band gambled "professionally," as Ronaldo put it. If they were not betting at knucklebones or dice, they were flipping coins with anyone willing to risk a bronze or a copper. The few tossed coins I caught from spectators I hoarded rather than risked at games, though Ronaldo had dutifully taught me how it was done, after which he had shown me how to cheat. With his lot, there was no such thing as a game of *chance*. The way I saw it, since I knew full well my own folk were cheating and I had no designs on infuriating any drunken strangers by doing the same, then I had best avoid the games altogether.

Mother Hagia spent her days peddling fortunes and magic potions. I believe she took in more coin than any of us, except for maybe old Lestros, the crippled pickpocket, who had such an honest face he could steal a person blind while smiling at pretty girls and bowing to the masters. Yet some of our take we came by legitimately, for there were always a few folk of discerning taste who tossed us tokens of appreciation for our real talents.

Cicero Plotinus was taking no chances; Saturnalia ended without sacrifice to the god. Having survived my first Pagan festival with my soul unscathed, I began to enjoy the vagabond life with unfettered abandon.

Each festival after that first Saturnalia drew me step after step deeper into their Pagan world. Though every celebration wears a different mask, the faces behind them are the same. Some are universal, some provencial; all are Pagan, all unlawful. One such rite which I witnessed with bemusement and fascination was the Lupercalia.

Each February fifteenth the goat-god Pan drives the wolves and evil spirits away from the herds, bestowing his divine protection over the sheep and goats for another year. It is probably the only beneficial thing Pan ever did for anyone, yet he is guest of honor at as many festivals as he can butt his way into, which is a considerable number. Drop into any celebration and odds are good that the hybrid goat-man will figure into it somehow.

During Lupercalia the young men of the estate or village emulate Pan by stripping down to nothing but tiny flaps of goatskin. Then, brandishing thongs of goat-hide, they run about the villages and fields and yell like demons. Undeterred by an absence of lurking wolves or visible evil spirits, they flail instead at any young girls who happen to be in their path. Now, one might expect that young village girls would wise up and stay indoors on this particular day, but, no, by some perversity of fate they invariably choose this day to be out in their gayest finery, wandering the fields, lingering in the woods, making themselves easy prey for the crazed goat-men. Then these foolish girls run screaming, not homeward, but into the trees with virtually naked mock-Pans whipping at their skirts. In view of Pan's reputation for abducting careless young women wandering the woods alone, one would expect them to show better sense.

I refused to take part in this ritual, but Mikato and the other lads joined in with raffish glee, and even Felicia felt no need for modest restraint. Nor did I take part in the sacrifice that preceded it, yet I confess that I watched the blood of the goat and dog spilled with a proper Christian horror mingled with a shamefully un-Christian fascination. My crucial and metamorphic confrontation with Paganism, however, did not occur until the Bacchanal.

The Greater Dionysia it is called, a three-day revelry in March, the grandest festival of the year. Of the old gods, even Jupiter is not so devotedly honored as Dionysus. Those who have never been to a Bacchanal can but dimly imagine the insanity which reigns over such a feast, yet I will attempt to recapture its heady flavor. Kegs of rich, undiluted wine are drawn by wagonloads to a secluded clearing, for there is nothing lawful about a Bacchanal, and the untamed wilderness is the only appropriate setting for the bizarre event. The celebrants arrive ivy-wreathed and masked in visages ranging from humorous to grotesque and terrifying, for they temporarily cast off their human identities and transform into Bacchantes—wild worshippers of the Lord of Wine and Revelry.

They arrived throughout the day. Some of the early starters were drunk by afternoon, had passed out by evening, and missed the night's proceedings entirely. Some rode donkeys, emulating Silenus, the besotted companion of Dionysus, and found themselves constantly unseated by mischievous merrymakers who switched at their beasts with oak branches. Unlike the old days when the god's madness belonged only to women, now both sexes danced fawn-skinned and garlanded, rattling and pounding the timbrels. Only Pan was missing.

At first I stood all agoggle at the outrageous costumes and weird masks. Everyone made much over me, and either the jest went round else they all had the same wine-soaked sense of humor, for scarcely a party arrived that did not laugh and congratulate me on having the best disguise of all—and I was not even in costume! Then the feast got underway: we drank and danced and drank and sang and drank and drank some more. As the night wore on, the songs became cruder and the dances wilder; the masks came off, and so did a goodly portion of the costumes.

Now, early on I realized that if I went round the circle of dancers one more time I was going to pass out from dizziness. I leaned panting against a tree-trunk and watched the impending orgy in a growing state of shock. At fourteen, I was as much up on the facts of life as anyone, and any gaps in my education had been quickly filled in by the uninhibited vagabonds. But countering this, my Mass days fidgeting in the back of the basilica had vehemently instilled in me a terror of mortal sins. The sight of this flagrant carnival of lust working up to its peak both confused and excited me.

Felicia, flower-strewn and flushed, whirled by and caught at my hand.

"Dance with us, Dominico!" she invited breathlessly.

I jerked my hand from hers as she was swept away with the roundelay. The dance was too fast, too wild, and I felt I would surely be trampled underfoot. I thought I'd best join Gorgi, who had crawled off to sleep in his wagon a good hour ago. But as I attempted to skirt the edge of the fire-lit clearing, Mikato swung out of the roundelay and staggered toward me.

"Hie, Dominico! Come and join the fun. 'Tis time you did homage to the God of Wine!"

He was dead drunk.

I shook my head.

"Afraid you'll soil your pure Christian soul?"

I should have seen it coming, but already the wine had befuddled my thinking. Mikato pounced on me like a demon, and before I could get some semblance of balance, he had dragged me to the center of the roundelay where a drinking contest was in progress to determine which man would be Master of Revels this night.

Hailing Dreeko and Ludi to his aid, Mikato grasped a handful of my hair, pulled my head back, and worked a full goblet of wine between my teeth. Choking and sputtering, I fought to escape, but out of sheer self-preservation I swallowed most of the undiluted brew. No sooner was the first goblet empty than someone passed him another one. A group of contestants gathered around to watch the fun, while Mikato threatened to turn me upside down and shake me by the heels if I failed to drink every last drop of the next one.

I downed it all.

Eagerly, the spectators produced another full goblet.

I resigned myself to my fate.

At one point I heard someone count five and bet on six.

By the time Mikato let go of me, I felt I had nearly drowned. I tried to stand, but the Earth immediately raised up and knocked me flat. The crowd cheered. Hands from everywhere grasped at me, lifted me high into the air, and sat me atop a wagonload of kegs. I had to hold with both hands to keep from falling. I peered down dizzily. To someone only three feet tall, it looked to be a long way to the ground.

Now a fragrant procession of pine torches swarmed around

the wagon, illuminating the clearing with a flickering glow and crackling pillars of smoke. Ronaldo climbed clumsily to the top of the barrels, provoking even more frenzied yells from the eerie gathering below. He took a sweeping bow and fell headlong into the throng, but the hundred-handed monster heaved him back onto the wagon. This time he held his footing.

"As first Master of Revels," proclaimed Ronaldo in thickly accented Latin, spreading his arms wide as though to embrace his subjects, "I decree—let the sacrifice begin!"

While several men went after a goat tethered nearby for this very purpose, Ronaldo continued his speech.

"We have a guest of honor! The undisputed Master of Disguise!" (Here he paused to let the whoops and yells die down.) "I give you Dominico . . . the Water Nymph!"

They thought this was hilarious. Worse, *I* thought it was hilarious. Now the Master of Revels hauled me to my feet, on which I swayed unsteadily.

"Tonight we initiate our little cousin properly! Mikato, prepare the initiate!"

Mikato and friends clambered up the wagon and stripped me of every stitch of clothing: I was too numb with wine to argue. When they jumped down, leaving me bare to the world, I could only stand steeped in hot embarrassment and stare foolishly back at the crowd. Laughter and whistles assailed my ears; my mind reeled crazily; my stomach churned. The bewildered and bleating goat was led forward, its throat cut open, and the blood collected in a libation bowl. Then the bowl was passed up to the Master of Revels, who took it precariously in both hands and held it over my head.

"On this solemn and unlawful occasion," intoned Ronaldo gravely, "I consecrate Dominico the Dwarf into the hallowed ranks of the Merry Revelers. Henceforth, his sacred name will be *Pan!* Lord of Mischief and Goats!"

Suddenly, warm, sticky goat's-blood rained into my hair, splashed over my shoulders, and trickled down my back and chest and arms. Now I knew I was going to be sick. Staggering to my knees, I leaned over the side of the barrels and retched violently. I was vaguely disappointed to see Mikato leap out of the way just in time, seeing as it was his fault I was sick in the first place.

"Pan! Pan!" shouted the drunken crowd. Someone tossed up part of a costume—a headdress with the horns of a goat sprouting from it—which Ronaldo plunked firmly on my head. I was blessedly unaware of what a spectacle I made: a naked, drunk-sick dwarf, dripping blood, crowned with a pair of goat horns.

Meanwhile, below, the orgy headed for its peak. Celebrants paired off with careless abandon. It scarcely mattered if they knew each other or not, and in some cases it didn't seem to matter whether the other was male or female. In groups of two, even three or four, they disappeared into the trees. For my part, my head whirled wildly, the Earth tilted, and the wagon seemed to bolt slowly out from under me.

Red-glaring sun struck angrily at my eyelids. Flinging one arm across my eyes, I groaned. I lay on my back beside a wagonwheel. No human sounds reached me—only twittering birds and rustling leaves. I rolled over and groaned again. My head drooped heavily. It felt ten times larger than normal. As I reached up to assure myself it had not exploded, my hand touched—a horn.

Appalled, I jerked the horned cap off my head and knelt in the dirt, staring down at myself with disbelief. My body was caked with dried mud, wine, and blood. Suddenly I remembered everything and wished I did not. Staggering to my feet, I walked dazedly toward the creek I knew to be nearby. My head throbbed vengefully, as if someone pounded my temples with mallets. In the green, late stirring woods, I glimpsed nude bodies, still twined together, sleeping off the night's revelry. I wished I was dead.

At the creek's edge, I slid down the shallow bank into muddy water. Gratefully I dunked my head in the cold liquid and tugged at the sticky blood-browned tangles of hair. I wanted to wash away every vestige of the Bacchanal from my body as well as my mind. Eventually, as I swallowed greedy gulps of cold water, I became aware that someone stood on the bank above. Ronaldo, Master of Revels, grinned at me devilishly.

"Ah, Dominico, a glorious morning for a bath, is it not?"

I glared up at him, hating him.

"*You!*" I spat. "*Traitor!*"

He started, taken by surprise.

"I? Because I have a little fun? Why, Dominico—"

"We made a bargain! You said no Pagan rites! I believed you, but no more! You've done me in!" By now my furious words burst forth in sobs.

Ronaldo knelt on the bank and reached his hand down for me.

"Dominico, come here," he said softly.

I struck out angrily, blindly, toward his hand, splashing water up across his face as I did so. He stared at me, water dripping off his nose and eyelashes. I stared back at him, shaken by the depth of my own anger.

Finally the vagabond chieftain shrugged. "I suppose I deserve that. You're right. I've broken our bargain, and I should never have done it. We were all drunk; so were you. I know 'tis no excuse and little consolation, but I meant you no harm."

I bent down to the muddy water and scooped cold handfuls over my face so that he would not see my tears. I was shaking and needing to vomit.

"The wine makes you sick," Ronaldo observed sympathetically.

"*You* make me sick!" I spat miserably.

He said nothing.

I bit my lip, heartily appalled at my own words. "I'm sorry," I mumbled wearily.

"No, 'tis I who am sorry, Dominico. 'Tis I who broke our bargain. Come up here now and we'll talk."

This time I accepted his hand up and shortly stood beside him, naked and muddy, but clean of blood. He smiled at me tiredly, and I could see that he, too, was bleary-eyed and wine-heavy this morning.

"I know you never wanted it, but what's done is done. We have made you Pagan."

I looked up in surprise. "I never consented."

"That makes no difference."

"But it does!" I retorted, not to be fooled. "'Twas against my will, and I cannot be held to account for it by man nor God! You cannot trick me!"

Ronaldo shook his head. "Lad, lad, what am I going to do with you?"

Abruptly, the anger drained from me, along with all color from my face, leaving me suddenly weak. I could only think he meant one thing. I tried to read his expression. Would he?

I looked up at him beseechingly, my voice wrenched with dread. "You won't . . . send me away, will you?"

"No, no, no, Dominico, no!" he exclaimed in surprise. "Do not imagine that!" He held my head between his two hands and gazed at me long, then he pulled me into his arms for a fierce hug.

"No," he repeated. "'Tis too late for that. I love you—I love you like you are my own son." He held me by the shoulders and grinned merrily at me. "Besides, 'twould be no living with Felicia if I did such a thing. Or Hagia. Or Brossos. Or Gorgi. Our folk would disown me."

I drank in his words yearningly. My heart had caught at the words *I love you* and *my own son.* I would forgive him anything: bargain breaking, Paganism. I stared into the depths of his dark eyes and wondered. *Ronaldo is Pagan and yet I love him. I have lived with Pagans and known nought but love from them. Can this feeling be abhorrent to God? Can it be a mortal sin to love these people? How can I love them and still despise what they are?*

Suddenly I saw the wall between us, so tangible I felt I could reach out and touch it, built there brick by brick by fear—fear of punishment, fear of death, damnation, and hell.

Who had built that wall? It didn't matter. It was I who kept it real by my stubborn belief in it. And more than anything I wanted no wall between us. I wanted only to tear it down.

Suppose it was a wall of lies? Suppose I ceased to believe in it? Torn between recklessness and confusion, I saw the wall as a phantom and watched it fade, felt it disappear from around my heart and mind.

Then I knew the truth. With the wall of fear gone I saw my true need, the need I had hidden from myself. I wished to be *one* with the family that had taken me in. Deep down I wished to be free of Christianity; I wished I, too, could be Pagan. I longed to embrace their religion simply because it was theirs. And now the fear was gone, and I saw not an angry God waiting to burn me in hell, but my own heart opening with relief to pour out all the love I had been afraid to release.

Ronaldo watched me questioningly through the bare seconds it took for my whole world to transform. I found my voice.

"Ronaldo . . . I want to be like you. . . ."

He waited, wondering.

"I want to be Pagan."

"Ah, think what you are saying, Dominico. I do not require it of you. It was wrong of us. . . ."

"No," I shook my head. "I love you. How can I be like a son if . . . if? . . ."

"You can, lad. I've let that stand between us, but no longer."

I smiled up at him. "I want to be the same as you."

"Do you mean, lad, you want to be a child of Isis?"

"Aye, 'tis just what I mean," I affirmed, and I heard the ring of truth in my voice. So did Ronaldo. Surprise and pleasure lit his face.

"You do not have to do this," he cautioned.

"I know."

"Ah, but such a procession we will make if Pan, Lord of Mischief, frolics before us!"

I nodded (not too vigorously, for my head hurt). "I want to be Pan. I want to be anything you want me to be."

Ronaldo laughed and shook me by the shoulders with rough affection. "Dominico, I'm glad you choose to join your soul to ours. The afterlife would be a hollow joy without your merry company. There's not one of us but would grieve your absence."

I smiled gratefully at his warm words. And I felt a growing surge of exhilaration, and maybe just a little trepidation, to deliberately embrace Paganism as though deciding which road to take: footpath or highway. I felt deliriously wicked, having stepped off the well-trodden highway and chosen the dark forest path, yet curiously relieved, sure in the knowledge that no matter what lay at the end (and I could not help thinking of that jackal at Osiris's feet) I would travel in good company at least.

"I think, Dominico, that we could both do now with Hagia's cure for wine-sickness. And you'll want to find your clothes before the others awaken. The day is for donning of masks again, for putting on disguises once more."

I hurried back with him to gather my scattered clothing, encountering only a few stirring revelers along the way.

IX

Little Dominico transformed himself into the young Pan whenever a celebration could withstand a visit from the woodland god. Of course, it was all in good fun; no one mistook the horned dwarf dressed up in goat ears and shaggy goatskin for the huge, capricious, dangerous Pan who lurked in dark forests and carried off mortals unawares. My Pan was one which folk could laugh with and enjoy. Children brought up in fear of the half-man, half-goat, chased me merrily through the lanes until they had me surrounded, and then I amused them with simple antics and fanciful tales. Their laughter rang like melody in my ears, nothing like the harsh, derisive taunts I had heard from childhood playmates, but joyous peals of delight for a small wonder invading the dreary confines of their lives.

Thusly we traversed Gaul, from expansive country estates to isolated rustic villages, sometimes feeling emboldened enough to enter a town or two. If this itinerant life seemed to agree with me, that was no illusion. It did indeed. As proof, I began to grow again. (I had not grown at all the two years I lived with my uncle. I knew so, because I had secretly measured myself by a notch on a hogpen post.) Now I grew, not by leaps and bounds, but by quarter inches and half inches. For every extra inch measured, I would whoop with triumph while Mother Hagia shook her head in pretended despair.

"Dominico," she would scold, "you'll be the ruin of us yet.

What will we do when we have a giant on our hands instead of a dwarf?"

I would grin mischievously and answer, "Anything I say, Old Hag."

"And how will we feed you, if you eat as much for a giant as you do for a dwarf?"

"I'll eat an ox a day!"

"How will we pull our wagons, then?"

"Why, I'll tie them all together and pull them myself!"

Exchanges of this sort usually ended in giggles and cackles. The old woman would from time to time give me an evil-tasting magic potion, which she maintained would make me tall and strong. Though I suspected that it was a trick to persuade me to drink something nasty and good for me, I pretended to believe her and dutifully swallowed it. My little spurts of growth, I was certain, had no connection with the doses she concocted, no matter how coincidentally the one sometimes followed the other.

Hagia knew all the healing roots and herbs; she sometimes took Felicia, Gorgi, and me to help her stravage them. She took us and the younger children berry picking and nut gathering, too, when the season was right. And Hagia told us tales, wonderful, exotic tales of strange peoples and gods. She made the stories sound as believable as if they had really happened, though I knew that most of them could not be true. And I gave little credence to her astrology, for I had been warned at Mass that astrology was witchery and devil's work, although her predictions seemed harmless enough.

When I at last agreed to let her read my stars, I was surprised to find she had the calculations already at hand. Quickly she unrolled her vellum star tables and, with a sharp stick, scratched in the dirt a spoked wheel marked with twelve strange symbols.

"The figures can be done anytime," Mother Hagia told me, adding more odd marks to the circle in a seemingly random arrangement. "But a true interpretation needs the presence and desire of the seeker. I've been waiting for you, little one."

She sat cross-legged on the ground. I did the same. The wheel lay between us.

"The nineteenth of October, fourteen years ago, Dominico, the heavens over Gaul looked so." Her gnarled hand waved over the circle.

I saw nothing resembling stars or constellations, just lines and squiggles, but I held my peace and waited.

"You are born under the sign of the scales—the judgment scales wherein the heart is weighed against the feather of Maat in the afterlife—you are the judge, the balancer. The scales swing wildly awry; you must bring them to rest. Such is your task. You weigh everything on the scales, even yourself. Only when you cease judging and measuring, when you clear the scales, when they sit empty and idle, only then will they balance." Here her droning voice stopped. She closed her eyes, and they moved behind her lids as though she searched for something. Then they opened and she resumed her flow of words.

"You are unable to find the balance now because you are chased by a scorpion. It stings at you constantly; it is your fate. Your scorpion drives you toward a crossing on the paths of destiny. Then the scorpion stings; its venom is spent; it dies.

"Until that time, no matter the choices you make, no matter which side of the scales you choose to favor, they will eventually tilt to the opposite. Destiny must compensate; fate must tip the scales and nudge you to your center, to a balancing point."

Now I grew restless. This talk of scales and scorpions was meaningless to me. I wanted to hear a tangible future, one which I could understand. After another searching pause, a shudder seemed to shake Mother Hagia's scrawny frame and she continued with a strange, hollow sorrow in her voice.

"Isis calls her children home! But this child she casts adrift. You will set out on a journey, not of your own choosing, but against your will. A journey over land and sea, a journey of both the body and the mind, a journey which, when completed, will bring you full circle. You will have been everywhere and nowhere. You will have learned everything and nothing. Aye, and then the scorpion will sting you, will destroy you, in your twenty-fourth year."

I straightened abruptly, eyes wide. That sounded serious! What sort of scorpion would destroy me? I wanted to ask, but I knew Hagia would not like an interruption. Her eyes were closed again. A smile played upon her withered lips.

"I see the golden-maned lion from the north. The scorpion-devourer. The Earth-walker. The song-maker. He is your balance, as you are his: the lion and the goat. Make no attempt to set *him* in your pan-scales," she cackled mysteriously. "They will never hold the weight.

"Ah, you are the sacrifice—chosen of the breath that sings on the winds. The goat dies and is reborn a song. Aye, little Pan, I see your death in darkness and your return to life. You wield a lighted staff. Now the lion will sing anew, for you are his song returned to him. The wheel is complete. The scales stand empty and still."

Her bony hand shot out and obliterated the mystic wheel, leaving only rippled finger-patterns in the dust.

"What think you, Dominico?"

"I have one question, Old Hag. Is it a good fortune or a bad one?"

She hesitated thoughtfully a moment. "Only you can know. 'Tis the right one. That must suffice."

I was disappointed. It all sounded grand and symbolic, but I had no patience at deciphering mysterious riddles. I frowned petulantly.

"Dominico!" I heard Gorgi shouting. "Come quickly! Grandfather will teach us the pole!"

"The pole!" I echoed, forgetting starry destinies in my excitement. "Oh, Gorgi, now?"

"Yes, now! Come on with you, before he changes his mind!"

"Hagia?"

"Go, child. Tomorrow cannot overshadow today—not for the young."

I ran after Gorgi hurriedly, shortcutting under wagons as I went. Two wagons sat in place, nearly forty feet apart. Stretched between them was the pole—forty feet of pole—lashed firmly to the latticed ribs of each wagon. The pole, which rested just beyond my reach if I stood on tiptoe, was thin enough to be resilient, yet thick enough to support the weight of an average-size man.

The troupe sat scattered on the ground about halfway between the two wagons. Even Ronaldo was there, taking his place with the rest. Excellent acrobat though he was, he did not compete with Brossos as polewalker. Indeed, who could? I joined the assembled troupe.

Brossos, lithe and lean even in his fifties, leapt upon the side of the wagon and walked nonchalantly out to the middle of the pole, hovered there for a dozen heartbeats merging his body motions with the rise and fall of the wood, and twisted sidewise to address us. I had seen him do all sorts of marvelous things on the pole, and at a much greater height than this, yet a sudden surge of blood tingled at my scalp. To try it myself! I wavered between fear and keen anticipation.

Brossos spoke softly. He talked of beginning by standing on

83

the end of the pole, steadying into one's center of balance, taking one step, centering, feeling the rocking motion in every muscle, stepping again. But, above all, walking the pole in the mind first, where all success or failure is born. He turned again and easily completed his stroll across the clearing. Clinging to the wagon ribs, he surveyed the troupe.

"Who will be first?" he mused. Eager or no, not one of us volunteered, for we knew he asked not us, but himself.

"Dominico!" Brossos beamed, his free arm stretched in my direction as though introducing me before an audience.

Taken by surprise, I came forward and accepted his hand up. Staring along the length of the pole, it seemed an impossibly long walk to the other wagon. I glanced uncertainly at the others, who watched with rapt expressions.

"You first, Dominico," smiled Brossos reassuringly, "because I know you can do it. Now, put your feet just so," he demonstrated, "and balance on the pole."

I placed my bare feet (in high summer my boots and I enjoyed only a passing acquaintance) as he had shown me. When I felt steady, I nodded.

"Look to the other end," Brossos said in a low, hypnotic voice which always seemed to instill me with a calm confidence. "There is your destination. Now, put a waking dream in your mind. Watch yourself, Dominico, balancing the whole length of the pole. Forget everyone and everything else. Slowly, slowly, walk the pole with your thoughts until you come to the end."

Ah, I allowed the familiar, comfortable tones in which he gave instruction to summon me to that lucid state of mind where balance radiated from the center of my being. Then, I set my imagination to work. My eyes tracked a ghostly image of myself clear to the other wagon, then they closed to re-create the scene from the inside—in my mind's eye. Perhaps I shut my eyes too hurriedly, because Brossos's voice came from just behind my left ear.

"Take your time, Dominico, and relax. 'Tis only an exercise."

I took a long breath and slowed the image. As soon as my mind-self touched the other wagon I opened my eyes and took the first step. I balanced carefully on the quivering wood and stepped again. Now I had to blend my centering with the barely perceptible motion of the pole. I took another step and another. Each step came more quickly now as I jubilantly realized I was not falling off the pole. But as Brossos is fond of saying, thinking of not falling is just another way of thinking of falling; they are two faces of the same coin as far as the mind is concerned.

I uncentered. The up and down movement of the pole jolted me and, both arms flailing, I fought to regain my equilibrium. I hung suspended in the air for one frantic moment, and plummeted to the Earth ingloriously. Rolling unhurt to my feet, I looked up to the pole in reproach. I had only walked about ten feet out from the wagon. Amid applause, whistles, and catcalls from my fellow troupers, I took my bows as if I had just crossed the yawning Chasm of the Underworld in the midst of an earthquake.

"Excellent!" Brossos boomed. "Now? Gorgi!"

The master acrobat's grandson scrambled up the wagon ribs. I took a seat with the others on solid, steady ground, pleased to receive a wink of approval from Ronaldo. Day after day we went through this, taking turns falling off the pole, this in addition to our usual practice. Even the worst among us—those who would never make polewalkers—participated daily. Brossos maintained it was a good balance and concentration exercise.

"A good falling exercise, he means," Mikato was heard to mutter, for the pole always whipped wildly under his weight.

I grinned impishly. "Just wait 'til he gets round to the blind-fold, cousin."

I thought I was only jesting, but Brossos soon had each of us trying it blindfolded. After a few days of it, he dismissed all the acrobats except Gorgi and me. Of all the troupe who had walked the pole consistently, only the two of us ever made it to the end with the blindfolds on. My theory was that the smaller and lighter the walker, the less erratic the rise and fall of the pole. Evidently the theory held true because I was certainly the lightest and twelve-year-old Gorgi the next lightest among the acrobats. Gorgi did better than I, for only a handful of times did I manage to walk the whole distance sightless. Brossos said I depended too much on my eyes and not enough on my instincts. True. I much pre-ferred to see where I was going. I confess to feeling more relief than disappointment when Brossos decided to concentrate on training Gorgi in the more difficult aspects of the art, for the lad possessed the natural grace of his grandfather. I had already suf-fered enough blind tumbles to satisfy me for a lifetime.

For those unfortunates who have never seen the master pole-walker at his craft, I wish to invoke a little scene. Imagine a Gallic town, nameless, because all towns seem so to wanderers like ourselves—a town in Aquitaine Superior, for in that province of Gaul the highways are few and far between—during the festival of, say, Lectisternium, since an eight-day outdoor feast at May's end is perfectly designed for our trade.

The street is thronged with people. The acrobats have finished their routines: pyramids, towers, shoulder-stands, hand-stances and all. Suddenly, the musicians change tempo, we bow reverently, and Brossos appears all in blue—blue linen breeches that knot just below the knee and a blue full-sleeved shirt sashed with black satin at the waist. He bows first to us and then to the crowd.

The pole is already in place, spanning the square from one second-story roof to another. Brossos climbs swiftly to one roof and stands poised before the pole for an instant. Casually, leisurely, he walks out over the square, each step of his bare feet a performance unto itself. Halfway across he stops, leans forward to balance on one leg, the other stretched straight back behind him, then he continues his walk, turns, repeats the stance.

Ah, a handstand! The crowd is stirred. Another handstand! And another! No! He is doing cartwheels above their heads! They burst into wild applause. Brossos balances and bows.

Now he removes his black sash. A volunteer is sought from the audience, someone prominent, well trusted in the town. The volunteer climbs to the roof and ties the sash securely over the acrobat's eyes. The crowd exclaims and then falls silent.

Blindfolded, Brossos stands still and intent for many hushed seconds. Then he walks, savoring every step, wringing out each precarious move. The throng has ceased breathing by now. Slowly, excrutiatingly slowly, he does the stances, the handstands, the cartwheels—each fluid motion brimming with grace and suspense. The spectators, staring awestruck, sway to the slow rhythm of cymbals and flutes. Brossos begins a final round of cartwheels from one end of the pole to the other, picking up speed, spinning faster and faster, and in the exact middle of the square he suddenly loses step. He totters wildly, battling to hold his balance, suspended over the upturned faces.

He falls!

His hands grope out blindly and grasp the pole just in time to catch his fall. For a moment he swings gently to and fro, bobbing lazily up and down.

The audience collects its scattered wits.

Now Brossos swings his legs forward and up and over and back until he is turning around and around the pole—now he lands upright on his arms and swirls his legs in and out and over the pole while his hands do a little dance over each leg as it sweeps by and the musicians merrily nudge the lively tempo upward—now feet and hands are on the pole and he is spinning heels over head and doing all manner of impossible things and one is certain there are times when neither hand is touching the pole at all . . . until at last he springs to a stand once more, executes a slow cartwheel, and walks with deliberate steps to the roof, where he removes the blindfold and waves it triumphantly over the throng.

Such a showmaster!

If I could hold an audience so spellbound with words and voice and gestures, then I would be master of my art indeed.

We collected a goodly hoard of coppers and denarii after performances like that one. In the towns we spent our money on knives, sweets, cloth, trinkets, and whatever goods we might need. By custom, each individual performer, gambler, or thief turned over to Ronaldo two of every three coins collected. This rarely amounted to much for the individual, but the common pot could build up swiftly, only to deplete just as rapidly when supplies were purchased.

For my part, I learned to spend my money quickly, else Mikato or Dreeko or someone would try and connive me out of it for some unsavory scheme. So I might buy a bracelet, a cap, a dagger, a mince pie, or Pan-pipes. Or I might buy a glass bead necklace for Felicia or a crock of honey for Hagia. I had very little; I wanted for even less.

All that mattered to me was my vagabond family and their love. And it was through them that Isis beckoned and embraced me as one of her own.

Deep within a Gallic birch grove, damp and verdant—on a morning crafted by forest sprites—each quivering leaf and blade shimmering a liquid emerald in the dawn mist—on a spring morning I sat on cool, moist earth and trilled the hushed and pungent air with a Pan-pipe's mellow tones. My playing was still uncertain then, yet the sound wafted pleasant and ethereal, muted as it was by the vaporous atmosphere.

From without my private melody-world, I heard Felicia calling my name. I guessed she followed the music of the pipes, so, at a mischievous sprite's urgings, I ceased my playing and crept into another leafy concealment not far away. When Felicia reached the first grove and found it vacant, impatience edged her voice. Suppressing my laughter, I played another tuneful lure on the pipes and eluded her again, slipping deeper into the umber. And so it went; each time Felicia discovered my hiding place, I had already disappeared, and my musical summons drifted from another part of the wood. Giggling now, the barefoot girl ran after me in earnest, but I was too adept at becoming invisible in the lush foliage.

Expecting nothing out of the ordinary, I plunged into a densely wooded grove of birch, and the vision which filled my eyes brought me to a bemused standstill. At first impression, the entire dewy vert appeared to be strewn with jewels! Quickly my reason dispelled the illusion, yet where the morning sun streaked the haze it illuminated clusters of gigantic crimson mushrooms and perfused them with the luster of irridescent rubies.

I stood entranced before the wooded fairyland of blood-red domes, some as large as four and five inches across, delicately scurfed with flecks of white. An elven harvest if ever I saw one! Indeed, I had infrequently found like mushrooms as a child, though never in such abundance nor so large, and I had been sternly warned by my mother that they were elf-fruit, treacherous to humankind, but much coveted by elves for their magical charms. And here lay growing a veritable garden of them!

Felicia must see this, I thought, impulsively skipping into the enchanted meadow and raising the pipes in a spritely call. She came laughing and scolding, clutching her skirt up to her knees to hold it free of the wet grass. Abruptly her merry expression transformed to one of awe and wonder.

"Oh, sweet Isis," she breathed reverently. "The Gift!"

Her wide, midnight eyes drank in the elf's ransom of wild mushrooms and then met my bemused stare.

"Do not touch them, Dominico; the goddess's gift may be taken only by her daughters. But do play—play the Dance of Isis."

Though I scarcely knew the tune, I did my best. Clumsily, haltingly, I piped out a semblance of the hypnotic strain. Felicia's dance was more graceful than my melody. She loosed her arms and legs and neck in slow, fluid motions, flowing easily through contortions that looked humanly impossible, until my piping faltered and she bowed low upon the damp earth.

Then she gathered mushrooms, as many as she could carry, gently plucking each one by the stipe, until she cradled a skirtful. She would not allow me to help her with the strange harvest by any means, so I merely followed, keeping a fearful eye out for angry elves as she hurried excitedly to Mother Hagia with her prize.

Hagia took one look at Felicia's red and white treasure and, cackling and gloating delightedly, called a bevy of women and girls to harvest the glen. That accomplished, they set to drying and toasting the crop. Then, in a secret ritual, for only the eldest initiates knew which parts of the mushroom would not cause deadly convulsions and madness, they pulverized the crop into a powdery form and stored it in a tightly sealed earthen jar. At the next full moon Hagia called the vagabond band together for communion with the goddess.

"Isis summons us," the old woman said. "She especially summons Dominico, for to him she revealed her Gift. Dominico, take this on your tongue and dream the dreams of Isis."

Having no idea what I was letting myself in for, I accepted the bitter essence. When all had partaken of the powder, a ceremony of music and song and dance began—a spicy mixture of flute, kithara, cymbal, and sistrum—but I never heard the end of it, for all too soon my body began to tremble violently and my nerves to go numb. The dancing jumbled into a confusion of sensations around me. Heeding my distress, Hagia took my hand and guided me to a secluded glen, where she sat me back against a tree and admonished me reassuringly to stay put whatever might happen and await the goddess. Then she melted into the trees.

The goddess was long in coming. I huddled in my cloak and watched the nodding forest; the early twilight gave the leaves an illusion of shifting sentient patterns, almost as though the trees and brush formed dusky faces that peered at me with subtle changes of expression. I felt the trees slowly become aware of my presence and turn their aroused attention in my direction. As I debated inwardly whether the plants knew that I suspected them of studying me, the blurred faces focused sharply into laughter.

Ah, do trees express their thoughts in leafy pictures? Might one read their minds by the motion of their leaves? Is it not queer that some trees seem to have more than one face, several in fact? Does that mean a tree is not one being, but a family of beings? Like the free folk? The many faces of a maple nodded and bowed to each other smugly, causing me to laugh aloud.

Of a sudden, the spell was broken, else the gloam had deepened, for the merry countenances distorted and changed before my eyes. The branches writhed overhead like many-headed Scylla, each leering visage more horrific than the last. The menacing heads lunged and snapped toward me at full cry, yet never quite reached me. I misliked this turn of events intensely. Squeezing shut my eyes, I shrank further into my cloak and wished it all away. Perchance these hallucinations might just fade; I wanted no part of the goddess's gift, not if it was to be this terrifying. But now I had about as much choice in the matter as a man who, having leaped off a cliff, decides he no longer wishes to hit aground. I opened my eyes and plunged into a chaotic nightmare.

A Medusa pointed her serpentine finger and spewed forth a sibilant stream of venomous accusations. I recognized the malefic apparition from a terrifying incident in my childhood; she had been a holy seeress wandering from village to village, consulted by the townsfolk on the cause of a rampant disease killing their livestock. By happenstance, a young dwarf caught her eye. Pointing her finger in just such a way, head flung back, eyes rolling wildly, hair all awry, she had looked to me like one of the dreadful Furies.

"Changeling!" the serpent-haired vision hissed viciously. "Imp! Here is your malady! A goblin child, for you know they switch their own for human babes at birth! And know you well, 'tis goblins' doings when the milk sours, the babe coughs, the wine spills, and the swine die! A changeling lives among you, and he curses you with his mischief!"

As I shook my head in dumb denial, I heard old Elgge speak up in her quavering voice. "Not so! I midwifed Dominic; the boy came from his mother's womb as he is! He's no goblin! Were my daughter here, she'd tell you the same!"

"You were befooled by goblin magic, old woman, unless he has goblin blood in his veins. Who is his father? His mother?"

My aunt glared at me askance. "The parents are dead. He'd be no kin to me!"

"Ayiee!" screeched the seeress. "A curse he brought upon an innocent pair! If you would save your herds, purge him of his evil nature! Drive the impish humor from his body! This pestilence must be scourged out of him if it would be undone!"

My uncle collared me roughly, only too eager to believe I was indeed a changeling. "I'll purge him myself!" he growled.

What a pathetic scapegoat I made, too much in shock to react with anything but numb disbelief. Was the world mad, or was I? They pushed me to a corner post of the hogpen and bound my hands round it. There were some few voices raised in my behalf—"Leave the boy be; he has nought to do with goblins"—but they were soon shouted down.

I shot a pleading glance over my shoulder, only to see my uncle raise high a stout stick. Quickly I turned my head back toward the pigsty. If I cried out with the blows, my voice went unheard amid the squeals of the swine and the shouts of the townsfolk.

"Papa!" I sobbed through my terror and pain. But my papa lay sprawled in my memory forever in his own blood. There could be no help from him.

At last the village priest came running and put a stop to the beating.

"If there ever was a demon in the boy," said the priest, "you have long since driven it out. Look at the child; you might have killed him. Is this how Christian men practice mercy?"

My uncle stood over me and declared: "He's a devil's spawn—a curse upon us."

"That is not for you to judge—only God. I forbid you to beat him again."

Elgge helped me to my feet—or was it Mother Hagia?—murmuring, "Don't you know a dwarf brings good luck, Dominico?" Her gnarled hands poured a libation of blood over my head.

Aye, it was Hagia, sprinkling liquid from a vessel on my face. It felt cool, for I was hot and trembling.

"So quickly, Dominico?" She crooned, "Isis is swift in you. Aye, the Gift can be frightening, but do not fear Isis, my dear; she shows you your soul."

Abruptly I had to turn and retch. Immediately I felt better. Hagia washed my face and gave me a little water to drink from her vessel.

"I can't do it, Hagia. Make it stop—please."

"It has just begun. I cannot stop it."

"*Please!*"

"You'll be fine, child. The harvest was good—I can feel that within me already. Isis overtakes you. You can but allow her. Look for her."

"I don't want to see Isis!"

"You will, though. She'll come to you."

"What will she look like?" I whispered fearfully. "Where shall I look?"

Hagia made a motion with her shoulders and hands that sent ripples of violet shimmering in the air around her.

"Each time, for each person, she comes differently, in a different guise. She can be all things because she *is* all things. She will come as she wishes to be known."

"Does she come to you, too?"

Mother Hagia smiled I think. It was hard to tell. Her face was fluid, and I could scarcely focus on her shifting expressions.

"I dreamed the dreams of Isis a hundred times before you were ever born, Dominico. I see Isis in all things, in all her aspects. The universe is her pageant."

Hagia stayed and talked with me until I began to calm down and see more clearly. Now I could see how ancient she was, wrinkled and brown and truly beautiful. Her white hair glowed an unearthly color, yet she was made of Earth and moonlight. And her lustrous black eyes were timeless, as ancient as the Earth itself, and as endless as the night sky.

I gazed into the eyes of Isis.

Enraptured, I understood that Isis regarded me wisely and lovingly through the eyes of Mother Hagia, for I saw both the Egyptian goddess and the human woman as one. I saw the Mother of all humankind lambent in the soul of Hagia. And Hagia spoke of Isis, spoke of the Queen of Heaven waiting just behind the fragile veil between life and death to welcome her children home.

I knew no fear of Isis, not if she dwelled within Hagia.

Now Isis took on another Earthly form and glided gently from the grey wood. Silently she wafted toward us, night-black hair shimmering with stars. As she sat with us on the Earth, I looked from one to the other: Isis the old withered woman nearing the end of her days and Isis the young girl in her first flush of womanhood—and I could not say which was the more beautiful. Yet the eyes were the same: ancient and timeless.

Isis-Felicia smiled at me and I smiled back. I knew she was Felicia, yet I knew she was Isis, too.

Now Gorgi drifted out from the darkness behind the tree-trunks. He merged wordlessly into our little circle.

Isis looked out at me lovingly from Gorgi's eyes.

And I have Isis-eyes, I knew.

Isis-Hagia talked with us of the unity of all things and the dance of life in which everyone is a part of everyone. She talked of the life force which binds us all together and to the living Earth, too. She spoke of the powers of the moon, and as I gazed up at the full moon gleaming white within a corona of rainbow rings and framed by dark clouds, it looked like one giant eye watching us from the sky. And the moon in the center of the rainbow iris was the bright pupil through which Isis gazed at us benevolently, unblinkingly.

I was mesmerized by that eye until slowly, lazily, the indigo clouds rolled across the radiant moon like a dusky blue-grey eyelid and finally darkened it entirely.

Isis winking.

Now we looked like shadows in the lightless woods. We linked hands and Isis-Hagia led us back toward camp. A cool mist permeated the forest, and from a distance the campfires shone a soft amber. And the human figures moving to and fro through the mist and the music looked like ghosts or dream-folk somehow passing from the dream-world to this.

Mayhap I am dreaming. Mayhap we are all dreaming.

Then we entered the bright camp and there was merry music and dancing, and everyone I knew now had those universal, loving Isis-eyes. As I joined the graceful roundel, so ghostly and unreal did it all seem that I was convinced we were all sleeping inside the silent wagons, our bodies slumbering deeply, while in our dream-selves we drifted out like astral ghosts and came together in the night.

The dancing ended, and we talked around the friendly camp-fires until dawn painted the sky dusky purple, aquamarine, and rose. And We were as One, and in every face I saw Isis smiling. Thus Isis revealed herself to me through her people—my people —through their hearts and souls and eyes. She embraced me in their arms, and I embraced her in mine.

X

 I never set out to be a thief. Circumstances pushed me unswervingly in that direction. Necessity conspired with opportunity, and I wandered without remorse into their snare. I offer no excuses, only reasons. I could have restrained myself, admittedly. I also could have starved.

Times were not always good, albeit I try to remember them so. Life was not all festivals and prosperity. Winters hit hard, and each winter struck harder than the last. By my sixteenth winter, the worst in anyone's memory except maybe Mother Hagia's, we slept the long, hungry nights huddled close together in the wagons like litters of stray puppies piled atop one another to keep warm. We were not the only ones to suffer. Between crushing taxes, crops confiscated for the armies, Germanni raids on the borders, and Saxon raids on the coasts, the poor folk of Gaul were left with little or nothing. If food could be found, it likely could not be bought, for who can eat copper or bronze, who can fill their bellies with silver or gold?

At first I provided the diversion. In most any village or town I had only to stand in one place long enough and I would draw a sizeable crowd. With just the least effort, I easily distracted the attention of nigh well everyone within sight or hearing. And, as I soon discovered, if I began a tale, I could mesmerize half a town if need be. In the meantime, Mikato and the others helped themselves to what little goods they might find unwatched. As long as we kept on the move, this ploy held little danger.

For stealth's sake, we split the caravan into smaller camps, concealing the wagons in twos and threes deep in the forests. In the hard core of winter we traveled only when driven. Midnight raids on surrounding estates and villages kept us from starving, though when the hunt for the thieves pressed too close, we had to move on. Living like this—going days without food or fire, knowing well that one pig or goose or sack of grain would hold off starvation a few days longer—this is what drove us to steal.

We were quite good at it, too. Ronaldo usually led our excursions through wintered woods or fields, a stealthy trek single file so no one could read our numbers. If it was an easy mark, the guards fell quickly, and we were in and out with the goods long before they revived, much less escaped their bonds. If it looked to be a bit more difficult, we spread out in pairs and crept in from several directions. A sound or shadow to attract a guard while someone took him from behind usually sufficed, but on rare occasions a whole estate might arouse, and then some of us must lead them a desperate chase while the real thievery was done.

Even the new concrete walls that some landowners constructed to protect their holdings could not stop us, for what was such a barrier to a troupe of acrobats? At any point of our choosing, we were over the wall in seconds, transforming easily from a human ladder to a human chain. Once inside we stayed together, for if one lone man should be caught behind the wall, it would likely mean his doom. Such a fate nearly befell us all one dark night in Maxima Sequanorium, and not all of us escaped unscathed.

The guards discovered us stealing cuts of salt pork from a storehouse. Instantly we were running—some charging the guards while others of us made off with our booty—but the cry had been raised. They must have expected something like this, because suddenly shouts came from all directions. Our retreat to the wall was slowed by Mikato, who had taken a pitchfork in the thigh. It made a deep and ragged tear through the muscles and left him gripping his leg and swearing between clenched teeth; Ronaldo and Brossos half carried him between them, staggering into the flimsy shelter of a henhouse. The rest of us scattered like the hens, taking care that we were noted, marked, and chased anywhere except near that small refuge. Dreeko and I, after dodging through pens of goats and swine, both finally took cover in an open building—a slaughterhouse from the smell of it—and peered out the unshuttered window.

A gang of half a dozen armed men, brandishing two torches,

made their way through the pens and buildings, thoroughly searching every hiding place, warily watching for any attempt to reach the wall. Soon they would surround the henhouse door where Ronaldo and Brossos hid with the wounded Mikato. Where was everyone else? Perhaps only Dreeko and I saw the danger they were in.

I would have given anything, just then, to be young Alexander the Great rushing forth with sword and shield, but I was not—I was Dominico the dwarf and a very frightened dwarf at that. Yet, I looked about for a weapon anyway, my eyes straining to penetrate the slaughterhouse gloom. The only relief I found in the darkness was a pale patch of white floating in the shadows.

What in the name of Isis was that? A face? A death mask? A demon? I squinted. No, it was only an ordinary goat's skull, horns and all, hanging on the wall—a common enough sight to a boy raised a goatherd, yet it had paralyzed me with terror before I realized what it was. Suddenly my mind groped backwards through time, a time when a small boy gazed up at an antlered giant—the Lord of the Forest—who told him, "Things are not always as they seem."

"Dreeko!" I exclaimed in a whisper. "Look! We can scare them at least! Divert their attention! Hi-yup!"

At the command, Dreeko hoisted me onto his shoulders. I could just barely reach the skull.

"What're you up to, Dominico?"

"If this works, they're going to think the devil himself is after them."

I pulled my hood over my head and peered through the skull's eye-sockets; it made a wicked looking mask, I imagined, with its tall, twisted horns and grotesque features. Dreeko concealed my feet in his cloak, while I clutched my own cloak tight with one hand and held the skull over my face with the other.

"Dreeko, can you see?"

"Aye. Let's go."

I had to duck my head as we eased out the door. The guards, all six, were at the henhouse, ready to enter. One saw us coming and dropped his torch with a cry of terror. Every man turned and stared, horror frozen on their faces.

Together, Dreeko and I must have stood eight feet tall. The moon was at kalends, so we could be but dimly seen outside the lone torch's flickering sphere. We advanced on them soundlessly, our cloaks fluttering with the night breeze, the skull face almost alive under weird shadows formed of uncertain torchlight.

They retreated.

Slowly at first, they backed off, fear twisting their faces; then, with a hoarse cry of *"Lucifer!"* one broke and ran. It took no more than that. He was followed by one after another. The torchbearer wavered, finally flinging the torch at us and fleeing after his fellows. Luckily, in his panic, he missed. Dreeko never hesitated. He smoothly skirted the still-flaming torch and floated relentlessly after them. I heard the door of the henhouse rattle behind me but could not look back.

Though we had them on the run, Dreeko seemed set on terrorizing the whole estate. I began to doubt the wisdom of his enthusiasm.

"Stop!" I hissed. "We go too far from the wall!"

He chuckled and kept going.

I whacked him soundly on the head.

"Idiot!" I steamed. "You'll get us killed!"

Now a small knot of men formed ahead—more torches and not a few spears gleamed before us. The men were entertaining second thoughts, not necessarily in our favor.

"Dreeko!"

The knot began to unravel and creep forward. Dreeko only carried us faster to our doom. With a bloodcurdling wail he charged into them at a dead run. Most scattered; a few spears flew harmlessly askew; we kept going.

"Damn!"

Finally Dreeko swerved off around a barn and began making for the wall. We had it in sight. Ronaldo awaited us on top. Then Dreeko stumbled over something in the dark, and I went flying, losing the mask and landing twenty feet ahead on the ground. Neither of us wasted any time; we ran for our lives, the guards close upon us.

Dreeko got there first, leapt upon a fence rail set fast against the wall, reached down, and flung me up to Ronaldo in one smooth motion. Ronaldo and I both stretched our hands back toward him—too late. The leading guard closed in and plunged a spear deep into his back.

There passed a moment of infinity I will never forget. One instant there was Dreeko, hands upstretched, a look of profound astonishment on his face, intensely alive—the next instant he was gone, no life in the empty eyes, dead hands slipping down the wall, his spirit fled to someplace unreachable.

I stared transfixed—horrified. Ronaldo jerked me off the wall. Hitting frozen earth knocked my wits back into me, and the two of us bolted for the woods. We caught up to Brossos and Ludi, who carried Mikato between them. Despite the blood he had lost, white-faced and teeth clenched, he held his grip on their shoulders all the long journey back to camp.

Nor could we rest there. Word went out to every campsite; we grabbed up everything, shoved it into wagons, and lit out for the highway. This was nothing new to us. From experience, we counted on no full-scale hunt on our heels until dawn, and by then we would be many mileposts gone and well off the highway. But our departure was still a dreary one. Felicia and Hagia stayed huddled in our wagon, soothing Mikato's wounded leg. I rode grim and silent on the driver's bench beside Ronaldo. He glanced questioningly in my direction; I could not look at him. Finally his quiet, steady voice broke the heavy silence.

"Dreeko knew. He knew the chance he took."

I stirred and shivered. "Aye, but 'twas my idea to pull such a foolish stunt."

"Foolish, Dominico?" he queried softly. "We might every one of us be dead or captive had you not. Dreeko understood that well enough, be sure, else he would not have been willing."

By now I was weeping convulsively. "But he needn't have *died*! Why did he have to chase them? We could have stayed by the wall!"

Ronaldo sat in his own silence for awhile. When he spoke his voice was no longer steady.

"Dreeko lost his life that we might escape. Will you deny him honor for his deed?"

I looked at Ronaldo then. Tears shone faintly on his cheeks in the dim yellow light of Ludi's lantern, which led our dead-of-night flight down a dark tunnel of highway. Our solitary guide in a world clouded and moonless.

I shook my head. "No," I whispered tearfully.

"Weep for him, then, but speak no more of foolishness. Speak of courage instead." Now his arm came around me tightly. "Your own courage, Dominico, as well as . . . Dreeko's. You, too, placed your life in danger. If Dreeko had been a step slower, if he had not flung you up to the wall . . ."

"He would have been over and gone!" I sobbed fiercely.

"He would now be in your place, weeping for you, or we would be weeping for the both of you." Ronaldo drew a shaky breath. "At least you are still here, little cousin."

"He saved my life," I sighed.

Ronaldo's arm tightened around my shoulder. "And both of you saved many of our lives. I wish Dreeko had not died . . . but I'm thankful you did not die with him, Dominico."

The next evening we camped at the end of a broad-rutted road that cut deep into a wood—an old logging road made by long, massive hauls of stripped tree-trunks—a road abandoned and frozen.

Here we held a somber ceremony for Dreeko. Felicia, tears streaming her face, playing a sistrum, led the sad, torchbearing procession around the camp. Then we encircled a square stack of carefully laid wood. Dreeko's sisters and mother laid his prized possessions on the pile: two bronze-washed wrist ornaments (how they had flashed when he juggled!), a red satin vest (his favorite performance vest), and eight carved-handled juggling knives (he would wish to perform for the court of Isis, we knew).

Then the torches were set to the wood and Dreeko's possessions burned on the pyre to release their essence from this world into the next. Sadly, we did not have Dreeko's body to lay out on the pyre. To burn his body would give his spirit instant release from his Earthly form so that he may more quickly step into the Ship of Isis and be sailed gently across the Styx into the Blessed Abode of the Dead. But his body was beyond our reach; he would have to wait until the dead flesh loosened before his spirit could break free. At least his possessions would be there awaiting him.

As Hagia flung incense on the fire, making the flames dance a brilliant green, and murmured an incantation committing Dreeko's soul to Isis, I looked up into the clear, cold night and saw that starry river that he must cross. It spanned the heights of Heaven like a faint, white ribbon of sparkling water. I believed Dreeko's soul had already escaped, already stood on the bank of that pale river, for I felt I had witnessed his flight from this world at the instant of his death. Dreeko's dying moment had struck me as more like a sudden departure than anything.

I smiled up through my tears and the smoke and wished him a swift journey and a merry welcome at the end.

When the ceremony ended, Dreeko's mother and sisters wept and hugged me. Mikato limped up painfully, using a shorn tree-limb for a crutch, though thankfully his pitchfork wound was not so serious as it had first appeared. Mayhap he would still be able to do acrobatics when his leg healed.

"Cousin," he said to me, "I've had no chance to thank you . . . I . . . if it hadn't been for you and Dreeko. . . ."

"Sure," I smiled wanly.

"Damn!" He looked away toward the pathetically small pyre smoldering in the clearing. "I'm the one who stupidly let myself get hurt, but Dreeko's the one who paid for it. It doesn't seem right, does it?"

I shook my head. "Death doesn't care about right or wrong, Mikato. It just lurks and waits to jump where it will—that's all."

Mikato looked at me strangely. Mother Hagia leaned close and spoke in her high, cracked voice.

"Death believes it is always right, children, for 'tis destined to have us all in the end." She nodded with easy finality.

Gorgi, who had been listening, shuddered. "Everybody knows that," he said later to me. "Why does she have to go reminding us all the time?"

South and west we traveled. Spring found us in Lugdunensis Superior province above the Rivers Loire and Rhone, where we kept to ourselves as much as possible. The festivals had all but died out, for Theodosius tightened the laws so that any official who so much as permitted Pagan feasts or rituals within his boundaries was considered to condone the crime and was dealt with accordingly. Our way of life was perishing and we had no place to go.

Mayhap we could have gone northwest to a less populated corner of Gaul, but that land was hard and poor, while we were already weary and hungry. Therefore, we journeyed south along the River Rhone, skirting the foothills of the Alps, and spent a lively summer flirting with the cities Lugdunum and Vienne.

I remember Lugdunum well. It was a market town filled with hustling and hawking vendors, and this sunny season the streets seemed always full to overflowing. Like stepping into a river it was and being swept along with the current past stalls and shops.

I loitered before a bakery, enticed there by the mouthwatering aroma that wafted from the ovens and effused a fragrant haven midst the more pungent animal and human smells of the street. I warmed a solitary copper in my fist and searched the tiered shelves of bakewares—dark round loaves, honeyed raisin cakes, broken pieces of crumbly white flatbread, little individual doughy rolls with jam fillings—and considered which delectable tidbit I might afford.

I took no notice of the open-air wineshop next door until slurred, boisterous voices interrupted my savory reverie.

"Oh, look at that, now. Did you ever see such an eyeful?"

"Can't say I have. Don't he look splendid though? Little bandy-cock all frumped up in tawdry like a popinjay!"

I gritted my teeth resolutely, determined to ignore these louts, purchase my cake, and go.

"Aye. What a dainty—what a charmer! What you all gawked out for, precious? A hobgoblin fest?"

I ground my teeth harder. They swaggered closer.

"Ain't you just devilish elegant, bandy-cock? Where'd a squat like you come by such fine plumery, eh?"

I turned and fixed them with a cold stare. They were two drunken laborers dressed in coarse dun and wheezing fermented humors.

"Oh, now, you've gone and puffed up the squat's feathers. Now, precious, it's just we've not seen a stunty swell like you since . . . why, since no-when!"

I considered my options. Reluctantly foregoing the sweetcake, I pointedly turned on my heel and stalked off.

They followed me.

"My, look at him strut. Ain't that rich now!"

"Aye, a runt-elf got up in frippery like a duke. Oh, stump-along, don't you cut a figure, though!"

We passed a shop densely hung with freshly-oiled, new-tooled leather goods. No one paid us any mind. I could probably bolt and lose them in the crowd, but the idea of running from these two swaggering oafs irked me beyond reason. One minced along-side me.

"Where you off to in such a huff, crook-legs? Look out you don't get stepped on now!"

In front of a butcher shop strung with huge cuts of smoked meats, I slipped narrowly between a tradesman and his wife and wended through their astounded brood of youngsters, leaving the drunkards in their path. They shoved, stumbled, thudded, and caught up with me again. I minded myself of Ronaldo's warning to avoid trouble in Lugdunum under *any* circumstances.

"None of that now, bandy-cock," slurred one. "Why, we just wants to follow you home and see what begot the likes of you."

The other sniggered. "Likely his mama got rutted by a troll!"

I stopped cold, turned, and eyed them malevolently.

"That's enough, dung-tongue!" I snarled. "And you, maggot-mind! Shut those festering wens you call mouths! You befoul the street with your stench!"

Oh, they turned fifty shades of red and purple before one let loose a bellow of rage and sprang at me, both hands grasping for my neck. Of course he grasped empty space, for I had moved aside and skipped behind him.

"Missed, ox-brain!" I crowed. "'Twill take more than slimy sewer-vermin like you to catch this bandy-cock!"

I ducked a wild swing of the other's arm and spun out of his reach.

"Try again, carrion-breath!"

They both lunged for me and staggered head-on into each other as I backflipped out of their way. I was in no wise afraid of these two. They were sluggish, clumsy drunkards; I was agile and quick and well practiced.

"Over here, you wormy piles of sheep-shit!"

Heaving lividly, they again tried to come at me from either side. I cartwheeled between them.

"What's the trouble, swine-face? Can't two witless lumps of ass-dung catch a dainty little runt-elf? Ha!" I laughed, dancing around them gleefully. "Come on, try it, pock-cock!"

They tried. I let them come close enough to overextend their wine-fuddled balance, then I flipped forward and rolled away. Both buried their noses in the dust. As they struggled to their knees I whirled around and delivered one a hearty, barefoot kick in the rear end. He howled. So did a gathering crowd of spectators.

"Get up, you scabby hind-end of a barbarian!" I sidestepped his angry lunge. "What kind of cowering curs can't stand up to one little hobgoblin?"

The other kicked at me wildly. I twisted clear, caught his upraised foot, and toppled him backwards. He thudded to the ground; the crowd roared and hooted. I bowed cockily. My mistake.

I raised my eyes to meet two fistfuls of dirt. Hastily I backed away, trying to brush the dirt from my eyes and avoid the man's hands at the same time. Fingers clamped my ankle and I stumbled over backwards thrashing like a beetle on its back.

Still gripping my ankle, he dragged me toward him and pummeled my face and upflung arms furiously with his fist. I attempted to ram my big toe up his nose. Yowling, he quit battering me to grab at the offending foot. Abruptly I threw my whole body over, wrenching my ankle but causing him to lose his grip, and scuttled away on hands and knees.

The other man's foot hammered me full in the chest. I flopped sideways with a grunt and tried to roll out from under his feet. The next kick skimmed my ribs. I kept rolling and rolled right up against someone's bare feet in the crowd.

I sat up with difficulty, expecting to be pounced on by two raging drunkards. Instead they swayed in their tracks and glared uncertainly over my head. I looked up.

There, looking mean and hard and menacing, grinned Mikato. He half crouched, balancing a long dagger in his palm, daring them to come closer. Beside him Ludi did the same. I blinked in surprise. Most of the acrobats and no few of the dancers, maybe a score in all, stood at my back, unmistakably reckless, tough, and none too pleased with the two beet-faced men. An expectant intake of breath swept the spectators. I got to my feet and grinned devilishly.

"Well, pig-pukes," I smirked, "not so brave now, are you? You're nought but ass-brained—"

Mikato's hand clamped firmly over my mouth. I rolled my eyes upwards at him. He still grinned dangerously. When he spoke his voice was smooth and acrid.

"I apologize for my little cousin, *gentlemen*. We try to break him of bullying innocent folk in the streets, but he's a bad one when he's out on his own."

The crowd snickered and guffawed. The drunkards' faces deepened to purple. Mikato let go of my mouth; his black eyes narrowed.

"Ah, but you two gentlemen did not *provoke* Dominico by any chance? If so, perhaps *you* had best apologize to *him*, else his wrath may be so terrible that I cannot assure your safety."

The spectators hooted and catcalled.

"Vermin-vomit!" I crowed. "Ox-offal! Worm-!"

Mikato stopped my flow of words again. I was enjoying myself immensely, and I noted that he must bite his lower lip to hold the malefic aspect on his face.

"The devil we'll apologize to that vile-tongued little. . . ."

The man's words died as he noticed the vagabonds had slowly spread out and very nearly closed the circle.

"On your knees!" ordered Mikato, still grinning.

When they made no move to comply, four acrobats gave them expert encouragement.

Mikato was not satisfied. "No—hands and knees, like the asses my little cousin thinks you to be."

A bit more encouragement and they were on their hands and knees. The crowd cheered. Some brayed loudly.

"Now apologize. Beg Dominico's pardon for your swinish behavior."

They were going to gag on the words, but the troupe prepared to wring an apology from them.

"Pardon . . . (mumble) . . . didn't mean . . . (mumble) . . . want no trouble. . . ."

"Eh? Louder!"

Suddenly Ludi elbowed Mikato and hissed—"Agents!"

Mikato looked past the crowd. I stood too short to see what he must have noted moving through the busy street—the tall spears of a civil agent's guardsmen. Necks craned. The fun was over.

"Worm-wits!" I flung at the kneeling drunkards as Mikato hauled me away by the shirtscruff.

With incredible swiftness the ring of spectators transformed into a preoccupied market-day throng. Mikato dragged me along, concealing his illegal dagger in his sash. We turned a few corners and halted. He cuffed me soundly on the head.

"Aah, Dominico! How could you be so stupid?"

"*They* started it—not me!" I retorted like a petulant child caught scuffling.

Mikato laughed heartily. "Do you think I'm fool enough to imagine, cousin, that you provoked a fight with two great lumbering drunkards double your size apiece? No, the cuff is for mucking it. You owned the show! You had them! What did you stop and bow for, you arrogant ass? And Ronaldo said no trouble! Come, we'll have to tell him what happened."

He started off, then stopped and admonished me gloweringly. "Stay close, Dominico. I'll not have you out of my sight while we're in Lugdunum."

I nodded.

"Mikato."

"What now?" He looked back impatiently.

"Thanks."

He flashed a quick grin and shrugged. Then with a jerk of his head he sauntered on. I trotted after him.

We did not stay long in Lugdunum. We were on our way to Vienne again when we heard the news that turned us aside.

Emperor Valentinian died, apparently slain by his own hand, but folk in Gaul felt otherwise. The young Emperor, at the willful age of twenty-one, had become too obstinate for General Arbogast to control. Just when Valentinian had a mind of his own, muttered folk in the marketplace, his master general found it expedient to dispose of him.

Now, Theodosius would not sit idle long after one of his generals murdered his co-ruler and laid claim to half the Empire. Soon, Gaul would again be the sporting ground for the Imperial Games.

All of us had seen our fill of usurper wars, so, while Theodosius no doubt gathered his mercenary forces, Ronaldo collected his little vagaond band and headed east through the Alps into Italia.

Now, I spent my boyhood in the forested mountains of northeastern Gaul—at least they called themselves mountains and I thought of them as such—but they were out and out imposters; they did nothing to earn the name. One sojourn even a little way into the magnificent Alps showed the anthills back home up to be the liars they really were. Why, they could not even honestly call themselves foothills!

It is easy to take the Earth for granted when her gently rolling surface lies sleeping under one's feet. But when she raises to her full height and touches Heaven, when she looms overhead and smites the senses with her sheer immensity, when she celebrates all her glory and majesty—peak to valley to cliff to canyon and on to peak again—reveling in her own wild nature and taking no notice of an insect that calls itself humankind, then the Earth commands a worship all her own. The human soul stirs in awed reverence and would joyously leap free to lose itself in this ageless monument of creation, except that the body jealously holds the spirit in rein. And good thinking that is on the Creator's part, else few who entered these mountains would ever come out again.

XI

 In desolate, rocky Umbria we joined the Flaminian Way on its southern route and merged into the busy stream of ox-and-mule-drawn wagons piled high with crates of geese or goods or whatever, people afoot carrying packs or driving livestock, even an occasional noble riding horseback. Our colorful ox-drawn wagons gave the people, coming or going, something new to stare at and ponder over momentarily as they passed.

Dressed in our gayest, laughing and joking from wagon to wagon, we broke camp near the stark Red Rock, ten miles north of Rome, along with pilgrims who had come to see where Emperor Constantine received his vision of victory under Christ's standard. We were not interested enough to pay the coppers it cost to stand on the exact spot where Constantine had slept; the denarii-per-wagon camping fee had been expensive enough.

Our last day of travel we crossed the Milvian Bridge over the River Tiber and passed between silent tombs standing eternal vigil along the highway. Even mausoleums and crypts could not dampen our spirits. We journeyed the afternoon in a state of high excitment—well, *most* of us anyway. Mother Hagia had been uneasy about Ronaldo's decision to go to Rome, and now the nearer we approached, the more opposed she became. She told her son she sensed trouble and disaster in Rome; he listened gravely, for she was Hagia, but she could not define her uneasiness, and he could easily define his reasons for coming.

Felicia and Gorgi and I clung high on the lattice-work of the lead wagon; the oxhide cover was rolled up on this sunny, warm day, more spring than winter. I believe we three spied the distant wall at the same instant. We let loose such a whoop that the oxen lurched forward a pace or two in startlement and rocked our perch dangerously.

"Oh, we're here, we're here!" chanted Felicia. "I can't believe it! I'm going to dance in Rome!"

Mikato laughed from the driver's bench and boomed, "Oh, aye, midst all its wonders the whole of Rome will halt and turn its eyes to see Felicia dance!"

Felicia tossed her head. "And when they do, I'll be much too grand for *you*, Mikato."

Mikato snorted.

"I rather think they will," I told her.

"Me too," agreed Gorgi.

Ronaldo leapt up onto the side of the slow-moving wagon. "Rome will turn its eyes to see all of us! 'Tis only a matter of time and opportunity."

Felicia smiled dreamily. "It *would* be nice to be famous in Rome. Lovely new clothes and gifts and parties . . ."

"And banquets," Gorgi chimed.

". . . and gold," smiled Ronaldo.

". . . palaces and baths," Felicia rambled.

". . . and circuses," added Mikato, joining the fun.

". . . and theaters," I said, for I had seen a play once in Vienne and found it thoroughly intriguing.

". . . and *death!*"

All eyes turned to Hagia, who sat on her trunk staring off to the clear horizon as though none of this journey concerned her.

"Mother," Ronaldo said softly, unsurely.

Hagia stirred and looked at him. "I do not trust Romans."

"Nor do I. But we are free folk. We'll break no laws. Rome has no grudge against us."

Hagia shrugged pessimistically.

"Now we are within sight, are your feelings any less vague, Mother?"

"No."

"As for me, I feel even stronger; 'tis worth the risk. Our journey has been trouble-free and swift, and we meet the gates of Rome under clear sky and fair weather. Good omens, Mother."

"Weather has nought to do with omens," she snapped. "It has to do with seasons and crops."

"What say your stars?"

"Nothing!" The old woman stirred irritably. "'Tis my *gut* says Rome is a fickle and deadly place."

"*My* gut smells profit. There's food and gold and silver galore in Rome; whyfore should we sit outside and starve?"

"Hmph!" Hagia stared back toward the sunny horizon. "Do as you please—you will anyway. But *I'm* not going in!"

Ronaldo sighed. "And you'll do as *you* please, Old Hag, I know. Fine. We'll need someone to stay with the wagons."

"The gate!" Gorgi crowed. "I see the gate!"

We turned to look, our excitement undiminished. Our caravan approached the Flaminian Gate.

Rome!

The Eternal City!

Soon we stood before the portals of a world apart: Heart of the Empire! Island unto herself! For me, Rome was legend. Emperors, generals, laws—even gods—might come and go, but Rome looks only to herself with reverence. For over eleven hundred years the city has thrived and built upon tradition and grandeur so ancient, so inviolable, that the citizenry worship her as a divine entity in her own right. Roma, they call her, and she has withstood foreign enemies, civil strife, senate wars, military takeovers, imperial usurpers, mad emperors, and rioting mobs. And Rome emerges ever victorious, still undisputed Queen of the Empire.

We camped our wagons in a grove outside the wall, for a fee of course. Nor were we alone; people flocked to Rome daily: farmers driven from their lands by barren soil and greedy estatesmen, jobless townsmen seeking a living, hunted men seeking anonymity, pilgrims come to see the city of Saints Peter and Paul. Whatever the reasons, an ever fluctuating suburb of carts, carriages, and wagons formed a permanent encampment outside the city walls. We were no exception; we paid our fees and raised our tents, and so long as we did nothing overtly illegal, we could count ourselves just another lot of supplicants come to taste the wonders of the Eternal City.

With ever heightening excitement we—acrobats, dancers, musicians, old folk and young—awaited the opening of the Flaminian Gate next dawn. We watched the stream of night-wagons leaving the city, for wheeled vehicles are allowed on the streets only during the predawn hours to carry goods and conduct commerce within the walls. We entered Rome on foot and joined the growing crowd on the famous Flaminian Way, which we had learned would lead us directly to the heart of the city.

I was overwhelmed with so many jumbled sights, sounds, and smells—one million people live within these walls—so I carefully kept sight of Ronaldo's bootheels, and trod stones that have felt the footfalls of a thousand years.

On either side structures of every shape guided our course, each one more massive and wonderful than the last. I had never imagined such a magnificent collection of mausoleums, temples, obelisks, columns, and arches all in one place. And so many aqueducts! Some three and even four arches high! Carrying water overhead in channels as wide as small streams!

Every exposed surface seemed to be marbled or frescoed or sculptured. We passed at least three glorious arches—Arches of Marcus Aurelius, Claudius, and Diocletian. Everywhere my eyes met mute stories in stone so graphic I need not be able to read words, only pictures. Fitting tales they were, too, for such imposing structures: tales of wars and conquests and captures and executions, all intricately detailed, even to the pain and despair on the captives' faces as they groveled at the feet of conquering emperors.

And the crowds! Rome crawls with people as an anthill crawls with ants. And scarcely does one of them ever glance at the centuries-old splendor, not even in the forums, where works of miraculous beauty calmly assault the eye no matter where one turns. Indeed, in the forums folk are so engaged in talking and bargaining and quarreling and harrying that one must raise his voice to be heard by the man next to him, thereby adding to the din. They evidently have no *time* to look about them; nowhere on Earth could people be so much in a hurry as in Rome. They are all on their way quickly to somewhere, though how they find their destinations in the maze of twisting avenues I could not say.

We wandered gawking through the narrow streets, entering the Forum of the Divine Trajan; we gazed up the spiraling relief carvings which climb to the dizzying pinnacle of Trajan's Column, where stands a statue of Trajan himself. We meandered through the great market and one busy forum after another (I lost count somewhere along the way) packed with myriad hordes of shopkeepers, hawkers, statesmen, and shoppers. We rounded the Capitoline Hill from which severe height gleams the golden roof of the Temple of Jupiter Capitolinus, splendid in the noonday sun.

Temples flourish in any little space they can squeeze into. Temples of Minerva, Mars the Avenger, Venus and Roma, Jupiter Victor, Mercury, Saturn! All of them are closed to worship by decree of Theodosius. Yet the city protects them; they are her history and her pride. The buildings, though empty and silent, are beautiful enough in themselves to inspire an awe befitting the gods for which they were built. Saddest is the tiny Temple of Vesta and the House of the Vestals in the Forum Romanum. The Vestal Virgins are no longer needed to tend the Eternal Flame since Emperor Gratian had it extinguished. Rome's hearthfire lies cold. Appalled Pagans foresaw doom to both Gratian and Rome. Indeed, Gratian met his doom soon enough; Rome still thrived unperturbed.

Her million and more citizens were going about their daily business as they have done for a thousand years. In the streets we made way for richly decorated sedans and litters carried by muscular slaves in matched tunics. If the curtain was open, we could glimpse a bejeweled occupant sitting or reclining within the shade—often a fine lady whose elegant coiffure was held in place by gold and topaz pins. We also stepped aside for senators, consuls, patricians, military police, and anyone who looked to be of the aristocracy. They were easy to spot. Some wore silken tunics and togas striped with gold and silver threads, but even the conservatives in traditional red-trimmed white were easily identified by the gaggle of clients squawking at their heels.

The markets smelled of spices, frying meats, fresh baked bread, garbage, penned animals, and close-packed humanity: Patrons and clients, merchants, tradesmen, soldiers, and slaves mingled in close proximity with assorted browsers, beggars, and vagrants. Our motley little band blended into this varied crowd so completely as to be virtually invisible. Freely we wandered the city, Felicia and Gorgi and I dashing here and there, calling excitedly to each other, pointing at this or that like rustic peasants at a fest. Ronaldo and Brossos stopped to talk with hawkers and loiterers from time to time, gleaning information on the workings of the social machinery, for we could not afford to be tourists in Rome. We must make a living and only one thing we knew for certain: If we did not wish to perform our arts in public squares for mere coppers, we would have to find a patron. To this task our chieftain and our master acrobat concentrated their matchless bargaining skills.

All day we spent in the city. I saw in Rome more splendor and more squalor than I thought to see in a whole lifetime. On spacious avenues one can stroll in the shade of covered colonnades artfully lined with fabulous statuary and soothing fountains. Nearby, secure behind the white walls of Caelian Hill, are the secluded gardens and palaces of the wealthiest people in the Empire. Yet, but a few streets away, a maze of narrow passages twists in dingy confusion, gutters reeking of spilth (a noxious substance thrown from chamber pots out windows—called *spilth* because that's the sound it makes when it hits the pavement—one learns to keep an eye out for it), overshadowed by the insulae: vast islands of wooden cubicles stacked one atop the other where hundreds of thousands live crowded together in poverty and filth. These tenements are perpetually dark, smokey, and ofttimes chill, for fires are restricted to charcoal braziers in the tiny rooms. Indeed, fire is a threat to quail even the most hardened urban heart; more than once an uncontrollable blaze has reduced entire sections of the city to smouldering rubble.

This was the Rome I saw the first time I entered the city. As winter faded into spring, and spring into summer, she unveiled a new face nearly every day, so that I despaired of ever knowing all of her wiles. At first our troupe was obliged to perform in public forums and reaped little for our work. There is nothing so jaded and insolent as a Roman audience, especially a plebeian one. The plebs hold no jobs, ply no trades, have nought to do all day but loiter in the streets and crowd into the games or circuses. These folk never need pray "give us this day our daily bread," for they already know whence it will come. They need only present a copper "bread ticket" at a designated station each day and they receive not only bread but regular stipends of olive oil, pork, and wine. The right to free bread is hereditary, copper tickets being closely guarded and passed along to descendants, and over one-fifth of the population claims the privilege. How it began I do not know; it is enough that it began. Now it cannot be stopped, for this is the infamous Roman mob. When the plebs clamor for more bread, emperors and senators alike take notice. Should the grain shipments from Africa run short, as has happened a few times, the mob can turn nasty. And more than one unpopular personage has ended a promising career torn in bloody pieces or pelted to death, dragged through the triumphal arches, and flung into the River Tiber. There is no one so powerful in Rome who does not secretly dread the many-throated cry, "*You to the Tiber!*"

This fear of the mob we counted on to provide us a living. To take the plebeian mind off rations and wretched housing, the city provides free entertainment fully one-half the days of the year. Our hope was to find a pleb-courting patron who would pay us good wages for our artful diversions.

The task proved to be a difficult one; slave troupes seemed to have cornered the market. Why pay free citizens a decent living when the same money will buy the players outright? To be sure, slave acrobats, dancers, and musicians were excellent—more polished, more richly costumed—but they had nought else to do but practice and be fitted for costumes ordered by their masters, while we must look to filling our bellies and keeping warm and dry. Slaves worried over none of these mundane details.

In contrast, our unique variegation of vagabond Egyptian, Syrian, Macedonian, and Gallic ancestry made us a decidedly more colorful lot. We were good. We were proud. We were freeborn. We knew our freedom and expressed it in our arts. The exuberance, the sheer joy of motion, the spontaneous creativity born of an unfettered life far surpassed, in our eyes, any performance a trained troupe of slaves had to offer.

Every morning we danced, played, and tumbled somewhere in the city, ofttimes playing two forums before noon. We performed in the Forum of Trajan, whirling roundabout Trajan's statue as though doing homage to the mounted warrior-Emperor. We paraded from the Capitoline along the Sacred Way, finishing our procession with a gala exhibition in the open plaza fronting the Amphitheater of Flavius, and wonder of wonders, the crowd milling there for the gladiatorial games drew back and took notice! We practiced our trade in the forum just outside the Theater of Marcellus near the arched footbridge that crosses over to the Island Tiberina and the Temple of Aesculapius, where we commanded a round of applause from a throng of theatergoers!

Early one morning in the Forum Romanum, as we made our bows and collected our meager take of coppers and denarii, a well-attired slave came forward and approached Brossos with an officious air. Ronaldo grinned, gestured for Mikato, and casually joined them. Here was the moment we had been awaiting!

As the four discussed business, I edged close enough to listen. Twice I noted that whenever the slave spoke of his master he unconsciously jerked his eyes in a particular direction. Gazing along the line of his glance, my eyes came to rest on a young man in a white toga standing on the Curia steps. So young, he must be new to the Senate, I thought, and now planning his campaign for popular support. Most elder senators scarcely bothered, seeing fit to show up only when the matter under discussion directly affected their own purses and prestige. This would be a wealthy one, who might hire his own entertainment to court the plebeian good will.

Yet the young senator took no interest in the hiring proceedings; his eyes were intent on something else. Curious as ever, I followed his intense gaze and discovered, with no little disconcertment, that he stared in rapt fascination directly at dark-eyed, laughing Felicia.

Did Felicia notice his unswerving attention? Certainly she did, else she would not glance so shyly toward the Curia and then turn quickly away, chattering nervously at another dancer, yet stealing a look now and then at her unexpected admirer. She blushed despite herself. The blossoming young dancing-girl, pretending with little success to be unaware of the handsome aristrocratic eyes that watched her, could not conceal from him that she was flattered. She glanced toward Mikato. Did he notice? No. Although the three vagabonds had assuredly marked the watching senator as our potential patron, they were too earnestly engaged in bargaining with the slave to mark the master's real interest. Only Felicia and I, it seemed, read his gaze. Oh, that Hagia had been there! Her sharp, old eyes missed nothing, and I would not have to stand pondering whether this was an evil portent or no.

The hagglers parted, the slave gave one quick nod to his master, and our new patron disappeared into the Senate House. Triumph glowed on Ronaldo's face like the fiery wine of the gods. His flustered daughter flung both arms around his neck and jubilantly kissed him on both cheeks; only one quick look did she turn toward the empty Curia steps before joining hands in a celebration dance. A trifle, I shrugged. Why should a harmless flirtation be cause for concern? I whooped aloud, turned ten joyous backflips, and joined the dance.

XII

The multitude hummed like a million bees in a hive. I stared along the freshly smoothed oval track of the Circus Flaminius: such a long distance to the other end and back! The crowd was still engaged in the lengthy process of settling into the awning-shaded stands when the Master of Spectaculars gave the signal to begin. I led off, as I had done a thousand times before into a thousand villages and towns, turning a series of flips and wheels in rapid sequence. Behind me followed the familiar vagabond troupe of acrobats, musicians, and dancers, but here the similarity ended; this was Rome, a circus spectacular, and trailing us I knew were jugglers, mimes, more exotic dancers and tumblers, trained horses put through their paces by trick riders, a dancing African elephant, and only Isis knows what else! We . . . I . . . set the pace, and it must be a fast one. All our headstands, towers, and pyramids must be done on the move with never a halt from one formation to the next. I balanced atop the quadrilateral pyramid as we made our dizzy spin down the track. When we rounded the spina, we split suddenly into two simple pyramids, leaving me topping one and Gorgi capping the other.

On the return trek along the other side of the spina, we passed the body of the procession; our pyramids broke into towers which toppled into sixteen separate tumbling human blurs. Now the spectators stirred with renewed excitement. Their applause peaked not for us, I knew, for I glanced across the spina; we were come abreast of the real attraction—one hundred chariots, each drawn by four horses harnessed side by side, each team high-spirited and high-stepping as though barely held in check—the contestants! The charioteers nodded toward the cheering crowd, but their real attention riveted on their steeds and their rivals.

By the time we halted at the end of the racetrack whence we started, our vagabond dancers and acrobats had mixed into concentric circles wheeling within and without each other in opposite directions; Brossos, garbed entirely in scarlet, dominated the center point, exhibiting a dazzling display of his magnificent acrobatic skills.

All the circus track was filled by now, a brilliant oval of exotic diversions, each act presenting its own grand finale, the chariots fanned in formation around the broad turn at the spina's end, rival sections in the stands yelling and waving colored scarves for their own favorite teams—red, green, white, or blue—what a deafening spectacle we created altogether!

Abruptly, on signal from the Master of Spectaculars, the performers fell still. I waited, sucking air in great gulps after the strenuous trek, watching for the next signal while the last of the cheers echoed and died down the length of the circus. The showmaster's hands dropped, and as I somersaulted toward the exit the entire parade took up again to complete its circuit around the track.

There were twenty-five races, four chariots competing in each. The chariots and steeds bore no ornaments other than the colors designating their teams, for to the charioteers this was not a show, but grim competition. Each race lasted seven turns around the circus, and even above the crowd's screams could be heard the thunderous hooves and rattling wheels. The races were not without spills, for there are no rules against sideswiping each other out on the turns; several damaged horses had to be destroyed, and a few charioteers were grievously injured.

The red team took most of the prizes; evidently it was not the odds-on favorite, for immediately a riot got underway, and fighting broke out in the Circus Flaminius stands. But this was a minor race, of little consequence, so the furor did not last long. The blue, green, and white teams would see other chances to qualify for the championship races in the Circus Maximus.

Our patron, whose name was Sividicus—Titus Fabius Sividicus—paid us well. We performed not only the circuses, but the theaters (the Balba, the Pompey, even the Marcellus) as a prelude to the plays. I must add that we were better than the plays, for Roman theater was disappointingly silly. Senator Sividicus attended every performance, sitting moodily in the reserved galleries and watching Felicia's every graceful, soaring move. He provided the troupe three spacious rooms on the second floor (preferable for its quick exit in case of fire) of a tenement built by Emperor Nero during the reconstruction of Rome (after one of the more infamous of the aforementioned fires).

Suddenly we had silver in our hands and all of Rome in which to spend it. Brossos saw to the acrobats' costumes first and made certain we practiced every day without fail. Oh, his spirits soared so he liked to never come down to Earth. He had a new balancing pole made for the theaters, the old one having been snapped sharply in twain during a flight for our lives in a Gallic forest. Ronaldo was in the same high spirits, making sure we appeared exactly when and where Sividicus wanted us, managing the sudden fortune that flowed across his palms. Mother Hagia refused to enter Rome at all. She preferred to keep our little camp outside the wall with an old crony and a very pregnant dancer and to ply her mysterious arts with the folk who passed or settled there.

I remember Gorgi and myself daring each other into posing as Christian pilgrims that we might explore the cities of the dead—the Catacombs of Callistus. Though the underground tunnels were dark and narrow, as confusing as the Labyrinth, Bishop Damascus had opened them up to pilgrims, cutting stairways, enlarging galleries, sealing off treacherous corridors, and repairing the martyrs' tombs. It was well worth the journey out to the Campagna for two adventuresome lads to purchase torches and descend into gloomy, winding tunnels underground—tunnels niched with graves of a bygone era, crudely decorated with sacred frescoed scenes by the worshipful hands of long dead believers.

"Imagine," I said awefully, "imagine if we were the first. Imagine no one knew about them and we came down into the catacombs with our torches and explored—just the two of us."

"Aye," agreed Gorgi, whispering dramatically. "Imagine we lost our way and we're searching for the way out."

"But we just go deeper and deeper and get more and more lost."

"And we find a treasure!"

"Guarded by old saints' bones!"

Despite barriers blocking off dangerous passages, freshly painted inscriptions (which neither of us could read anyway, being blissfully unacquainted with letters), and silent, somber pilgrims, we were in our own world and might have been bold explorers in danger of losing ourselves in the catacombs for eternity.

However, the pious pilgrims did not appreciate our irreverance. At length we were summarily collared and expelled from the catacombs. We emerged blinking into the bright sunlight, to the reality of hermits and religious mystics hawking holy relics to well-to-do pilgrims: a scarf soaked in the blood of some saint or a piece of bone or lock of hair of another.

Gorgi was all for hastening back to the city and exploring the Cloaca Maxima next, but I persuaded him that the great sewer was rampant with excretion, rats, scorpions, and desperate criminals. Whether all this was true, I only guessed, but I had Gorgi wide-eyed. I felt I could convince anyone of almost anything.

Within days my belief was put to trial. It was one hot summer evening just after the merging and deepening of late-afternoon shadows, when all decent folk have gone home to supper, yet when the more unsavory elements of society creep out into the darkling streets, anticipating night's black cloak. As I wended the narrow lanes homeward, still unfamiliar enough with the city to verge on being hopelessly lost, I abruptly found myself face to face with a congregation of street urchins. They seemed to have crawled out of the stonework, so suddenly did they appear from doorways and alleys. I spun about; more urchins materialized behind me.

In truth, "urchins" is a misleading term. Though they looked to be no older than Gorgi, they were byproducts of Rome's lowest strata. "Street toughs" we called them—immature, unpredictable, and unquestionably dangerous. My heart skipped time like a flutist with hiccups. I stood hemmed in by a full dozen boys and a smattering of girls.

"Hie, lads," gloated a dirty, barefoot youth, "look what we caught us this time. A bloody dwarf."

"Aye," chimed one of his mates, "a regular bandy-legs."

The first boy sauntered up to me, an insolent grin on his smudgy face. I would have liked to back off, but as there were only more of the same behind me, I held my ground.

"Whatcha doing out without your keeper, runt?"

The question had no real answer so I said nothing. My heart pounded. What did they want? By now I was totally closed in by a tight huddle of grimy faces, arms, and legs. Their apparent leader began poking and tugging at my pockets and belt, deftly relieving me of the small dagger I had not been foolhardy enough to draw.

"Got any coin, bandy-legs?"

"No," I said truthfully.

They satisfied themselves on that point quickly enough. The leader jerked at a fistful of my hair, inspecting a glint on one ear.

"What's this now?" he grinned, tugging at my hooped earring playfully. "Silver, is it?"

I winced as he pulled harder; one of them laughed.

A girl's high-pitched voice: "Ain't he the stunt what does tricks in the Forum?"

"That's you, is it?"

"Aye, the same," I confirmed, glad of the interruption.

"Oh, what luck, mates. We was just wishing for a show, wasn't we now? Bandy-legs come along just in time."

Tired though I might be, I was perfectly willing to give them a "show" if it would get me out of there in one piece, but these toughs had seen too many arena games. Simple acrobatics have not enough blood in them. And they were armed. They carried that versatile street weapon—the "spike"—a stout stick, blunt at one end and sharpened to a lethal point on the other.

Suddenly I found myself enclosed in a thicket of these long spikes as the urchins widened their circle to form a human arena.

"Do us a headstand, runt," ordered the ringleader, poking my shoulder sharply with his stick.

When I balked, a few of them stabbed at me menacingly, and a painful prodding it was, too. With a terrible lucidity I perceived the only possible outcome of their little game: They would get their show, and I would be left a bleeding and bruised lump of flesh on the street, possibly alive, more probably not.

I drew myself up to my full height of three-feet-plus-one-half and squarely confronted their leader with a boldness born of fear.

"Do you know," I charged, "just who you are poking with those little sticks of yours?"

"No, stump, who?" jeered the amused tough, glancing gleefully at his fellows.

I jammed my hands on my hips, forced my features into indignation, and slowly rotated to survey the fierce, youthful faces, wastrels in the Eternal City, destined to live and die scrounging the streets of the metropolis.

Inwardly, my mind ran a reckless race to conjure a tale fit to stake my life on, for it had come to that. My slow turn brought me to face their leader once more. I fixed him with a glare.

"You dare beset Dominico the Dwarf! I who routed an army

of Burgundians alongside Cernunnos, Lord of the Forest, when I was but a child! I who once brought to bay the Wild Huntsmen! Why, I've been set upon by trolls and dragons and a horde of Huns and lived to tell the tale! Am I to be afraid of pointy sticks?

"Oh, if I told you of the frightful creatures I've run afoul of and survived, you'd beg pardon for your insolence! Do you know that once upon a dark night—darker even than the Catacombs when the last torch has sputtered out—far on the cold, misty marshes bordering the Black Forest, I discovered myself to be stalked by werewolves?

"Aye, all I could make out was their great, red, vulpine eyes glowing hungrily at me from the shadows, but close upon me I heard their stealthy paws and rumbling breath as they skulked along either side of my path.

"What was I to do? Why, nothing! There was nothing to be done but tramp along and get a good grip on my dagger. They shadowed me until I reached a clearing in the tangled foliage, and then they closed in. As the clouds unshrouded the moon I saw their long, white fangs bared in the icy light.

"Suddenly their snarling died, and the wolf-creatures slunk back and cowered away. A towering, black-cloaked shape now stood in the clearing. All I could tell of his face was that he had the same red, vulpish eyes as his slavering wolves.

" 'Dominico!' the figure hissed horribly, pointing one clawed finger at me.

"I froze as if ensorcelled, for indeed I was. I no longer possessed the power to move; this dread being held me in thrall. Then he laid me a task; he bade me go where he willed and retrieve for him a ring from the King of Demons. And I, being spellbound, thus set forth to do the bidding of the sorcerer."

Of course, I invented this fantastic tale as I went along, and by now, having almost forgotten my original predicament, I was transcended by my own fabrication. So were the street urchins. Their dark eyes grew wider and wider as I described a fearful journey through enchanted mountains and into deep caverns. I seized on whatever came to mind; I disremember all the details now, but I do remember that I enjoyed myself incredibly. Night had descended quietly, bringing with it the cool sea-breeze, and the urchins huddled in a rapt circle around me. By the time I reached the height of the story, I had them by the tale.

"At last, in the deepest, furthest cavern I found the Demon King's throne, flanked by two iron pedestals burning feeble-flamed in the dank air. And on the throne rested the remains of the King of Demons. His skeleton sat in state; the rich red robes hung loose from the bare bones. His skull, tilted at an unnatural angle, stared balefully with empty eyes, and the grimace on the parted jaws was gruesome to behold.

"Horrified as I was, my eyes sought the bony hands resting on the throne's iron arms. There it was! On one long, fleshless finger shone the ring.

"I wanted nothing but to run away from there, such terror did that grisly king strike to my heart, but I was still under sorcery and whether I will it or no, I must take that ring!

"Reluctantly, tremblingly, prayerfully did I stretch forth my hand," and here in the telling I reached slowly with thumb and forefinger toward the ruffian leader's tense fingers as he rigidly clutched his spike, "carefully I touched the ring and then THE DEAD HAND GRABBED ME!"

The boy yelped as I clutched his hand; they every one jumped; a couple of girls giggled nervously. I sighed and smiled grimly, loosed my sudden grip, and allowed a silence to settle about us. Finally a small boy whispered—"What did you do?"

"Do? Why, I was caught tight, wasn't I? I looked him straight in the eye-sockets and said, 'Do you know who you have hold of? You dare lay hand on Dominico the Dwarf! Why, I've been set upon by a gang of savage street toughs and lived to tell the tale!' "

Their ghostly faces registered at first only blank perplexity, then all at once they broke into astonished laughter. I laughed with them, no less surprised by the end of my story than they.

"And now, young ladies and gentlemen," I addressed them, "If you'll kindly direct me toward the Insulae of Nero, I'll be on my way."

"We'll do better than that," avowed the young leader. "We'll take you."

Hence, I arrived at my doorstep escorted by those who know the crooked byways best, the nameless street urchins of Rome. Ever after that, if they waylaid me it was for a story.

XIII

The boat trip down the Tiber to the seaport Ostia is a short one. The River Tiber, which is clear when it enters Rome, is brackish brown when it emerges from the city and stays so until it reaches the backwash of the sea. A few of us journeyed there for a sightseeing holiday, departing Rome well before first light and returning long after sunset. We scavenged the shore of the warm, blue Tyrrhenian Sea, loitered on the docks, and watched the ships come and go, gawking at their foreign crews and intriguing cargoes: lions, elephants, leopards, crocodiles, and apes for the games; African grain; slaves from Britannia, Syria, and Parthia.

Still vivid in my mind is the most dashing, forbidding figure I had ever seen. He was Persian—swarthy, glowering, and heathen. What an exotic picture he made, gorgeously bedighted from jeweled turban to curled slippers; from his wide satin sash hung a murderous-looking scimitar, and the set mouth behind his coiled, black mustache bespoke a dangerous temperament.

So impressed was I that on returning to Rome I had a like costume made: a white turban set off by a giant eye of red glass, a crimson vest and pyjamas, a white silk shirt emblazoned with a gold-embroidered sash, and an exquisite dagger-sized scimitar that I had to haggle for all I was worth to procure.

What a proper harlequin I looked! I admit I reveled in outlandish garb whether performing or not, so I cared not that I looked the harlequin, only that I looked a proper one. Inadvertently, though, I attracted the speedy attentions of a heretofore merely annoying element of society. Whole streets in some sectors were dominated by prostitutes. Provocatively draped women and girls displayed themselves on window sills and balconies and posed in open doorways, faces daubed with paint, brazenly whoring their wares to whomsoever would pay. Now, how they made their living was no concern of mine, except that whenever I passed, some of the more foul-mouthed wenches amused themselves by taunting me at full pitch in embarrassingly tasteless terms, so that I ofttimes found it convenient to circumvent those streets.

Besides, I have been Pan at the Bacchanal. How sweet could pleasure bought from a practiced prostitute be, I consoled my stung pride, compared to the impulsive abandon of a beflowered young girl, flushed with Dionysian exhilarant, who glances unabashed invitations to Pan, the goat-boy? What of the moment when she slips from the dance and Pan gives chase? Like a shy wood nymph she flees the circle of torches and runs into the dark forest, Pan in intent pursuit. A grasp at her fawn-skin tunic and, amid delightful shrieks and rapacious laughter, both tumble into the leafy umbra. Then her round, budding breasts and warm, moist secrets are Pan's; her hands are hot and searching; for the nonce they revel in each other's desires, until the wine and the moon overcome them.

There is no deceit—she believes that I am Pan no more than I do—merely harmless fantasy. I know by some folks' standards I should work myself into a mire of guilt and shame, but I have experienced no redeeming value in feeling either guilty or shameful. In truth, I can dredge up no remorse at all. I rather recall those uninhibited young nymphs with fond nostalgia, and I regret my woodland romps with no more sincerity than I regret breathing.

In Rome, however, I found no opportunity to do more than dream of those joys.

Until now.

Subsequent to my newly acquired fashion, which hinted I might also possess a coin or two above a copper, the same shameless mercenaries who had been pointedly scathing before suddenly took to enticing me with their well-rehearsed pleasures.

One wench with a look seductive and vulgar and a glory of hair dyed yellow-gold and henna-red cascading in alternating waves of color from crown to tip—the rage in Rome this summer—leaned on an ancient wooden balcony-rail and revealed a voluptuous bosom promising to spring free of her loosely be-ribboned dress any moment.

"Come up, dearie," her voice sang clearly over the noise of the rest. "Half price for you, honey buns. If your pecker is sized like the rest of you," she chuckled lewdly, "won't you be only half the trouble, though?"

I almost pretended to ignore her and to keep going. But some imp stopped me midst the raucous laughter of whores and patrons. I tugged off my turban (for the afternoon was too warm suddenly), scratched my head, searched with care into my sash, and solici-tously held one small coin aloft.

"Half your usual price, you say?" I called up to her in the curious silence our listeners provided. "That'd be a half-copper I reckon, sweet tits!"

Riotous guffaws roared while the sunset-tressed whore looked ready to catapult a barrage of verbal abuse and mayhap a spilth pot upon my person, but of a sudden she changed her mind and curved her red lips up in a smile both wicked and enticing.

"For you, sweet boy," she cooed, "a half copper it is. You'll only take a *minute*." (She mimicked an accent very Aventine Hill.) "I'll bet you don't know enough about a woman to *begin* to know what to do with her."

I gazed up at the gold/red haloed woman who leaned over the balcony. Her opalescent breasts were as mesmerizing as twin moons at ides.

I grinned delightedly.

"Be sure—I bet I can figure it out—given the woman."

She winked and beckoned up the stairs with a lilt of her chin. "Come up, luv."

As I leapt up the rickety stairs, not believing my good fortune, another balcony-lady sassed her. "Half-copper! Curiosity starved the cat, Clarissa."

Clarissa whirled and cocked a curvaceous hip and eyebrow. "Do I look like I'm *starving*, Erin?"

She looked delicious. Delectable.

Erin smiled. "You look *voracious,* me dear."

"You mind your pleasure and I'll mind mine," Clarissa re-turned brassily as I cleared the last step and landed reverberously on the unsteady balcony, which swayed and vibrated with alarm-ing vigor.

"Eager little lad, aren't you?" she said, laughingly catching at her doorsill just in case the balcony chose this moment to collapse.

123

I followed her inside with less hesitation than I might have felt in other circumstances, the precarious balcony being sufficient impetus to overcome my shyness.

"You ought to get that fixed," I gasped. "'Tis going to fall."

"Perhaps. There are certain persons I'm hoping will be on it when it does. My, my, aren't you a lovely young thing? You sure you're old enough for this?"

"I'm seventeen," I asserted. She was years older than me—maybe thirty—pretty and shapely under her facepaint and faded garment of diaphanous green. She smelled nice and so did her room, redolent of fresh herbs, like our wagon, only less potent than Hagia's collection.

I watched her arch a red-dyed eyebrow and study me with lively brown eyes.

"Seventeen," she mused smilingly. "So old? Dressed pretty, too." She twined a scarlet-painted fingernail through a long strand of her colorful hair. "All those lovely red curls, too."

She turned and sizzled away, giving my delirious eyes a chance to rove over something other than her promises. In the center of the room stood a low, long, polished maple table. On either side lay two worn, red velvet dining couches. Beyond awaited a curtained bed.

Clarissa turned abruptly between the table and bed to face me, gold and red tresses falling across her smooth shoulders.

"Your half-copper . . . what *is* your name, dearie?"

I swallowed dryly. "Dominico."

She smiled conspiritorially. "Your half-copper, Dominico, so I don't feel so wicked and indulgent."

I had forgotten entirely. I spun the coin across the polished tabletop, where it revolved and circled and clattered to a finish. I looked toward Clarissa, not entirely certain how to proceed in these situations, feeling terribly inexperienced and excited at the same time—apparently, by the look in her eyes, just the way she wanted me.

"Come over here, Dominico," she beckoned, sitting invitingly upon the bed. She raised scarlet-tipped fingers to her beribboned bosom and pulled loose the bow that barely held her modesty together. "I have something for you."

We cooled our throats with sweet wine, then she reached for her crumpled dress. I took the hint and retrieved my clothes.

"I've a living to earn, sweetie," she said, deftly tying her ribbons. "Has been fun, but 'tis time for the sundown customers. I have my eye on one I don't want Erin snatching up her stairs, which she'll do if I'm not there."

"Aye, I understand earning a living." I looked at my half-copper lying on the polished table. Now that I had enjoyed her intimate touches and she had been so disarmingly delighted with mine, the paltry coin looked like the insult I had first meant it to be. I wondered whether she would be insulted or pleased with what I would do next.

She stared questioningly when I took back the coin. I unhooked from my trampled turban the red glass bauble, setting it gently on the table.

"This'll look nice with your hair," I said, suddenly bashful.

Now I searched the seam of my sash. She was likely usually paid in denarii, but I had better than bronze. I found the single argent, the only one I'd ever owned and had kept all week just to pull out and look at. I spun the silver coin across the tabletop.

"Buy yourself a pretty new dress to go with it, too, luv." I grinned, feeling a little shy and a little bold, and very flashy.

She caught the coin expertly as it spun off the table. She was not insulted.

"I could see you were a right generous and proper young gentleman, Dominico. You will come back, won't you?"

"I've no more argenti, Clarissa, or I would."

"Honey buns, you're all energy. All excitement. I feel like a young girl with an eager beau. Anytime, Dominico, anytime." She held the red bauble low on her beribboned bosom. "A gold dress, I fancy, trimmed in crimson. *You* know where to find *this*."

Now I grinned. "With an invitation like that, be sure, I'll be back."

I fairly danced out her door, and then proceeded more cautiously, having forgotten the rickety balcony and stairs. Erin tore her eyes from potential patrons to watch me. I blew her a kiss and caution to the wind, and cartwheeled ecstatically down the last ten steps.

I told no one but Gorgi, and he was fittingly envious, almost regretting his time occupied in long practice hours with his grandfather, mastering the difficult acrobatics of the pole. I thrice ventured on return escapades to see Clarissa, but those are other tales, such as the night the balcony actually did collapse. . . .

With Gorgi busy and, it seemed, everyone else but me, I had

unaccustomed hours on my hands. Felicia, when she was not with Mikato, was always being called to dance solo engagements somewhere. I took to wandering the streets alone more and more. I never tired of looking at the city. Rome was a wonder and a mystery to me. She had a presence of her own, and she had a thousand stories to tell. The best time to study her was early afternoon, when virtually everyone else languished indoors for the siesta hour, when the lanes and avenues of Rome were as near to deserted as they were apt to be, when none but the most ambitious or crowd-shy citizens strayed forth to join the vagabond nation of cats that prowled the streets.

One afternoon, vagabonding on my own, I spied a familiar face and figure slipping stealthily from a private gate onto the street. Felicia? Here? On Caelian Hill? Ah, she must have had a dancing engagement. But so early in the afternoon? During siesta?

She startled when she saw me, threw her mantle up over her hair, and turned quickly away.

"Felicia!"

She seemed about to hurry on, but instead spun about to face me.

"Dominico!" she cried, panic and accusation straining her voice. "Have you followed me?"

"I have not!" I told her indignantly. "Do you think I am a sneak? Be sure, I am not!" I noted her drained complexion. "What's the matter with you? What's wrong?"

"Nothing," Felicia shrugged unconvincingly. "You merely startled me, Dominico."

I knew her too well to be deceived. Something was very wrong. What had Felicia to hide?

"Do you do this sort of thing often, Felicia?" I pried.

"I don't know what you mean, cousin. What sort of thing?"

"Come on, Felicia, you know very well I'm going to figure it out sooner or later, so why don't you just come out with it now and save me a lot of bother?"

She hugged the mantle close about her sagging shoulders and sighed. Then she began a slow stroll up the street. I fell in beside her.

"You know I dance for Sividicus."

"Aye."

"That's not all."

I waited.

"Now I do more."

126

"Oh."

"Don't say it like that Dominico! I meant to do nought but dancing, by the Serpent, I swear it, but. . . ." She fought a catch in her voice. Then she turned solemn eyes to me. "You know, do you not, that I entertain at his dinner parties? Have you any idea what Fabius Sividicus's private parties are like? What goes on?"

I shook my head.

"I hope you never do, cousin."

Suddenly she looked wearied, far older than her seventeen years, no longer the carefree child who exclaimed with me over the wonder of Rome. A bitterness welled on my tongue—not at her, but at the whole accursed city that could so hurt one I loved in so short a time. Silence stretched between us.

She stopped walking and gazed at me fearfully. "Please say *something*, Dominico. Oh, don't think ill of me!" She knelt and clutched at my hand, her midnight eyes pleading.

"I *never* think ill of you, Felicia. Truly. One of my best friends is a . . . a lady of commerce."

"A whore, you mean?" She looked surprised.

"Well, 'tis hard for me to think of you as. . . ."

"I am a whore, am I not? I lie with a man for favors, do I not?"

I tried to imagine Felicia, like Clarissa, in a provocative state of undress, and succeeded too easily. I reddened and dropped my eyes, embarrassed by my own vivid imagination. Felicia was too much like a sister for me to feel comfortable conjuring erotic portraits of her.

"See!" she cried. "You cannot even look at me—not even you, Dominico!"

I met her eyes quickly. "'Tis not so, Felicia. I . . ."

"You despise me! Ah, I knew 'twould be—!"

"You don't know what I think!" I retorted brusquely. "Not at all! I'm thinking you could take lessons from a balcony lady I know whose pride and alacrity in her art is the same as you have in dancing."

"*Lessons!*" She looked incredulous, even indignant, mistaking my meaning but at least rising to her own defense.

"Either you believe in what you do or you are ashamed of it. She believes in herself. If you are ashamed, then you should not be doing it."

Her wide, black eyes stared into mine wonderingly.

"I . . . I bought us privileged engagements. I did it for everyone. And at first it was . . . exciting and daring, but Fabius—he becomes strange and . . . *perverse*. He's not a good man, Dominico. He likes to see people hurt." She dropped my hand abruptly and stood upright. "Now I feel horrid and degraded when he touches me."

"Then do it no more! Refuse!"

"He'll drop the troupe."

"Let him!"

"You don't understand! He's powerful—and ruthless. He can ruin us—he *will* ruin us!"

"'Tis a noble sacrifice, Felicia, but isn't it a bit much? Ronaldo wouldn't have it for a second."

She sank onto a marble bench beside the still-deserted avenue. "Oh, Dominico, I don't know what to do."

"I do. Come out of the city. Come with me to Hagia, tell her about it, and she'll think of something." I tried to sound light-hearted. "Mayhap she'll mix up a fall-out-of-love potion and slip it to Sividicus or. . . ."

She stared at me in dismay. "No! I can't!"

"Why not?"

"She can't protect us. And anyway, she'll know—"

"Know what, cousin?"

"She'll know I'm with child!" Felicia blurted. "She'll make me stay outside the city, then Sividicus . . . oh, 'twill all come apart!"

I loosed my breath in an involuntary whistle. I recalled how she had blushed when Mikato teasingly attributed her newly bulging abdomen to rich Roman fare, and how her costumes lately concealed her supple brown belly behind shifting veils.

"Why . . . that's . . . truly, I don't know what to . . . I mean, do you not know whose child? . . ."

Felicia came to life, eyes ablaze. "Mikato's, of course!"

"How can you know? I didn't think . . ."

She gestured impatiently. "Whenever I've lain with Sividicus I've poisoned his seed. I do not poison Mikato's seed!"

"You *what?*"

My amazed expression made her not-quite smile.

"There are secrets Isis gives only to women, my cousin. Secrets men know nothing of."

I stared at her for a long moment, trying to unriddle this girl/woman I thought I knew so well.

Resolutely, I came back to the matter at hand. "Why don't

you tell Mikato you carry his child? Tell Sividicus you're betrothed to the father of your child and give him the shove. The troupe can well do without him; our reputation is high enough now."

"It looks that simple to you, does it?"

"That simple."

She shook her head and smiled briefly, as if I had said something amusing. Abruptly, she sprang to her feet and started walking again.

"You don't know Sividicus, Dominico. He'll take revenge, I know he will. If he cannot have what he wants, then he'll spoil it for everyone else. What will Mikato do when he finds out what I've been doing? What will Father do?"

"How will they ever know?"

"Sividicus will make certain they know."

"Then go to them yourself first. They won't despise you either."

She regarded me almost gratefully, then shook her head once more. We walked in silence for a long while, in and out of the arched shadows of the four-tiered Aqueduct of Nero. Then she knelt and met my gaze with a decisive look.

"Thank you for listening, Dominico, and for giving me no reproach. I could talk of this with no one but you. But this is my trouble, and I must deal with it. Promise me you won't tell anyone else of this."

"Don't make me promise that, Felicia."

"*Yes,*" she said fiercely. "Swear it. Swear by the Styx—no, swear by the Gift of Isis you won't tell. *Swear,* Dominico!"

I sighed, incapable of refusing her anything. "All right, I'll keep your secret. By the Gift of Isis I swear it. But Felicia, I don't like it."

She smiled slightly. "I know you don't. Believe me, cousin, you've been more help than you know. Something you said . . . I think there may be a way to confront Sividicus so that he dare not . . . I must think on it further. Just leave it to me, and speak no more of this."

I did my best. Though I kept it to myself, I surely worried over it enough. After several days I could bear it no longer, so I caught Felicia aside and insisted she tell me what she had in mind to do. Her answer was designed to frustrate me: After the Armilustrium, she promised, I would know if her plan succeeded.

Armilustrium fell on October nineteenth, a full two weeks away, and our most momentous performance yet would also fall

129

on that date, for celebrations had been arranged all over the city. Armilustrium: the lustration of arms and the laying up of the shields. In antiquity it signaled the end of the warring season; now would the weapons be put aside until spring. Certainly there is no such winter truce anymore; I doubt there ever really was—not in practice, anyway.

Ironically, the festival of laying up of arms is still celebrated in true Roman spirit—by staging (Christian outcry notwithstanding) the most spectacular gladiatorial games of the season. And, doubly ironic, it falls on my birthday. This portentious birthday was going to be my eighteenth. It promised to be an eventful one.

The day before Armilustrium a triumphal procession of sorts took place along the Sacred Way; it proved to be the talk of Rome. Symmachus, the City Prefect, had imported an extraspecial attraction for the morrow's arena games, and the illustrious patrician played for public acclaim by making a grand show of his generous contribution.

I saw them as they were paraded through the streets: twenty-nine Saxons, captives of war, shackled together and made to endure the taunting Roman mob. Each man bore chains from wrist to wrist and ankle to ankle, and one longer, heavier chain, linking the right ankles of the prisoners, held them in line.

They passed close to me, very close, as I stood pressed back against the crowd. I heard the clank and drag of their chains; I smelled the sweat and fear on them. Tall warriors, they were, almost giants. Their long manes of yellow hair and beard made them look more akin to lions than men, and their lake-blue eyes glittered with almost unnatural brilliance. Staring straight ahead, with never a glance right or left at the jeering throng, the shackled barbarians made their grim journey through the streets of Rome, their last journey, destined to end ultimately in the Colosseum, the Amphitheater of Flavius.

I saw the faces—each man's countenance as he passed in procession: pain, fear, humiliation, pride, rage, defiance, and hatred—*savage* hatred.

One limped; he stumbled. Ignoring sharp goads from the guards, the barbarians halted to a man, while the captives before and behind helped their fallen comrade to his feet. Then the dreadful march resumed, and the twenty-nine Saxons were swallowed into the Flavian Amphitheater's vorant mouth.

Staring at the dark gate, I felt a strange ache inside that I could put no name to. Near to bursting with sorrow, my heart cried out for the barbarians. I would not go to the arena to see them die on the morrow; only once, in a moment of insensibility, had I accompanied Mikato and Ludi to the games, but I did not watch long. The crowd had sat shaded beneath festive-colored striped awnings and screamed for blood. There was so much blood spilled that new sand had to be spread again and again, yet the mob cried for more. Starving and tormented animals tore each other to pieces to feed the blood lust. Hacked and hewn gladiators raised their hands for mercy from the crowd—they did not often get it. Even from the topmost gallery, from which the arena floor looked to be hardly larger than a copper, the sights and sounds were ghastly. Behind tight-clenched eyes I could still hear the sickening crunch of a skull crushed under a mace amid the cheers and laughter of the crowd. *Laughter!*

Pale, sickened, I fled the gallery and retched over the outer arcade ballustrade. Still I could hear the death roar of the crowd. I betook myself as far away from there as I could go. For weeks I avoided the amphitheater on game days, for the sound of the blood-hungry mob within set my stomach churning. It would be that way tomorrow. Symmachus would likely force the hapless captives to battle each other to the death—under threat of an even worse fate. No, I could never watch that.

Next dawn heralded stunning news. Rome seethed with rumor. All twenty-nine Saxons had killed themselves in the night, strangled each other to death in their dark cage. It was said the last survivor, when he had choked the life from his only remaining comrade, beat his brains out against the cell wall.

Symmachus was in a fury. His big event spoiled, he appeared on the speakers' platform in the Forum. Ah, his disgust was unbounded; he was beside himself with indignation. The throng packed in the Forum jeered at their Prefect, railing him. Some seemed genuinely upset that the promised show had been ruined, but others grinned and taunted him, enjoying his embarrassment. Symmachus denounced the insolent Saxons and their barbaric act of cowardice in most eloquent, condemning terms, construing their dishonorable suicide as a personal affront to himself, to the spirit of competition, and to the good people of Rome. He ended his speech by concluding that the Armilustrium games were better off without men with so little pride or honor.

Cowardice? Dishonor? Surely, I puzzled, out of all these people, I am not the only one to see where the true honor lies. I pictured those proud Saxons in the black cells beneath the arena floor, choosing to die nobly at one another's hands rather than butcher each other for a bloodthirsty mob's amusement.

I recalled their expressions. On not one face had I read defeat. The twenty-nine Saxons were the victors here, by my reckoning. They had cheated Symmachus, cheated the mob, cheated Rome. The triumph was theirs. Who dared call them cowards? A furtive tear rolled down my cheek; quickly I brushed it away. Eighteen years old today—I ought not cry—not here in the Forum Romanum.

XIV

Despite the minor hitch in the gladiator department, Armilustrium festivities continued on schedule. Spectators packed the amphitheater for a wild beast hunt, and the Circus Maximus race concluded in a bigger riot than usual. Our troupe took no part in the spectaculars. Indeed, we took no notice, for we were preparing for a more illustrious engagement—a late afternoon performance in the Theater of Marcellus.

Be sure, we had played the Marcellus before, but this was to be no vulgar public show; Sividicus had planned an invitation-only affair for some of Rome's most distinguished and renowned citizens: senators, patricians, rhetoricians, architects, scholars, poets, philosophers, high-class courtesans, and notorious opulent swells—a select twenty thousand. Even the City Prefect would be in attendance.

Preluded by magicians, a lyricist, and trained leopards, our little company of vagabonds was the featured attraction: musicians, dancers, acrobats all. We took special care; the stage in the half-moon shaped theater was narrow, so our split-second sequences (never give an audience an instant to blink, unless it be in breathless anticipation) required careful timing. Brossos' pole suspended conspicuously across the stage. Torches stood at ready for when the sun sank too low to illuminate the roofless theater.

Backstage, expectations ran high. Everything was at ready, except that Felicia, the star solo dancer, was missing.

The dancemistress was frantic, Ronaldo and Mikato were annoyed, but I was worried. What could cause her to be gone so long except for that business with Sividicus? Yet, surely she would not jeopardize the performance of her life! How little I knew Felicia's mind.

The show began, awnings flapping in a cool afternoon wind—no Felicia. The magicians conjured their repertoire of illusions—still no Felicia. Then, just as the tenor went on with his lyre, she swept through the stage-door, sparkling and jingling and screaming like a Siren. Sividicus stormed in right behind her.

A senator backstage of a playhouse! An unthinkable breach of protocol! Yet here he was, grasping Felicia's jeweled arm and spinning her around.

"Get your hands off me!" she shrieked wildly. "Let go or there will be no dance!"

"You'll dance," Sividicus told her between clenched teeth. "The choice is not yours."

"Isn't it?" Felicia spat back angrily. "I'm no slave, Fabius! I do as I will!"

Out on stage, the lyricist's fingers fumbled momentarily as the dancing girl's voice shrilled throughout the theater.

"As you will! You forget I hold your career, your whole family's future, in my power!" His grip tightened convulsively on her arm.

Felicia's response was laughter. "Indeed? Think again! Perhaps it is *we* who hold *your* career in *our* power!"

Mikato now shoved between the two of them and faced the senator squarely. "What is it you want, Sividicus?"

The senator was cool, very cool. "This matter is between Felicia and myself, mountebank. You have no business in it."

Ronaldo intruded. "I have business in it." Glancing sharply from Felicia to Sividicus, he awaited an explanation. Felicia turned all shades of red under her father's gaze, but she held her head high.

Sividicus sneered, his eyes on Felicia. "Your lovely daughter is playing dangerous games with your future, Ronaldo; I suggest you set her straight."

"And I suggest you speak straight!" Ronaldo snarled.

"Felicia?" Sividicus invited her to speak first, an unbecoming smirk twisting his lips.

She hissed at him like a cornered cat. "If it is to be said, let it be from your mouth, not mine!"

"As you wish." He addressed the gathered troupe smugly.

"Do you really believe your mangy talents have brought you to perform before the elite of Rome? No! *I* have done it! *Fabius Sividicus!* And Felicia buys my patronage with her body. For all these lucrative engagements you so pride yourselves on, your little darling barters the pleasures of her flesh. While you've been playing at tumbling, she's been playing at whoring."

Shocked silence prevailed; all eyes fixed on Felicia. Ronaldo stared at his daughter; her head remained high.

"In the name of Isis, Felicia . . ." Ronaldo began, but he was cut short by a terrible bellow of rage.

Mikato lunged at Sividicus, only to run up against Ludi and Brossos; they knew the penalty for assaulting a senator could likely be a slow death. His attack was checked, but his fury remained unabated; Mikato whirled on Felicia.

"*How . . . could . . . you?*" he shouted, accentuating each word with a trembling fist. By now the backstage ruckus had become unavoidably apparent to the theater audience; the lyricist ceased plucking his lyre altogether, his solo ruined. Sividicus, in agitation, signaled the leopard trainer to go on stage.

Anyone who knew Felicia could predict her reaction to Mikato's accusation. She screamed. Defiance sparked from every inch of her lithe form.

"*Stop it!* Stop shaking your fist at me! Stop staring at me! *Yes,* I traded my favors for fame, and a good bargain I made of it, too! You wanted work, didn't you? Well, take a look at where you stand now and thank Felicia!"

Excited by her voice, the caged leopards began an ill-tempered rumbling as their carts rolled past.

"Now I'm through!" Felicia told Sividicus boldly. "And there's nothing even you can do about it! My unborn child will see to that!"

"Child?" wondered Mikato. "What child?"

"*Your* child!"

"Or *his,* Felicia?"

A full-throated roar shattered the tense atmosphere. The leopard trainer signaled in the negative to Sividicus. Fuming, the senator snapped at Ronaldo.

"Send your musicians on!"

Ronaldo ignored him.

"Whose child?" insisted Mikato.

"I'll have you flogged!" Sividicus threatened Ronaldo.

Felicia burst again into sharp laughter. "You'll have no one flogged, Fabius. You've the cream of Rome out there. Suppose we don't perform?"

Mikato shook Felicia by the shoulders until he captured her full attention.

"How do I know the child is mine?"

Two snarling leopards rocked their cages, clawing at each other through the bars. I lost patience.

"Just take her word for it, Mikato. She told me the same and she never lied to *me!*"

Mikato stared at me, dumfounded. "You knew?"

Like more logs on the fire, this flared his anger anew; he shook Felicia again. "You kept it from *me*, yet you told Dominico!"

"He believed me at least!" she cried, jerking free of his grasp, her dark eyes flashing. "'Tis more than you can say!"

Sividicus confronted Ronaldo. "If you don't go on now, I'll ruin you! You'll never play Rome again!"

"I'd wager," Ronaldo told him levelly, "that Felicia is right. If we don't go on, Sividicus, 'tis we who will ruin you. Is not Symmachus in the audience? He cannot be in a very good humor after this morning's disaster. What will he say of *this?*"

Sividicus fell silent. The Roman aristocracy was unaccustomed to being kept waiting. Already they tired of the fiasco and stirred restlessly. Punctuated by leopard growls there could be heard disgruntled mutterings and indignant expletives. From the sound of it, many people were leaving.

The senator became distraught. "All right, the game is yours. I'll double your pay—or triple it! Name your price, only go on immediately!"

Ronaldo gazed at his daughter, a strange, triumphant light burning in his black eyes. We stood breathless, waiting to hear the price. Slowly, a knowing smile curled the corners of his mouth.

"I've had a bellyful of Rome—and Romans," he said, speaking not to Sividicus, but to us. "We do not perform. We leave the city—tonight—now—to *freedom!*"

No one argued; no one questioned; our chieftain had spoken. Sividicus darkened to purple, the cords in his neck straining for a new threat. It never came.

"*Yi! Yi!* Look out!" Ludi and Gorgi shouted us gleeful warning as two of the leopards leaped from their cages. They were loosing the beasts. Stomping, waving, whistling acrobats shooed the frantic cats out across the stage toward the soured audience. Ah, the panic was heartwarming.

Brossos, grinning, called us back into order; Ronaldo led his people out of the theater and into the golden afternoon, abandoning the speechless senator to his ignoble fate. We wasted no time dawdling, for Ronaldo trusted Sividicus not a whit. We left Rome by the swiftest route: past the baths of Agrippa, between the Pantheon and the baths of Nero, across the Campus Martius, past the Column of Marcus Aurelius, and onto the Flaminian Way. By dusk we were out of the city and well on our way to the campgrounds.

When we arrived at the near-deserted wagons, still decked out in our finest costumes, none of those in camp needed to ask why we were there. They set at once to packing. Oh, it was just like the old days, yoking the oxen, throwing everything into wagons, and pulling out into the night.

Mother Hagia had taken one look at Felicia's exhausted, pallid face and clambered her into a wagon. Now Ronaldo and I sat on the wagon-bench, while Mikato walked ahead with a lantern, leading the oxen along a narrow, starlit byroad. I drank in the serene autumn air and welcomed the pleasant creak and roll of the wagon.

Ronaldo spoke. "I hadn't forgotten, Dominico. Today is your birthday."

"Aye, it is."

"You've not had much of a celebration, I fear. We'd planned one after the performance."

"Ronaldo, I couldn't ask for a better end to it."

"Nor I."

"Think you Sividicus would really come after us?"

Ronaldo's silhouette shrugged.

My thoughts reflected on this Armilustrium day. No wonder I was tired—and hungry, too. A yawn fought its way from out my throat.

Ronaldo's voice, quiet and thoughtful, wafted through the sleepy haze which drifted across my mind.

"Dominico, yesterday I saw a chain of Saxon warriors taunted in the streets. They defied Rome with their lives, and today Rome named them cowards. I wondered then—what do we here? Do we care less for our own honor? Aye, we are well away, lad, well away."

Never had I felt so proud to sit beside Ronaldo as I did in that moment, beneath those billion stars, following that lonely road, the universe a still, black pool outside the bright glow of Mikato's lantern.

XV

Sividicus did indeed exact his revenge. I have no proof it was his doing, yet I know it, as one knows death lies nearby when the carrion-birds descend.

Little more than ten days out of Rome, we had traveled northeast up the Tiber and disappeared into the protective embrace of the Apennines Mountains. Feeling at last free, we pulled the wagons into one close camp and prepared a celebration of thanks to Isis. We felt ourselves her children come home. Even Mother Hagia's apprehensions vanished in the peace of the wilderness; she bemusedly agreed her fears must have been the result of an old woman's bodily humors.

Early in the afternoon, Mikato and Felicia shared bread and wine and made their marriage vows; then they disappeared into the forested hills to a hidden retreat—the traditional marriage sanctum prepared in secret by the groom—where none could seek them out and disturb their wedded passion. Such was the custom born through generations of vagabond wanderers, descending from a time when the bride was likely to be a maiden stolen from farm or village and whose father would come searching for his kidnapped daughter. To be sure, two of our family were a couple of Gallic village girls who had run off with the gallant and dashing acrobats, but fathers are lax nowadays and glad to be rid of their daughters. So we staged our own hunts, which were but merry-go-noisy send-offs.

Having chased the newlyweds well along their way, the rest

of us returned breathless to camp in high spirits, soaring with expectancy, for now our time had come; tonight we would commune with the goddess in the sacred rite of Isis.

Mother Hagia moved among the celebrants, muttering an incantation in strange, ancient tones, and, omitting only the uninitiated children, on each tongue she placed a carefully measured pinch of dry powder from a ceremonial earthen jar. Each participant quickly washed the bitter substance down with a swallow of strong wine and awaited fervently, apprehensively, the Gift of Isis.

As I swallowed repeatedly against the residual bitterness in the back of my throat, I sought to calm my mind, to clear it of all expectation and fear; for to commune with the goddess is to die and be reborn, and the sleep of Isis is fraught with unimaginable dreams, visions inconceivable except to one who has partaken of her gift. The goddess can be terrifying, yet she may also be exquisitely beautiful.

Naturally, the more I tried to think on mundane matters, the more surely my thoughts were drawn to Isis. Vividly I recalled my initiation. Was it not quite four years ago? Could it be so recent? Oh, aye, I had not long been anointed in goat's-blood and given the festive name Pan; I had only just plunged my soul into the Pagan life, only fourteen years old and wandering the deep forests and green meadows of Gaul. Then Isis had called me. How many times since then had I shared the Gift with my vagabond family? I had never counted, but I might guess half a dozen—or more.

Nausea shook me and I retched up the contents of my stomach. Suddenly I awoke to my surroundings. My senses shifted into intense focus—sharp, clear, alive—as the potent magic took possession of my soul. A light drizzle glazed the clearing—not even enough to sputter the fires—and dropped unnoticed upon the wedding celebrants. The Dance of Isis was well underway.

Ah, a beautiful dance it was, too. As the dancers slowly passed each other about the circle their hands came together, touched, and parted in a graceful roundel, and each hand left a translucent ribbon of color in its wake. Around and around the dancers flowed, weaving a shimmering wreath of rainbows that hung in the air like fragrance.

Fascinated, I watched the ever-changing ripples of light streak and fade, in and out, over and under, around and around, until I lost sight of the dancers altogether; they melted like phantoms into lucent motion. Mayhap I, too, was fading. I waved my hand before my eyes. My fingers, trailing a silky substance behind them, spun a vaporous web of delicate violet. Again, I felt more ghost than body, so easily did I merge with air and Earth.

Rising to my feet as though bodiless, I started toward the circle intending to join the dancing, but distracted somehow, I wandered restlessly and marveled at how smoothly the substance that was me flowed without effort through the substance that was air. The ground surged, a fluid earthly substance that simply rolled beneath my feet, feet which now seemed so remote, slipping along the rippling ground. Thus the Earth carried me away into the living forest.

Feathery black clouds brushed across the silver face of an opalescent moon at full ides—so bright that I must avert my gaze—suffusing the earth with strange gossamer light that clung to everything—leaves, branches, boulders, grass, my hands—I could even feel it trailing in my hair like cobwebs—everything unshadowed now glowed with a shimmering cloak of moonstuff.

Magic! Whirling leaves spun a silver aura; bare wet branches and rocks bristled with sheen and glister; an astral essence pressed and nudged and hugged me all around; my phantom self vaporized into a universal fluidity and all flowed together in the Dance of Isis.

Why, the Dance *was* Isis! They were one and the same, ever in motion. All were in the Dance and One with Isis. And Joy was but to know it and flow with her. Such a Secret I had uncovered!

Indeed, my spirit spread out in great ripples until there was no separating myself from the forest, the wispy clouds, the frozen white globe suspended motionless in a vast blackness, and on beyond even the moon-shy stars, a great *existance-holding-togetherness* that, even as my mind stretched to comprehend it, swept me up into purest, indescribable joy.

Ah, Sweet Isis!

When, a timelessness later, I felt myself embodied again, the sensation was odd, ludicrous in fact. It scarcely seemed possible that such a free-flowing essence could ever be crammed and stuffed into something so small and confining as a corporeal form. Yet, paradoxically, the sensation was not unpleasant. My body fitted me perfectly, or I fitted it, and felt quite delightful and comfortable, like a pair of favorite, well-worn boots.

Why, at this moment, nothing felt finer than to be a dwarf in a dripping black woods in cold autumn. Why, nothing felt finer than to be me. I laughed aloud and turned nine back flips in a row. As for curses—I snapped my fingers in the face of the universe and shouted "Ha!"—to Hades with curses! How could this body—any body—have an evil nature? Why, it was life's child itself, Earth's child, like trees and squirrels, toadstools and rain, born and nurtured in the womb of creation—Earth's womb. What could be more holy? Life in the Earth Mother—eating her fruits, drinking her milk, breathing her breath—spirit clothed in nature's own cloak—returning Earth to Earth in the end. . . .

Which reminded me of more mundane joys, like fire and food and bed. Feeling pert and sagacious and joyful all at once, I set to finding my direction back to camp, not an easy task even though dawn seeped into the night sky, for I had wandered far and erratically. I started downhill, half recalling that I had climbed upward earlier. Soon I hit upon a stream I judged would lead not far from camp.

Whistling with merriment despite my exhaustion, I almost stumbled unaware into the death-snare. As it was, I halted in confusion at the sounds of screams and yells and pounding hooves. My heart drumming, I began to run frantically in the direction of the melee, but before I had gone far two horsemen plunged from the trees, and sighting me, charged down upon me like death on twin nightmares. Soldiers!

I dodged into the underbrush. Still they came. In, around, and out of bushes and brambles and thickets I led them, ducking into whatever looked the most impossible to get through, like a rabbit chased by hounds. Thorns and branches tore at my face and hands, vines and creepers grappled with my feet, yet I began to hope that I might actually lose them, that is, until I found myself at the brink of a sudden steep ravine. I scampered along its edge, trying to find a place to descend that would not plunge me to the rocks and wild river below. One horse crashed through the wood somewhere off to the side; the other pounded not too far behind me. Escape looked hopeless. I heard the riders laughing, as though this chase for my life was great sport.

Suddenly, there! A little below me and just ahead, a long, slender tree-trunk lay fallen, bridging the ravine. I never slowed my pace, never hesitated, never thought twice; with a burst of speed that surprised even me, I slid down to the tree-trunk—all that lay between me and a sheer drop—crossed its shuddering length at a dead run and scrambled up into the brush on the far side. Then I lay panting, scratched, and bruised, peeking through the undergrowth at the two soldiers across the ravine. Disgruntled, they blamed each other for letting me get away, but neither was about to follow me, for the ravine was deep and the slender bridge treacherously flimsy for a full-sized man in leather and mail.

"It's only their dwarf," growled one. "Not worth the trouble. We've done the job here anyway."

They turned the horses back into the trees. Afterward, laying low and listening intently, I heard only a few diminishing traces of men on horseback, then all went quiet in the cold, dawn-lit forest. Even the birds seemed reluctant to announce the day. Agonizing over what "job" the soldiers had done, I crept from my hiding place, recrossed the ravine, and made my way stealthily, fearfully back to camp. I dreaded the worst, prayed desperately that it not be so.

Even my growing dread did not prepare me for the sight: amidst overturned wagons, scattered and trampled possessions, lay the bloodied and twisted bodies of all the people I loved.

I stood unmoving at the edge of the clearing, my vision unaccountably blurred. For one crazed instant I thought that if I went no further I could hold off the awful truth, that this reality might not be after all. But reality was relentless. I stepped, as I must, into the scene of carnage.

Though many of them had evidently been in flight when they were overtaken and struck down from horseback, a good many lay wrapped in their blankets around the now dead fires, slain in their sleep. Perhaps they never even knew they died. Others, I could tell, had fought back. They were hewn down all the same.

I walked horror-stricken in a nightmare from which there would be no waking, mercilessly drawn from bloody heap to bloody heap. I had to know if one of them—*anyone* of them— still lived. Each familiar face was an agony to me. They were all dead, hacked with swords, spitted with lances: Ludi, Lestros, Mother Hagia, Brossos, Gorgi, everyone, even the little ones and babes. When I came to Ronaldo I could go no further. I sank to my knees in a mire of anguish and shock, my heart wrenched so cruelly I thought I must die. I stared at his face contorted with rage and death, his black eyes still open to see the blow that had split the top of his skull. The horror cut too deep for tears; for a bitter eternity I knelt there, unable to move or think or accept.

Numbly, I was aware that I had not seen Felicia in the clearing, nor Mikato, so when I heard the rustlings in the wood at my back I stood and turned and waited.

They came, hands gripped together, the same fear and dread that must have been on my own face when first I arrived now turning to horror as they realized their fears were truth. For a second Felicia stared at me searchingly, as if I could explain it away; I shook my head helplessly, too full of grief to speak. We stared at each other; all was said in the deathly silence of the camp. Then Felicia and Mikato began the same agonizing ritual I had suffered, moving ghostlike from body to body, from face to face.

Harder even than seeing Ronaldo's body, for Mikato, was finding Ludi, sprawled on his face, a dagger still clutched in his hand.

"I should have been here," he whispered to Ludi's bloody back.

Felicia left off smoothing the grey strands of hair from Hagia's sleeplike face. She stumbled over to me, looked at her father's face, then turned quickly away with a sharp moan as though a blow had been struck her. Slowly she composed herself and then, with a shuddering breath, turned back to him and gently closed his eyes and grimacing mouth. For a long time she knelt before him unmoving, head bowed, tears flooding down her still face. I stood silent beside her, knowing no words of comfort for either of us.

"Oh, Dominico," she suddenly murmured, the words wrenching from deep in her gut. "I have killed him. I have killed them all."

PART III

XVI

Winter at Ravenna stung sharp, with a raw and bitter cold, a harsh contrast to the mild, sunny winters west of the Apennines Mountains. Ravenna on the eastern coast was as far as the three of us traveled, for Felicia fell ill. She had never been the same since that dreadful dawn four months gone, nor had any of us, but Felicia felt the blow the worst. Now, six months into carrying her child, she became weak and listless, beset by a grim melancholia that neither Mikato nor I could lift.

We had not thought far ahead. Indeed, thinking was agony. We had gathered all the coin our vagabond band had possessed and some few valuable trinkets. The rest we burned with the families in their wagons; we could not send the dead to Osiris emptyhanded and bereft of all possessions, for they have earned the right to enjoy such comforts in the afterlife. It was hard, the burning of the dead. Merciful, how the eyes may see and not see at the same time. How the mind sees what is whole and unsundered because it cannot bear the stark carnage the eyes look upon. We kept one wagon, and Mikato was able to find one of the scattered oxen. Thus with heavy hearts and bleak thoughts we traveled east. How did it matter where we went? All that had been joy to us was forever gone.

We could not speak of it. It was too monstrous to speak of. We could scarcely think. But we wept. We remembered, and we wept.

Hard it was, to turn and find no bright, creaking wagons following, hard to turn to see the empty road—and hard not to turn—reminding ourselves a thousand moments what would not be there.

Hard to stop moving and hear . . . nothing. The evening silence weighed like a burden we could not set down, could never set down, remembering a million words we would never hear again.

Hard to halt the words meant for ears that would not hear—would never hear again. Hard not to see those faces—sweet faces, hard not to hear those voices—merry voices calling each other—calling us—from one end of the caravan to the other.

Empty road. Empty silence.

And the anger. The bewildered uncomprehending *why?* raged against the Sky, against the Earth, against the Gods. *Why?*

Now and again we met tears in each other's eyes and looked away, blinking, swallowing the pain, not knowing how to face it in the other.

Felicia sat on the grass, hands clenched around her knees, rocking, staring at the river—eyes as unfocused as the water's formless surface.

I could bear no more. I came to her softly and laid my hands on hers, curled my fingers around hers.

"Felicia. . . ." The words caught tight in my throat; tears came instead.

Her hands gripped mine.

"*Oh*—Dominico—" she whispered hoarsely. We reached out to each other, wrapped arms around each other, and held on, weeping aloud.

And Mikato, needing us, was drawn to our circle of sorrow, and we welcomed him in tears and open arms.

Felicia reviled herself unceasingly for the massacre, sure that Sividicus had sent soldiers after us. That likely was true, but she was convinced that the guilt was all hers. No amount of argument would persuade her otherwise. I tried to say to her words that I thought Ronaldo would have said, that she could not take the burden for all that had happened on herself, that fate laid the road before us and we wended it as best we could. And Felicia would listen and smile sadly and thank me. But the little solace I gave her was soon gone and she sank further into bitter regret.

Now, in Ravenna, hunger did nothing to ease her descent into the megrims, and her gravid condition clearly frightened Mikato,

148

as it did me, for I remembered my own mother's death in child-birth. Without nourishment, Felicia and her babe had little chance of surviving. Daily, Mikato and I stravaged the seaport for food. Oh, there was food to be had aplenty; the storehouses of Ravenna brimmed with grain imported from Africa. But the price! Hard times beseiged the Empire and grain was scarce, but Ravenna cared nothing for that; she held a fortune in her storehouses and would have nought but gold or silver for her grain. Only the army, the city consuls, and the wealthy would taste that golden hoard. We had long since spent all our coin and jewelry, trading them for food at well under their true value. Our ox had been stolen and likely hung in someone's curing house by now; the garrison had been in no mood to listen to the tale of such riffraff as us. Now all our tumbles, tricks, and thievery could not bring a coin above a copper. We were in dire peril of starving.

"Dominico," Mikato declared, returning to our stranded wagon after a fruitless morning, "put on your finest. I feel lucky today." A glint of hard determination replaced the hopeless look that lately haunted his eyes.

"'Tis devilish cold for satins," I grumbled. "Woolens will be lucky enough." Hunger did little to lighten my disposition either.

Mikato uncorked the last of our sour, watery wine and passed earthenware cups to Felicia and me. Felicia, shivering in spite of the blankets wrapped about her, smiled at him faintly, but it was clear her condition was worsening. Mikato raised his cup and hesitated, looking first to Felicia and then to me.

"To the three of us," he said solemnly, saluting me, his sober gaze still meeting mine. "May we each one prosper, wherever we may be."

Odd, I thought, Mikato rarely expressed such sentiments; the strain was telling on him. I saluted him as jauntily as I could and drained the wine greedily. It glowed warm and comforting in my empty stomach.

Felicia came to life a little and wished us good fortune as we left the wagon for the chill winter wind. Our trek was a cold one. I hooded and wrapped myself in the old woad cloak, its wool greyish and worn after all these years, scant protection against the late-February blast, for when the winds whistled over the great marshes below the River Po their icy sting could turn even a temperate winter afternoon into a frigid one.

Obviously Mikato had a destination in mind, the way he strode purposefully through the streets, but I did not ask where because his mood seemed sullen and grim. He did not speak, but glanced at me from time to time. We descended stone steps to a waterfront wineshop. Before the door, Mikato paused and looked down at me strangely. I looked back, trying to read his mood. *There is something he is not telling me,* I thought. Then he turned abruptly through the doorway. I followed.

Though shipping was down for the winter, the noisy establishment was crowded as always with merchants and port-bound seamen of many lands. With a sigh, I held my hands to the fire while Mikato looked around. I misliked dealing with a crew of this sort; it invariably ended in a drunken brawl and someone getting hurt, usually me. Like the time I balanced blindfolded on a winecask for wagers, rolling atop the long table until someone decided to jiggle the odds a bit and jerked up the end of the table. I fell off backwards and ended up in the middle of a cross-table fistfight.

At Mikato's quick nod, I trailed him into a side wing of the tavern where he approached a small, wiry, black-skinned man sitting at a private corner table. The man, an easterner by the cut of his full-flowing robes, waved us to join him. As we sat, the man—an Arabian, I guessed—looked me over and gave a satisfied nod. I began to feel this had an uneasily familiar air about it.

"Good," spoke the easterner, using the Greek. "Excellent."

Bemused, I glanced at Mikato. He drummed his fingers nervously on the tabletop.

"Well?" Mikato demanded, staring at the man.

The easterner reached somehow into the folds of his robes and produced two money bags which chinked heavily when he plunked them down; he pushed them across to Mikato.

"As we agreed," the man said with a flashing, gold-capped smile. "One hundred solidi. A fair price for the dwarf."

Comprehension was slow to dawn on me, not because it was not obvious, but because I wanted not to believe Mikato could do it. I stared at him, stunned. I think my heart stopped beating, and I could draw no air, like a man who has had the breath knocked out of him.

Mikato looked not at me, but at a moneybag as he fumbled at its drawstring. Dazedly, disbelieving, I watched his smallest move. He poured a few coins into his trembling palm, making sure they were truly gold, and let them fall back into the bag.

"Mikato?" I whispered, half pleadingly.

He turned hard eyes to me. "I have no choice!" he rasped, his voice thick and fierce. "*Understand!*"

He could not meet my incredulous gaze for long. Shame and grim determination coloring his rigid face, he concentrated on jerking tight the drawstring with stumbling fingers.

Something within me shattered, piercing my heart like a thousand daggers.

"For the love of Isis! *Mikato!*"

One last instant his gaze locked to mine. We both knew. There was no turning back. The damage he had done could not be undone.

Mikato rammed the moneybags beneath his cloak and sprang from the table, knocking his chair over like a man panicked. Frozen, I watched his fleeing form wend through the tavern. At the door he hesitated, as though he might look back. I half rose to go after him even then, but a sinewy hand clamped on my shoulder. Without turning, Mikato plunged on out to the street, leaving me to stare at an empty doorway—all that remained of four years living, laughing, crying together; all that remained of my beloved vagabonds.

I felt empty, as though all of me had been devoured by a hulking, bleak nothingness.

Two more easterners, conspicuously armed with sword and dagger, emerged from another table in the shadows, clearly bodyguards for a man who could carry a hundred solidi into a wineshop. Briefly I wondered if Mikato would get home safe with so much money, then I shook off the thought before it sucked me into grief.

"Now, my little gem," the foreign Greek voice said smoothly, "you come with me."

No question about it, since one of the guards clamped my upper arm in an iron grip. Half led, half carried from the tavern, I scarcely noted the journey through the cold streets, nor the apartments we entered, nor the words spoken to me as I was pushed into a tiny room and the door latched sharply at my back.

Felicia! He had done it for Felicia, of course. Yet knowing that made the hurt no easier to bear. Frustration, bitterness, and rage boiled up within me so suddenly that I felt drowned in my own bile. I truly came near to choking, so tight did my throat stricture with anger and misery. I had trusted Mikato, and his treachery cut like a sword to the heart.

The penuria door opened; the robed easterner entered followed by a servant.

"You are," the black man informed me, "the property of Hassan Khafar-Ra Ibrahim-Rashid—myself." This was as near I could catch the spiel of names he chanted at me. He snapped his fingers at the servant, who laid a dish of food at my feet. I looked down at it stonily.

"As part of the bargain, you will be well fed and well treated. I am a man who keeps his word. You will be comfortable here while I finish my business in Ravenna—then, to Constantinople. Therefore, my rarest of gems, eat, wait, be patient, and rejoice that your future rests in the capable hands of Khafar-Ra the Renowned."

Another snap and they both left abruptly. I stared wearily at the steaming plate of fish, boiled egg, pickled olive, stuffed dates, and hot white bread—delicacies all. The wine smelled strange, like dates, a sickeningly sweet smell that made my empty stomach turn a forward flip or two.

The Renowned what? I wondered blankly. Is this how the man eats all the time? "As part of the bargain," he had said. So Mikato had bargained me this banquet. I sighed, covering my eyes in anguish, blocking out the square little storeroom with its one high window too small even for me to squeeze through. Perchance my cousin sincerely thought he had to do what he did; mayhap he persuaded himself he had my welfare in mind as well. Rationalized, the whole miserable muck made a kind of pitiful sense. I recalled Mikato's salutation over the cups: "To the three of us. May we each one prosper, wherever. . . ."

To the Styx with him! I could not begrudge Felicia the gold to buy her grain, but, gods, the way it was done! Would I not have come willingly to save her life? Could he not have told me? Ah, "Come along, Dominico, be a good lad and don't fuss. I'm going to sell you to an Arabian fellow who'll feed you like a lord and take you off to . . . Constantinople?" If the sacrifice was to be made, could he not have had the grace to let me do it myself? I shook my fist and cursed his name.

"Mikato the treacherous! The deceitful! The villainous, perfidious, odious, execrable, putrid, vile! . . ."

Eventually I ran out of maledictions, my bitterness and resentment beyond words. Clutching my head in despair I sat before the cooling feast.

"Mikato the maggot," I muttered, dredging up one last epithet, vowing in my grieving heart never to speak or think his treacherous name again. With dismal relief I regarded the food, too hungry to care how dearly it was bought. As I bit voraciously into a tart pickled egg, I instantly broke my stern resolve and wondered forlornly how Mikato could possibly explain to Felicia where had gone her little cousin Dominico.

XVII

How does life go on? How is it, when one's heart is shattered beyond bearing, life goes on relentlessly? Two mortal blows in a row, and I am still breathing—and eating and sleeping (mechanically and fitfully) and weeping (Gods! Why cannot I convulse and die of tears?)—as though my empty little life still matters. As though anything matters at all.

After two days dark confinement I was bundled onto a tall mule already burdened with hide-covered packs in a long caravan attended by well-horsed and fully-armed guards. Khafar-Ra the Renowned took no chances. My wrists were bound securely to the pack ropes in front of me. When finally my stubborn, useless instinct for survival roused me enough to try freeing my hands, the attempt proved futile; furthermore, a guard rode close by my mule just in case I did succeed. So I gave it all up in a wistful fog of despair and resigned myself to a long, lonely journey to Constantinople.

The caravan visited briefly the markets at Bononia, Verona, Patavium, and Treviso, and at each stop the train grew, for whenever Hassan Khafar-Ra etcetera made a goodly purchase, he must buy a new beast to carry it. The man was wealthy beyond belief!

Ofttimes Khafar rode his horse beside my mule, for the man loved to talk, and he had a captive audience. Dispirited as I was, numbly hearing his patter, his constant cascade of words filled the hollow spaces in my head which would otherwise be flooded with torturous memory. So I listened like a drowning man clutching at a twig and heard much of him. He was Arabian by birth, but he had traveled widely and lived all over the East, from Constantinople to Alexandria.

He was a merchant of no little renown in the East, to hear him tell it, and I easily believed him as I watched the gold flow. On this particular trip, he had arrived at Rome the previous autumn by ship and sold a load of Egyptian spices, cloth, ivory carvings, and plunder from royal tombs. He began new purchases in Rome, journeyed on to Florentia, and then to Ravenna where he picked me up for a trifling hundred solidi. Now he began the return trip overland to Constantinople. I harbored only a vague notion of how far that might be, knowing only that it was the capital at the easternmost edge of the Empire, therefore I assumed it must be a fair distance.

Khafar's tremendous success, he told me confidentially, sprang from an uncanny ability to find the valuable, the beautiful, and the unusual (I suspected I fell into the unusual category) and then tempt the right people to pay enormous sums for his wares. Why, in Constantinople, he admitted modestly, an item brought a higher price simply because Khafar himself had procured it. He confided that although he did not generally deal in slaves, in my case he had made an exception. In fact, he seemed to feel I should consider myself quite honored to be so singled out by Khafar-Ra. He expected a multifold profit off me, for dwarves were now in demand in Constantinople—if not, they should be, and would be, too, by the time he put a word into the market.

In demand for what? I wondered.

Unexpectedly, I found myself enjoying the Arabian merchant's company, for he had seen half the world and found plenty to say about it. Sometimes he let me get in a word or two. He lamented that my Greek was atrocious and my Latin barbaric and corrected my speech continuously. He took my education right in hand, calculating that by the time we reached Constantinople I would be fair-spoken enough in Greek to greatly enhance my worth.

Early April, just past Aquileia, my spirits began to climb from their long depression; the old vagabond began to stir within me. I took a fresh look at my surroundings: the peaceful, awakening spring-clothed hillsides; the familiar, pleasant clatter of beasts' hooves on a hard road; the smell of earthy air and damp animals; cold rain and wind sharp enough to rouse curses to frigid lips; blessed warm sun dancing upon grateful skin; and ropes stinging and annoying my wrists by day, shackles hampering my feet at night.

I named my mule Nero and attempted to give him orders, which he ignored, being unswervingly devoted to walking just four feet behind the mule in front of his nose, deviating from his course only to snatch at stray greenery infiltrating the fringes of the highway. Sighing, I weighed the hard facts of the situation, juggled a few fanciful but unlikely alternatives around, and came to an astounding conclusion: I was going to Constantinople.

"How long, Khafar-Ra," I ventured the next morning, having carefully gathered my wits, "how long did you say 'til we reach Constantinople?"

Khafar continued tying my hands to Nero's pack. "Three months, with the Holy One's favor."

"So far? I thought sure I must have heard wrong the first time. Do you intend to keep me bound day and night for three months? 'Tis wretchedly tiresome, and I warn you, any moment I may go mad and gnaw through these ropes with nought but my teeth."

Khafar's strange black face smiled amicably, but his eyes narrowed in suspicion. "Do you imagine I should risk losing such a rarity as yourself, my unpolished gem of gems?"

"No indeed," I cheerfully agreed. "I should not risk losing myself either, if I were you. But suppose I don't wish to get lost. Suppose I am perfectly content to go clip-clopping right along to Constantinople with no trouble at all."

Khafar's grin widened as he mounted his horse. For the hundredth time I marveled that he never became entangled in his yards of robe.

"I would think, Dominico my jewel, that you were up to some deceit and intended to escape the moment opportunity presented itself. I would be right, would I not?"

Now I grinned. "Admittedly, you would be absolutely right any other time and in any other circumstances. I'll venture to boast I'd have escaped well before now if I'd thought it worth the trouble."

"Ah!" His eyes glittered with amusement and interest. "And why do you think it not worth the trouble?"

I shrugged. "In the first place, where would I go? I don't know this country, and I'll admit that a dwarf alone in the Empire is likely fair game, so I run a great risk of finding myself worse off than I am now, humbly begging your pardon. Not to demean your treatment of me, which has been beyond reproach, except for the ropes of course, nor your company, which, though not exactly roaring, is pleasant enough."

The Arabian glanced at me sidelong as the caravan slowly bumped and straggled into a forward motion. "I cannot tell you how gratified I am that you do not find my company . . . roaring, as you put it. But you cannot think to flatter me into setting you free."

"I know better than that. I'm only trying to be truthful, and the truth is I'm in a hard situation and I'm trying to make the best of it. Need I point out to you why, even though I could easily retrace our route back to Ravenna, there is little reason to return? I have nought to go back to."

He nodded thoughtfully. "True enough. Was it not your cousin? . . ."

"Forget my cousin! Look you, Khafar, I'm a vagabond clear to my Pagan-ridden soul—a man of the road. So where am I now? Why, on the road! Headed where? Why, Constantinople! What vagabond could pass up the chance to journey the whole of spring-time clear to the far end of the Empire? Ah, and I freely admit your glowing descriptions and marvelous tales have set my anticipation to a keen edge. Might I add, too, that I couldn't travel in safer company, knowing you are not about to let anything happen to *this* rare gem."

Khafar laughed heartily. "Dominico, you almost convince me! But I do not believe you have forgotten why I take you on this journey at all. When we reach Constantinople I will sell you to some bored aristocrat in need of fresh amusement."

I stared at him prancing his horse beside my steadily plodding mule. "Well, now, you are not a man who minces his words, are you, Khafar? Aye, that's a hard fact to swallow, be sure. But 'tis swallow it or choke on it. Seems to me you are a straight fellow—a man of your word. I also am a man of my word— mostly—and you are a reasonable man—a *bargaining* man. Now, I propose we two strike a small bargain. 'Twill be to your advantage, for I will assuredly lose my fine edge as an acrobat if you keep me bound three months, and there goes my sale value. Whereas if I am free to keep limber and practiced, why I'll be worth more, won't I? So, you give me leave to ride free of these bonds, and I give you my word I'll not try to escape your watchful company—at least not until we come in sight of Constantinople." I smiled winningly. "I must give myself *some* out, you understand."

157

"Completely," said Khafar. "I understand you well enough to know I should be a fool to trust you, but"—he slipped a curved dagger from his robes and slid it beneath the knot, slicing it neatly apart—"you have your bargain."

"Ah," I sighed, rubbing my wrists contentedly. "May your Holy One bless you with robust health and purest gold all your days, Khafar-Ra," I said, and meant every word.

After that, I had no complaint; it was an incomparable journey, albeit we spent the first month of it wet, being thoroughly rain-drenched daily. Beyond Aquileia we crossed the tapering point of the cressant Alps; far to our left towered gargantuan fortresses and castles of rock, an impregnable limestone wall of sheer needles, chimneys, and towers. In my mind's eye I imagined giant heads and shoulders looming up from behind the mountain ramparts to bellow angrily and hurl huge boulders upon our trespassing caravan. Most of the distant peaks still wore shining helm and mail of snow, like a slumbering white army of Titans.

East of the Alps, in Illyricum, the highway met with the River Savus and wended its quicksilver course southeasterly. We invaded pine-sheltered forests and crossed myriad mountain streams, alternately bathed in brilliant sunshine and cold spring rains. From the freshly verdant river valley, we could see wintery mountains to our right, cloud-wrapped and grey; our road ran through deep gorges and a wilderness of blue spruce, fir, and larch, giving way to newly green oak, beech, and shiny maple as we descended gradually into lowland woods.

Abruptly the Savus opened onto sparsely scattered pastures of sturdy cattle, goats, and horses and meandered on down through fertile fields planted with spring wheat, barley, oats, and rye. We passed beneath fragrant blossoming orchards, too, of apple, pear, and plum. Oh, a rich and fruitful land! Illyricum was not at all like settled and weary Gaul, where the land had been ravaged and plundered until scarcely enough survived to support the armies and the dwindling populace. Yet the wilderness here still thrived! How had Illyricum withstood the Empire's avarice? Even though we saw scars, too, of widespread lumbering in the thick forests, and mining of iron and copper, Rome had found this rugged country harder to destroy.

By the end of April we had crossed perpetually foggy marshes and the army's field headquarters at Sirmium. Then we passed the scrutiny of the military garrison at Singidunum, a closely guarded center of industry and trade. Here the River Savus blended anonymously with the Lower Danuvius on its long easterly journey to the awesomely distant Black Sea. From Singidunum the Via Militaris forged virtually straight through to Constantinople, and still Khafar expected two months traveling!

At first the road followed the broad, flat plains of the River Danuvius fluted by green hills, but then the countryside became more rough and rugged by the day until we found ourselves in a narrowing canyon—the tail of the Carpathian Mountains to the north, the head of the Balkan Mountains to the south, and the increasingly tumultous blue and white Danuvius racing between. Then, abruptly, at Viminacium, the Via Militaris cut southward, up the rocky gorge of the River Margus, and sliced through the southern bluffs. Now we were again in the mountains.

The Arabian's guards became even more watchful and wary.

"Do we fear an attack, Khafar-Ra?"

"Quite possibly."

"From who?"

"Whom."

"What?"

"From whom. The proper grammar. . . ."

"Oh, *whom*, then, plague it! I'm just trying to get an answer to a simple question! From *whom*, pray, do your vigilant guards anticipate this rude interruption to our erstwhile peaceful journey? How's that, eh?"

He ignored my sarcasm. "Bandits rove these mountains. We carry a goodly cargo."

"Do tell. As one of the goodly cargo I wish to know, why, O Foolhardy One, do we shortcut through them?"

"Because, O Brainless One, the threat of hill bandits on the Militaris does not begin to compare with the peril of Huns along the northern highway. Via Viminatium is overrun with hordes of them, plundering in swift-horsed raids. They strike! Then across the river and away! We would be unlikely to come through with our heads, much less our mounts and goods."

"Ah, a most sensible consideration, I grant you, yet it seems to me the safest course would be to carry your wares back the way you came—by sea."

"Safest? Not during early spring storms. And infinitely more expensive. A vessel arriving from the west is easily marked and taxed at the harbors in Constantinople. The harbor taxes are enormous, much more so than those taken at the highway gates. And doubly so in my case, little jewel, for in Constantinople it is well known that I am of a high Arabian clan and a devotee of Zarathustra, which makes me taxed as harshly as a Jew."

"Is that so? Is Zarathustra a heretic, then?"

"*Him?*" Khafar-Ra chortled. "Zarathustra is an incarnation of Ahura Mazda—of God! The Church is not happy with that; it makes their claims embarrassing—that their Christ is the *only* incarnation of God. They hate my religion as much as they hate the worship of Mithra, and they hate them both the more because they came out of Persia. Once it wouldn't have mattered. All religions were at least tolerated in the old Republic, as long as the people were law-abiding and paid their taxes.

"But now the Church makes religious policy. Now it would have everyone's soul under its dominion, willing or unwilling. Take a bit of advice from me, my Dominico. Stay clear of the game of theology in Constantinople; it is a very dangerous pastime."

I looked at him quizzically, wondering at his seriousness.

"You'll find scarcely a man or woman," he went on, "from the lowest street beggar to the royal heir, who will not stand half the day and debate the fine points of religion. Do not become ensnared in it, for to disagree with the wrong person could mean your death. Especially do not entangle yourself in any of the Christian disputes. The safest policy is to quickly claim ignorance of such an exalted subject and bow out at once. One is better tolerated as a godless, unworthy Pagan than a Christian of an opposing opinion.

"Praise them, admire them, tell them you envy their grace. If you have ever yourself been God-touched, do not even hint of it to a Christian."

"God-touched? I don't understand."

"You know, little gem, if you are God-touched. As when Ahura Mazda floods your soul with light, and you are upflung into an ecstasy of understanding and illumination—in kinship with all things living and unliving. Then you are God-touched. Or when Ahriman plummets your soul into the dark storm, and all is alien and enmity and engulfed in meanness, misery, and anguish. That, too, is God-touched, of a fearful sort. But there is no mistaking when you are swept into the divine madness, whether Dark or Light. It happens."

I stared at the twitching ears of Nero lurching over the cracked and weedy stones. Yes, I thought, I had been God-touched. I shivered, though warm sunlight glanced off the treetops and danced lightly through the green shade. Was Isis of the light or the dark? She seemed both.

I put the question to Khafar-Ra.

"Isis? I would venture that, as Ra is the sun and Isis the moon, if he is of the Light (which he is), then she is of the Dark, yet it is difficult to determine which Powers the lesser deities may serve—and dangerous to guess. I believe the moon is changeable enough that Isis might wax and wane in her loyalties. Best, in any wise, to avoid the many guises of the Great Powers and look straight to Ahura Mazda of the Seven Holy Lights, whose flame in our hearts does vigil against the Seven Darknesses. The choice—whether you submit your heart to Powers Light or Dark—is yours. Do you yet worship Isis? Mistress of the Night?"

"I have."

"But now? . . ."

"I don't know. I'm not sure I trust her. . . ." I fell silent, watching sunlight play among forest shadows, listening to leaves shift restlessly in a fickle wind.

Not many days later, as I wandered beneath the trees, relieved of my body's urgent morning need, Isis awaited me with her Gift. I stumbled upon the blood-red domes, speckled with white foam and silver dew, clustered in a shady birch grove. I halted disturbed and uneasy before the half-dozen crimson mushrooms. Did Isis attempt to make amends and soothe my bitter doubts with a divine offering? Or did she seduce and wile me into some poisonous snare, tempt me into madness and death? Midst the dew-bowed grass—the long blades bended as if in homage to the Goddess's fruit—I stood rooted, afraid to spurn her Gift, afraid to take it.

Presently I realized my eyes burned and stung with tears. So clearly in memory's vision I saw another such grove on a long ago spring morn and the sable-haired young girl who danced merrily to the trilling of my Pan-pipes. My loss rushed at me anew. I would see her no more. Nor any of them. My vagabond family was gone, annihilated, and I was alone—irrevocably and utterly alone.

Now Mikato's treachery stabbed at me again, like a dagger to the heart. I bit my lip and blinked back the tears; I would not weep because of *him*. And Isis? What had been her part? While she whirled me away in an ecstatic dance through the dark forest, she let death take my beloved people, let Roman murderers hack and bloody her own faithful children. Why was *I* spared? So that one I believed my friend might turn on me and sell me of a sudden as though I were nought but an expendable possession which he found expedient to dispose of? As though it were his *right!* Better I had perished with the rest, with Ronaldo and Hagia and Gorgi and. . . .

I shuddered, struggling with the bitterness that threatened to engulf my heart. It felt more cruelty than blessing that Isis had lured me to safety with a deceitful ecstasy which ended in horror and anguish. I started grimly at the seductive fruit of the Goddess. I vowed I would never bow to Isis again. I was done with her. I turned my back on the scarlet snare, abandoned the white-columned birch grove, and stalked resolutely back to Khafar-Ra's busily breaking campsite.

If the Arabian merchant noticed my stern jaw, he said nothing, but put me to work to earn my keep.

The caravan met no trouble on the stretch through the rugged hill country. Perhaps the sight of fifteen wickedly armed guards discouraged any would-be waylayers. In less than a fortnight the Militaris brought us to the city of Naissus. Khafar beamed with relief; the most dangerous part of the journey lay behind us.

At Naissus we halted two days while Khafar did business at the bazaar. And he had spoken the truth; he was well-known even here, for among the many Greek accents heard along the main thoroughfare, those of the more prosperous merchants called the name Khafar-Ra in jocular greeting. There followed much exchanging of news, joking, and bartering. The most talked of news was that Emperor Theodosius had at last gathered a formidable force and would soon be riding west to crush the traitorous Arbogast, the former Master General who had set his own puppet emperor upon the throne soon after young Valentinian's suspicious death.

Khafar the Renowned dealt only with select merchants of high reputation, and even then he offered them only a carefully chosen sample of his goods. A great many of the merchants eyed me speculatively, but the Arabian merely laughed and waved them away, saying they could not possibly meet his price for such a *rara avis.* Later he confided to me that it would not hurt his bargaining power if word of his priceless dwarf happened to reach Constantinople ahead of the caravan. I began to see the whyfore of Khafar's self-proclaimed renown.

The greater portions of May and June we spent crossing Dacia and Thrace. The highway ran mostly through wilderness and a few lone cities, such as Serdica high in the mountains and Philippopolis low in a river valley, in both of which we stopped to visit the bazaars.

Then we entered the Rhodope Mountains, whose dense pine and oak vales, chestnut and poplar slopes, irridescent with bright summer wildflowers, reminded me so much of Gaul and filled me with so much peace and longing that I wished we might never reach Constantinople. I would have been content to dwell in those enchanting hills forever. I believe Khafar divined my mind, for of a sudden a guard traveled ever at my side, and my ankles were again chained together at night.

When first I saw the Arabian approach with shackles and chain it gave me a painful jolt.

"Ah, no, Khafar. . . ." I protested, taken by surprise.

"Regretfully, little gem, this is necessary. You need not look at me with such reproach. The temptation to escape grows greater within you with each milepost we pass, does it not? I see you gazing into the mountains and dreaming; you may go free no longer."

I swallowed back my disappointment and met his eye with a grim smile. "I should have expected it." My voice was thick; I said nothing more. Of course I should have expected it! Did I think he would change his mind, go softhearted on me and let me escape or set me free? What a fool I was! Inwardly I cursed myself for letting it hurt. Well, I would not be caught by surprise again.

Khafar locked the shackles. "I will do well by you," he said by way of consolation.

I glared off into the darkling forest without reply.

There was one bright moment in the remainder of the journey that made me forget my troubles and brought back a measure of my good humor. Near Adrianopolis, not far from the battlefield where Emperor Valens's Legions had fallen to Fritigern's Visigoths, the caravan met a westward-moving force of armed horsemen.

Theodosius's Legions! The bright crimson and bronze vanguard forced the caravan's horses and laden mules off the highway. We crossed the wide, trampled shoulder and stopped in the weed-choked drainage ditch to watch them pass.

They passed at an easy gallop, still at the fresh beginning of their long ride. They would follow Via Militaris straight through to Italia. Theodosius rode to do battle with Arbogast over the Imperial Command of the West.

"There!" I heard Khafar breathe sharply. "The Emperor!"

I had only time to see that Theodosius, surrounded by his Guard, looked massive and bullish, confident and splendid, riding under the banners of the Eagle and Chi-Rho. Then followed legion after legion of the disciplined Roman armies, riding in uniform columns of bronze helms and red plumes.

Khafar signaled forward, and we resumed our trek in the ditch. Nor did we have a chance to regain the road all that day.

Not far behind the legions rode another army, long yellow hair glowing under the bright sun like a rippling field of golden wheat. They were burnt bronze and arrayed in tough leather trousers and vests, and each shield and helm brandished a distinctive ornament as if each man carried his own banner.

"Visigoths," Khafar informed me. "That one there, the center leading, would be Alaric. King of the Goths, he calls himself."

I saw that he was proud and fair and looked very young to be leading an army into battle. Intent on his own thoughts he passed us, followed by the thunder of his robust barbarians.

I needed no telling that the next horsemen to ride past were Huns. They fit the image of all the tales I had ever heard. Squat, yellow-skinned, scarred, and slant-eyed, they looked to be the ferocious warriors of the plains that terrorize the dreams of folk living near the eastern frontiers. I stared round-eyed, taking in the flying braids and topknots, the grim flat faces, the scored hide-shields, the wicked lances and swords.

Hard on the heels of the Huns rode more of the Roman cavalry, presumably to keep the Huns in line. Then followed an army of black-skinned men garbed in brightly striped robes and fairly bristling with weaponry. Arabians! Khafar waved a long, sinewy arm wildly, shouting aloud in a quicksilver Arabic tongue. Some of the desert horsemen saluted his greeting with glittering barbed scimitars and shouts and grins of their own.

Then followed an endless train of supply wagons and foot soldiers of all manner of tribes and clans, trampling the mounds of horse-dung beneath boots and sandals. At last, as afternoon leaned toward sundown, the road cleared and nought was left but the ringing of the pavement.

"Whew!" I whistled, as we spread into a dusty clearing to camp. "I never knew the armies were so . . . so *many!*"

"I expect," Khafar said musingly, "that Theodosius will have sent much of his infantry and the bulk of his supplies by ship. They'd put in at Salona in Illyricum, most likely. Command of Illyricum Prefecture is disputed, but Theodosius holds it for now."

164

"Looks to me as though he's going to recapture all the West before long."

"I trust he will. Stilicho's legions are still holding Italia. Arbogast will try to meet the Emperor before he can join forces with Stilicho."

Silently, I wished Theodosius victory, not forgetting that it was Arbogast's soldiers who murdered my father. Aloud I said only, "I would not now trade places with Arbogast for all the wealth of the Empire."

"Nor would I," agreed the merchant.

With an inward sigh I watched my hands unbound from the mule's pack and my ankles shackled for the night. All too soon we would be in Constantinople. I dreaded the inescapable fate that awaited me: in that foreign city I would be sold to a stranger who would hold my every breath in his power.

XVIII

Constantinople resembles Rome just enough to give one the uncanny feeling that he has stodged himself on too many oysters and stuffed cabbages and is suffering the aftereffects—a Rome distorted in the unearthly, indigestible traversity of dreams.

When Constantine the Great looked for an eastern capital he chose the Grecio-Asian city of Byzantium, for it commands the Bosporus Straits, the only waterways between the Black Sea and the Marmara and, by the way of the Hellespont, the Mediterranean Sea itself. Constantine renamed the city New Rome—though folk put their own name to it, as folk will, and called it Constantinopolis, the City of Constantine. The Emperor had constructed forums, courts, a senate house, and an imperial palace—all fair replicas of those in Rome—and, as many Roman emperors had done before him, he plundered Greece of her unmatchable art to add splendor to his city. As chance would have it, New Rome, like the original, was situated on seven hills.

Emperor Constantine, however, was not satisfied with mere appearances. He relocated some of Rome's most aristocratic families, conscripted them in fact, to begin a new aristocracy in his capital. He even went so far as to transport en masse a representative body of plebs and put them on the bread ticket, for what would New Rome be without the unruly Roman mob? Awesome is the power of emperors! It is as though they possess the numen of the gods; if they will a thing, no matter how preposterous, it is done.

It is but sixty years since Byzantium became Constantinople, but that is time enough for this far eastern city to become a Rome that is yet not Rome. As one enters at the wall built by Constantine and travels along the wide arcade-lined avenue atop the hilly central ridge of the city, its streets give one that dreamworld feeling. Stolid basilicas and baths, Roman arches and domes, Greek columns and statuary, are bedizened with the most fantastic mosaic designs imaginable. It is as though someone let loose color-blind, deranged architects with a galaxy of colored marble. Yet an uncanny sense of having been here before is invoked by the familiar architecture of the Church of the Holy Apostles where Constantine is buried, the newly constructed Forum of Theodosius, and the busy Forum of Constantine with its great column crowned with the Great Emperor's statue. By the time one reaches the Augustaean Forum at the end of the narrow penninsula, with its near replication of the Forum Romanum, the urge to pinch oneself awake is overwhelming.

Here the perverse similarity ends. The promontory overlooks the Bosporus Strait, whose zigzag course is anything but straight, and whose turbulent currents sweep down from the Black Sea and into the Marmara. The shore across the Bosporus is oversprawled with the crowded city's overflow. To the northeast, the forum overlooks a narrow, deep-water arm of the straits—the Golden Horn. Across this natural harbor lies an island city, walled off from the desert beyond, cut off from the two mainland cities by the watery arms of the Golden Horn and the Bosporus Strait. Since there is only one bridge across the Horn, and that one far from the city proper, much commerce between the three sectors of the city is conducted in boats, and carefully, too, I might add, for in places the boiling currents are capricious.

In Constantinople people are as thick as flies on a dungheap. No, I exaggerate—flies outnumber people at least ten thousand to one. They swarm amid filth and refuse that is sizzled to a hearty stench in the hot summer sun. And what an incredibly picturesque swarm they are—the people, I mean, not the flies. Skin of every shade and hue is fashionable in the city: black, brown, dusk, olive, yellow, bronze, tan, ruddy, and for every race seen I must have heard a dozen languages. The streets are an endless carnival. I never in my life saw so many outrageous, extravagant costumes in one place, not even at a midnight Bacchanal. They clashed in every garish and lurid color ever devised by the mind of a lunatic dyemaster.

As for beggars and derelicts! Now, Rome claims her fair share, but Constantiople breeds enough maimed and mutilated and diseased wretches to make the Eternal City look like Paradise. An ordinary, everyday, nondescript dwarf like myself would never draw a second glance from a crowd in this city. Most of the beggars who clamored around Khafar for coin, to be shoved back brutally by his mounted guards, were crippled and twisted, or missing ears or a limb or two, as though bones had been broken and left to grow back crooked, or a member chopped off to produce a lopsided effect. To my horror, I learned later from Khafar that this was indeed the case; the vicious vermin that own these pathetic beggar-slaves butcher their flesh to give them as grotesque an appearance as possible. I also learned that many of the crook-backed dwarves I saw were deliberately raised in cramped cages from childhood, forcing their bones to grow stunted and malformed. Thereafter, whenever I saw the mutilated multitude, I could have wept with fury and pity.

We spent the better part of my first day in Constantinople seeing Khafar's merchandise and beasts ferried across the Horn to Galata, a suburb cut off by swift water from the rest of the city. Once there, through the crowded streets we twisted toward Khafar's household.

I was housed with the servants while the Arabian took care of his business. Nothing could have induced me to attempt an escape. Constantinople was not a place in which I wished to find myself "fair game." Khafar took nearly a week to arrange for my disposal, as I thought of it; in the meantime he had me outfitted in the gaudy silk robes which were currently in fashion. Khafar assured me that he had my best interests at heart, as well as his own; I was as good as sold into the noblest Pagan household in the Empire. I was keenly aware that all that stood between me and the fate of those mendicant victims of butchery cast into the streets was the ability and honor of the Arabian. I honed my acrobatic skills, vowed to mind my tongue and not lapse into vagabond Greek, and hoped Khafar's honor ran deep.

Then the day came. We rode to the water in a cushioned sedan carried by eight armed servants and crossed the Horn on a large oared boat rather than the ferry. Still the unwieldy vessel made a harrowing voyage. I wondered how many people never reached the other shore and what the going odds might be.

On the western mainland we traveled up through the Augustaean Forum past the Imperial Palace gates and the Hippodrome. The entry portals of the immense racecourse stood open, so that I could see a long row of monuments along the spina; no race was in progress, but throngs of robed people flowed in and out of the circus portals. From the look of it, a riot was brewing, for some groups shouted and cursed and made obscene gestures at others. Khafar bade the servants move quickly, and as we jerked and jarred through the milling crowd I decided the ruckus must be between two rival factions wearing charioteers' team colors—blues and greens about to have a go at each other. We escaped the melee just before it turned into a raging battle.

The Forum of Constantine was a little quieter, but no less packed. A fantastic, gigantic bazaar was in perpetual progress, folk buying and selling anything from vegetables and livestock to fine fabrics and shackled slaves. The going commodity, though, was water. Despite several aqueducts that serviced the city, during the oven-hot summer months water was always in short supply. Carried in jugs and skins by mule from the outlying rivers, water was bartered in the marketplace, its price varying with its cleanness. Some stalls offered a drink from a small cup for a copper, and the lines at those were long. I was taken aback. I had always thought of water as something free and abundant, like air. And always there were the pitiful wrecks, mangled hands outstretched—if they had hands—beseeching a copper or even a fig to sustain their hopeless lives a little longer. The drive to live must be strong, I thought. Would I cling to life so desperately if I were to share the same fate? I hoped I would never be forced to find out. My heart ached when I looked at them, and I wondered, *What sort of world is this?*

Not far from the Forum of Theodosius we halted in front of embossed bronze doors set in a plain concrete wall. One of the sedan servants struck a heavy bronze knocker and the doors swung open almost instantly. A portal slave bowed low and ushered us into a large, plain courtyard, sedan and all. Here we alighted; we had arrived at the House of Themistius.

From the courtyard we were led through the vestibule into an elegantly tiled and spacious atrium. Statues of Apollo and Artemis stood back to back, pouring water into a shallow, oblong pool.

Beyond the atrium the tablinum opened upon a clear view of a sumptuous garden and splashing fountains surrounded by a long peristyle colonnade. I caught my amazed whistle before it escaped my lips; I had never seen the inside of such a luxurious house. And all that water in this dry season!

An ancient white-headed man stepped down from the tablinum. He wore simply a long tunic, unencumbered by toga or ornament, and he took each step carefully, as though unsteady on brittle bones.

Khafar performed an elaborate bow. "Your Most Venerable Dignity."

The ancient snorted. "Don't put yourself out Khafar-Ra; you don't give a fig for my dignity." The sharp old eyes turned to me. "So this is your prize? Why do you have him all made up like a fop?" Not waiting for an answer, he lowered himself onto a polished walnut couch and crooked a knobby finger at me.

"Venerable Themistius," Khafar announced smoothly as I approached the old man, "allow me to present Dominicus of Rome, world-traveled acrobat renowned throughout the West, a most talented and gifted dwarf."

Themistius ignored him; his alert eyes steadied on mine. Though Khafar had instructed me otherwise, I returned the stare. I could not help it; at such close range the old man's piercing gaze demanded it.

"Ever even been to Rome?" Themistius asked abruptly.

"Yes, your . . . ah . . . Ancient," I addressed him hesitantly, dispensing with Khafar's "Dignity" and substituting a venerable title of my own.

The old man chortled, enjoying the merchant's sudden discomfort. "Ancient, is it? So seventy years looks ancient to you, does it, boy?"

I nodded. "Aye, very."

Khafar panicked. "A thousand pardons, Patron! Dominicus means no insult to your lofty age. What he means is. . . ."

"Quiet!" croaked Themistius in annoyance. "I don't need you to tell me what he means. The boy knows exactly what he says. In wiser ages than this the title Ancient was an appellation of respect. I find it most perceptive of him." Then to me: "Played which theaters?"

"Marcellus, Pompey, Balba, Circus Maxi . . ."

"What about the Julius?"

I frowned. "I know of no such theater in Rome, Ancient."

He nodded. "There isn't. An acrobat, eh? How good are you?"

I grinned. "Very."

"Then let's see it."

I shrugged out of the airish red and yellow striped robe; beneath I wore "foppish" yellow linen pyjamas and tunic, which I thought were splendidly flashy myself. I did a series of seemingly casual backflips, handstands, forward flips, and cartwheels, sharply reminded once more how much I missed having a whole troupe to work with. I bowed breathing deeply.

"What else can you do?"

"Why . . . I can play the pipes, juggle a bit, tell a fair tale. . . ."

"Can you read?"

"Read, Ancient?" I stammered. "I . . . why . . . no."

"Think you can learn?"

I stood straighter; my chin lifted. "Be sure I can, Ancient. I can learn anything anyone will teach me."

He nodded again and regarded me musingly. That seemed to be all the questions, but then suddenly he rasped another.

"What religion are you?"

I stared at him blankly.

"You heard me clearly. What gods do you worship?"

I cleared my throat. "None, Ancient."

"*None?*" The old man leaned back with a chuckle. "An uncommon answer, indeed. And why not?"

"I find the gods treacherous," I told him evenly.

"Ah!" The Ancient's eyes lit up. "So Dominicus has examined the gods' credentials and tossed them out on their rears. Well, well." He rose painstakingly and faced the merchant.

"I extend you my apology, Khafar-Ra," Themistius said gravely. "I was certain you were trying to pass off your usual trumpery. Instead, I believe your gem is rarer than you know." He climbed the three steps to the tablinum and struck a tiny bronze gong. A slave appeared through a side opening.

"Praxos, prepare one thousand solidi to be paid to Khafar-Ra for the purchase of one dwarf."

I stared, astounded, as Praxos lifted an appraising eyebrow toward me and disappeared again. One thousand solidi! Khafar smiled like a cat in a bowl of cream.

"I knew well your sagacious scrutiny would quickly discern his true value, your . . . Ancient."

"You knew I wouldn't haggle with you, you thief. Ah, Nemone?"

The woman who had entered glanced at me. "Praxos sent me."

"Yes, yes, of course. Take Dominicus and find him some serious attire. And see that refreshments are served for Khafar-Ra and myself."

She nodded and turned. I took my cue and followed her, pausing to look back once.

Khafar bent his head. "I am almost sorry to end our most agreeable acquaintance, Dominicus. May the Light ever shine before you."

Solemnly I imitated one of his own elaborate bows. Then I hastily joined the waiting Nemone. Now I belonged to the House of Themistius.

XIX

Not all members of the House of Themistius were overjoyed with my arrival.

"This is just one more incident to prove my point," I overheard Daphne arguing with her husband (Themistius' middle-aged son) Apollonius. "Look how much gold he paid for that dwarf! Outrageous! And why? So he could trot him out at last night's dinner and embarrass me in front of *my* guests! Why, I've never been so mortified in all my. . . ."

Apollonius interrupted her tirade soothingly. "Now, dearest, I don't believe Father purposely did it to embarrass you. He finds Dominicus amusing and thought the guests would enjoy him. You know how he likes to liven things up."

"Liven things up! That crotchety old man likes to *annoy* me!"

"Father finds those social events a bit of a bore is all. . . ."

"No one invited him! And you're changing the subject, Apollonius. The point is, he's obviously senile—throwing a thousand solidi away on a . . . a . . . *tumbler,* talking philosophy with a *dwarf,* and educating the mannerless creature right alongside his own grandchildren! He's not in his right mind; you shouldn't allow it."

"Daphne, this is still his house and he *is* spending *his* money. And my father is a shrewd man; he isn't senile just because he does things that seem, well . . . *frivolous* to us."

"Frivolous? No one in his right mind . . ."

"Daphne!" Apollonius snapped irritably. "Father is *the* most

173

respected scholar of philosophy and natural history in Constantinople, and you will only make a fool of yourself if you repeat that inane opinion in educated company."

"Well there was highly respectable company here last night, and they were aghast when that dwarf told that indecent tale about the Arabian sheik and his seven hundred wives."

"*You* were aghast—and a few of your cronies. Some of the guests laughed so heartily they could scarcely finish dinner." Apollonius chuckled. "I found it luridly amusing myself."

"Oh, you're as bad as Themistius. I'm serious, you tell him, Apollonius. Tell him neither he nor his dwarf are welcome when I am entertaining guests. I don't interrupt when he has those long-winded philosophers here going on for days at a time about elements and virtues and invisible particles and such nonsense. Now, do I?"

Apollonius sighed. "I'm sure he'll be reasonable about it when I've presented your request in more sensi—"

"Reasonable, ha! For all the high-blown talk about *reason* in this house, your father hasn't a reasonable bone in his . . ."

Here I ducked away quickly, but not quickly enough to avoid being caught eavesdropping by watchful Praxos. But I got away with nothing worse than a long lecture on propriety and a stern warning. I acquiesed, saluted him smartly, and gave him my most amiable grin. Praxos half smiled, shook his head, and sped me on my way.

The household was not a large one. Along with Apollonius and his wife Daphne were their eldest son Alexandros and two smaller children, Pericles and Astasia. Themistius's widowed daughter Athene also lived there with her two daughters, Sapphone and Phoebe. The house slaves were Praxos and Nemone, who were married and had a young son named Hector, plus Mercurius, old Endymodes, and myself.

Dawn each day began with a paean to Apollo, though even had a wall been open to the east, the mass of the city would have blocked any view of the sun topping the horizon. Despite the reverence to Apollo, it was not a household that worshipped deities. Themistius revered the light of pure reason, restraint of the emotions, and moderation in the sensations, strict fidelity to personal ethics and seeking after truth. Apollo was the symbol personifying his ideal man. I often heard fondly-quoted maxims: "nothing in excess—know thyself—curb thy spirit," and all members of the household were expected to live by them.

After the greeting to the sun, and breakfast, then followed morning lessons; no one's education was neglected. Themistius himself taught philosophy, logic, and ethics to scholars who gathered in his garden for the privilege of hearing him. I was put to studying with the youngest—Phoebe, Pericles, Astasia, and Hector—because I knew nothing of letters and had to start from the beginning. We were tutored by Athene. She set me immediately to copying Greek letters and learning their names. I found it not very difficult and in less than two days had passed up five-year-old Hector. Athene moved me to sit beside Astasia, who was seven, and began teaching me to arrange letters into words.

At first I felt a proper fool—eighteen years old and taking lessons with a lot of fidgety children—and Astasia giggling and edging away when I first scooted beside her on the bench, my wax tablet propped on my knees, but I drew funny pictures with my stylus and made her laugh aloud and earned us both a reprimand. And Daphne would have been mortified if she knew what a favor she did me with her blundering meddling. She invaded the study before the week was out, displaying not a shred of the much-touted restraint, and forbade the children to have aught to do with me. She warned Athene that she would be held personally responsible if I was allowed to corrupt the innocents and threatened to sell me to the cheapest slave-merchant if I told so much as one tale or said one vulgar word in her children's presence, regardless of what Themistius had to say about it. Athene cooly informed Daphne that she felt capable of handling any situation that might arise in the study, that she intended to rely upon her own sound judgment, and for Daphne to tend to her own duties and leave hers be. Daphne flounced off in an immoderate huff. The children stared at me wide-eyed with renewed fascination and respect.

I privately resolved to take Daphne's threat seriously and do absolutely nothing that might jeopardize my presence in the household, for I knew my circumstances could only worsen drastically at the hands of the slave-merchants. Besides, I had discovered an unlooked-for joy where I had expected only drudgery and dismal servitude. Never before having spared letters more than a cursory glance, I was stunned when I read my first words etched on Athene's tablet, simple as they were; then when she smoothed the wax with her stylus and bade me write them—I did! I could! I was reading—and writing! And I hungered for more. And Athene, with the same gentle seriousness with which she instructed the children, taught me fully as much as I could manage at a time.

At first the task looked near impossible—to memorize an infinity of possible letter combinations, to see them as words—how did one do it?—until one morning, during still another patient demonstration from my tutor, the secret dawned on my groping brain with surprising lucidity: The simple relationship between letters, sounds, and syllables became as clear as a cupped handful of cold spring water. Thereafter, reading seemed as a game of knucklebones, except that with the bones only thirty-five different combinations may fall; with letters the possible throws number in the tens of thousands!

Soon Athene moved me to study with ten-year-old Pericles and her own thirteen-year-old daughter Phoebe. In addition to Greek, twice each week we spent half the morning on Latin, and once I learned to apply the magical secret to the set of Roman letters, I quickly surpassed Phoebe and Pericles, for Latin was practically my native tongue, after Gallic.

Several months afterward Athene informed Themistius that it was time both Phoebe and I further our studies, meaning we should learn under Endymodes, the tutor to Sapphone and Alexandros. Themistius selected worn scrolls of Lucretius and Herodotus, heard each of us read, and with sincere praise to his granddaughter and me, agreed.

Old Endymodes—who, though not as ancient as Themistius, was old enough to have tutored Athene and Apollonius, and now tutored *their* children—old Endymodes made scant attempt to conceal the fact that he thought his time better employed doing other things than teaching literature and philosophy to a dwarf. He glared down his long nose at me in distaste. He crisply welcomed Phoebe, who had been promoted into his tutelage under duress, and seated us side by side at a wide bench with a slanted writing table which I could not possibly reach without standing on the bench. Alexandros snorted gleefully at my discomfiture; at fifteen years of age he had thus far spared no more than a passing crass remark or quick-knuckled rap on the head to an odd-looking little slave, but now I was to be in his company daily. So Alexandros snorted and Endymodes's short staff sang in the close room before it cracked sharply against Alexandros' skull. Sullenly, Alexandros turned back to the scroll he was reading. Sapphone, nearly seventeen, gave her younger sister a reassuring smile, for Phoebe had jumped frightfully when the old tutor rapped her cousin's head with the staff, and now she was near tears. And I—I felt horribly, conspicuously unwelcome, but I stubbornly swallowed my misgivings as a wooden box was impatiently procured to seat me higher on the bench. I could endure disdain and scorn—counting that as part of the bargain—in exchange for the learning I craved with an endless thirst now that I had tasted of it.

Endymodes was not as formidable as he had first seemed. He was stern, to be sure, and discipline as well as criticism were swiftly meted. Yet, he never once used the staff on the girls, and I only felt its sting when I crossed the bounds of propriety, for I have ever been troubled with an imp-spirited tongue, and Endymodes would not tolerate my impertinent outbursts. In my private opinion Alexandros got off with less corporal discipline than he deserved; he was grudging and sullen, ofttimes even smart-mouthed and argumentative if he thought the old tutor might be too preoccupied with another pupil's stylus or scroll to strike at him. Endymodes must have grown as weary of giving him constant reprimands as I was of hearing them, but he never let up, and intractably kept his master's grandson at his lessons.

In the beginning Endymodes spared me merely perfunctory attention, yet I was all eyes and ears when he worked with Phoebe beside me. Ah, but I could *not* contain my questions, and gradually Endymodes's impatience gave way to willing instruction as he realized that I was as eager to leap at learning as a charioteer's steeds are eager to tear around the circus. The old tutor could not but respond with all his skill to such an apt and ready pupil, even a dwarf-slave from Gaul. I soon heard my share of his carefully measured praise for lessons well-learned and answers well-spoken. Alexandros's dislike for me never abated, but Sapphone helped me at my work as often as she helped Phoebe. So I ignored Alexandros and steeped my mind in the rational wisdom of the Greek and Roman philosophers.

Following the noon meal, the House of Themistius habitually retired for an afternoon rest, especially during the summer months when even the sun-scorched garden was abandoned for stifling, but sheltering, rooms. Almost everyone, slaves included, took a short or a long nap, and all household activities were quiet and subdued, for Themistius invariably slept three hours and did not like to be awakened by unnecessary patter and chatter.

As the weather cooled I became more and more restless in the afternoons, having little inclination to sleep. Ofttimes I read scrolls in Themistius's scriptorium, if I asked permission of Endymodes or Themistius before they retired; I was not allowed to "paw through scrolls like a tradesman at a bazaar," but must wait for

177

them to deliver one to my hand. Themistius usually gave me a choice—though I scarcely knew what to choose—while Endymodes always had a particular work in mind that he thought I should be reading; so if I knew what I wanted I went to the Ancient, and if I did not I went to the tutor. Sometimes Athene or Sapphone also came into the scriptorium, or Praxos, or even Apollonius taking his leisure before resuming his daily business contacts, which had to do with investment in an argosy of ships and imports, as I understood it. My whole world centered on what I saw or heard in the household, for I could count on one hand the number of times in a year I left those walls.

Just once, as that first winter began its pass into spring, did my vagabond spirit overcome my careful indoctrinization into restraint and reason. Too restless either to sleep or read or daydream in the garden, I found myself one afternoon pacing past the penuria. It suddenly occurred to me that a little wine would mellow my mood and sweeten the afternoon, and here was the storeroom right at my need. The room had no lock, for no one had reason to steal household stores. I pushed open the penuria door and entered, leaving it ajar to let in the light.

I located the large jars of common wine and was looking about for a drinking vessel when I spied the flasks of expensive blends high on a shelf. Those flasks would be easy to drink from and— I grinned to myself—why not have the finest? Of course it took some cautious climbing up the shelves to get hold of one, and then a short drop to a sack of meal to come safely down, but I found that no difficult feat; I was not an acrobat for nothing! I uncorked the large round flask and took a few appreciative swallows of the strong, rich wine. Ah, it had been a long, long time since I tasted wine so invigorating. I sighed with pure joy.

Then occurred to me the likely possibility of someone discovering the penuria door open and finding me imbibing the best wine in the house. They would not be pleased, nor would I. Yet I did not favor closing the door and sitting in airless pitch dark. Cautiously I peered out and saw no one stirring. They were all probably just dropping off to sleep or settling down to sewing or reading and would not be emerging for a couple of hours at least. I stepped out, fat flask bulging under one arm, and closed the door softly behind me. I crept to peer around a corner. Where might I go? I thought of the atrium. No—Apollonius might pass through on early business. I thought of my tiny room. No—Mercurius, who shared it with me, would be snoring, not to mention appalled if he awoke to find me. . . . My reason matter-of-factly informed me that I was about to plunge myself into deep trouble; the undaunted vagabond that inhabited my soul cheerfully agreed and urged me on. I thought of the garden. Yes—the grape arbor. Quickly I took one more long drink in case I got caught between here and there, shed my sandals, and silently padded barefoot on tile to the garden. It was deserted, as were the empty doorways that faced it. No one observed my nonchalant stroll between the leafy hedges and beneath the twisting grapevines that climbed thickly over a lattice-work arch. Inside was a low concrete bench that rose in a scroll-like design at either end. I grinned smugly. Anyone would almost have to come around and look directly into the arbor to find me.

Settling myself comfortably on the bench, I rested back against a curved arm and unstoppered the blessed Dionysian brew. Ah, yes, it had been a *very* long time. . . .

I had finished off about three-quarters of the flask when I felt that a stroll about the garden was definitely in order. Feeling incredibly pleased with myself, I half floated along the pebbled path through a hazy proliferation of neatly trimmed hedges and early-budding rose bushes that hinted here and there of the brilliant display of effusing colors to come. Some of these orderly rows I had pruned myself. How civilized I was become! I snickered at my own domestication as I pissed on a thorny rosebush. Who would ever have imagined that Dominico the vagabond, little Pan of the Bacchanal, would become Dominicus the houseslave in one of the oldest, most reputable conservatories of Greek sobriety in the eastern Empire? What a joke on me! I cackled aloud, then spun furtive glances around the open doorways to see if anyone had awakened, whereupon I burst into a burbling fount of giggles at my own guilty skulking. I clamped a hand over my snorts and sat down in the middle of the path in a futile attempt to regain some semblance of composure. Finally I gave up and clasped my knees, rocking with laughter. And why should I not? What was wrong with a little pure drunken glee now and then? Would do some of these staid folk good, I reasoned smugly.

When Praxos discovered me I was turning cartwheels around the rim of the fountain—falling in occasionally, splashing and laughing and shushing my noise, clambering out and turning cartwheels again—making quite a commotion I suspect. He fished me out of the fountain by the nape of the tunic and hauled me dripping to my feet. I grinned up at him, unable to wipe the smirk from my face; to me he seemed most comically upset.

"Shut up, Dominicus! Fool! You've wakened everyone in the—*stop it!*"

But I had slipped his grasp. "Ha, ha! Catch me if you can!" I crowed like a cock just come of age. I turned a backflip from him and sidled away unsteadily along the garden path. Praxos leapt after me, and I eluded him gleefully.

"Dominicus!" he hissed. "You don't know what you're doing!"

Dimly I was aware that faces and forms filled the doorways; I heard the exclamations of children. Ah, an audience!

Drunk though I was, it still took Praxos some trouble to catch me again. This time he kept a tight grip. He dragged me past the outraged face of Daphne (I giggled at her), past the worried face of Athene (the word *folly* introduced itself into my muddled brain), to stand at last beneath the severe countenance of Themistius. (*Now you've mucked it, Dominico.*)

The Ancient fixed me with a steady, silent stare. I blinked back unsteadily, for by now the world reeled about me, and I was held in place only by the firm grasp Praxos had on the back of my tunic. It occurred to me then that Praxos was doing his best to lend me some semblance of sobriety, but no one, least of all Themistius, was deceived.

Disappointment swelled the Ancient's voice. I had broken the bounds of obedience and reason, he told me sorrowfully, broken faith with the trust he had accorded me, and shown my ethical restraints to be sadly lacking in strength or conviction. Worse, I had disgraced the ideals taught me in his house. He ordered me to confine myself to my room until his judgment was not clouded with anger and disillusionment and he felt better prepared to decide on suitable punitive measures. Praxos tightened his hold and nudged me past Endymodes's forboding frown and Sapphone's sorrowed expression.

No one came into my room, not even Mercurius. I had plenty of time to think about "punitive measures." The wine and the worry would not allow me peace. Fitfully I arose from the pallet, paced a while, sat forlornly by the wall, paced again, then splashed water over my face from the basin. Possibly the worst I would suffer, I strained to reason with wine-soaked faculties, might be a sound beating. But suppose Themistius decided I was unfit to remain under his roof? Might he not do as Daphne was probably this moment urging him? What if he should sell me off? I trembled, suddenly cold, conjuring all the horrors I might have stupidly let myself in for.

If only he will not sell me, I pleaded with the Fates, or whichever powers set men up for such disasters, *I swear I will be the model of servitude and sobriety.* But I felt in no wise reassured; I knew too well that it was useless and foolish to try and make bargains with life; life would do as it pleased, regardless.

They waited until the wine had worn off, leaving me exhausted, shaking, clammy, queasy, and in turmoil. In such sorry condition I came meekly before Themistius, unable to even attempt concealing my distress. All the household was assembled to hear my fate. Themistius sat sternly on a bench in the evening-shadowed garden; I stood, small and shivering, on the pebbled path.

He fixed me with his most piercing stare for long moments before his best lecturer's tone crackled out. "Dominicus! How do you feel?"

I tried to swallow with a thick, dry tongue. "Not so good, Ancient."

"*Eh?*"

"*Sick,* Ancient."

"You look it. I wish my grandchildren to witness—*and think seriously on*—the aftereffects of your foolish, irresponsible fit of indulgence as enthusiastically as they observed its immediate effects this afternoon. What were you thinking?"

I shook my head weakly.

"Were you *thinking?*"

"No," I whispered.

"No. How would you feel about showing us a few acrobatics right *now?*"

I paled a shade whiter at the thought.

"*Father!*" interceded Athene's gentle voice.

"Shush! I didn't ask him to do it; I asked him how he felt about it. Dominicus, I have striven to impart to you the greatest of treasures—the finest ideals life holds and a mind sharpened by knowledge and wielded with wisdom. You have flaunted your drunkenness in the face of every virtue my house honors. I do not hesitate to admit that I am grievously disappointed; I thought better of you than that. In light of your previous occupation and background, in which restraint and reasonable decorum were no doubt unheard of, perhaps I understand a little; yet that does not negate the severity of your misconduct, and in order to make certain it is never again exercised in this household, consequences must be equally severe."

I sucked in a deep breath, my heart pounding frantically in my temples, feeling I might suffocate on the spot. Thoroughly ashamed and terrified I waited out his deliberate, interminable pause.

"Endymodes and I have conferred and agreed upon the most suitable and effective punishment. Dominicus, beginning today you are banned from the scriptorium for one full month."

For a second I feared I heard him wrong. Then a wave of dizzy relief swept over me. Banned from the scriptorium! No more than that? My face lit with graditude.

Along with Alexandros's derisive snorts I heard Daphne's indignant protest. "*That's* the punishment you give him? You continue to indulge and pamper this obnoxious dwarf even now? After he willfully . . . under your own roof . . . in front of your own grandchildren . . . *my* children!" Her voice finally sputtered out, choked with indignation.

"The punishment is sufficient," Themistius told her testily. He turned back to me. "I believe you will find, Dominicus, that your banishment will grow wearier, rather than easier, as the month progresses, so you need not look so relieved. Now, all of you, go on about your business and I'll hear no more on the subject." The last statement was directed deliberately toward his daughter-in-law.

As all turned to leave, Sapphone showed me a quick grimace of sympathy as she went. I approached Themistius seated on his bench.

"Well?" he snapped, though his eyes danced merrily. "A complaint? Already?"

"No, no complaint, Ancient," I said swiftly. "I . . . I am sorry, Ancient, that I dishonored you, after all your teaching, after your kindness. Thank you. Thank you for another chance."

"Another chance? At what, boy?"

I licked my lips hesitantly. "I feared . . . the slave market. . . ."

"Ah!" he smiled. "Now I understand. No wonder you were so relieved." His voice was kindly. "You feared too much, Dominicus. Such a thing was never under my consideration—nor will it ever be."

Now I smiled at him. "Thank you," I repeated. "I'll not dishonor you again, I swear it."

"No need to swear. I believe you won't. Now get on with you and see you don't disturb my nap again. And try to stay out of Daphne's sight while you're at it."

I nodded and fairly danced away, my fears laid at rest. Perhaps one can, on rare occasion, make bargains with life. The Ancient was right, though, about one thing: I thought that interminable month of idle afternoons would *never* end!

XX

"Ow! Hey!" I protested, dodging away as hard knuckles rapped sharply and unexpectedly on top of my skull. It was Alexandros, in a long white and red striped tunic, smelling freshly scraped with sweet-scented oil.

"Ha! Got you, Dominicus! That's for your smart-ass, show-off answers this morning! Playing it up good to Endymodes and the old man, aren't you? I don't like being made to look bad, especially by a half-sized slave."

"You should've known those answers," I growled, backing a safe distance. "Endymodes has us read on them often enough, and the *old man* expounds on them frequently, which you'd know if you'd ever come to his discussions. I imagine that's why Themistius asked you them. *You* couldn't answer, so *I* did!"

He sneered. "That's what it takes to be in with those two old goats, is it? Applaud their boring discourses and parrot them back? Good little parrot."

I tried to ignore him and walk past, but he pushed me back against the peristyle. "Aw, now, I forgot; you're Grandfather's pet parrot. You won't be angry now, will you?" he apologized sarcastically, still crowding me back between himself and the peristyle. "You won't run tattling to the old man, will you now, Dominicus?"

As his hand reached out toward me I jerked my head back,

expecting his usual trick of grabbing a fistful of curls and twisting me up to my tiptoes. Instead, with a hateful grin, he patted me on the head with maddening solicitation.

"See? There's a good little parakeet, Dominiculus. I wouldn't want to hurt your feelings. Not Endymodes's and Grandfather's pet dwarf. Oh, no, you tell them I've been *nice* to you."

I stood glowering up at him while he burst with arrogant laughter. I had to fight the urge to punch him hard right where I could reach best and hurt him most. But one thing Praxos had impressed upon me: A slave does *not, ever,* strike members of his master's household, no matter how provoked, not even to defend himself. I understood even then that Praxos was specifically warning me against Alexandros. So I held my rage and endured yet another condescending pat on the head before Alexandros had amused himself enough and strutted away.

I stomped into the household bath, red with fury.

"What's the matter with you?" Mercurius wondered.

"Alexandros!" I snarled.

"Oh. Sure he's been his usual uncivil self today. What of it?"

"He patted me on the head and called me a parakeet."

Mercurius shrugged dramatically. "Dominicus, you're going to have to learn to live with it. Ignore him. You think I enjoy his company? Tending his bath just now was a verbal lashing. Nothing I did pleased him, but I remind myself that it doesn't matter because nothing *is* going to please him, so why worry over it when he berates me? It does me no harm, except to my pride, and pride in excess. . . ."

"Yes, I know . . . is arrogance," I finished for him gruffly. "And I have never seen a more arrogant ass. . . ." I glanced up as Praxos emerged naked from the bath. He looked at me questioningly.

"Dare I ask whose ass you are discussing?"

"Guess!"

"Not mine, I hope."

"Dominicus has had a pleasant-as-always chat with Alexandros," Mercurius told him, arranging a bench parallel along one side of the massage table.

"Mmm," Praxos mumbled noncommittally and stretched his full length prone upon the table. "Ready?"

Mercurius gestured to the bench. "Stand up here, Dominicus, so you can reach across him. Cup your hands and I'll pour you the proper amount. The oil-rub and the scraping are the most important phase of the bath. Now, I'll take this side; start with the shoulder and do as I do."

He began spreading almond-scented oil across Praxos's left shoulder. Hesitantly, feeling slightly embarrassed, I tried to copy his motions on the right shoulder. I had never rubbed oil on a naked man before and was not certain how I should proceed. Praxos twitched his shoulder beneath my palms.

"You're tickling!" his muffled snicker complained.

"You touch him too timidly, Dominicus," instructed Mercurius. "Move your hands boldly, like this." He put his hands over mine and pressed them firmly hand over hand across Praxos's back. "Do my eyes deceive me? Why, Praxos, I believe the impudent acrobat is embarrassed!"

"I'm not! It's just . . . well, maybe I am a little. It seems so . . . *immodest.*"

Mercurius laughed. "Barbarians worry about modesty, not Greeks—and certainly not the aristocracy!"

Praxos rose on one elbow and said lightly, "There's no reason to feel immodest. Any domestic slave worth his salt knows at least the rudiments of the bath. Should Themistius, or Apollonius, or even Alexandros, require you to attend to their bathing you *will* do it, like it or not." He grinned. "Be glad you have a patient body to practice on and a meticulus teacher. By the time we're finished you'll be so skilled in the bath as to be priceless." He lay his head back down on his arm. "Go on—and *forget* modesty."

Mercurius replaced my hands on the nape of Praxos's neck. "Thumbs on each side of the spine, in close, like so. Now stroke downward and outward firmly. Don't think about who you're rubbing; concentrate on the feel of the muscles and what you're doing."

Still feeling strangely abashed, I imitated Mercurius's movements. Praxos settled to a more comfortable position.

"That Alexandros," he said conversationally, "*is* growing up to be an arrogant prig, isn't he?"

"Prig isn't precisely the word Dominicus used."

"No, but for *modesty's* sake, we'll pretend it was prig."

"He's insolent to everyone in the household, including his parents. The only one he hasn't crossed is Themistius; he avoids him when he can."

"The avoidance is mutual, I think. Themistius doesn't like his sullen attitude. Apollonius hopes he'll outgrow it."

186

"Where do you suppose he was off to this evening? It wasn't the gymnasium; he smelled too sweet for that."

"I wouldn't be surprised if it was the circus or the games."

"Not running with the blues or greens, I'd wager. He was wearing red and white."

"Not likely. I can't see him on the Christian teams. I'm sure their doctrinal squabbles are well beneath him. The whites—pleasure is their religion. The reds—drunken brawls and stealing seems to be their main occupation. I'd guess the whites for our arrogant prig." Praxos grunted suddenly and jumped beneath my knuckles.

"Sorry," I said. "I didn't mean to jab."

Praxos waved my apology away. "Just took me by surprise."

"Pressure should be steady and circular," Mercurius reminded me. "You don't want to make your man jump, but, then again, don't worry if you hear a groan or two. It means you're getting the knots out."

I nodded. "Um, you know I wonder, what have chariot teams to do with Christian doctrines? In Rome the colors have no such connotations."

"Fortunate for Rome," said Mercurius. "You mean Christians are not drawn up in battle lines over details of dogma?"

"I don't think so. Oh, every great while the priests and monks get all worked up into going out and chastising the heretics, but they're the only ones who bother. And chariot races are," I shrugged, ". . . just chariot races."

"Well, not so in Constantinople," Mercurius informed me. "This city is a breeding ground of fanatics. . . ."

"An imbroglio of religious factions," added Praxos.

"I believe they gather here just to find rival factions to fight with."

"What about the blues and greens?" I persisted.

Mercurius snorted. "A green will not agree with a blue on anything—and vice versa. Why, if a blue will take an Orthodox Trinitarian stand, a green will take an Arian Extremist one. If a blue clamors for a sanctified state religion, a green will decry it. If a blue will grow his hair long and affect barbarian trousers, a green will shave his head and lengthen his tunics. They roam the streets in gangs, and woe to the rival color they catch out alone!"

"Why? What are they fighting over?"

"Who knows?" scoffed Mercurius. "Doctrine!"

"It started out an argument over the nature of divinity," said Praxos. "The Athanasians wanted a God of three equal divinities;

the Arians wanted a Father God of greater divinity than the Son, who would be both divine and human."

Mercurius laughed sharply.

"Amused? I remind you that thousands upon thousands of people, some entirely innocent of malice or dogma, have suffered torture and died wretchedly over this one difference of learned opinion. Of course, the question is pointless; it cannot be proven either way, and neither side could have the capacity to delve completely into the nature of such a being, if one in fact existed. But the bishops argued their cases before Emperor Constantine, and the Emperor decided on the exact nature of divinity himself."

"So he chose Athanasians," I said.

"Right. Problem solved. The Arians bowed to the Emperor, slunk home, and changed their heretical ways. Right? *Wrong!* Nothing changed, except that fanaticism on both sides flamed even hotter. In Constantinople the controversy raged on until it threatened to destroy the city."

"What happened?"

"Wait!" Mercurius interrupted. "Hold the discourse a moment, Praxos, while I give Dominicus a little practical instruction. Or do you wish to leave here slick as a basted goose? Here, Dominicus, is your scraper." He positioned my fingers over a carved piece of smooth ivory, gracefully curved and fitted to the palm. Guiding my hand firmly, he began to peel the oil and grime from Praxos's skin with deft, sure strokes. "Not too lightly. Angle the edge and press just hard enough that you scrape away the gritty layer of dead skin."

"But not so hard you scrape me raw!"

"Don't worry," I said wickedly. "I've skinned many a hare in my time."

Praxos groaned.

The scraping was indeed the most difficult task. Mercurius was as quick as I was cautious. The oil-rub and scraping should go thrice as quickly as they had already. It was some time before I relaxed my stiff concentration and bade Praxos go on with his tale.

"Where were we?" he asked.

"Constantinople."

"Oh, yes. Constantinople created her own version of the controversy—a pitched battle over the patriarchy of the church. The two factions clashed in a grisly battle to capture the cathedral. Over three thousand died. I didn't see it, but they say the floor of the cathedral ran with blood. Theodosius settled it, upholding Constantine's decision, but neither faction has forgotten what happened to friends and families at the hands of the other."

I whistled in amazement. "So all the Christians in the city split into two warring camps and somehow aligned themselves with chariot teams—blues and greens? Why, that's . . . that's . . ." The idea left me speechless.

"Not *all*. There are many other Christian sects mixed into this brew—Gnostics, Monotheists, Manichaeans, Nazarenes, Apollinarians—the list is endless."

I grinned. "Season with an assortment of Jews, Zarathustrians, and Pagans, stir with a stick, and the pot is boiling over."

"Precisely."

Mercurius slapped Praxos on the buttocks. "Turn over."

So the talk went. The more I heard of Constantinople, the more I felt that the House of Themistius was an island of tranquillity midst a sea of insanity.

Deep in winter word came that Emperor Theodosius had died in Mediolanum. Now his two young sons ruled the Empire—Arcadius here in the east, Honorius in the west. Without the old Emperor's strong rule, fierce rivalry arose over who would command the Legions. Between warring generals and Alaric's rebelling Goths within the borders, and marauding Huns without, the reign of the two boy-Emperors was fraught with strife.

XXI

While mayhem tore at the Empire, life went on in Constantinople as usual. Oh, folk grew apprehensive and there was anxious talk of the barbarian peril, but as the months stacked up twelve deep folk submerged their fears in their pleasures and theological controversies as before.

In the House of Themistius scholars and students still gathered each day, not only in the mornings for the formal discourses, but also in the late afternoons and early evenings, often staying to dine abstractedly and continue a particularly intriguing discussion on through the last fruit-bowl.

This island of tranquillity countenanced many differences of opinion, but they were amiably debated. Tempers might flare, but reason took precedence over angry defense of favorite theories. Themistius's distinguished guests prided themselves on being the living intelligensia of rational philosophy. Their ethical code did not allow censure of another's beliefs as long as one seemed to arrive at them rationally and caused no harm by them. One thing they found intolerable in their midst was religious fanaticism, surrounded as they were by the sea of insanity. Irrespective of religious convictions (whether Pagan, Gnostic, Jew, or Christian) *all* were of the Hellenic literati.

The gods came under the same intense scrutiny as everything else. The consensus generally held was that no one could prove the existence of any one god, much less to the exclusion of all other gods. Themistius argued that either all the gods existed as

190

is (which he in no wise believed for an instant), therefore man might just as well resign himself to suffer a confusion of deities meddling in his life; or none of the gods existed (at least not as religionists depicted them), therefore man could emit a sigh of relief and tend to the business of ordering his own life by use of his natural rational faculties.

As to the nature of divinity, the old philosopher would shrug. If a rational man can believe that it be possible for three different gods to be in reality one god, then can he not just as sensibly believe that a multiplicity of gods might possibly be one and the same deity? Why should God stop at three? Why not an infinity of divine persons?

No, he would counter his own question. Any divine being capable of creating the vast and complex universe should have no need to father a confusing hodge-podge of gods to govern it, petty little cliques of deities who certainly displayed no ability to create a universe themselves even should they work collectively, which they gave no hint of doing. Indeed, they scarcely even deigned to recognize each other's existence. Is this how divine beings behave? If so, men are faithfully patterned after them. (Here his little jest always evoked a chuckle or two.) All this aside from Themistius's stated opinion that the universe is *not* orderly and of deliberate design, but random collision, joining, and rejoining of atomic properties.

Thus, hypothesized Themistius, the gods were nought but products of the great minds of ancient philosophers, genius intelligences, but human nonetheless. The gods had no other existence than as symbols in the shared conscious history of man: personified symbols of the ideals, dreams, longings, and failings that characterize the human race. And, to Themistius, the symbol of the highest ideals and attainments the human mind could envision was Apollo.

Sun-bright Apollo. Apollo of reason, truth, and enlightenment. Apollo of perfection.

And I let the walls of reason surround me like the walls of the House that kept me. I retreated into the serenity of study to protect my deepest feelings—feelings long shaken by all the hurt I could take, or would take. It seemed only reasonable to defend myself as best I could. So I cooled my heart's fever in the bottomless wells of philosophy, for philosophy was safe, as were history and literature, engaging my head in fascinating pursuits that had nought to do with my heart. And, after daydreaming over Homer, skimming Hesiod and Herodotus, struggling with excerpts from Plato and Aristotle, delving into Pliney and Tacitus, and pondering upon Lucretius and Epictetus, why, I fancied myself quite a scholar.

Ah, but my walls were not impenetrable.

The first blow of the catapult merely annoyed me: "I'm surprised Endymodes hasn't had you read this, Dominicus," said Alexandros lightly as he spread a scroll across my reading table, "since it *is* Plato and it applies directly to you. . . ." He leaned over me, holding the scroll open; I clamped my hands on the table edge, expecting the tall stool to be kicked out from under me, which had happened by "accident" a few times before. Alexandros merely tapped a particular line with his forefinger. "There . . . read right there."

I stared at the words. They read ". . . *and any defective offspring of the others will be quietly got rid of.*" Leave it to Alexandros, I thought, to search Plato until he found a reference like that just to make me . . .

"Read it aloud, Dominicus, so Sapphone and Phoebe can hear it."

"No." I wanted to shove backwards and knock him over, but I dared not.

"I'll read it then." Alexandros pronounced the line in erudite tones. " 'Any defective offspring' (that's you, Dominicus) 'will be quietly got rid of.' What do you say to that?"

I shrugged brusquely. "So what? I hadn't heard Plato was particularly admired in this house."

"Not usually. But Endymodes made a point of reading us this very passage when Grandfather bought you, and he elaborated upon . . ."

"*Shut up*, Alexandros!" Sapphone commanded fiercely. "We don't want to hear it!"

"But you did hear it. Of course you remember, don't you?" Alexandros persisted innocently, readying to launch a second blow. "As I said, Endymodes elaborated upon the theme, saying how Plato referred to the Spartan method of disposing of defective infants, exposing them on a mountain to be devoured by wolves or freeze to death, so that Sparta maintained a healthy, productive populace. Endymodes said that it is an expedient and necessary practice if a society is to keep from deteriorating with each generation, as does the derelict strata in Constantinople."

"Some of those people," I said tightly, measuredly, "were made that way on purpose."

"Well, yes." He shrugged it off. "But Endymodes particularly pointed to you as an example. He said it would be criminal . . ."

Sapphone jerked at his shoulder angrily. "Alexandros, *stop* it!"

"If you were allowed to breed your inferior stature and base nature. In a well-ordered society you would not have been nurtured past your first draw of breath. . . ."

"*Alexandros!*" This time the angry voice crackled from Endymodes, who stood tight-lipped and white-faced in the doorway.

I stared at him, stiff with shock and anger myself.

Alexandros skulked back, grinning. "I thought Dominicus's education needed broadening, mentor."

"How *dare* you!" Endymodes strode into the study.

"I only repeated your own words!" said Alexandros airily. "If they are true, why should you mind them repeated? Unless you are ashamed of them."

Endymodes paused and met my accusing, unwavering gaze. I wanted very much to hear what answer he would make. The silence in the room rang in my ears. Endymodes dropped his eyes and paced away. Ah.

"You believe this." My words fell with flat finality. It was no question.

The old tutor took a long breath and let it out in a sigh. "In general—yes. In the particular—no."

I looked back at the lines on parchment. "Plato leaves no room for choice between the general and the particular." Again I met his eyes with challenge, refusing to dodge the fiery hail about to come catapulting over my defenses. "Either you believe it or you don't."

Endymodes paused for long seconds before he answered. "I fully realize that there is always an exception, Dominicus. You were spared, and, as it happens, society has not suffered; I suspect you have much more . . . potential than anyone guesses. Now that I have had closer acquaintance with you, I will admit I am moved to state that, yes, it would have been a misfortune if your talents had died in infancy. Yet if my emotions say one thing, my intellect says another.

"Dominicus, you are perhaps one in a thousand who has some worthy contribution to make; your mind is sharp, your skills as a scholar barely uncovered. Yet such a likelihood could not be predicted with any degree of accuracy at your birth, nor at the birth of any defective infant, nor even at the birth of your own offspring. No, reason tells me that for the good of the whole society, the practice is sound. One weeds the garden so that the productive and esthetic plants may be properly nurtured. The gardener does not regret the death of the weeds. Emotionalism must not be allowed to cloud the clear sight of reason."

"And reason must prevail," I muttered dryly, staring into the blind fog of emotion that obscured the parchment before me.

"It is the superior faculty."

"Ah, yes." Absently I began rerolling the scroll, looking at no one, saying nothing more. I was burning inside. What did they think I was, anyway, that they could so bluntly—

Sapphone's indignant voice sliced the silence. "Well, *I* don't believe it! It's a cruel thing to do to helpless babies, and a cruel thing to say to Dominicus!"

I heard Alexandros' derisive snort. "Women! Ruled by their emotions, eh Dominicus?"

I neither looked his way nor gave indication I had heard. I sought some dark cell in which to wrest my roiling feelings.

The silence in the study pulsated and suffocated like a head-wrenching fever. I wanted to be anywhere but here, but I was *not* running from them. I would take anything they said or did and never give them the satisfaction of seeing me cringe.

Endymodes cleared his throat and spoke in terse, abrupt phrases. "Dominicus—prepare a recitation on the major theories in the history of natural philosophy—along with any refutations or substantiations you can find. I will hear your summary tomorrow—you'll need to begin your research in the scriptorium immediately—you are dismissed for that purpose."

I climbed down from my stool, refusing any other acknowledgment of his words, determined not to let him see my relief at being excused from the room. Alexandros hissed something taunting under his breath as I passed, but I made no effort to decipher it.

Some of Themistius's students were reading in the scriptorium while others listened to his discourse in the garden. I felt no wise up to facing anyone; I wanted only to be alone. I walked on past the scriptorium and kept going until I found refuge in the peaceful solitude of the atrium. The brilliant slanting rays of early morning sun were just beginning to streak in through the sun-roof and touch the air with warmth. The gently plashing water in the fountain filled the room with soothing murmurings, and the perfect, serene faces of Apollo and Artemis revealed no touch of mortal pain. I sat on the cool tile edging the fountain and stared blankly at the liquid rippling surface, trying to control the emotional turmoil that gnashed madly at my soul.

Alexandros had intended it to hurt, and it did. I didn't care, I told myself—I would not care—I would never care. Grimly, I ground my teeth and set about strengthening my defenses. My walls were not yet high enough nor thick enough, no one would pass them again. Moments later Sapphone discovered me in the atrium.

"Dominicus," she said hesitantly, her leather sandals scuffing softly across the tiles. "I've been looking for you. . . ."

"What for?" I did not look up. "You're supposed to be at study."

She sat beside me, hands clasped whitely together in her blue-gowned lap. "I couldn't stand it; I told Endymodes I was coming to find you; I told him . . . Oh, Dominicus, I'm so sorry!"

"What're *you* sorry about?" I tried to keep the sharp edge of anger out of my voice, but there it was. I took a deep breath and rephrased. "It wasn't your fault, Sapphone."

"I should've said more on your behalf, but I was so shocked. Alexandros—I'm not surprised—he's cruel and he loves to do that sort of thing to people. But Endymodes—he's got things twisted all wrong—he's worshipped intellect so long he forgets people have feelings."

"Best to know the truth," I muttered.

"Truth? Surely you don't believe . . ."

"What they said of me? Not that. But at least I know who I'm dealing with—what they think. Anyway, it's done and there's nothing more to be said about it." I glared at Apollo.

Her hands fidgeted unhappily. "We should talk about this."

"No we shouldn't."

"Yes we should. It helps feelings to talk them out."

"The only thing that will help is to forget about it." I sighed and looked up into her distressed face. "Look, I have to be rational about this. The facts are the facts and there's nothing I can do to change them. If Endymodes thinks I'm a weed in his garden, well *fine*—let him. It isn't his garden anyway. As for Alexandros, who cares what that arrogant brat thinks? I'm here because my papa did *not* feed me to wolves, because Themistius thought I was worth a thousand solidi, and Endymodes must live with it because he's a slave like me; and if he has to rationalize some saving grace in me to make it palatable to him, then I'll just have to settle for that, won't I?" I was becoming uncontrollably sarcastic and cynical in my speech without really wanting to. I took another deep breath, closed my eyes, and cast about for that elusive calm center within that was always there yet often so impossible to find. This time I found it. I met Sapphone's sharp eyes and continued quietly.

"Reason is a powerful weapon, you know; it can convince one that just about any situation is bearable and enable one to rationalize it comfortably. My intelligence reminds me that I can never change what I am, nor people's opinions of me, nor the fact that I no longer have any choices in life—except one: either wail in despair and rage and strike out blindly against the whole universe, or face it undeceived and unflinching in the light of reason."

"*Reason!*" Sapphone unexpectedly snarled. "*Intellect! Rationality!* I cannot tell you how utterly sick I am of hearing those words! Does no one *feel* in this house but me? I thought *you* did, Dominicus!"

I stared, startled by the vehemence in her voice.

"I can say it aloud, now that my wedding is but a month away—how glad I am to be leaving! Dominicus, there is more to a person than mind! Have you noticed that it is only intellectuals who tout the superiority of reason over feeling? They laugh at emotion as a woman's weakness. Well, I say it is her strength! The man I am marrying thinks my tears and joys and my angers and loves are wonderfully alive! Thank Aphrodite that in this age women can choose their own husbands and not be bartered like cattle or slaves."

She glanced quickly at me. "Oh, Dominicus, I'm sorry. This isn't fair to you, is it? But you used to be alive like that, when first you came to us. You were all heart and merry eyes, and one could read your soul on your face. What happened to you?"

I glared into the restless waters of the fountain, seeking to focus on the colored tiles in the still depths. A thousand tiny things had happened to me, and for each one I had placed a new stone to fill the chink in the wall.

"I cannot afford it anymore," I told her flatly.

"How can you afford *not* to feel?" Sapphone cried. "Ah, I wish I could tell you what it's like to love. . . ."

I know, I thought hollowly. *I don't want to remember.*

". . . and to be loved. To be cherished for oneself, just for being who you are, without having to explain everything you say or

196

think or feel with some *rational* justification. I wish I could tell you what joy it is to know someone who is simply glad of your whole being, who . . ."

I stood abruptly. "I don't want to hear it."

"But—"

"Take your impossible joy elsewhere."

"Not impossible, Dominicus—"

"For me it is! Here—in this house—it won't happen!" My own vehemence shook me. I veered away from the black pit of the future I glimpsed—a lifetime of emptiness, *deadness,* in the House of Themistius—and dropped a shield of cynicism between me and it. "Besides," I added sarcastically, "it wouldn't be allowed. I might *breed.*"

Sapphone stared at me for a moment, quietly, then she dropped her gaze to her fingers; they worried at a cracked piece of tile.

"That's not the kind of love I mean," she said in a subdued voice. "Just . . . someone . . . whose whole heart is open to you . . . who loves you as you are . . . no matter what. . . ."

I wheeled and stalked away. She tread perilously near carefully locked rooms of memory that I wished left undisturbed, desolate rooms once filled with the warm tears and merry joys of a folk who were all heart and loving.

"Dominicus! Where are you going?"

"To the scriptorium." My voice grated roughly. "I have a recitation to prepare."

"Endymodes only assigned it to let you out of the room. . . ."

"To spare my feelings? Belatedly thoughtful of him. He'll doubtless still expect to hear me tomorrow." I had paused but briefly, not turning around, yet not wanting to leave.

"Wait, Dominicus! You'll need hours to research all that; I can save you the trouble. I've had to give the exact same recitation; I can give you the whole summary easily."

Now I turned and looked at her doubtfully. Truth be known, I scarcely relished entering a scriptorium of virtual strangers and then striving to concentrate through my turmoil on scroll after scroll of deadly-dull hypotheses and counter-hypotheses. Yet . . . I hesitated.

Sapphone smiled. "I promise, we'll speak only of dry philosophies and nothing else. Agreed?"

"Agreed," I nodded, both relieved and wary. "If you can stick to your promise."

"I will," she retorted, lifting her chin. "My rational faculties can adhere to the topic of inquiry as well as anyone's. So come back and sit down and stop scowling. We'll talk enough theories and hypotheses and jejunities to stuff a scholarly goose."

I smiled weakly at her banter and resumed my seat on the fountain's rim. I was anxious to immerse my mind in a safe subject.

"All right. I'm listening."

"First we'll get comfortable." So saying, she kicked off her sandals, pulled her skirt to her knees, and lightly swung her legs over into the fountain, kicking foam in the water playfully. She reached down into the water and splashed it at me.

"Come on, Dominicus," she laughed.

I did the same. The delicious coolness lapped at my ankles. I wriggled my toes and splashed back at her.

"Who shall we discuss first?" I asked, grateful for her cool diversion.

"Heraclitus. Remember his old adage—one can never step into the same river twice, because by then it will be a different river?"

"Aye, I remember. Nor would the person still be the same as he was when he stepped in the river the first time. He's right about change, I'm sure. Everything *does* change, every moment—it's built into nature, to keep things moving, isn't it? And 'twould be pretty dull for my money, if it wasn't."

Sapphone laughed. "You'll get no argument from me there! Life *would* be dull if everything stayed the same forever. Well, as you know, Heraclitus also postulated fire as the universal element. He said everything in existence is formed of the density or rarity of fire."

"Ha! When Heraclitis stepped into his elusive river why did he not get his feet scorched if 'twas fire?" I skimmed my feet in waves through the cool liquid. "Anyone with senses can tell this is not composed of fire, however rarified. Besides, if all was fire, everything would burn itself out, wouldn't it? Everywhere would be heaps of ashes."

"Why, what of Parmenides, then?" countered Sapphone flippantly. "He would say that is illusion; our senses cannot perceive true reality at all—they deceive us at every turn. There is but one element, one underlying matter, one unchanging, immutable . . . *everything!*" She fanned her fingers once about the sun-bright atrium. "If our senses tell us differently, they lie."

"Rubbish! What have we to rely on if not our senses? They are the food of our minds. My sense of sight guides me through the door so I do not hit the wall, and I find it uncannily reliable (if I am not drunk). My sense of touch tells me the hearthstone is too hot for comfort, so I move away. My sense of smell tells me rain is coming and it comes, tells me fish is roasting and it is. My hearing tells me when someone calls my name, and who is calling . . . you get the drift. It's just not reasonable to suppose that our senses are not reliable to a substantial degree. And, anyway," I grinned impishly, "if our senses are unreliable, and mind bases its thinking on what the senses perceive, then so is our reasoning unreliable—therefore Parmenides, according to his own hypothesis, was a fool to credit his own reasoning."

Sapphone laughed delightedly. "I hadn't thought of that. Oh, do tell that to Endymodes—I expect he'll purse his lips and sputter himself into a dither over that one."

I shrugged and made a mental note to do that. "Who's next?"

"Democritus."

"Oh, do we even discuss him in this house? I thought the infallible Lucretius disapproved of Democritus."

"*No* philosopher is infallible. Even Grandfather, who respects Lucretius as one of the greatest minds to put words on parchment, will be the first to insist on it. Indeed, I *know* he can be wrong. Have you read Lucretius on the subject of women and—um, conception?"

I glanced sidewise at her in surprise. She almost—but not quite—blushed. And for good reason. In the passage she referred to, Lucretius wrote rather graphically that women "wriggled" and employed "lascivious movements" during lovemaking in a clear attempt to divert a man's seed from its proper path—thereby avoiding conception. He stated that a woman writhing in bed is using tricks of prostitutes to avoid pregnancy and to make intercourse more enticing to men. Wives, he claimed, had no need of it, that in fact a woman conceived best when postured in the manner of four-footed beasts.

It was *I* who blushed.

"You read it? I wouldn't know from experience, of course— not yet—but I asked Mother about it and she says the very idea is utter stupidity, and that the great philosopher obviously never consulted any woman on the matter."

I could well believe that. But I had no intention of discussing further the subject with Sapphone. I had enough trouble already wresting with midnight fantasies of the pretty granddaughter of Themistius.

"You said you'd stick to the subject, Sapphone."

"I am," she replied, looking amused and piqued. "We were discussing Lucretius's credibility, were we not?"

"Democritus," I reminded her.

"Oh, yes, Democritus. He described matter as being made up of tiny seeds, too small to be perceptible to the eye. He named them atoms and claimed all existence consists of nothing more than millions upon millions of atoms in constant motion, combining and recombining to form the various elements. Then to account for the continuous motion of the atoms, he postulated the existence of—"

"Vacuity!" I exclaimed. "Philosophers are quite fond of vacuity, don't you think?"

She giggled. "Now, I *wouldn't* repeat that to Endymodes, if I were you, Dominicus."

I looked up at her, wide-eyed and innocent. "Why, Sapphone, surely you don't think I meant that sarcastically."

In answer, she splashed me with water.

"I simply meant," I went on with an offended air, "that there must be empty space for atoms to move about in and allow for the atoms in, say, stone, to be denser than the atoms in air—there must be something—or rather *nothing*—between the atoms if some things are to be more solid than others."

"Right. And, so far, Lucretius would quite agree. Now here is where he and Democritus differ. Democritus says that all this change and motion follows some great design, some intricate, purposeful pattern unknown to us. He contends that the motion of each atom is absolutely determined by the movement of the whole design. 'Nought happens for nought,' he says."

I grinned at her. "He also said, 'Nothing exists except atoms and empty space; everything else is opinion.' So that's only *his* opinion, isn't it? No, Lucretius would not like it. Democritus's universe would cause all thought and action to be determined by the whole design, thus negating free will and choice. Be sure, Lucretius would admit to no design to the universe on the simple grounds that no rational purpose is discernable. He'd say it's random collision of atoms, attracting and repelling continuously, and if any gods presume to make a design of it, they've fairly bungled it thus far."

"And which do you think it is, Dominicus?"

"How should *I* know? That's *the* question, isn't it? The one scholars debate over until they are fury-red and murderous. Besides, they're both really ingenious theories, for who can prove

200

or disprove either one?" I smiled slyly. "It seems to me that philosophy is an open trade. All it needs is one part logic and nine parts imagination. I may just try my wits at that game. I expect I might be good at it."

She laughingly agreed. "I expect you might! You probably have enough vacuity in your brain to match any philosopher."

I snorted and splashed her vigorously. Sapphone splashed me in retaliation; I counterattacked, and she defended herself. We called truce only after thoroughly drenching each other.

XXII

 Next morning I gave my recitation. I did not miss the fact that Endymodes dispatched Alexandros to the scriptorium first thing, for which I was glad. Endymodes listened and interrupted in his usual manner. He pronounced my summary satisfactory and my delivery excellent, though, as usual, some of my remarks he termed "unduly impertinent."

Old Themistius, however, enjoyed my impertinent remarks, so I made no attempt to squelch them. I think he questioned me during the informal evening discussions with colleagues just because I was likely to say something outrageous without really meaning to. Guests not accustomed to me often glared at me askance, as if I had no more business than a trained monkey expressing an opinion in learned company. But Themistius would ask, and I would answer, and I soon learned it was far easier to arouse their mirth with a flippant answer than be credited with a serious one, so impertinence was my trade.

Sadly, Themistius, who enjoyed my company so much, suddenly one day fell senseless in the garden. Athene had him carried to bed, where he lay unable to move or speak; only his shallow breath and flickering gaze told us spirit and mind still dwelled within. I knew he must purely hate it, if his reason was intact. He would see no virtue in living in such an incapacitated state.

A loyal circle of his colleagues and students came to give their sympathy, but they would not stay long, being shocked at his condition. Sorrowful and embarrassed, they stood and knew not what to say to his unresponsive form (except the eyes, which fixed them with an expression they could not read.) Athene and Nemone attended him, lifting the frail frame and coaxing down his throat wine spiced with the physician's herbs or broth or honeyed milk. They cleaned his wasting body, which had lost control of urine and excrement, and changed the bedding continuously. The younger children were allowed in only once to see their grandfather and leave him their flowers, except Phoebe, who liked to come in and freshen his room with garden herbs and sing little songs the while.

Daphne made her appearance, tight-lipped and, I thought, a little smug. Athene would not let her go in alone for fear of unkind words she would say to the Ancient to upset him. When Daphne opened her mouth to speak to him, Athene shoved her forcibly from the room, and the two of them argued in the garden until Daphne's voice shrilled angrily and Athene slapped her. Daphne thereafter sulked. She complained to Apollonius, but her husband quietly agreed that Daphne's presence would at the least annoy Themistius—yet he gravely admonished his sister for slapping his wife, who was, he pointed out, the mistress of the house. Athene replied that Daphne was not *her* mistress—the daughter of Themistius—nor anyone's while her father still lived.

Apollonius looked in on him twice daily, as did Praxos and, less frequently, Mercurius.

Alexandros went in briefly, at the angry, disappointed insistence of Apollonius. After that, he avoided coming home at all.

Sapphone, sad and hushed, came once with her husband, and stayed the afternoon. She emerged from her grandfather's room with moist eyes and hugged her mother and sister. In the garden she told me she was happy in her new household, and she confided that she hoped to be with child soon—perhaps (and her eyes glowed) she was even now. Then she dropped her voice to a whisper, and with a secret smile and not a trace of embarrassment, said that Lucretius was a fool indeed, and that a woman who could lie moveless in her marriage bed was a cold fish—or had a cold fish for a husband.

When Sapphone presented me to her husband he greeted me with cordial curiosity, said he had heard much of me, and hoped we would next meet under happier circumstances. He seemed a good sort for Sapphone; he embraced her comfortingly in the grape arbor while she wept.

Endymodes spent a punctual hour with his old master each day, reading him favorite scrolls—mainly on the dispersal of atoms and the inevitable, yet complacent end of a life well lived.

Each evening I came and told him a tale—for the Ancient ever enjoyed diversion and laughter (in moderation, of course)—but it was hard, for I scarcely knew if he wished I would go away and leave him be or if he was glad of the momentary diversion. I drew from childhood Gallic folk legends and a raven's-hoard of vagabond lore and merry jest-tales. I wondered if he thought them silly and superstitious, but I subjected him to them anyway. Only his eyes flicking toward me at whiles told me he listened, and twice I thought I saw a fleeting, ghostly smile enliven his lips, so I was encouraged to believe he enjoyed them.

He seemed to be getting stronger—for a while. Then a new stroke hit him, and within days he was dead. Ah, I would miss him. I wondered if his atoms scattered and his spirit was no more, as he believed would be, or if he stood glaring about him, finding himself in some abode of deathless souls. Either way I felt certain he was glad it was done with.

Themistius always said that Pagan philosophy would die with him; likely he was right. His passing scarcely made a ripple in Constantinople, but to family, scholars, and his students, the loss was deep felt.

And I felt it strangely. I became restless. Oh, the house was a pleasant place, with the fragrant garden and lulling fountains, warm sunshine and cool tiles, beckoning scriptorium and quiet company. Yet sometimes I paced the peristyle like a caged beast. Not that there stood anyone to keep me from walking out the vestibule gates. But Constantinople, still foreign and frightening, sprawled out there with open tentacles. I scarcely knew my way about the city, and I feared the beggar-masters might snatch me up and I would forever and irrevocably regret having set foot past these portals.

I resolved to be Stoic about it. After all, I had no real complaints about my life here. Yet, just when I thought I had safely rationalized my mind and heart into contentment, just when I thought I had gratefully accepted my small place in the universe, I would discover in my breast a fugitive sprite longing for freedom in the hills and forests, crying with a need so ellusive and intangible that I could put no name to it, seeking . . . seeking a *why* to my life. And when the ache grew unbearable, the need unassuagable, I resolutely returned to the scriptorium and buried my thoughts in ancient knowledge. Oh, aye, I drank, breathed, and dreamed knowledge. I was obsessed with knowing. And I was very, very confused.

Suddenly my position in the household became tenuous. I had belonged to Themistius. When the Ancient died his shipping trade and property, slaves included, all went to his son Apollonius, except for a generous sum of solidi to his widowed daughter Athene, plus a one-twentieth allowance in shipping profits. Apollonius cared not a fig whether he had a dwarf-slave or no; his wife Daphne only wanted me out of her house and replaced as quickly as possible by a docile ten-or-eleven-year-old girl to be her personal slave. With Sapphone gone to a house of her own, I still had Praxos, Nemone, and Mercurius to count on as friends—but slaves can offer each other little more than moral support, for we have no say in household matters.

It looked to me I might likely be sold at any moment.

About that time Apollonius's younger son, Pericles, moved up from his studies under Athene to study with Endymodes. Pericles was twelve and now determined to do everything his seventeen-year-old brother did, eager to be just like Alexandros. Between the two of them they plagued me relentlessly. Phoebe tried to take my side, but she was just fifteen, quiet and shy, and overwhelmingly intimidated by her aggressive cousins. Only Endymodes's strict discipline and swift-striking staff kept the morning studies from becoming unbearable. Endymodes treated me decently enough, always with his customary reserve and careful impartiality. But I dreaded morning lessons and spent more and more of them reading alone in the scriptorium.

Athene found me there one morning and told me she was leaving the household; she was purchasing a seaside villa, small, but adequate to her own needs. However, before she moved, she was thinking of buying me outright from Apollonius and perhaps gifting me to Sapphone. She would feel better, she said, if she knew I was assured of a gentle mistress and a good household.

So it is come to that, I thought, not surprised, glad to see my future take a familiar form. I had no idea what Sapphone's husband's household might be like (I knew only that he was not yet its head), but the House of Themistius (pardon—House of Apollonius) had gone sour on me, and suddenly a change, *any* change (within reason, mind you) sounded sweet. And to know the mistress of my fate would be Sapphone was a heartfelt relief.

But next day I chanced to be in the garden, secluded in the

little grape arbor, thinking of nought but how it would feel to leave this secure, familiar house for another, when I overheard this conversation approaching along the path:

". . . because," Apollonius was saying in his sternest tones, "you spend none of your time studying and all of it running about the streets with that circus crowd. . . ."

"The whites do *not* run about the streets," Alexandros countered indignantly. "Those are the other colors. You know absolutely nothing about the whites, Father."

"I know indolent good-for-nothing swells when I see them, and that's what you and your friends look to me. Doing nothing but spending enormous amounts of money on fancy clothes and expensive wines. Where do you think that money comes from? Hard work and attention to business—that's where! And I can well imagine how much you lose betting on the races." Apollonius's hand went up to stay his son's protest. "No, I've checked the tallies. Your team's not been winning for months."

"Not *winning!*" sputtered Alexandros furiously. "You give me the big lecture about my friends and my life, but it really all boils down to that! It'd be different, would it, if the white team *was* winning? Is that it? Why you—you *hypocrite!*"

"Watch your tongue with me young man! No, that's not the point, whether you're winning or not—"

"*You* brought it up."

"The point is the disrespectful attitude these whites have. I don't like the way you talk to me or the tone of voice you use toward your mother—or your aunt Athene. I did not raise you to be rude and haughty with your elders."

"Yeah?" sneered Alexandros. "Then who did?"

A short pause, then Apollonius's voice dropped to deeper, gentler tones. "Maybe I didn't raise you at all," he said quietly. "Maybe I thought I was too busy and let slaves do the raising for me. And now, son, it's too late for me to go back and do it right . . . but it's not too late for Pericles. Your brother thinks the sun and moon of you, Alexandros, and he'll do anything you do without thinking it through. I'm going to spend more time with him, let him have a hand in shipping and merchanting, show him what my world is like. . . ."

"So you want *me* out of the way," Alexandros accused him bitterly. "So you *exile* me."

"Rome is hardly exile, Alexandros. It's not as though I am

sending you to Britannia. But the University in Rome keeps strict rules," his father admonished. "It tolerates no barbarian affectations and no drunkenness. The games and circuses are off limits to students, and should you break the rules they will not hesitate to give you a good flogging."

"Father!"

"A couple of years in Rome will do you good. And if the University cannot make you see reason and straighten up, then perhaps it will be the Roman Legions for you."

"*Father!*"

Apollonius chuckled. "I thought that would get a rise out of you. Keep that in mind, son. Be sensible and enjoy this opportunity. You'll take the usual Mediterranean voyage—Athens, the Aegean, Alexandria—on one of our own vessels. I've already made guesting arrangements along the way, and you'll winter in Alexandria. Endymodes will accompany you—"

Alexandros groaned. "Endymodes!"

"Yes, and you will cooperate with him absolutely. He'll keep you at your studies and see you enrolled in the University. He'll be in correspondence with me. Understood?"

"Understood," Alexandros capitulated.

"Good. We'll go to the auction next week and select you a personal slave to take along. A sober, conscientious domestic. . . ."

"My choice?"

"Within reason, yes."

There stretched a long, thoughtful silence. "Well, then, I would have Dominicus."

Startled, my head snapped up from its idle prop of hands. I made no more move than that, lest I be caught listening, but my ears pricked up like a hound's.

"Dominicus? Out of the question. I said within reason."

"Why not? He's sober and conscientious—and clever, as well. Old Endymodes likes him. And he can help me with my studies because he remembers *everything* he's ever heard or read. Why, I wouldn't need to take notes, even, if he sat the discourses."

Another long pause, then Apollonius said narrowly, "And you think you can bully him about, is that it?"

"No, sir, no. Well, just think—I'd probably be the only student in the University with a dwarf, especially one like Dominicus."

"Alexandros, Dominicus is much too valuable to be wasted

on frivolities and entertainments. Besides, Athene approached me this morning about purchasing him and sending him to Sapphone."

"Because Mother wants to be rid of him. But, see, he'd be gone with me. Anyway, Dominicus is *from* Rome, isn't he? He *knows* Rome; Endymodes and I do not. With all the reasons for taking him, it makes no sense to go and buy a slave we haven't tried."

Another of those damnable long pauses, then Apollonius's voice: "I will speak to Athene. I promise nothing, but I'll consider it."

They wandered on out of the garden.

I realized I had been holding my breath only when I felt it go out in a rush.

Ah, to Rome! On a ship! And to see all the world between! I did not for a moment believe Alexandros's fallacious arguments for taking me along. Be sure he meant to bully me. I wondered how I might fare caught between overbearing Alexandros and severe Endymodes on a long sea voyage.

Then again, I might be sent to Sapphone, which would not be so terrible. I knew her heart, liked her well, and her husband seemed a good man. But to go to another household nearly the same as this—how I wearied of peristylium walls and domestic duties.

No, I had no love for Constantinople, but still . . .

I would not like being personal slave to Alexandros. I knew too well his tyrannous disposition, and yet, and yet. . . .

Rome was so very near to Gaul, to home, I might . . .

I stopped my spinning thoughts and tried hard not to hope or dread either possibility, for the decision would not be mine. I would go just where they wanted to send me, whether I wished it or no. I had to bring all the Stoic logic I knew to bear and not let my heart think of choices. I must be ready for whichever fate would be doled me. So I pondered doggedly on matters of philosophy. Whether I be fixed in some intractable plan or pushed and shoved along by random collision could make no difference to me. I reminded myself: *I am a slave and must live with whatever is given or taken away by others.*

All that interminable day I tried not to care that Apollonius and Athene between them were arranging my life. I only half succeeded. I was a knot of anxiety and frustration within.

Finally, finally, they called me aside after the evening meal I could scarcely swallow. They sat on a bench in the shadowing garden; I climbed upon another and sat cross-legged, my heart pounding in anticipation.

Apollonius began maddeningly to inform me of two opportunities that had come up, not knowing I was already aware—oh, how aware!—of both. Athene brought up some pros and cons of each—all those things I had struggled *not* to think on all day lest I want one answer too terribly much. And at this moment I knew I had deceived myself. I wanted one answer so badly my heart ached.

Get on with it! Get on with it! I cried inside. *Tell me!*

"And so," I heard Athene saying in the stiffling summer air, "Apollonius has at last agreed with me in this: we are letting the decision be yours, Dominicus. Which would you do?"

Stunned, I gaped at her. She was giving me a *choice?* The one answer for which I was totally unprepared? For the moment I could only stare in astonishment while her words slowly penetrated my brain.

Then, suddenly, it took all my self-control to constrain an exuberant *whoop!*—from turning ten backflips in a pure release of caged tension. As it was, I could not wipe away the grin that spread itself all over my face.

I knew the source of my restless yearnings. I was overcome with vagabond fever, a nigh well incurable malady. After two years confinement . . . ah, sweet vagabonding joy . . . I was going . . . going! . . .

Athene read it in my face, for she was not surprised when I said uncalmly, "I would go to Rome—to *Rome!*"

"I thought as much," she said with an understanding smile.

Apollonius nodded, pleased. "You have much to prepare. Alexandros sails within the month."

XXIII

Wisps of black cloud flew like ghostly dark gulls under a grim grey sky. The Bosporus wind that drove from the north blew uncommonly chill for early October, and the cold waters of the Horn ran choppy and swift by fits. The sailing vessel moored to the dock dipped and rose on the waves, making the short walk across the boarding plank an interesting one. Our goodbyes already said—

"Sapphone, understand, please. It's not that I would not like your house, nor you for mistress, but . . . it's like living in a lovely, peaceful prison, but a prison nevertheless. And this. . . ." I swept my hand to the tossing ship, ". . . this is . . ."

"I know. You're a vagabond at heart still, Dominicus. I shall miss you, but I'd not hold you back."

She stooped and kissed me fleetingly, almost shyly, on the forehead. I smiled in surprise.

"Take care," she whispered. "If Alexandros is unbearable, write, and I will see you get home."

I nodded, not spoiling her generous concern by explaining that this was not home to me, nor could it ever be.

"Goodbye, Sapphone."

"Good luck, Dominicus."

. . .

Our little party stood on deck to watch the sailors cast off and to take a last look at Constantinople. The Greek, Cretan, and Phoenician crew hoisted sail and the north sea wind nudged the ship out into the Horn. The Augustaean Forum and the Palace Seawall slid past. Suddenly we entered the strong current of the torrential Bosporus Strait and picked up speed. By the time we swept into the Marmara Sea, the ship was under full sail.

Such a giddy feeling, riding waves and wind and watching the land melt away—exhilarating, too, much like flying would feel, I imagine. Indeed, we rode high in the water and I felt as though the powerful wind that billowed the sails might lift the vessel clear of the sea and fly her across the sky like some dream ship.

Alexandros and Endymodes went on below decks, leaving me gripping the rail and staring at the broad green sea in spellbound fascination. The spell was heightened by a familiar voice behind me that roused old memories.

"Well, little jewel, what do you think of sailing?"

I spun about. "Khafar!"

The dark Arabian grinned and leaned against the railing, gesturing a hand lazily in a familiar greeting. "Myself."

"By the gods! What a stunner!"

"Stunner? Is this the Greek taught you in the House of Themistius?"

I grinned with delight. "You took me by surprise! You sail to Rome with us?"

"To Alexandria. My trip with you was my last from Rome and will remain so until the barbarians are contained. A caravan would not likely slip past Alaric."

"What a lucky happenchance this is, that we should sail on the same ship."

"Happenchance?" His dark eyes danced. "Not at all. I was making arrangements to go to Alexandria when I heard that the grandson of Themistius was also going—and taking his dwarf along with him. I thought to myself: I've not seen that rascally vagabond these two years—what pleasant company for a long voyage—I wonder how he fares? You look well, rarest of gems."

"I am. And you? You look prosperous."

"Yes, and getting soft and dull. I need travel. And trade. I've had a long rest, but now I look forward to bringing a caravan of camels up the eastern provinces. Ah, Egypt, Arabia, Palestine, Syria, Cappadocia, Galatia! I've relatives in all of these. I believe this time I will bring home a wife. And you—you return to Rome at last."

"Do not forget Athens and Alexandria. I will be a man of the world by Rome."

"That you will," he agreed, looking me over. "How you've grown since I last saw you!"

I scoffed. "You know very well I have not grown, Khafar!"

The Arabian grinned. "Would you rather I said you have aged? How old are you now, O Ancient One?"

"Twenty-one this month. And I have got a beard, too."

Khafar leaned forward and squinted. "Where?"

"Shaved, of course. Apollonius allows no 'barbarian affectations' in *his* House," I mimicked.

"Of course. Tell me, I did well by you, selling you into the House of Themistius, did I not?"

"Aye, well enough."

"You are happy, then?"

What a question! I regarded him briefly and shrugged.

"I am neither happy nor unhappy, Khafar-Ra. I simply accept my life," I said, gazing profoundly out to sea, feeling every inch a proper Stoic.

"That is no answer."

I sighed. "It's the best answer I can give. What does the happiness of one little slave matter to this world? One tiny stitch in a magnificent tapestry? I must be content that my stitch is necessary."

Khafar looked as though he might say something contradictory, but he kept his peace. We watched black clouds overtaking the ship across the eerie green-grey sky that loomed above the fitful sea.

"Dominicus!" old Endymodes called. "What are you doing up here? Come below before the storm strikes!"

Long resigned to obedience, I turned. My robe flapped in the wind like the sails overhead.

Khafar clutched the rail with one hand and bowed. "Until later, Dominicus."

The sound of the name from his mouth struck me with distaste.

"Dominicus is a slave," I told him. "I wish you would not call me so."

"Ah. Perhaps Dominico the vagabond is not so content as he thinks."

I shook my head. "Dominico no longer exists. That life is gone, Khafar."

"Then what shall I call you, my friend?"

I thought a second, smiled briefly, and shrugged. "Dominic, I suppose. Just Dominic. 'Tis my name, you know."

"*Dominicus!*" Endymodes screeched.

The Arabian dipped his head. "Until later, Dominic."

I waved and scuttled across the pitching deck.

The storm sped quickly past, but it was rough while it lasted, and frightening, too, from the innards of the rolling ship. I felt I would rather ride the storm on deck, at least to see the great waves that struck so suddenly, but I feared I would be swept overboard. Besides, the sailors wanted no passengers underfoot while they battled rough waters.

Indeed, I soon learned to stay clear of the sailors altogether, for they jeered and called me runt and threatened to throw me as a tasty peace offering to any sea monsters we might encounter. I had no doubt that they would, should the occasion arise, for they seemed a hard and callous lot and unlikely to feel any compunction for doing so, except that I belonged to their employer. With the unpleasant possibility in mind that they might just claim I was swept overboard, above deck I at first stayed close to either Alexandros, Endymodes, or, more often, Khafar. Otherwise the voyage went well. Given the queasiness I have often felt in my stomach over various matters, I was happily surprised that I did not become seasick at all. I had little to do but fetch things for Alexandros, and see to his wardrobe and rubdown, and we all spent a good deal of time lounging on deck and enjoying the increasingly pleasant weather.

Excitedly, we assembled at the railing when our ship sailed into the Hellespont. The strait is named so because here Helle fell from the back of the golden ram and drowned. The sea narrows into a long channel, running forty miles from the Marmara to the Aegean Sea. It is never wider than five miles from shore to shore. Endymodes pointed out the place, only a mile wide, where Xerxes, the Persian king, built his famed floating bridge of boats and marched his army across the Hellespont to invade Thrace. Here also ended the tale of Hero and Leander when both drowned.

Our passage was swift, as the current runs toward the Aegean. We were fortunate that capricious winds and treacherous fogs did not endanger our progress and that we were allowed a clear view of the cliffs on the northern shore and a glimpse of fabled Illium to the south—at least where the city once stood; there is nothing there now.

Emerging full into the Aegean Sea we passed the isles of Imbros, Lemnos, and Tenedos, turning our sails south along the coast of Asia. We skirted the rocky heights of Lesbos, where Sappho wrote, then we rounded the isle of Khios and brushed the shores of ancient Ionia where we put in at our first port: Ephesus.

After uncounted days on the sea, it felt strange to walk the plank to the dock and to exchange our sea-legs for land-legs just when we had gotten used to them, but we were excited to see Ephesus. The city is built on a level green plain dotted with steep hills, a river valley meeting distant mountains. This country is the birthplace of Apollo and Artemis, and the Amazons dwelt here. The long, rocky mountain of Coressus is one of the places Pan is said to have lurked. Some say Homer was born here. It is a place brimming with history and legend.

Ephesus is beautiful, also, full of marble arches, aqueducts, columns, and statuary. In this amphitheater Saint Paul preached Christianity and was shouted down by enraged worshippers of Artemis. They imprisoned him on a hill near the sea. The city claims that Saint John fought wild beasts in the amphitheater, though that he could have survived is a wonder to me. It is also said that the Virgin Mary spent her last days a few miles from here, and Mary Magdalen also.

Most wonderful of all are the ruins of the Artemision—the glorious Temple of Artemis—most ancient monument to the sister of the sun, mistress of the moon, she who is the fertile mother and also the virgin huntress.

Sadly, marauding Goths half destroyed the temple about a century ago, and it has never been repaired. Nor will it ever be. Since the edict of Theodosius denying protection to Pagan temples, pieces of the Artemision are being plundered constantly. Once the temple roof rested on one hundred and twenty-eight marble columns, each one towering fifty-feet high. Many of them still stand, their height and symmetry soaring against the blue heavens, somehow appearing airy and delicate in contrast to their ponderous size. The remainder are fallen and broken or rolled away in pieces for less lofty uses. The graceful statue of Artemis still sits amidst the ruins, her timeless face as yet untouched by the destruction around her. Her bosom, however, has been brutally desecrated by outraged Christians who took offense at her multitudinous, munificent breasts.

Some say that is why the sea is receding from the harbor. The ravaged Artemis has abandoned Ephesus and taken her blessings with her. Now each year the city constructs longer and longer wooden piers to extend the docks across the desicating harbor. Pagans say the sea is the milk of the goddess, and now the city will die for destroying the source of her bounty.

We set our sails to sea again! We swept past Samos and Ikaria and west across the Aegean Sea. We skirted myriads of islands, all with fabulous names, wonderful tales, and wild, rocky coasts—an archipelago of Greek history and story scattered sporadically upon the clear blue sea.

At last we sailed into the Achaean Provinces. With Mount Hymettus far to our right we put in at the port of Piraeus, from whose docks we could just discern, gleaming in the sun, the square-topped shape of the Acropolis.

Athens! The city covers the stony hills and plain like one vast, intricate sculpture. Though the sun would be sinking soon, we would have nothing but to journey straight along the avenue of the Long Walls into the city. Even Alexandros could not help being awed by the mother-city of the civilized world.

I can scarcely describe it. The moon shone full and silver in a blue-black sky. The Acropolis shimmered resplendent with moonglow. As we ascended the steps to its summit, the most beautiful, the most perfect structure on Earth rose before us: the Parthenon! Within, the fifty-foot statue of Athene, wrought of ivory and gold, appears to live and breathe in shimmering torchlight. Without, ancient Athenians are carved in frozen procession in honor of Athene. Sculpture is everywhere, delicately painted in gold, blue, and red. Below, on the level plain, the moonstruck temples and buildings glow with a silent, pristine beauty. No, I cannot truly describe it. One must go and see for oneself.

We spent some days in Athens, following in the footsteps of the philosophers and Saint Paul (so far we have been nowhere that the apostle has not been before us). We declined to visit any more of the Grecian penninsula, for news had it that Alaric's Goths marched toward Athens, and no one could say for certain what their next move might be. They had already destroyed the Temple of Ceres at Eleusis. So we set sail south through more of the Cyclades and into the Cretan Sea.

Out here in the vast depths, the sea sparkled with a deep blue that paled the clearest sky. And when the sun sank red and fiery behind a cloudy horizon the whole western waters might have been liquified gold. Gentle waves and favorable winds provided peaceful, dreamlike hours of musing upon the waters. Then Crete glided into view.

Our eyes searched the mountainous island peaks to catch a glimpse of Mount Ida, the birthplace of Zeus. Such a forbidding, desolate place for a god to be born! We passed the city of Knossos where Minos sent Theseus to be devoured by the Minotaur. That was in the days of her glory; the Palace and the Labyrinth are lost now—some say destroyed by earthquake and fire, some say by the gods.

We took the long voyage around to Alexandria, returning to Asia by way of Rhodes—where the hundred-foot tall Colossus of Apollo no longer stands—sailed past ancient Xanthus, famed for its exquisite marble, and landed at beautiful Attalia, miles of sanded beaches the like of which I had never seen. Next we sailed the coast between Cilicia and the Isle of Cyprus, so near to each other that we could see both shores from our ship. Here we spied a Roman galley striking for the island. Its decks seemed overly crowded with men. As it drew near we saw that they sat chained together in a mass.

"Slaves to the copper mines," said Khafar. "Syrian, likely. Some Armenian and Arabian perhaps."

I knew of the famed copper mines of Cyprus. As I watched the slave ship pass with its fated cargo, I counted myself most fortunate. Many times my uncle had threatened to sell me into the salt mines of the Rhineland. Indeed, at any point in my life I could have suffered toiling underground or begging the streets in a wretched state. Instead, here I stood enjoying a leisurely cruise to Egypt with but minimal duties to pay my passage. Silently I thanked the gods (if there be gods,) all of them, Christian and Pagan, for granting me as untroubled and clement a life as they have thus far.

"I wonder," I mused, watching the ship melt into the shoreline, "do you think we have choices in life, Khafar-Ra? Do we decide our own fates?"

"You wonder much, little gem. What brings this on?"

"That ship of slaves. This voyage. Your presence." I shrugged. "I guess I've been thinking about it for a while."

"Do we have choice?" murmured Khafar. "It seems so."

"Yes it does. It seems I myself decided whether to stay in Constantinople or come on this voyage. Yet now I wonder if I could ever have chosen any differently than I did, given who I am and my very nature. On my life, Khafar, I could not have said, 'No thanks, I'll stay.' Do you understand what I'm trying to say?"

His reflective black face turned from the horizon toward me. "Yes, I know exactly what you say, Dominic. Given the time and the circumstance, given your experience and knowledge, and given your psychic state of the moment, you had only one avenue open to you. You could only choose exactly as you did."

I leaned my head against the rail and grinned up at him. "I'm glad *you* understand it, O All-Knowing One. Now enlighten me."

He remained contemplative. "Ah, but I'm not sure I *do* understand it—not any more than yourself. I am merely reminded of when I brought you to Constantinople—when I could have let you go in the mountains you were longing toward. Many times since I have wondered why I did not."

"You have?" I blinked in amazement.

"I have. I think, my friend, given the same choice today, I would set you free."

I stared long at his serious face.

"I was very . . . hurt over that." Then I shrugged. "But business is business."

"I could have afforded it."

Now I realized he was more distressed over the incident than I.

"Now, look you, Khafar. I was hurt *then*. Today I'm glad you did not. Else I wouldn't have spent two years learning in the House of Themistius. Else I would never have known the wonderful, old philosopher at all." I winked up at him. "Else I'd not be standing here gazing upon this beautiful sea and talking choices and paradoxes with you, now would I?"

The Arabian regarded me for many judicious seconds. Slowly he smiled.

"It *is* a paradox, as you say. I am content to hear directly from you that I made the right choice, Dominic."

"If you made a choice at all, eh?" I reminded him impishly. "Given the time, the circumstance, and your psychic state of the moment, remember?"

"I've assumed I was in the grip of Darkness when I did not free you. Now I wonder if it wasn't the Light guiding my hand."

"Mayhap there is no difference."

He shook his head. "Let's not argue *that*, jewel of jewels. We'll be at it from here to Alexandria."

I sighed sagaciously. "'Tis pointless anywise. The answer is likely just another paradox that cannot be unraveled."

For several moments we watched the far eastern shoreline, each of us lost in his own thoughts.

"I wonder, Dominic," Khafar said at length, "if you are glad to be here today, then what does that make of your cousin's decision to sell you to me? You were very bitter. . . ."

"I am *still* bitter," I cut in.

"So bitter you would not speak of him. . . ."

"Nor do I wish to now. Khafar, you are rapidly ruining my day."

"You are still hurt."

"I'm *angry*," I corrected, tight-lipped and glaring.

Khafar queried me softly. "Yet you would not stand here now if he had not. What makes his choice any different from any other?"

I struck the rail with my fist. "He had no *right!* It was treachery! He . . . he had no *right!*" I repeated in a frazzled whisper.

"Perhaps he truly had no choice, as he believed, as we have been speculating. Perhaps he could not have chosen differently, given the time, the circumstance. . . ."

"Not fair," I muttered, pressing my eyes wearily against my knuckles, fingers locked tight around the railing. "You are not playing fair, Khafar."

"What makes his failing any worse than another man's?"

"Why do you defend him?"

"I do not defend him. I just remember that you carried so much bitterness and would not speak of it. . . ."

"I don't wish to speak of it *now*, either."

"You have not forgiven him."

"*No*, I have not forgiven him!" I shouted, whirling on the stubborn Arabian furiously. "*I cannot forgive him!*"

"Or you do not wish to?" he provoked mildly.

Now I turned my back to Khafar and clenched a fist in frustration. "I don't know! Maybe *I* don't have any choice about *that*. Maybe I cannot even *wish* to forgive. What's it to you, anyway?"

His voice came to me subdued, almost lost in the slapping of sails and waves.

"I merely hoped, as a friend, that you had been able to unburden your heart. That's all. We can drop it, Dominic."

Slowly I turned back to face him. "No. Not yet. I'll tell you

218

the difference. I trusted him, and what he did broke all the bonds of trust. Oh, I know what you are saying, Khafar, and I even realize that possibly you are right. But what my head knows has no power over what my heart remembers . . . or feels. Aye, I am hurt and angry and bitter—and I cannot help it. Furthermore, I don't even *care* that I cannot help it. And now—*now* we can drop the subject for good, if you don't mind."

The Arabian dipped his head in a gesture halfway between a bow and a nod.

"Dropped, Dominic."

We stayed overlong at Antioch, where the scholarly gentlemen looked me over as though I were some sort of specimen they would like to dissect. We stopped briefly at Tyre, where the royal purple is made from snails and from which the excellent wood of the cedar is shipped across the Empire. I have heard, though, that the grand old cedars in the Lebanon Mountains are felled faster than new ones grow to replace them, so that the supply diminishes yearly. Rome, I'm sure, will not be satisfied until the mountains are denuded.

Tyre is on a peninsula. It used to be an island. Then Alexander the Great built a tremendous causeway of rubble over which he marched his army and war machines. That was some seven hundred years ago. The causeway still joins the island to the mainland.

As we sailed down the coast of Palestine, Khafar-Ra recounted for me the Jews' struggles with the Romans. I gazed to that dry and forbidding shore as he spoke. In my mind I saw the Jerusalem Temple burned, the city leveled, every last survivor taken captive to slavery or for the games, and nearly a thousand men, women, and children dying by their own hands at the fortress of Masada rather than be taken alive by Romans. A few years later the Jews rebelled again. They were taken by force from Jerusalem and forbidden to re-enter the city. A great many, Khafar told me, now live in Alexandria.

Alexandria! The immortal city of Alexander the Great! I begin to feel that Alexander and Saint Paul had been everywhere in the Empire, for we go nowhere that one or both did not precede us and did some spectacular feat. I feel that we follow their heels and have just missed them at each stopover. We will catch up with them soon, no doubt.

The evening before we reached Alexandria, we could see the beacon of the lighthouse on Pharos Island even though we were still far away. Sailors claim the light can be found for hundreds of miles. We docked at Alexandria in bright sunshine. The first half of our voyage was ended; we would winter in Alexandria. Before we debarked, Khafar and I said goodbye, since our paths would not likely cross in this huge city—he guesting in the merchants' quarter and I in the royal quarter, the Brucheum. Khafar was pensive.

"I will miss you, little gem. This has been a magnificent voyage. I wish there were some way to continue our acquaintance."

"I know. Endymodes told me."

He eyed me sharply. "Told you what?"

"That you approached Alexandros and made an offer of three thousand solidi for me—and Alexandros turned you down flat."

"You weren't to know that."

"Look you, Khafar, I've plenty of masters. I don't need another. I rather prefer you as a friend."

"I would have freed you."

I smiled. "I believe you would. But what good to be free in Alexandria? How would I get home?"

"I could have taken you. What good to go home a slave?"

I sighed. "Better than never at all. Anywise, it's a moot question, isn't it? Alexandros refused your offer. Besides, Rome's a big city, Khafar, easy to get lost in—or out of."

He looked at me askance—a mock scandalized expression. "I have not heard this—no! Still, I would expect it of you, O Reckless One."

Now Endymodes and Alexandros approached along the deck.

"Good fortune, Dominic, in your endeavors. The Holy Lights go with you."

That familiar, elaborate bow: would I ever see it again? I returned a flamboyant bow of my own.

"Goodbye, Khafar-Ra. Sweet water and serenity be yours, and may our paths cross again one day."

XXIV

Take an obelisk of somber Egyptian architecture, carve upon it a frieze of graceful Hellenic design, gild it over with a thin veneer of Roman vulgarity, and Alexandria is the result. The people are as diverse as the city's origins—folk as black as charred wood or as yellow as ocher mingle with the subtler shades of cinnamon brown and apricot pink. Piercing, hawk-browed features and slanting, almond eyes contrast boldly with the classic profiles hailing from the northern Mediterranean shores. Conspicuously rare here are the tall, yellow-haired Germanni, and all those I have seen are slaves, descendants of captives in old wars.

In Alexandria I spent a good deal of my time in the library and museum—in what is left of them anyway. The ill-fated Greater Alexandrian Library has been burned so many times, it is a wonder it is still standing. Caesar burned it once, and Aurelian destroyed much of it, but many of the scrolls were saved and many more replaced by Antony. Nearly fifty thousand were kept in the Serapeum—Temple of Serapis. I would like to have seen it—the giant statue of Jupiter Serapis guarding the Daughter Library within his temple—but I am five years too late. Theophilus, Archbishop of Alexandria, led a mob of Christians who toppled the statue and burned the Temple of Serapis along with most of its scrolls. There was fought a bloody battle as Pagans struggled to save their burning temple. Librarians plunged into the inferno and carried out as many of the great books as they dared, but untold quantites of irreplaceable literature was lost to the world forever. Now the Greater Library and Museum do but hint at their former wonders, and all that marks the site of the Serapeum is the impavid red granite Column of Diocletion, like a ninety-nine foot spear thrust upright into the Earth, pointed into the Sky.

Endymodes immediately enrolled Alexandros under the tutelage of the distinguished scholars in a private college near the Museum. Me, he put to work in the Library; he paid the copyright fees, purchased ink and papyrus, and enrolled me in the dictation sessions scribing a volume of Pliny the Younger. It was interesting at first—I kept my hands busy and my mind occupied, and I became quite adept at keeping up with the reader—but in less than a handful of weeks my attention began to wander. There was such a wealth of fascinating information around every turn of the massive, lofty-spaced building! Soon I was on the roam for any sort of diversion I might happen upon. I was in the right place for it, too.

The Library and Museum occupy the same complex, part of which is "under repair," though I never saw evidence of any actual work going on. It is neither deserted nor quiet. Scribes are at writing desks copying manuscripts for themselves, patrons, or masters. In one wing several voices drone on morning to noon, afternoon to evening, reading from scrolls to roomfuls of busy scribes who hastily record every word on papyrus; they or their employers pay well for the privilege of transcribing not only the classics but the newest works on a multitude of subjects. There are private nooks, too, for studying and scribing on one's own.

Across the foyer from the Library is the Museum—the most complete forum of history's greatest minds. This is where the mathematicians and geographers taught, where Euclid perfected geometry, where Eratosthenes calculated the circumference of the Earth to be of immense girth, where Hipparchus mapped the Heavens, where Hero and Archimedes devised their mechanics, where Herophilus explored the anatomy of condemned criminals (whom I hope were already dead when he did so). The Museum is brimful of fascinating charts, maps, diagrams, and crackpots. Some fired-up evangel is always there orating or arguing over this or that; it's an extremely noisy and wonderfully diverting place.

When I grew bored scribing history and philosophy, I used the dictation fees for my own interests. I discovered many maps of the known world by various historians and geographers. I paid the copy-fees and spread several of them around me on a drawing table. It was a long, meticulous, fascinating task, for the maps did not all agree. It was frustrating, too, to let Africa disappear into unknown territory, likewise India and East Asia, for all that land must go *somewhere*. Still, I took a varied handful of maps and drew them into one, and I was justly proud of my handiwork.

As I took a close look at my map, I saw that I had journeyed almost halfway around the Mediterranean Sea—the Mid Earth Sea—center of the Empire—center of the world. Small as it looked drawn on parchment, I remembered how many months journey it was from Rome to Constantinople and how rugged was the terrain represented by that flat parchment. Placing a finger near Augusta Treverorum in Gaul, I traced my path thus far, coming to rest at Alexandria, Egypt. I smiled wistfully. *Would that Papa might see me now!* Then I traced the sea route from Africa to Rome, coming nearly full circle! Gaul looked only a short hop from Rome, but I reminded myself that those lines on parchment were in reality the Alps and I must either cross them or go around. My imaginary journey went no further, for beyond reaching Gaul my mind could not envision. What did I expect to find? What was I looking for?

While I was pondering the future, an unlooked-for incident touched upon me in Alexandria and turned my mind toward pursuing yet another path of understanding. It happened at the burning of a household of Arians by Athanasians. I came upon the riotous torching of the house one evening on my way home. The fire was just beginning to kindle, for the mob still shouted abuse and flung torches into the house; the members of the household still fought the mounting flames or fled with precious possessions. A young lady stumbled into the crowded street. In her arms she carried a large cylindrical basket, clutching it tightly. The crowd would not let her pass, but tripped and pushed and shoved her until the basket was wrenched from her arms and fell rolling under their feet. The lid shook loose and the contents spilled out across the pavement.

What valuables did the girl rescue from the flames? Jewelry? Clothes? No, nought but scrolls! Scrolls were strewn into the street. In terror and anguish the young lady fled through the crowd. They were being easy tonight—no one caught and threw her into the flames, no one stoned or flogged her. It was enough for the crowd to burn her home and triumphantly wave aloft the precious basket and fling it back into the fire. Scattered remnants of the scrolls were trampled and shredded beneath their sandals, but one bulky parchment flew from the doomed basket, tumbled and rolled across the street, and came to rest just at my feet.

My scavenger instincts still ran deep. Without hesitation I snatched up the scroll and concealed it in the loose folds of my robe. I backed slowly away from the scene of riot and flame and hurried home with my prize. I carried it boldly into the guest house, bid goodnight to the vestibulum slave, and slipped into the penuria where my little mattress nestled midst our baggage. I struck my lamp, untied the cord, and unrolled the parchment to see what I had found.

Several scrolls were rolled together. They were the Gospel as Recorded by Matthew. I had never read any Christian works—the House of Themistius did not have them—but I thought I knew what they said, having heard much of them in my childhood.

I studied the Greek lettering. The hand was small and close and precise. My eyes skimmed down the page. Though I had not intended to, I burned a week's allotment of oil and read the half of Matthew that night. The gospel was still the story I remembered. I found written there no trace of argument over divinities, trinities, doctrines, or heresies. Instead I read the wonder-filled story of a man of God, told with simple eloquence. The tale let Jesus speak for himself—and very outspoken he was—in succinct statements and expressive parables.

Puzzled, I rerolled the scrolls. I must have gotten hold of a rare gospel, I concluded. The others must contain the articles of dispute that set Christians to killing one another.

I slept restlessly that night, having too little time to sleep before sunrise. I greeted the sun with the paean to Apollo, as taught me by Themistius, and snatched a handful of olives and a chunk of bread from the kitchen. Then came my duties to Alexandros: replacing the garments he threw out of his wardrobe looking for something to wear, shaving his face close and clean, attending him through a grumpy breakfast. Today was Sun's Day, and he had plans for an outing with fellow students. The Library was closed on Sun's Day, a day holy to Christ and Apollo and Horus, but Endymodes had me scribe a letter for him to Apollonius because his own writing was becoming shaky and nigh unreadable. When at last I found myself free, I betook me to a secluded corner of the garden, unrolled the scrolls, and finished the Gospel of Matthew.

The story affected me strangely. So filled with tales of love and forgiveness and mercy, I decided Matthew's must be a minor gospel and not given much credence by the Church. The other gospels must contain the commandments to persecute and revile

224

those who believe differently. If Jesus recommended it, he never mentioned it within Matthew's hearing, and that Matthew was sharp—he scarcely missed a word. And the passage that struck me in the gut, unaccountably blurred my eyes, was the one in which this most-wise Jesus said we must forgive our brothers—seventy times seven if need be.

I thought of Mikato.

I did not feel forgiving, only angry and bitterly sorry. I knew I should not hold his desperate act against him all the days of his life—nor mine—but my heart was unwilling to forget the hurt he had done me. Tears streaming because my heart felt cold, because I couldn't forgive my brother—could scarcely even think of him as brother—I murmured my first prayer to the Christian Lord since I was a little boy.

"Forgive me my anger, for I cannot be rid of it. Forgive me the bitter feelings I cannot loose. *You* can forgive him, no doubt, but I am not finding it so easy. Help me. . . ."

I felt no differently after I prayed, except that I knew I had asked for that which I never thought I would want. I wanted a heart free to remember Mikato without rage or accusations, free to remember him as I had loved him. I locked the prayer deep within my heart, along with the hurt which bestirred uneasily in its dark catacomb.

And didn't I feel like a thief? The manuscript was not mine.

And a fool? Alexandros caught me in the garden.

"Say, Dominicus, what is it you're doing, hiding out here?"

I had been reading and reflecting longer than I imagined, for here he was back and the sun going down.

"Nothing. I'm not *hiding*."

"Reading again? What now?"

Alexandros reached for the scrolls, but I snatched them away.

"Ah-ah-ah," he admonished. "Hand them over."

"No. They're not mine."

"Stolen, then. Give me them *now!*"

"No."

I saw I made a mistake. Alexandros narrowed his eyes.

"You'll not refuse me, slave. Now or ever."

He charged over, grabbed my wrist in one hand, and struck me backhanded across the face with the other. He struck me twice, thrice, four times before he took the scrolls and let me crumple to the pavement.

He smiled omnipotently and unrolled the scrolls. "Now I will see what it is you hide in the . . . gospels? Dominicus, you're reading gospels?" He laughed derisively. "I wouldn't 've suspected *you* of Christian sentiments. Ah, this is rich!" He raised his voice to a shout. "Endymodes! Endymodes, come here, you must see this! The prize pupil!" He laughed nastily at me again as I stood slowly on my feet, tasting blood and feeling a buzzing in my head.

Endymodes hobbled into the garden on his staff, holding aloft an oil lamp in the dusky shadows.

"See, here," Alexandros smirked. "Your clever little dwarf reads gospels, Christian gospels, secretly, in the garden. What do you make of that, Endymodes?"

Endymodes blinked at me, startling at my damaged face.

"Well, I suppose Dominicus may read what he likes. He reads a great many things."

"He's not going to read this one. Hand me the lamp."

"No, don't!" I cried.

Alexandros stopped short of putting the scrolls into the lamp and cocked an eyebrow at me quizzically, dangerously.

"Why should I not destroy this doggerel?"

"It isn't doggerel. It's a good work, well written. And old, too, scribed in an obsolete hand. It's probably worth something."

"To you?"

"There's truth in it." I looked appealingly to Endymodes and back to Alexandros. "You shouldn't destroy it."

"Dominicus is right," spoke Endymodes, "the manuscript is old and not to be lightly cast aside."

Alexandros glanced from one to the other of us, then with a cool smile he set the end of the scrolls aflame.

"As did Christians to the Sarapeum, so do I to their gospel."

Endymodes and I watched it burn in silence.

"For all you know, Alexandros," I finally said, "that manuscript could have been scripted by the hand of Saint Matthew himself."

Alexandros dropped the last of the ashes and turned to me with mocking, stern deliberation.

"And now for you, Dominiculus, and your defiance. You will not say, 'No, Alexandros,' to me. I am your master—" he snatched Endymodes' staff from his crooked hands and descended steadily upon me, "you will not forget it."

XXV

 I stared straight up at the camel's swaying head. The homely visage stared back down at me from a ridiculously long neck, like a cobra hovering over a mesmerized mouse. And the beast had not even stood up yet! The long knobby legs were still folded beneath the hulking body.

"Surely you don't expect me to *ride* that!" I said to the dragoman standing beside the camel's head.

He grinned. "There'll be nothing to fear once you are on her back. Or would you rather walk behind her?"

I shook my head and glanced doubtfully over to see Alexandros and Endymodes being helped to mount their beasts. Before I could reconsider my own ascent, the dragoman seized me and flung me onto the carpeted camel's humped back, where I clung for my life while the creature immediately heaved its rear-end into the air and struggled to its feet. I felt like I rode a mountain in an earthquake.

After I grew accustomed to the jerky motion of the beast and the long drop to the dirt, I looked back toward the Nile, its meandering blue waters emitting a living green aura of vegetation from its banks. Coming thus far upriver by barge, our little party now rode astride a caravan of hairy hills lumbering along a dusty, palm-shaded road, heading west into the neverending desert.

In the distance three perfectly geometric mountains floated above a hazy horizon, seeming no more substantial nor connected to the Earth than the bank of clouds that stretched away behind them. The Pyramids! The closer we traveled, the more solid, grander, more indescribably gigantic they became. That men should undertake to build mountains!

I gazed upward in awe toward the peaks of limestone. What were they? Tombs? Monuments? The Pharaohs they were built for are long gone to dust—only silent stone remains. Still, they command a bemused admiration. I guessed each one of those pyramids must have used up the lives of a million slaves who toiled and died under the whip of Egypt—so that now thousands of years later we might come and stare—and wonder why. Did one of those laborers ever step back and run an eye along the vast edge of a pyramid and call it his handiwork? Who could say?

We looked upon the face of the Sphinx also that day. It did not look back at us—it scarcely noticed us. Etched in gargantuan blocks of stone, head raised loftily to capture the sun, eyes far-watching to the blue horizon, the Sphinx appeared as ageless as the Earth. Our lives are as brief as the flash of a firefly in its impassive face. It appears to ponder the deepest secrets of the universe, but I recall that mortals fashioned the Sphinx, too. Without human hands, this mysterious creature would be so many chunks of rock. The wisdom written in its calm features belongs not to the gods, but to humankind.

I imagined time as the Sphinx might view it—circles of change as sure and true as the revolutions of the stars: days, seasons, years, lives, nations, empires—all coming and going, rising and falling, on and on. . . . We call Rome eternal. How have we the temerity to believe it? Wrought by accident or design, in the unrecorded dawn of history the face of time became etched on stone—perhaps the ages themselves etched it there. I stood transfixed in my little moment of time and looked into infinity. Soon, soon, I would be no more, and the Earth would never notice I had come and gone.

That evening, to my map I secretly added three triangles and an outline of the Sphinx at rest, as if to say, Dominic, too, was here.

We sailed from Alexandria in the spring.

News was not promising. General Gildo of Africa was in revolt; Gildo refused to ship African grain to Rome; Stilicho sent Gildo's brother with an army to make him see reason. Meanwhile, a heretical sect took advantage of Gildo's revolt to attempt its own overthrow of Rome's religious authority in Africa. Western Africa was all battleground. And if no grain was shipped to Rome, there would be no bread. If there was no bread the plebs would be hungry. And if the Roman mob was hungry . . .

We sailed anyway.

My spirits soared to the rhythm of sea and sky where vagabond clouds were driven, like our sails, on the wings of the wind. I watched sun, moon, stars, and clouds pass silently overhead and leave no trace upon the motionless sky. Behind our ship the waters merged ceaselessly, leaving no trace to mark our passage upon their restless surface. Bemusing, too, I thought, that to find one's way upon the sea, one must map the stars. And to gaze up on a clear night from a lonely vessel tossed upon wind-driven waves, and to rove the slow-wheeling stars, to peer into the face of infinity—so visible, yet so unreachable—makes one wonder at a universe so immense that the eyes cannot contain it, and the mind can comprehend it only in fragments. Yet the paths of the stars were as familiar to me as strokes drawn by my own hand upon my map. Each constellation rose over the whispering dark horizon in unvarying order, telling its own tale as clearly as if words were written in stars.

We sailed into a storm—a rip-roarer of a storm with gales and squalls, thunder and lightning—which tossed us capriciously from wave to wave. No place in the vessel, nothing we touched, was not wet and cold and clammy. Endymodes lay in the chill cabin wrapped in a damp blanket, sneezing and shivering, sick with fever and a hoarse cough that rattled uneasily in his chest. I had difficulty keeping charcoal burning to warm the dank room and heat his wine. Alexandros, huddled in his own cabin, demanded the same services from me, though he was not ill.

At last we sailed through the Straits at Messana into the Tyrrhenian Sea. We followed the warm coast of Italia and looked upon the new green of a brilliant Roman spring. We glided past Mount Vesuvius. Three hundred years ago the volcano had erupted ash and fire, burying two entire cities, not a trace left of them save a few lines of Pliny. Soon we sighted the red roofs of Ostia glowing in the sunset.

When I left Rome three years ago, I was a boy, unlettered and free. I returned a man, a scholar, and a slave. Would I trade all my learning to regain my freedom? I didn't know. Sometimes my head buzzed with words like a hive of frantic bees and gave me no peace. Other times the realms inside my head were all the peace I could find. And the knowledge was mine, not to be snatched away from me so easily as freedom.

How strange to come to Rome again. How wonderful to hear the Latin tongue! My pulse quickened as we crossed forums and streets I knew intimately. Every building, every statue, looked just as I remembered it. But different now. The city had not changed—I had. I saw Rome with new eyes. The grand architecture I once thought so beautiful now looked ponderous and ostentatious. The metropolitan excitement now seemed like aimless frenzy. I had been too long at sea.

Since the grain shortage was not imminent—was merely a bothersome possibility—Rome raised the goods' tax on outlying provinces to forestall it. Should the campaign in Africa go badly, well . . . Rome was beginning to feel the blows as food prices catapulted. And a curious law had come into effect since I was last here.

For a city that adopted fashions and fads overnight, only to discard them just as quickly, Rome had taken an unusually patriotic interest in clothing. When last I saw Roman gentry, barbarian trousers were the rage. The young ladies—and some of the gentlemen—wore their hair long, gold and henna dyed, and woven into elaborate topknots and beaded braids. Young gents stalked abroad in colorful trousers with sandals laced around up to the knees. Ladies wore soft kidskin slippers laced with chain and leather thongs up bare legs and long, slitted tunics, and both sexes flashed bronze, glass-inlaid arm-and neck-bands of Germanni design.

But no more. The new law was stringent and explicit: Barbarian trousers and beards (especially beards), braids, jewelry, or other articles of barbarian design were forbidden, and not a blond head did I see, save on an occasional slave. (Chestnut brown and Egyptian black were the colors tasteful this season.) Lawbreakers were punished with permanent exile from the city. Rome was uneasy, and there was a growing anti-Germanni feeling within the populace. The Senate did not dismiss lightly encroachments of the western borders by barbarian tribes, nor the steady advance across the Empire by Alaric, King of the Goths. And it galled Rome to depend on barbarian soldiers in the legions to protect her from tribes that might be their cousins. Aye, Rome was uneasy.

We moved into apartments off Trajan's Baths because Alexandros wished to be near the center of the city. The baths were elegant and spacious. The pools steamed with noisy splashing and shouting—naked men gawking at me in my sweet little tunic, and me gawking back at them, perfumed dandies flexing their muscles and parading up and down like prize wrestlers before a match. I hated oiling and scraping Alexandros between his dips in the pools; he would never be satisfied and made disparaging remarks at me to make the other boys laugh. He was seventeen and willful and arrogant and witty, and the lads loved him.

Endymodes enrolled him in the University of Rome under five tutors in six basic courses: rhetoric, philosophy, history, geometry, thesis, and grammar. Alexandros attended classes from early morning to noon; afternoons he studied in the university scriptorium and whiled hours at the baths; evenings he dined out.

Dinner parties were not too bad at first. Each gentleman gave a formal dinner for six to twelve friends, expecting reciprocal invitations. Every guest brought along his own slave to serve his food, fill his cup, peel his grapes, wipe his fingers, lace his sandals—all those things too inelegant to do for oneself. Alexandros liked to show me off, his dwarf who could juggle the dinnerware and tell tall tales, and I didn't mind as long as we were in genteel company, for there was interesting talk around the tables as the boys lounged on couches and we slaves stood behind their elbows ready to jump to their bidding. But gradually Alexandros gravitated into a crowd of wealthy young sots, whose entertainments were of a cruder sort. They ran afoul of as many of the university rules as one humanly could in one season: drunkenness, gambling, gaming, whoring, public vulgarity. The hosts of Alexandros's parties fell into a competition to discover new diversions. A midnight excursion to a brothel left we slaves cooling our heels on the street with cold torches while the revelers cavorted within. (I never saw Clarissa. We walked down her old street once. The balcony was still down, the buildings condemned, vagrants living in the derelict shells.) A drunken afternoon at the circus betting on chariot races left Alexandros broke for the week because with loud loyalty he bet on whites every time and every time they lost by miles. A stealthy day at the Colosseum left me sick, though I did not watch I could smell the blood and hear the blows and the cries of the spectators and the wounded. An outing to the theater sank to an excuse to shout abuse and throw eggs at the performers.

I needed no reminding that I performed on this very stage not so very long ago. It rankled me to sit and watch my boorish master fling eggs at actors on a stage where I once tumbled and bowed midst applause and cheers—though the play *was* exceptionally bad, even for Rome's usual puerile and ribald exodes. The plebeian audience possesses neither the patience nor the passion for an Orestes or an Oedipus. Yet I recalled with pride that the audiences had thrown no eggs at us! The dazzling vagabond troupe! Then the sadness shadowed my heart. Those joyous days, those wonderful people, were gone forever. I must not think of them, not here, with these louts who would goad me mercilessly if I wept. I swallowed my heartache and stared fixedly at the image of Apollo carved above the far tiers.

Alexandros held his parties in private dining establishments from which he could order a selection of menus and various entertainments. *His* favorite entertainment was gambling at dice and knucklebones. Alexandros was spending and losing extravagant amounts of his generous weekly stipend. He would have bullied Endymodes for more, if Endymodes had not followed Apollonius's precautions and placed the money in trust with a local solicitor who could not be bullied or cajoled.

One night, while drinking and brawling in a gambling house, Alexandros took a wild swing at a gambler who accused him of flipping a bone on the sly to change his throw (which he did, no doubt), but Alexandros missed and was knocked to the floor, where his opponent ground the heel of his sandal into the back of Alexandros's right hand. None of his buddies, of course, leapt to his rescue; they stood back in drunken befuddlement until the proprietor intervened and saved the hand from further damage. Alexandros stumbled home cursing and carrying on so that Endymodes sent me for a physician in the middle of the night. The doctor charged an enormous fee to come tell Alexandros his hand was not broken, only bruised and lacerated. Alexandros avowed the physician was wrong and insisted his hand be bandaged thoroughly. The physician complied and charged another fee for the bandaging.

But Alexandros got his money's worth from that bandage. As far as anyone else was concerned, he warned me, his hand was broken. He took me with him to lectures the next morning, and all humbly and earnestly, told each of his mentors that his hand was badly fractured in fighting off two thieves who attacked him on a dark street. He regretted he would be unable to write for some time, but as he feared his studies would suffer, he asked special permission to bring his scribe to class to write any notes or assignments for him, just until his broken hand mended.

They fell for it. All except the thesis and grammar instructor, who glared suspiciously at the bandaged hand and at me. He glanced sharply at Alexandros and agreed, indeed, that his grammar and composition were sloppy and that he had best do *something* to improve them and, yes, if his hand was truly injured he could use a scribe—and if it was not, he would see him flogged for sloth and mendacity.

I was in. I confess I did not mind the deceit. Attending discourses and classes was no hardship. The most difficult was geometry, requiring my mind to dance in complex patterns and theorems it was not naturally inclined to follow. The most boring was philosophy, for I had studied most of it before. The most instructive was rhetoric, if I could keep my mind on it. But the most wonderful were thesis and grammar. Master Umbrusus Elusius taught both and, ah, how the man could lecture! He was portly, silver-haired, and dignified, and an architect of spoken and written language. He never spoke hesitantly, searching for words, or dryly as other tutors did. No, the words rolled deeply from his diaphragm in cadent phrases like an orator reciting poetry, grammar impeccable, vocabulary fine-tuned. Even the abstractions of which he spoke, the construction of a sentence to the organization of a thesis, astounded and held me spellbound.

As we wrote practice sentences, paragraphs, or extrapolations, Umbrusus stalked from desk to desk and critiqued the work. When he stood over me, even if my neat hand scribed just what Alexandros dictated, each word of criticism or praise I took to heart, though they were not meant for me.

The worst part was spending every morning with Alexandros. At first he dictated lessons to me, enjoying the novel privilege and envious attention he thought it brought him. Of course, when assignments needed to be completed in the scriptorium, he left it to me—he needed his rest before the evening carousals. Soon I engaged him in furious whispered debates in classes over what I would or would not write, for by then I knew more about it than he did and felt justified in insisting I be allowed to do it right, if I must do it. He saw the sense in that, besides, it saved him having to think too hard of an early morning.

Alexandros took pains to convince even his outing companions his right hand was broken—before leaving the apartments he wound the bandage thoroughly across his palm so that he could not bring his fingers together with his thumb—and though some friends may have suspected the ruse, none of them could care whether I did his writing for him or not. He stretched the deceit out for six weeks, but I knew his hand was not hurt more than a few days because I felt the back of it hard more than once within the week. But finally Master Umbrusus made him unbandage it in class and examined it.

"My compliments to your physician, Alexandros," Umbrusus said dryly. "Considering the gravity of your injury, your hand has healed remarkably, without mark or scar. Now, if you wish to ensure full recovery of its dexterity, I suggest exercise."

He plucked the quill from my hand and held it out to Alexandros, who looked as though he might protest.

"Unless," Umbrusus added, staring down at him sternly, "you prefer me to first consult with your physician."

Alexandros jerked his head.

"No sir."

"Write."

Hastily Alexandros took the quill and, in his confusion, forgot even to pretend stiffness as his fingers flew. Umbrusus arched an eyebrow at me, probably accusing me for my complicity in the deception. I tried looking innocent.

"Send your scribe home, Alexandros. If I let him stay, everyone will be bringing scribes to do their thinking for them."

The room burst with laughter, and Alexandros, tight-jawed, sent me out. Reluctantly, I left, avoiding Umbrusus's penetrous stare. I went home and told Endymodes what happened.

What thought Endymodes? He knew of the deception and it galled him, but he was helpless to prevent it. Many mornings he stayed abed with a hoarse cough and rattling breath, and when he did rise, somedays he barely had strength to walk across the room. I heated him garlic soup and steamed his bread over the brazier for supper and brewed him hot, honeyed wine to soothe his throat and help him sleep. It was left to me each dawn to rouse Alexandros, ill-tempered and hung-over, and to take curses and cuffs for my trouble.

When I told Endymodes, he was sitting up on the bed. He thumped his staff on the floor furiously and pulled himself stiffly to his feet.

"The boy will dishonor his family. Before he goes further, his father must be informed of *everything!*" He took the hot mull I proferred him. "Thank you, lad. You know, I hoped to spare him this, but Dominicus, scribe me a letter to Apollonius."

I climbed the stool to the writing table, more than willing, knowing Endymodes's shaky, arthritic hands oft made his writing painful and indecipherable. Endymodes spared Apollonius nothing, from his son's recent deception to the gambling, drinking, and carousing in unsavory company. I wrote every word with bold, vengeful strokes. I had just rolled the parchment and was attending to Endymodes's instructions to deliver it immediately to the shipping clerks and schedule it aboard the next vessel for Constantinople. Unlooked for, Alexandros strode through the door, home long before school should be quit for the day.

We looked guilty as hell.

"Here, now, what are you two up to? What's this?" Alexandros put out a hand for the scroll.

I froze.

"Dominicus!" He snapped his fingers. "Give over!"

Resigned to a difficult scene, I sighed and held the scroll up to him.

As Alexandros unrolled it, Endymodes quavered, "Your father must know! My duty! Every word true and you know it!"

Alexandros read the letter furiously, more purple and rigid with every sweep of his eyes. He shook the letter at us, staring, then he ripped it to shreds. Grabbing up Endymodes's staff, he advanced upon the old man.

"Alexandros!" I yelled, jerking at his tunic. "I wrote it, you steaming sot! The letter is mine!"

He turned his rage on me. "Dominicus! Slimy little sneak! Sewer rat!"

He fetched me a blow alongside the head and knocked me half across the room. Before I could regain my feet, he leapt at me, flailing the stick as if I really were a rat he would kill. In the close apartment there was no escape from his fury, which heightened with every murderous blow—punctuated with hysterical words.

"There—will—be—no—letters—except—I—dictate—them!"

He strode to the parchment box, flung it open, and slapped out a new sheet on the writing table.

"Come up here!"

Reason told me to obey. I climbed dizzily onto the stool and picked up the quill with numbed fingers. Head spinning, I scribed as he directed: how well his studies were going, how cooperative he was, how pleasant the weather. I was so boiling I could have written it in my own blood—literally—but I wrote precisely as he said in a painful script. When I finished, Alexandros whisked it away, perused it suspiciously, and thrust it into the hands of the old tutor.

"Sign it!"

Endymodes looked despairingly at me. My right eye was swelling shut, my nose bleeding, and I sucked blood from a bruised lip. I was not certain I could climb off the stool without falling. With a trembling hand, Endymodes signed the letter. A smirk twisting his face, Alexandros rolled, tied, and sealed the parchment, all in heavy silence except for the shrill singing that assaulted my head. As a parting gesture he kicked the stool out from under me, and only a quick grab for the writing table saved me from falling flat on the floor.

I watched him go, hating him for bullying me and hating myself for letting him.

"Foaming lunatic!" I spat blood—holding to the table until the room stopped careening.

"Dominicus!" gasped Endymodes. "You're hurt!"

"Aye." Grimly, wearily, I retrieved the stool and climbed back up to the table.

"What are you doing?"

"Writing Apollonius another letter."

XXVI

Alexandros treated me with a vengeance. At parties he made bets on whether I could stand on my head for an hour or do one hundred backflips without passing out, and I had better do it, too, or I felt the staff for his losses when we got home.

One sultry evening at an intimate dinner in which the ladies in attendance were paid escorts, one of the ladies expressed curiosity as to my sexual endowments. Alexandros laughed uproariously and commanded me to drop my tunic so that all the company might have curiosity satisfied.

He was in a capricious humor, and the foul look in his eyes told me I was dead if I did not.

In a stark silence and all eyes on me, I dropped my tunic to the floor.

"And . . ."

And my underwrap.

Giggles and whistles, oohs and ahs, greeted my nudity. Oh, they had a good time exercising their wits at my expense, while I stood before them in quiet humiliation.

Alexandros bade me turn about so that everyone might get a full view.

Tonight the mere sight of a naked dwarf was high comedy. Burning with mortification, I grit my teeth and endured their ridicule.

Alexandros allowed as I had sufficient endowment, he might

237

charge a stud fee and see if there was profit in breeding dwarves. I sickened at the thought of helpless dwarf babes raised in slavery and mockery by the likes of these. Alexandros rallied the ladies for the first volunteer in the experiment. There was much laughter, but no volunteers. To these who admired only strength and beauty, I was grotesque and comic. They gasped mirthfully until tears flowed and another serving of wine was called for all around.

I remained standing under Alexandros's arrogant sneer, shamed and humiliated, until he gave the nod that I should retrieve my garments.

What held me in the power of this hateful lout? Why did I not simply bolt for freedom? Ah, if it were that simple! There was Endymodes, for one. He gained strength daily, but had still not recovered from his illness. Sometimes all that stood between him and Alexandros in his rages was me, and I could dodge the wild fists much quicker than Endymodes. There was reality, for another. When I was seventeen and a cocky acrobat, Rome was an adventure, and I was indestructable and immortal. In the four years since then I had known senseless death, treachery, and slavery. I never felt more vulnerable and mortal; Rome never looked more dangerous. And a runaway slave with no means would fare badly on the streets, even were I not apprehended, flailed, and branded. Escape the city? Flee to Gaul? Truth be known, I had never been absolutely on my own before—I had no place to go, no sustenance, no protection.

I had no protection against Alexandros, either, but I had hopes that the letter I sent to Apollonius would somehow rectify the situation. It would take a minimum of one month for Apollonius to receive the letters (both scribed in my hand—likely they would even arrive on the same vessel), two months before I could look for any reply, or three if Fortuna was busy elsewhere. Yet, as the two-month drew to a close, I both dreaded and longed for the awaited answer. Ideally, Apollonius would himself arrive to take matters in hand. Had I made it clear how unbalanced Alexandros was become? No, for his mental state had since worsened. I feared that a mere written reprimand would arrive from Apollonius, and Alexandros would fly into a fury and murder me on the instant. Still I waited—waited for Alexandros to cripple me, Apollonius to answer, a miracle to happen.

Then I learned that time might be running out for me in ways unguessed. Alexandros made clear that I was expendable one evening at a drinking, dicing party. He was betting wildly and had lost all his money and now had none left to stay in the pot. A fellow student, Crispus had won most of the throws, and the other players were dropping out.

"You think you have me beat, eh, Crispus!" roared Alexandros. He looked around to me and beckoned.

Wary, I approached to just beyond his reach.

"Hear this! Dominicus against your five hundred, Crispus! Have we a bet?"

Crispus turned a greedy eye on me and grinned. "One last bet? Your dwarf against my lot? Fair enough, Alexandros."

Crispus! A more loathsome, unsavory rotter he could not have chosen with whom to gamble my life—for it *would* be my life. Everyone, even Alexandros, knew Crispus gamed his slaves illegally in private bouts. It was common knowledge among *slaves,* at least, that his did not last long. Stunned, I watched Crispus rattle the dice hollowly in the cup. I heard a low voice behind me as one observer remarked to another, paying me no more mind than if I were deaf or witless.

"Alexandros is drunker than I thought. His dwarf could fetch a cool five *thousand* on Palatine Hill."

Gods! Why did they not tell HIM that?

Crispus let fly his dice and rolled ten.

Alexandros rolled seven.

I trembled in relief to the sounds of Alexandros's triumphant crows and Crispus's sour curses. Alexandros had to be drunk all right. He had a thesis to be finished tomorrow. What if Crispus had won? Sober, he would never have gambled his only hope of remaining in the university and enjoying the continued financial support of his father. By now he was so deep in deceit, and I with him, that he could not likely do without me.

Early in the fateful two-month, Alexandros had hit upon a new scheme for cheating, unique, I'm sure, in the annals of academia. It occured to him that there stood large decorative urns on pedestals between the pillars which supported the lecture hall's domed roof. It occurred to him also that I might fit easily into one of them. Early one morning when I roused him for classes, he sent me through the predawn streets to the university to try the doors. What reason to bar the lecture hall? There was nought in it but writing tables and stools and the lectern. I slipped into the hall, which was just beginning to lighten through the high-arched windows, and found, indeed, that I could climb onto the low peristyle which connected pedestal to pillar around the hall, grasp the lip of an urn, swing up and slide into the ceramic vessel. Getting out, I realized, was going to be a bit harder. I settled snugly in the interior and soon heard the students arrive, and then the noise settled as the history master entered. I could hear perfectly, and the sunlight streaming down through a window trickled enough light into the jar that I could have written on parchment (which I did the next time, smuggling in parchment, ink-pot, and quill to leave hidden there), but the same late summer sun that afforded me light also warmed the urn considerably, so that by midmorning it was hot and stifling inside, and sweat trickled down my nose and back and cramping legs. By the end of the last subject (rhetoric, through which I could barely stay awake) I was in misery. Noontime, after the hall emptied, I took some trying time getting out; my hands were slippery with sweat and the lip of the jar was hard to get a grip on from the inside, but I made it out, thinking if I had to do this again I'd be wise to bring a grapple and rope.

Of course I had to do it again . . . and again. More and more frequently Alexandros didn't bother to get up for classes at all—then he would send me back again in the afternoon to explain that he had taken ill and would be out a day or two. Sometimes it was true; he really was sick—hangover sick. And Master Umbrusus Elusius would raise an incredulous eyebrow as though he knew perfectly well I hid in the urn daily to cover his assignments. Between writing Alexandros's papers, running his errands, holing up in the sweltering urn all morning, and attending to his revels most evenings, I was exhausted and weary-eyed. Is it any wonder I slept through geometry and rhetoric? I did badly in those subjects and twice took a thrashing from Alexandros for having no geometry done and no idea how to do it. Naturally Alexandros fared badly in rhetoric; he had to do his own speaking, and what little I knew was not enough to get him by.

Inevitably it all came to a reckoning. They told me there came a dramatic pause in the rhetorician's speech, and a whopping snore reverberated the silent hall. Then another. And another. The students broke into snorts and snickers while the furious mentor made stern investigation into who dared sleep through his rhetoric.

I only knew that I awoke to a shout, awoke staring up into the red face of the rhetorician glaring down at me through the mouth of the urn. Ah, what a scene ensued! The mirth of the students as I climbed out of hiding. The fury of the tutor. The demand for Alexandros, who was absent. The messages sending for the other tutors. The delegation of students sent to find Alexandros and accompany him hither immediately. (They found him at the baths; his hair was still damp when they hustled him into the lecture hall.) The assemblage of the university masters. The assemblage of the students—his peers.

A tribunal of judges was selected: two from the freshman class, one the history master. The master rhetorician presented his charge that Alexandros was conspicuously absent from classes and had in fact sent his personal scribe secretly in his place. The rhetorician was superb. He convinced *me* straight off, especially when he snapped open the scrap of parchment I used for notes and read from it a portion of the morning's history notes. The history master nodded solemnly at his words read back to him. More charges were presented against Alexandros, these by classmates who knew of his escapades and now jumped at a chance to get in on the speeches and impress their tutors. Alexandros sat angry and speechless. His drinking and gambling buddies eyed each other nervously, wondering when their names would come up. Then Master Umbrusus Elusius took the floor.

"I would speak with the *scribe* of Alexandros before this assembly."

Uh-oh. Umbrusus pulled up a stool for me, and I climbed onto it before the murmurous assembly. Alexandros watched me murderously. Umbrusus held aloft a slim scroll.

"Alexandros submitted this thesis to me day before yesterday. It was not written by Alexandros."

Umbrusus unrolled the scroll and presented it in front of my nose.

"Dominicus. . . ."

He remembered my name!

"Did you write this?"

"Umm, yes sir. That's my script."

"I *know* it's your script. I'm asking if you are the *author*. Is the *content* yours?"

I glanced toward Alexandros, who was wishing me dead. But I would not lie for the likes of him to Master Umbrusus Elusius.

"Yes sir, I wrote it."

"Ah."

Indignant mutterings bestirred the hall. Umbrusus rerolled the parchment, his eyes fixed grimly on Alexandros, giving the mutterings direction. Then he paced, stopped, spun, and addressed me in a voice that echoed to the domed roof.

"This is undoubtedly one of the most brilliant freshman theses I've read in years."

My eyes widened. "It is?"

He smiled. His voice dropped to its usual volume. "Most original. Most enjoyable."

"Thank you, sir," I breathed, his praise racing to my head like good wine.

He turned to sweep his gaze over the assembly. "The moment I read it I knew Alexandros could not have written it himself. This thesis was written by an assiduous and contemplative scholar, if somewhat overly imaginative in conjecture, all of which Alexandros is not. Since it was written in Dominicus's script, I presumed, naturally, that he was its author. However, I could not explain how the scribe came to know so intimately what I looked for in extrapolation. Our master rhetorician has today discovered how it comes about that Dominicus the scribe knows more of the lectures than Alexandros the student. We have had a hidden scholar in our midst."

He pointed the end of the scroll at me. The history and philosophy masters glanced at each other in amazed accord; the geometry and rhetoric masters, with good reason, were less impressed. Umbrusus strode back to me.

"Dominicus," he brandished the scroll, "who taught you to write like this?"

"Why . . . you did, sir," I answered bemusedly.

Laughter invaded the somber assembly. Umbrusus beamed.

"Yes. I did. Thank you. But not entirely. Someone must have instructed you before you came here."

"Oh. Endymodes taught me. Alexandros's tutor."

"Taught you to treatise philosophy like this?"

"No sir. That would Themistius, Alexandros's grandfather."

"Where is this Themistius? In Rome?"

"Oh, no, he's dead!" I blurted. "Everyone knows that!" How, I wondered, could a university master not know of Themistius?

More laughter erupted.

"And this Endymodes? Is he in Rome?"

"He is."

"Ah. Now we are getting somewhere."

"No we are not!" declared the history master. "Speed this up, Umbrusus—it's lunchtime."

The assembly concurred.

Umbrusus shrugged. "Proceed."

The history master looked to Alexandros.

"What is your defense? Do you call someone to defend you?"

Alexandros glared darkly over the ranks of students.

"Crispus!"

Crispus looked him steadily in the eye and shook his head.

"Aluisius! Persus! . . ." Alexandros named aloud every one of his reveling companions. Every one declined.

"Do you speak on your own behalf, then?" rapped the history master.

Alexandros shook his head sullenly.

The tribunal conferred, the master speaking rapidly and forcefully to the freshmen. The history master rose to his feet.

"We have agreed. For deliberate fraud, for flagrant disrespect for the University of Rome and its ethical and academic standards, Alexandros Perce Themistius goes on record as expelled from the university as a malingerer and a cheat, never to be reinstated. May it be further recorded that he received twenty lashes before the assembled student body, and we are being lenient. Sentence will be carried out forthwith, and maybe we'll all be home by siesta."

A senior student came forward with the whip, which was a single cord of leather and not tipped with lead or blades, for it is the university's intent to castigate the students, not slash them to shreds. They stripped Alexandros's tunic down to the waist and bade him lean over the peristyle. He gripped the edge with sweaty hands, and the senior did the flogging—twenty lashes red and sharp across the back—and it is to Alexandros's credit that he grit his teeth and did not cry out until the eleventh or twelfth strike. I did not particularly regret seeing him whipped, for he had made me feel pain often enough, nor did I feel sorry for him when the last lash was done and he loosed his grip and slumped to the floor, his back a mess of welts and blood and sweat.

The student assembly dispersed. Some of Alexandros's reveling companions looked at him pityingly, guiltily, as they passed his kneeling form. He did not look up. He was shamed and dishonored and no longer one of them. I had no sympathy to spare him, for he had made me feel humiliation often enough, too.

Umbrusus approached me. "Dominicus, I wish you to bring this teacher Endymodes around tomorrow afternoon. I would like to speak with him."

"He's been ill, sir. He could never walk this far."

"I'm sorry to hear that. I will come around tomorrow afternoon myself. Unfortunately, I have an engagement this evening

243

that cannot be broken. However, I am most eager to speak with him, concerning you, Dominicus, and a future for you at the university, with proper application to your master, of course."

"You mean working for you, sir?" I could scarcely believe my ears.

"No, no, lad, I mean studying. A slave may attend the university; his master need only pay the fees. For you, we might even capture a scholarship, once I submit this thesis to the master assembly."

I was overwhelmed. Finally I stammered a "Thank you, sir." I even forgot for the moment that Alexandros was sure to kill me as soon as he caught me. Then I remembered.

"Master Umbrusus, Alexandros will have murdered me by tomorrow."

"Will he? Perhaps you had best accompany me home this evening."

I thought of Endymodes alone and Alexandros in a rage. I shook my head.

"I'd best go see to Endymodes and tell him what happened."

Umbrusus nodded and strode over to Alexandros, who was pulling himself painfully to his feet. The mentor ordered two lingering students to help Alexandros to the university's physician with a message that he should be treated and kept overnight. Then he warned Alexandros that he would be dropping by the apartments tomorrow, and if he found that Alexandros had laid a hand on Endymodes or me, he would take steps to have him confined to a garrison and marked as dangerously deranged, until his father could take custody.

Alexandros acknowledged his words with a sharp, bitter nod and eased his tunic up onto his back, wincing at the pain. Without glancing in my direction, he shook off the student's helping hands and walked stiffly out the door.

I ran directly home and told Endymodes all that had happened. When I came to the parts about Umbrusus praising my thesis, coming to meet my teacher, and wanting me in the university, my eyes glowed and so did the old tutor's. But he was also angry.

"That the grandson of Themistius should so disgrace his House! Expelled! A cheat and a liar! Publicly dishonored!" He coughed violently at his outburst. Hastily I fetched him wine. He took the cup in shaking hands and drained it. He regarded me with watery eyes.

"How I wish I'd been there to see him whipped. But I've failed,

Dominicus—failed my responsibility to the House of Themistius. How will I face Apollonius?"

"*You* didn't fail!" I told him. "*Alexandros* failed. He's out of control—*anybody's* control—and that started long ago in Constantinople. One old man and a dwarf are not enough to contain him. We should've known that; Apollonius should've known it. Take none of the blame on yourself; Alexandros has earned it all."

The wet eyes blinked and the pale, thin mouth smiled. "This has been hardest on you, Dominicus. You're a kind lad and you deserve better. I've seen you by lamplight, poring over the little map you keep hidden beneath your mattress."

I startled, surprised he knew of it.

"An old man alone day after day." He sighed. "Curiosity got the better of me. I am sorry, Dominicus."

I shrugged. "I don't mind you finding it, Endymodes—just Alexandros."

"Ah, yes, Alexandros. I'm not sure why you've not run away from him before now, but I'm grateful you have not. You've been strength and comfort to me, my boy." He clasped my hand in his cool, dry one. "I have not much living left, but you've a whole lifetime before you. I've worried over you, hoping Apollonius would soon come."

I smiled, that he should state the same worry and hope for me as I had for him.

"Our worries are soon over, Endymodes."

He shook his head. "Tomorrow is not yet here, Dominicus. I want you to know that I see how wrong I was—terribly wrong—to believe that conditions of birth reflect human worth. Will you forgive my stupidity?"

I nodded gravely. I had not thought of that incident in a long time, but he had a need now to set matters aright.

"Thank you, lad. And tell Sapphone when you return to Constantinople that I learned I was wrong. She was ever angry with me after that."

Sapphone. I smiled wistfully. *Constantinople.* Even that was beginning to sound good. Then I shook myself back to reality.

"Nonsense. You'll tell her yourself when you get home. And tomorrow Master Umbrusus Elusius comes—to see *you!*"

Endymodes sat up straighter, eyes gleaming. "I must bathe and bring out my best tunic—the long, blue one with white scroll and quill trim—and show these Romans how to dress in style."

I laughed. "They *don't* know figs about dressing, *do* they?"

Endymodes spent the afternoon bathing and sprucing and then resting from his labors. I cleaned up, too, wondering what the morrow would bring.

The night brought Alexandros.

It was bound to happen. That was what was so despairing about it. He staggered in, noisome drunk. The room was lit only by moonlight streaming blue across the gloom. I feigned sleep and watched him covertly. He stumbled about a while, blind and hazy. Finally, he managed to take an ember from the brazier with the curved, sharp-ended tongs. He struck the lamp to life and stood blinking and swaying. Then he saw my huddled form. He dropped the ember, hinged the tongs wide open, and charged. Had I not rolled away with a start, he would have gored a hooked tong deep into me. I bounded to my feet in alarm. He buried the hook in my mattress and now tugged and wrested, unable to free it. Of a sudden it tore free and he came at me again. By now I had moved so that the table stood between us. He tried to reach me but could not, befuddled as he was. Furiously he rammed the table straight at me. I ducked. With a shove he toppled the table over my head—it came crashing down behind my back, leaving me trapped between the table-bottom and him. He raised the tongs and I stared at death.

Whack!

Endymodes's staff slapped him straight across his raw back. Bellowing, Alexandros arched backwards and turned on Endymodes—grasped him by the neck with one hand and shook him savagely. I snatched up the fallen staff and went for Alexandros's legs. With a howl Alexandros struck out at Endymodes with the tongs and flung him against the wall. Then he spun on me. I fended him off with the staff and sidled desperately around the table. The staff stuck sideways and I had to let go—Alexandros tripped over it and staggered to hands and knees. He still held the deadly tongs, killer eyes fixed on me, and he'd be getting to his feet any moment now. . . .

In panic I grabbed the brazier by one handle and swung wildly at him. A corner of the brazier struck across his head just above the right ear; charcoal showered the room; Alexandros fell on his face.

I stood in heavy silence, broken by my own gasping breaths. Then came a thudding on the wall from the next apartment and a muffled shout to hold the noise down or else. Then nothing.

Confusion held me fast for a few long seconds, then I staggered around the overturned table to Endymodes. He lay sprawled on the floor, his neck crooked at a sharp angle, a gash where the tongs had ripped across his cheek, his eyes and mouth gaping open.

Dead—Endymodes dead. Trembling, I reached out and closed those staring eyes, closed the colorless mouth as I gently, persistently, shifted his head to a more natural (comfortable, if I but thought about it) position. I sat back on my heels and gazed in shock.

Gradually I became aware that the room was studded with red-glowing embers. I snapped instantly to my senses; here at the end of the hot, dry summer, flames could catch and spread frighteningly fast. Hastily I scrambled with scoop and whisk, regathering every charcoal, stamping out every tiny glow. I had no desire to set fire to the city.

You think you're in trouble now, Dominico, I hissed to myself, *burn Rome and see what happens.*

And I was undoubtedly in trouble. Alexandros still lived. He lay out cold, his hair matted in a still pool of blood, but he was breathing.

And I had struck him down. There would be no escape from his wrath tomorrow. Even if I went now to Umbrusus (assuming I knew where to find him on Saturn's Day, which I did not) Alexandros would be perfectly within his rights to drag me to the garrison and have me drawn and quartered, or mayhap castrated and both hands lopped off, or if I was lucky, condemned to the salt mines. Or mayhap he would just kill me outright, as he did Endymodes.

I approached the broken figure on the floor. Poor Endymodes. He had been excited about Umbrusus Elusius honoring him with a visit tomorrow. His lifelong humble work given due recognition at last. Now that would never be. And Umbrusus had planned to enroll me in the university tomorrow. Now that, too, would never be.

I glared at Alexandros, prone and insensible.

"Why are *you* not dead, you cockroach?"

I clutched my head and rocked in despair. What could I do? Go to Umbrusus? How long could he protect me from Alexandros's legal right to invoke full punishment on a slave who knocked him out? Not long, I feared.

Flee the city? Become a runaway? I wondered at my chances

of being caught and suffering full punishment for that also. *I can only be drawn and quartered once.* Rome felt like a huge trap closing in on me.

I decided to go home. To Gaul. Where in Gaul, I had no idea. But I must go and I must go quickly. I glanced down at my short tunic—it would not do. From our baggage I pulled my long yellow-and white-striped robe and shrugged it on over the tunic. I laced my sandals. None of these were proper clothes—not for traveling on foot. Though the night was warm, I rummaged for my bleached wool cloak and wide strips of legging for cold weather, sure I would need them, hoping I would need them. For now, I spread the cloak on the floor, raided the larder of flatbread, cheese, figs, and honeycakes, and made a bundle of it. Now I slipped my map from beneath the mattress, rolled and tied it with string, and tucked it carefully into the bundle.

I looked about to see if I had missed anything. As my glance fell on Endymodes, I felt I could not just dash away without some sort of goodbye. I took his long blue tunic with the fancy white quill and scroll borders and laid it carefully over him. Perhaps they (whoever Alexandros called to take the body) would cremate him in it. I wanted to say a prayer, but to which gods? I truly did not know. I assembled them all together in my mind's eye: Apollo, Artemis, Zeus; Horus, Isis, Osiris; Jesus, Mary, and Joseph . . . all I could recall on such short notice . . . and I prayed that they accept and guide the soul of Endymodes—my teacher and my friend—to wherever good souls go. Amen.

I checked one last time to see if Alexandros had not conveniently died and saved me a lot of trouble, for if he had I could call it a drunken accident, and who would dispute me? Unfortunately, he was not only breathing, but was beginning to make a sound suspiciously like snoring. No luck there.

I slipped into the night and headed for the north gates of the restless city.

PART IV

XXVII

I escaped Rome hidden in the back of a freight wagon which carried me north toward Florentia. From there, traveling at night, avoiding well-trafficked ways, I disappeared into the Apennines Mountains.

I lived by "stravage and bramble" as the vagabonds called it, thriving off Demeter's autumn fruits, though at times the goddess's generosity bordered on what estatemasters would call thievery.

Days and weeks blurred together as I made my way toward the southern passes of the Alps, urgent to put as much distance between myself and Rome as possible. And the truth is that were it not for the kindness of simple folk, Christian and Pagan, who helped me along the way, I would never have made it.

There were shepherds who shared their supper for a tale at the campfire, and the monk who shared his for nothing. There was the goodwife who gave me milk and hot bread and kind words, and the charcoal hauler who let me ride and doze for miles beside him on the wagon-seat, just for an extra hand at unloading.

I reached the Gallic provinces in the midst of a winter frost, and I might have died had it not been for a poor Christian widow to whom charity was more than a word, who would not turn away a hungry, homeless dwarf who stumbled half-frozen upon her doorstep.

They sheltered me through the winter, the widow and her five children, and I worked alongside her boys, shoveling charcoal for the ironworks. And at night I taught her eldest sons their Latin letters, for it was their mother's dream that they improve their lot and leave the ironworks, and not die of lung fever like their father.

Truth, the whole village took me in, and for me it was a haven of peace, warmth, shelter, and family. But with the spring came the tax assessors, who asked questions about the newest and smallest worker at the ironworks, and I had no doubt they would soon conclude I was a runaway. I had to move on, not only for my own sake, but for the sake of the folk who harbored me.

Stealing down mountain to valleys where spring had already blossomed, I haunted umber forest shadows and sun-brightened meadows. Sometimes I made my home in a natural cavage underneath a rocky overhang. I had flint and iron for fire, myself for company, my wits for survival. I fished and scavenged by day. I stole down to village or farm by night. I had not lost my touch; I could always come away with something, be it eggs right from under the hen, peas right off the vine, plums right out of the tree.

Only rarely did I openly approach a village or dwelling. Shy and skittish, I might appear suddenly in the meadows to astonished goatherders and hail them in the old Gallic tongue. For a handful of tales they would share fire and supper, and as they later nodded off around the campfire I would quietly disappear into pale, moonlit meadows where the grasses whispered grey and ghostly in a night-wind.

Or I might waylay a lone traveler on the road and relate a long tale of magic and dwarf stones—a little invention of mine—to while away the walking hours. Then when my listener was thoroughly charmed I would tell a woeful down-on-my-luck story and mourn that all I had left in the world was one magic stone. By that time, if I read my mark aright, the listener would trade almost anything for that stone—anything from a few coppers or a bronze dagger to a forest-green cloak or a leather belt buckled with a bronze boar's head. I would feign reluctance, but I would always trade, having a whole pocketful of stones and an unlimited supply lying in high mountain streams. I selected the stones carefully, taking the brightest ones polished smooth by the cold rushing waters and laying them out in the sun to dry. The most unusual, mysterious specimens I collected. Oh, a proper charlatan I felt, chuckling merrily to myself after a particularly profitable transaction.

Growing bolder, I ventured into a small village now and again with nought but a handful of stones and a headful of stories of faraway places. I kept to the back-forest folk, never venturing near towns, taverns, or inns. After retreating into the wilderness with supplies, I often saw no one for days and weeks at a stretch.

Spring deepened into high summer, and the wilderness was alive with color and fragrance and intoxicating air. The meadows sang with birdsong and windsong and riversong—Earthsong.

The wonder of the mountains and forests is their solitude. The grandest of feelings is to stand on a high precipice overlooking a cascade of tumbled rock, windswept treetops, and waves of spring meadows painted all over with wildflowers. Now a dizzily swooping descent into verdant valleys, now a sudden ascent of mountain range crested by granite peaks rising one after the other into the purple distance, until they melt into the clouds and seem to parade right up the sky. As my eyes drink in such a fantastic panorama of Earth and Sky, at that moment I am lord of all I behold. I stand firm in the clouds with the world spread below my feet and laughingly name myself Emperor of the Earth.

Then the most awe-inspiring chill is to watch the sudden approach of massive stormclouds that rumble and flash an ominous warning and roll across a placid sky with brooding blue-black masses and dazzling white-hot streaks and flares of lightning. Swiftly, darkly, the storm is upon the mountain. I see and smell the veil of summer rain long before it washes over the nearest ridge, chases me under a low-hanging ledge, and lashes petutantly upon the shelter's edge. Once I huddled, amazed and afraid, shivering from an indefinable crackle in the acrid air, while directly overhead the clouds clashed so violently I feared Heaven and Earth must split asunder with one deafening crack. Each staccato dance of lightning exposed every crag and crevice of my shallow cave and etched the jagged terrain below in a sizzling glare that seared an eerie image forever in my mind.

A devastating disappointment it is, too, watching the last flicker of campfire sputter out under a deluge of wind-whipped rain and hail and to resign oneself to a cold, wet, stormy night. Then the world's most welcome sight is dawn's white fog slowly receding, revealing an ever-widening clearing of shadowy trees out of its milky mist. Slowly the world awakens hushed and luxuriously green. Birds shake the water from their feathers and break into excited song. The heavy, humid air softens the gentle dripping of the rain-drenched forest, and the moist Earth stirs and creeps to life. Each fresh-washed leaf, fern, flower, tree—each vale and glade—suffuses the air with pungent fragrance and tantalizes my nostrils with earthy delights. (I am certain Heaven must smell like this. If not, then I am not going.) Life flourishes everywhere—a multicolored crust of moss and lichen dapples each rain-glazed rock and rotted log; tribes of wild mushrooms sprout up from the tangled forest floor; tiny intricate flowers bloom in delicate arrays smaller then the iris of a woodpecker's eye.

Then comes the glorious moment when the sun at last bursts forth from behind grey clouds and slants long rays of hazy golden light across the meadows. For an instant silver droplets sparkle on leaf and blade, frond and web. Then the rocks take on a ruddy glow of their own, and the sun-flamed trees come ablaze with inner light—dark smouldering evergreen and velvety glowing emerald. Fields of wildflowers shimmer in sunlight, brilliant oceans of color. Stilled lakes reflect the clouds like pools of sky downpoured and collected in earthen basins.

And at day's end there is no serenity to compare with watching the burning amber sun sink below low-lying indigo plains and paint the sky with light and cloud—midnight blue and dusky purple, ember orange and burnished pink, molten silver and bronze. Then the magic hour of twilight transforms the daylight world into a mysterious land of shifting shades and shadows, where trees stand in sharp black silhouette against a pale, color-washed sky, and the air settles in pockets of warm and cool across the greying meadows. Then the birds at evensong sound lonesome and mournful, and a solitary hawk wings high and free across a darkling sky.

How like magic, then, to watch the night gradually overshadow the world, to recall that where just scant hours hence was a vault of pure impenetrable blue is now a deep velvety black universe sprinkled lavishly, whimsically, with a spectacular sparkle and glitter of stars. I wonder who named the stars and why—I find the great scorpion climbing the southern heavens—I wonder which tiny point of light Heaven might be—I seek out brilliant Venus, ruddy Mars, and elusive Jupiter and wonder if the gods know they are planets, or if the planets know they are gods.

Then I wonder whether perhaps the ancient philosopher Lucretius may have been right, that there exist no gods to toy with our lives, that the universe is one magnificent galaxy of suns—thousands of suns shining on thousands of worlds like this one and on the unnumbered folk who people them. In such reflective moments I am visited with a strange sense of aloneness, a feeling that I and my joys and sorrows and yearnings are meaningless, and I am hopelessly lost in the enormity of a universe I cannot even begin to comprehend. As I lie back, fingers locked behind my head, wistful eyes roving the stars, a poignant and piercing loneliness sweeps over me. I roll to face the Earth, press my forehead into the cool grass, and battle a sinking feeling of futility.

Betimes I wondered what my life had come to, tossed hither and thither by the winds of fate or chance. I did not even know what life was *for* or what I was supposed to do with it. A tumult of philosophies clamored in my brain. They gave me no answers, no peace. Sometimes the sense of loss and futility was so maddening I pounded the Earth in rage. And Earth patiently surrounded me with her presence and her power while my rage was spent. The Alps, even at their most turbulent, were peace. Their solitude was all the peace I had—or needed, I told myself.

One cold night, drawn out by the full moon's haunting light, I found myself staring down at a bright spark of campfire. In its ruddy glow human figures moved to and fro, and I heard their voices clear in the still night air, faint and tinged with laughter. Unseen, I cupped my chin in hands and watched them from my solitary hilltop. My belly was full; my cloak was thick and warm; I had abundant firewood in my rocky hideaway. But tonight I was lonely and craved the voices, faces, and companionship of human beings.

I appeared unannounced at the edge of their firelight. Startled and amazed they stared. I noted the hobbled mules, the wagonloads of wood.

"My papa was a woodcutter," I said simply.

Their stares broke slowly into smiles, and they bid me welcome to their fire. I heard their news and talked of my travels. And that night I was no one but Dominic of Gaul, son of a woodcutter, home from my journeys. And it felt good.

Solitude drove me from the heights. Solitude and autumn. I left aloft pines, spruce, and fir; mountain goats, windy paths, sudden snows. I ventured down through forests of great oak, maple, beech; steep grassy cow-pastures, patches heavy with juicy berries, sleepy little country villages. I descended into groves of chestnut and walnut; orchards and vineyards; harvest-ready fields of barley, oats, rye, and wheat; estates, roads, inns, and towns. I entered the heartlands of Gaul.

What a grand freedom it was to saunter jauntily along the middle of an imperial highway illuminated only by a round argent moon gleaming like a gem in the night, while the great oak forest loomed on either side with ready concealment in its dark brambles, should unexpected company come galloping down the road. A bulging knapsack slung across my shoulders, rag-bound feet making only the faintest whisper with each rollicking step, I sometimes sang a lively walking tune if I was not too wary of being surprised in my song.

Once I followed a beekeeper above sweet-smelling orchards and entertained him with my chatter until he forced upon me a pot of honey just to keep my mouth otherwise occupied. Betimes I would crouch near a country road, garbed in forest green and brown, so thoroughly blended with the thick foilage as to be invisible to passing eyes. Then when a decent-enough looking fellow came along, I would emerge from the green shadows and hail him boldly from the oaks. The traveler without fail came round with a start and stammer as though he stared a wood sprite in the face. I suppose I made quite an uncommon sight—dressed in earthy colors; leaning on a stout, crooked stick; long, thick curls tangled and wild; sunburnt and red-bearded; gazing up from a child's height—a prize dwarf if ever there was one. I relished his momentary befuddlement. Tramping together we might trade gossip, tales, and a magic stone from my collection. Still, I kept a fair distance between myself and my walking companion, for I was ever wary of being taken and sold into slavery again.

However, winter would eventually be coming on, and I had no liking for hiding out in the cold on my own. Already the Old Straw Woman stood vigil in the fields—the largest of the sheaves ceremoniously frocked in woman's clothing and placed to oversee the autumn labor. Already much harvesting was underway. I figured I could find ready listeners for my tales when men and women came weary to supper and fire after the day's labor. They would have coin, too, for it looked to be a good harvest year.

For the first time in my adult life, I was free to wander among my own folk, the rustic people of Gaul. True, there were jests and snorts and rib-nudging at my first appearance in inn or tavern, but soon, to most folk, I was "the storyteller." I could conjure tales and sights from all over the world, curious and exotic tales never heard before in this part of the Empire. And if I abruptly came up against my reflection in mocking eyes—"Hey, Meta, look at that! How'd you like to plant a big fat kiss on that?"—I dismissed it out of hand. But later the jests would echo in my head, and I would wonder what I was doing here. Alone, in the mountains, I had been simply myself, simply Dominic, for who was there to take my measure?

Yet I wanted company. And most folk were friendly, ready to talk, eager to listen, so I found company, fire, food, and coin most everywhere. When harvest was done I jingled denarii in my palm and eyed the road before me. Boldly (there's nothing like coin to make a man bold) I set my steps along an imperial highway toward the northern provinces. I did well on the road, too, for people and goods flowed steadily, the emperors and generals having moved their wars to distant provinces this year.

Somewhere in my wanderings I passed my twenty-third birthday. Life was good—I was free, young, and world-traveled, opinionated and impertinent. Vagabonding as I pleased, I lived in taverns, inns, and barns, and if coin was scarce, I could always talk a meal and a roof out of someone.

I worried briefly if I was not taking chances stopping off at inns along the highways, for though they room civilians, they also serve imperial agents and messengers. If ever the escape of a dwarf-slave who struck his young master was reported outside Rome . . . well, an imperial agent remembers these things. The first agent I shared fire and supper with made me fairly quake, but I had to face it out sooner or later. *He*, at least, had never been alerted to a renegade dwarf, judging from the easy way he propped his heels on the table after supper, swilled his wine, and talked weather and politics with me. He avowed he was right glad to see another traveler on the road, winter slowing traffic as it did. Said it was a relief to talk to someone who had seen a bit of the world, too. Some folk are misliking of imperial agents and avoid them, but I found most of them are not bad company, and there is no one like an agent for an earful of news.

XXVIII

'Twas my own fault—my misfortune. I've no one to blame but myself. Cocksure and careless, I forgot I was fair game in some circles.

Near the town of Vesontio, during a bone-chilling rain, I took refuge at a dilapidated inn and post. I stood dripping and shivering just inside the doorway and surveyed the noisy, crowded common room. All the lamps blazed, the fire roared high and hot; the inn was bright and over-warm and sweetened with the stench of humanity and honeyed mull.

As I edged my way through the close-packed bodies I caught snatches of conversation amid the din. The roads to the south were flooded, bridges awash, causing this astounding crowd of stranded travelers to press close together in the common room without deference to wealth or class.

Miraculously I found a space on a bench and squeezed into it, dropping my knapsack at my feet under the table. I nodded amiably to my neighbor on the right, who stank unbearably, and he gave me a sour look in return. Shrugging, I turned to the man on my left. He was groomed and well dressed, but wore a glum, doomed expression. Perhaps he had been sitting next to the other man longer than he liked.

I had to grasp the skirt of a busy serving maid to gain her attention.

"Mull," I said, "and a bowlful of whatever you're serving."

She stared at me suspiciously. "You got coin?"

"Maybe. How much?"

"Ten coppers."

"Robbery."

She shrugged and started away.

"All right," I called, fishing at a pouch inside my tunic. I slapped a bronze piece into her palm.

Now the scrawny, smelly man on my right showed yellowed teeth and raised his cup to me. "Salute, mate."

"Salute, yourself," I said noncommittally.

"Name's Mingus."

"Dominic," I said reluctantly.

"Come far?"

"Far enough."

"Aye," he nodded, as though I had said something profound.

"You in trade?" he persisted.

"No."

Fortunately the serving maid plunked before me a mug of mull and a bowl of ragout with a crusty chunk of hard bread. I dug in, ignoring the scrawny man on my right.

He was not to be ignored. "I'm out of work, meself. What business would you be in?"

I took a long drink of sweet mull. "Dragon hunting," I told him solemnly.

His gaze narrowed. "What'cha take me for?"

"Why, I'll take you for whatever I can, friend." I grinned at him.

"Ha! You'll take me for nothing!" He peered at me fuzzily through rat-like little eyes. "Dragon hunting, eh? Ain't no such thing as dragons."

"A lot you know. They don't live down here, of course, but up in the high Alps, in caves. They crunch up iron ore raw and cook it right in their boiling hot stomachs. Aye, dragons are the only creatures on Earth that cook their dinner *after* they eat it!"

He snickered noisily. I winked and continued shoveling down my own supper.

"What'cha want to be hunting dragons for, anyway?"

"Why, treasure! Don't you lowland folk know *anything*? Why, a dragon's worse than a tax collector. They just love treasure— gold and emeralds, rubies and sapphires—they leave piles of gems just everywhere."

The man snorted rudely.

I swigged more mull.

"You got any of that dragon treasure on you, mate?"

I swallowed slowly, watching the man's sly face.

"As a matter of fact, *mate,* I don't."

"Maybe I'll just have a look for meself," he grinned. He leaned over me, his long arm fishing beneath the table for my knapsack.

I met him under the table, a dagger at his throat.

"Maybe you won't," I told him.

Slowly, very slowly, he raised up, the dagger point pressing upward under his chin.

"No need for that," he squealed, eyes bulging.

"You're right," said a terse voice from the man who sat on my left. "There's no need for that because if you attempt to steal his pack I'm going to have you arrested by those city guardsmen over there."

The scrawny thief cringed. I held the dagger point against his throat for a long moment, letting his panic sink in. Then I eased up. He scrambled off the bench and away.

"Thanks," I said to the glum-faced man on my left. "I'd have a lot of explaining to do if he persisted."

"Murder," he sighed. "Messy business. Put that stickler away or *you'll* be arrested." He waved down the serving maid. "Let's have a pitcher of good wine over here. Some Falernian, if you have it." She moved with much more alacrity when he spoke than when I had. The man was middle-aged and balding, dressed in a respectably conservative tunic. He had a rather harried, officious air about him, as though wrapped in worries.

"Dominic," I introduced myself, extending a friendly hand.

He took my hand perfunctorily, as a man accustomed to greeting many people he scarcely knew or cared to know.

"Rufus Publius, of Vesontio. And you? . . ."

"Of Gaul," I answered expansively.

"Ah." He smacked the word, as though to indicate he understood I might have reason to be unspecific about my origins.

Good Falernian wine arrived, a pitcherful, and I noticed he paid in silver. We saluted each other's health and grumbled about the weather, he especially, for as it turned out he was a City Consul on the way south with the military tax to garrisons on the Rhine.

A miserable, thankless job, being a Consul, he complained, constantly struggling to meet the ever growing tax quotas. I was truly sympathetic, though I felt disinclined to admit that I had never paid a tax in my life.

"Where did you say you were born?" he asked abruptly.

I was adept at answering sudden questions.

"Ah, if only I knew," I sighed. "I was abandoned at birth, left a mere babe on a mountainside. The usual tragedy."

"Raised by wolves?" he guessed.

"Why, sir, you are truly astounding. That's exactly . . ."

For the first time the morose councilman laughed. He clapped me on the back and refilled both our cups.

I reminded myself to ease up on the drinking. It was contrary to my habits to get drunk among strangers, no matter how friendly they seemed. Nothing destroys a man's judgment like strong wine.

"And what is it you do besides hunting dragons?"

I did not mind the questions. Many people have an insatiable curiosity, especially about me. Playing on that curiosity was my livelihood.

"Well, you might say I deal in wishes. Wishing stones."

Publius did not look impressed, but he was not my sole audience. Men across the table, laborers from the look of them, listened intently.

"Here, let me show you." I ducked under the table and delved in my pack. When I reemerged my listeners were leaning forward for a look.

"A magic stone." I opened my hand, revealing a rock of purest white veined with amethyst. "Made by dwarves, deep beneath the mountains."

I turned the stone to catch the light; silvery flecks glinted in its surface.

"Anything your heart desires—the power within the stone will make it happen. Tell you what, mates," I said to the listeners, "I'll let go of this stone if you've something useful to trade for it." I looked from face to face. "You'll never find a better bargain. Make me an offer. What's it worth to have your fondest wishes granted?"

A large man across from me frowned. "Hold on! If that stone is so magical, how come you're in such a hurry to trade it off? If 'twas true, you'd keep it for yourself."

I rolled the rock in my fingers and grinned light-headedly. "Why, if I was so ignorant I'd trade my head in for a melon." Maybe I had been drinking more than I knew; Consul Publius poured more wine into my cup.

"Any high country babe knows a dwarf stone only works once for the holder. Then 'tis useless to him, and he must pass it on to someone else. You don't do idle wishing on a dwarf stone! No, sir, you keep it and think on it and wish carefully. Then when you're ready you take the stone and hold it up to the light of the moon at full ides"—here I raised it aloft admiringly, and it did look uncannily like a chunk of the moon—"and make your wish. But before your wish can come true you must first pass the stone along to another. So naturally I'm right eager to pass it on. Believe me, mates, this *one* stone will keep the whole lot of you comfortably awash in wishes."

Some of the men looked skeptical, and I noticed the Consul wore an expression of dour amusement. But leaning over the seated listeners with a greedy avarice on his ferret face was that rascal who had tried to steal my knapsack. I reminded myself to watch my back.

Someone offered a copper for the stone.

"A copper!" I snorted. "Why, this charming lass over here won't even give me a crust of bread for a copper—will you, darlin'?"

The serving maid almost smiled. "Not a crumb."

"Anyone have anything to *trade?*"

The big man across the table, a farmer maybe, placed two late-season apples on the table.

"Now *there's* an offer," I nodded. No one topped it, so I handed over the stone and scooped up the apples. "You've got yourself a magic stone, friend. Remember, under the moon at full ideas, then pass it along to someone else."

The man rubbed the stone with his thumb. "What did *you* wish for, then?"

I winked at him. "Maybe I wished for apples. What do you think?"

He guffawed loudly. "I think I just lost two apples."

I saluted him with my cup and drained the last of the wine. The hour was late and most customers were settling to sleep on the floor. I noticed the scrawny man slinking about, his beady eyes watching me, and I wondered if I dare fall asleep.

Publius slapped a hand on the table. "My city guard is over here. Bring your pack and settle in with them. You won't have unwelcome visitors in the night."

"Well, now, I'd be properly grateful, I don't mind telling you."

I followed him across the common room, glancing sidewise at the scarecrow man, who looked woefully disappointed. I grinned, none too steady on my feet.

The councilman had half a dozen guardsmen with him. While

I searched for a place to lie down, Publius spoke to one of the guardsmen in a low voice, explaining my situation, I gathered. I turned to set my pack down; I heard movement behind me; something struck the back of my head.

I went down to my knees in a red haze, then something struck me again and I sprawled forward into darkness.

When I finally struggled back to consciousness, I wished I had not. My head pounded as if horses galloped over it, my shoulder ached terribly, and my hands were wrenched behind my back and bound.

Rough hands forced me to my feet, and in a spinning haze I saw that early light seeped through the shutters. My mouth felt like wool; I could not speak, could barely stand.

"Here now. What're you taking him for?" It was the man who had traded me the apples.

"He's under arrest, by my order, the City Consul at Vesontio."

"What for?"

Publius gazed at me steadily, brandishing my dagger.

"Carrying a weapon."

He emptied a bagful of colorful stones at my feet.

"Sorcery."

He looked me up and down critically.

"No doubt he's a runaway, too."

The muttering farmer had no choice but to leave me to my fate.

Speechless, I stared at the man I had been drinking with in the night, discovered I was about to be sick, and swallowed hard. My knees buckled, but I was hauled to my feet and out into the inn yard. Oxen were being hitched to wagons. Publius spoke to a man who made a show of respectful deference to the City Consul.

Among the many crates on one of the wagons was a wooden cage in which a thin, miserable-looking hunting hound lay listless. I felt sorry for that wet, caged creature. I felt even more sorry when the Consul ordered it dragged out of the cage and onto the muddy ground. The hound whimpered but lay where it fell, too weak to move. A collar and chain were removed from the dog.

"Put it on the dwarf," said Publius.

I struggled against them, but the leather collar was quickly fastened around my neck.

"I hoped Count Lagos would be pleased with the gift of a new hound, but sadly, this one won't do." He spoke dispassionately to me. "Perhaps the Count will find you as amusing as I did."

263

Someone jerked the chain and I stumbled forward. Two men heaved me into the cage and chained the door fast behind me. In disbelief I watched the Consul walk away. Then the wagon lurched into motion. Stunned, I staggered against the wooden bars in an effort to keep my feet. The hound lay still in the mud; the rodent-faced man squatted on his heels, grinning at me as he bit into one of my apples; the men in the yard watched without protest—no one would dare.

I sank to the floor in despair, the first dark moment of a miserable journey of several days. I huddled in the cage at night, nothing to warm me in the cold but the clothes I had been wearing when captured—no cloak, no blanket, no hope. That first night after they unbound my hands I tried shinnying up the rough-hewn bars to reach the latch, but the chain that ran through the bolts was secured somewhere on the solid top of the cage—somewhere out of my reach. I shivered in the center of the cage, listened to the rain, and wondered what this Count might want with a dwarf.

Basilia squatted on a hillock overlooking the southernmost sweep in the wide river. Here the clear waters spread from the east to fill the broad riverbed between the densely wooded hills of the Black Forest on the north and the jagged ridges of the Jura Mountains to the south.

The wagon passed by the squared-off border outpost and its permanent surrounding settlement of civilian hangers-on. I heard a constant bustle from both the garrison and the town; Basilia must be always at ready, for it holds this very strategic pass on the border between the Roman Empire and Germania so the Alamanni do not pour through the gap like an armed flood.

At the edge of the garrison a small delegation of camp women cajoled the drivers and guards to halt and take advantage of their hospitality. Bawdy banter went back and forth until promise was made the men would stop by after their goods were delivered.

One gaudily painted young lady held up her colorful skirts and ran gaily beside the wagon-driver who hauled me in the cage. She saw me leaning against the wooden bars.

"*God's blood!*" she called to the driver, pointing. "You'll not be taking *him* to Lorrach, too?"

The man confirmed he was.

The woman stopped short and watched me go by in the wagon,

her expression of gaiety now one of pity. Then she made the sign of the cross.

I stared back at her wonderingly. When she was nearly out of my sight I saw her turn slow steps back toward town, head bowed, no longer gay. A sense of foreboding made me shiver from more than just the cold.

The oxen pulled the wagons upriver to Rauraci, which was once a powerful and flourishing city, most of which now towers aloof and desolate from a high plateau overlooking the river. Where the fortified remnants of Rauraci huddled on the Rhine's southern bank, we crossed over a great wooden bridge wide enough to accommodate two chariots abreast. Now across on the Germanni shore of the river, we wound bumpily up a split-log road into the Black Forest.

I clung to the stout wooden bars of the lurching cage and stared up at deep green sheltering pines that climbed the steep mountain slopes. Beneath the umbra shadows snow laced the forest floor. A cold, wispy breeze mingled a piney fragrance with the fresh scent of clean snow and rich mud. I craned my neck and looked farther up. Away off to the east, partway up the mountain, protruded a round tower with a strange conical top, looming dark and imposing above the treetops. Then the road dipped and I lost my first glimpse of Lorrach Keep, and I was near overwhelmed with dread.

XXIX

Lorrach Keep was a disorienting mixture of old Gallic stone fortress and Roman garrison. Where the ancient circular walls had crumbled they had since been patched with concrete and rock. Where gates of stolid wood once swung, now stood formidable gates of iron. In ancient times the roughly curved base of the stronghold wall rose flush beside the bank of a moat; now the citadel edged a deep, boggy ditch sodden with melted snow and spongy mosses—adding a heightened effect to the uneven wall. A cylindrical stone structure frowned severely over the gate; flanked by two stark turrets on either side, it reminded me of a gigantic cornuted devil's head.

As the oxen's hooves clomped hollowly on the heavy-beamed bridge, and the ponderous iron gates swung slowly outward with a strident shriek, my blood ran cold and I felt the lifeless hand of death touch my soul. Nonsense, I told myself sternly, this place could be no worse than any other, nor could these walls be any harder to climb. Still my fingers clenched the wooden bars in fear when I saw the heads. In late stages of decay, human heads were impaled on spikes along the top of the wall. Wisps of long yellow hair or beard still clung to a few of the skulls. Barbarian heads.

Then the wagon passed under the portal and into a grey wasteland—a cold floor of trampled mud, a conglomerate of stark Roman outbuildings dominated by the ancient citadel.

A bone-scraping screech of metal brought me around in a panic. I had just time to catch a heart-rending glimpse of evening sunlight glowing softly green and gold across the forest; then with a hollow clang the iron gates grated shut against the shining Earth. My heart sank.

The tribute wagons stopped near a storehouse for unloading. The Vesontio Consul's representative had me released from the cage, but he fastened the leather collar and chain back around my neck.

"A nice touch the Count will appreciate," he muttered as he tested the buckle. When his eyes met my beseeching stare he turned abruptly away and took the end of the chain.

"Consul's orders—not mine—you're for Count Lagos."

At an impervious tug, I followed him across the frost-hardened mud toward the great hall—if such a grim citadel can be called a hall. The massive circular stone structure was erected in misty antiquity, certainly not by Romans, most probably by my own Gallic ancestors long before Caesar ever heard of Gaul. It looked to me like a gigantic chimney, and indeed, black smoke did billow out the roof and high windows. The twin towers were attached to either side, conical and pointed on the tops.

Just to the right of the double oaken doors we passed beneath a chain and pulley suspended from the wall by a wooden beam. From the chain hung a great iron hook, stained a dark reddish brown. Beneath the hook, too, a large reddish brown splotch stained the earth.

To the Consul representative's disgust I caught at the portal, weak-kneed, in sheer terror. He jerked at the chain and dragged me inside.

I blinked in the smoky, feebly-lit interior of the vast citadel. Dusk-light seeped in through high empty windows sunk into the three-foot-deep ageless stone walls. Heavy beams imbedded into the stone supported a ceiling perhaps two giants in height. In the center of the ceiling a round black funnel disappeared into a sooty smokestack.

I dropped my eyes. Below lay a circular pit filled with tables and men and a glowing coal bed.

Lucifer's pit—the words hissed relentlessly in my head. I fought to bring my panic under control.

We stood on a six-foot-wide ledge that encircled the sunken hall. Along this ledge stood a ring of tall, wrought-iron tripodial pedestals, twenty-four I counted later, which spaced the circumference of the hall. Each pedestal blossomed at the top into a heavy iron brazier, burning oil with a hissing flame, sending sooty black smoke twisting up the center chimney. Every pedestal was linked to the next by a loosely hung chain of heavy black iron—the whole arrangement imposing a disturbing impression of enchainment. The only two tripods not linked by chain were the two directly to the left and right of the stone steps descending into the hall.

The hall was sunken about nine feet. Heavy tapestries hung the walls, depicting battle scenes in dark opulent hues. In the center of the circular room a low rim surrounded a much smaller circle, a shallow depression in the stone floor, a coal bed sparkling to the rim with gold-hot embers, smoking and sizzling like a lake on fire.

Around the smouldering pit stood six long tables angled end to end in a hexagonal formation. The benches at the tables were seated with men in legion uniform without helm and armor. I recognized Equestrian insignia.

On the opposite side of the dining hall, seated on a tall chair atop a stone dais, appearing hazy and wavery through writhing heat above the embers, the Lord of Lorrach brooded over supper in his sunken hall.

I tried taking a deep breath to steady myself, but the hot, stuffy air did me no good. Nothing but iron will got me down the thirteen steps to the pit floor while all eyes watched our descent, the council representative gripping one end of the chain and me collared at the other end.

My whole being seemed trapped in chains, and I could only move where they pulled me. My whole being desperately wanted to run, but I knew exactly how far I would get—just five steps before I jerked up short on the chain.

As we rounded the bed of hot coals (perhaps it was eighteen or twenty feet across the diameter) I had a clear view of the Count of the Rhine Frontier—gaunt and pale, a short, black beard closely trimmed, a long red cloak brooched at both shoulders and belted over a fitted long-sleeved black leather tunic, military trousers and nonregulation boots knotted over the calf—a thirtyish man whose classic profile bespoke a bloodline of pure Roman aristocracy.

Count Lagos regarded me complacently while the representative unraveled his pompous greeting and presented me as "a gift prompted by the high esteem the Most Illustrious Count arouses in the humble breast of his faithful Consul at Vesontio."

Lagos made vaguely amused sounds—a bare semblance of laughter—from behind an unpleasant smile.

"He's short on his tribute again, I take it," the Count hissed.

The representative answered hastily, "The Consul offers you one quarter for your troops as is customary. . . ."

"One quarter is not enough!" snapped the Count, a fist striking the armrest of his chair. "My troops *must* be supplied, even if his city does suffer! Your Consul forgets that the frontier army is all that holds a barbarian horde from raging down the valley and annihilating his precious city! I have the garrisons Basilia and Vindonissa to oversee *and* these forests to secure! Do you imagine the Germanni respect your borders out of courtesy? No? They would be amassing for attack in these hills this moment if they did not so fear Count Lagos. My men must be hardy and well supplied. A quarter tribute is no longer sufficient. My tax agent assures me that Vesontio can spare one third in kind. Tell your Consul to see that it does."

"It has been a poor year, Excellency."

"Ah, and shall I beg the Alamanni and Marcomanni rabble not to attack this year because my men are shorted?" Count Lagos sneered. "Or perhaps you would suggest I sent them a rag-tag dwarf as a *bribe*."

The representative almost whined, "Our Consul thought you might find some amusement in the dwarf, your Excellence."

"Then I accept it as a token of the good Consul's *high esteem*. Audience is ended." The Count waved him away. "You may join my officers for supper and deliver my reply to Vesontio on the morrow."

The representative, tight-lipped, found a place at the right-hand table. Lagos leaned back and eyed me with disconcerting speculation. I stared up at him, knowing I looked a proper tatterdemalion in worn and torn homespun. Then I remembered where I stood and that he represented the Emperor. I bowed briefly.

"Ah," he said, satisfied, "it has manners. Is it amusing?"

I glanced around briefly before realizing that he addressed *me*.

"I suppose so, Excellency. I'm skilled at telling tales."

He snorted in surprise. "Why the little beast speaks the Emperor's Latin, too!"

Under the roomful of laughter, I straightened my shoulders and collected as much height as I possessed.

"I read and write both Latin and Greek, your Excellency. I studied at the University of Rome under Master Umbrusus Elusius." Then in a desperate bid for a way out of here, "If you care to contact him, he will provide me impeccable references."

"References?" Amusement tinged his voice. "I've no use for an over-educated hobgoblin."

I swallowed a hot retort.

"Still, a puff-head dwarf does promise some interesting diversion."

I misliked the sound of that. I gave him close scrutiny; he fixed me with a dissolute and sanguine eye, a look that bespoke a foul disposition.

"What tricks can you do?"

I sighed. "Very few anymore, your . . ."

"No good!" The Count snapped forward in his chair. Then he assumed a tone of reasonable argument. "Any tame malformity worth his supper does tricks."

"I'm not a tame—!" I choked off, suddenly heedful of my foolhardy retort.

Lagos cocked an eyebrow toward the listening men and smirked. "Not malformed?" he traduced in false innocence.

I did not need to turn around to see the jeers and stares behind me; I could hear the laughter plainly enough. How could I argue *anything* in the face of so much concerted ridicule? I clung to what dignity I could.

"Not tame, at any rate!" I blurted—unwisely.

Now Lagos flung his head back and emitted a mirthless sound. "Not tame, little imp? At least not yet, eh? Well, well," he suddenly hissed in a deceptively soft and sibilant voice, "we will remedy that easily enough."

The Count's vicious smirk insinuated that he would take a perverse pleasure in taming a stubborn dwarf. In the watchful silence that stilled the hall, I knew I trod on dangerous ground. Though on the verge of panic, I stood like chiseled stone.

"Show your tricks, then, you shrunken monstrosity. I trust you'll not be so imprudent as to forget them." He pointed to a waiting slave. "Remove the collar."

So the hateful collar and chain were taken from my neck, but I felt no relief. Weary, hungry, stiff from the long, cold wagon ride, I dared not disobey. I wondered grimly what would be my fate if in truth I had not known any "tricks."

Docilely I put my hands to the floor and did slow flip-overs to loosen up. No music, no vagabond troupe, no applauding spectators—nothing but the grim hall, feet and hands slapping stone, stiffling air, the mutter of men and the clank of cups, the hiss of embers and the roar of oil fires. My performance was grueling and nerve straining. I had not really tumbled for months, save an occasional spontaneous burst of flips and wheels and handstands that sprang forth on lonely grassy swards when I could not contain my joy. But this—my heart was nowhere in it. With leaden feet and trembling hands, I determined to see it through to the bitter end. And bitter it was. When I stumbled, which was often in my distress, the company of officers clapped, cheered, and shouted insults; whenever I stopped to catch breath and balance they pounded on the tables and called for more. Haltingly I glanced toward the Count, and his dark stare and imperious gesture set me spinning again.

I could not go on. I had not the supple body of my boyhood; I was unpracticed, ungainly, exhausted. I collapsed face down on the cold stone floor, gasping for air.

Fire streaked across my face. My hand jerked to my cheek, and I saw the whipsman recoil the lead-tipped whip. My face burned; my hand came away smeared with blood and sweat.

"Get up. I've not given you leave to stop."

Wretchedly, I forced my weary muscles to move and tried to go on. By now I was dizzy and the circular hall spun faster than I did. I collapsed again, and the whip struck again, now across the back of my neck.

I jerked, and stumbled to my feet.

In less than two backflips I fell again, flat on my back. The ceiling receded in darkness. The whip bit, slashing through my shirt. Painfully I rolled over and crept to elbows and knees.

I could not get up.

The whip stung my back, once, twice.

I pushed against the floor with my hands and could not see them. My muscles quivered and I fell forward. My breath burned in painful gulps; blood hammered hot in my head; my heart felt it must burst open in my chest. They might whip me to death, but I could not get up.

The Count laughed long and loud.

"Pathetic performance," he sneered. "Trust the Consul of Vesontio to try and bribe Count Lagos with such a useless creature."

Laughter fell around me. I pressed my hot forehead against the cold floor and tried to breathe, prayed silently, desperately, to be gone from here.

"Yet I do possess an artful appreciation of the absurd. Our dwarf must have a suitable name. What shall it be?"

Names, ludicrous and lewd, bandied about the hall with riotous glee. I tasted salt on my lips and realized I was quietly weeping.

"*You! Dwarf!* On your feet!"

Somehow I managed to get to my feet, wiping a sleeve across my face. I winced; the sleeve came away blood streaked. I gazed up at the sneering man seated high upon the dais. It seemed to me the room had dimmed considerably.

Lagos raised a jeweled finger for silence. "A proper Roman name," pronounced the Count, "befitting his dignity. Stumpus Runtus Monstrosito!"

The hall echoed with laughter. I trembled in horror and misery. My worst nightmares had come to claim me: that I would be trapped and taunted and tormented with no hope of respite or escape. Dumbly, I heard that epithet bantered about the hall. I could only stare glassy-eyed at the black onyx ring on the Count's right forefinger as he rubbed it absently beneath his close-bearded chin.

"Well, well, Monstrosito. How tame are you now?"

Suddenly the ringed hand reached to a platter on a stand, delicately lifted a large chunk of beef between forefinger and thumb, and flung it with a slap upon the flagstone at my feet. I looked dazedly from the meat to the cold reptilian smile. What did the man think I was? A dog? I did not pick it up.

That onyxed finger said much: It flicked just barely to the side; the whipsman let his coiled, black lash snake out across the floor; he drew the lead tip slowly over my rag-tattered feet. I gazed along the slithering whip to the whipsman, who with one eye (the other was patched) awaited a signal from the Count. My alternatives were clear—pick up the meat now or perhaps eat it off the floor after a further taste of the lash. Humiliated, I reached to take the scrap of meat, but a growl stayed my hand.

The low, vicious warning stopped me cold. The gigantic black wolfhound must have been lying behind the dais, out of my sight. Now it crept forward, a deep-throated snarl curling its lip, bare fangs exposed. Even hunched at the shoulders, the huge hound looked me eye to glittering eye as it stalked forward, a menacing growl in every breath.

"I wouldn't make any sudden moves, Monstrosito," the Count said casually.

Trembling, I eased my hand back. The hound came on, and scarcely ceasing its rumblings nor taking its watchful gaze off me, gobbled the meat down in two voracious gulps.

272

The wolfhound continued to snarl and took a step toward me, hackles bristling. I froze.

"*Caesar! Down!*" snapped the Count. The hound backed down and crouched beside the dais, eyeing me. Lagos laughed.

"How unfortunate for you, Monstrosito. You've let Caesar eat your supper. You'll be quicker next time, I trust."

I had long since lost any appetite and now my heart lodged in my throat. I heard the Count order his winecup filled, and he stepped down from the dais, setting his cup on the right-hand table. Then he took the leather collar and rebuckled it around my neck. I flinched as he pulled it tight where the whip had cut across the back of my neck. Lagos cupped his hand hard under my chin and jerked my head back so that I must look straight up at his face as he loomed over me.

"How tame now, my little malformity?" he smiled downward.

I stared up in nought but terror. That pleased him.

"Tell the Consul," he said, glancing toward the representative, "that I find his *gift* amusing after all." Then he tossed the other end of the chain to the whipsman and seated himself at the head of the table.

"Secure him in the slave quarters."

The whipsman jerked the chain and pulled me forward; I stumbled to keep up. My eyes, pleading, met those of the council representative. He looked away and quaffed his wine. The next jerk sent me sprawling. Midst catcalls and laughter I staggered after the whipsman, across the circular hall and up the thirteen steps—half-dragged I was, the steps being too high for my short-legged gait.

Across the grey frozen courtyard I was pulled, past a spew of Roman outbuildings to the back of a long, narrow rectangular building. I was dragged into a dim, cold room—the slave's quarters—and given over to the hallmaster.

"And what'm *I* supposed to do with the little bug?"

"Secure him," replied the whipsman, "until the Count calls for him."

The red-faced, beefy man pulled me to a corner where an iron ring was imbedded in a support beam. Someone fetched another hoop of iron open at one end and fashioned to be closed by a bolt. The hallmaster slipped the hoop through the iron ring and the end-link of the chain. He then closed the loop using a bolt and wrench. Judging from the force he put into bolting it, it would be nearly impossible to loosen without the wrench. I could still unbuckle the collar, though, if they did not bind my hands.

I thought too soon. He inspected the collar.

"The bugger'll be out of this as soon as my back is turned." He whipped off the collar and proceeded to force another bolt through the aligned buckle holes, enlarging them to accommodate the bolt. Then he strapped the collar back around my neck and bolted it in the same manner as the chain.

All the while he made crass comments and guffaws at my size and shape.

"There now, he'll not slip out of that too easily." He sat back on his heels and eyeballed me speculatively. A lewd grin split his greasy face.

"Let's see what his cockles look like."

I stood like stone, resigned to enduring this further humiliation, as he untied my trousers and lowered them.

"Ha! Let's see what they can do, then." With that he squeezed my genitals in his grimy hand.

I swear I did not do it on purpose, though it seemed so. I was as startled as he. First a look of disbelief and then of beet-faced rage distorted his face. He stared at his hand and, bellowing, struck me backhanded, sending me spinning on my face against the dirt floor.

"*Piss in my hand,* will you!" Next thing I knew he jerked me up by the chain, hauled me off my feet in midair, and shook the chain furiously.

"I suppose you think that's funny, eh? Well, I'll show you what *I* think's funny, you piss-faced little . . ."

I did not think it funny at all; I was choking to death. A whipcrack stopped his tirade, and he dropped me abruptly to the ground. The hallmaster grasped his sliced shoulder and glared at the whipsman in affronted anger.

The whipsman grinned. "I'd hate to hear you explain to Count Lagos how you killed his new pet—and why."

The blood drained from the hallmaster's face as he considered this consequence of my sudden demise. After glowering ineffectually back and forth between the whipsman and myself for several seconds, he spat on me and stomped off.

Of the few slaves in the quarters witnessing the little scene, not one so much as cracked a smile. They avoided the hallmaster's glare.

The whipsman, still grinning, recoiled his lash and left.

Ignored, I clutched my trousers together and crept into the dim corner. There I huddled, shaking, eyes darting to take in the gloomy slave hall and its gloomy occupants. Above my head there hung a damp water-bucket with a drinking ladle hooked over the side. I would have given anything for a drink of water, but the bucket hovered well out of my reach.

I dropped my head to my knees in despair.

Oh God, don't leave me here.

And so I came to Lorrach Keep.

XXX

I saw much of the Keep, for Count Lagos took a fancy to having me led behind him on the chain while he inspected the grounds. The ancient circular hall—the Great Hall, it was called—commanded an expansive courtyard within the encircling wall. The smaller buildings were all Roman: storehouses, smokehouses, barracks, officers' quarters, baths, stables, kennels and such. Most prominent were the slave quarters, common kitchen, and common hall, which were housed in one long rectangular structure. At one end was the common troops' entrance, which descended a few steps into a dark, wood-beamed hall lined with tables and benches, where the six hundred regular soldiers dined. The far end formed a large brick hearth in which a fire was kept blazing from before first dawn light on into the night. Directly behind the great fireplace, sharing the same chimney, lay the common kitchen. Behind the kitchen was the slave quarters—a cramped, cold room barely warmed with the heat that seeped in from the kitchen fires. I spent most my days and nights chained in a far corner, always cold.

The outer wall of the old fortress had been well repaired. It stood about twenty feet high, and the inner surface was so smoothly mortared that I spied not a fingerhold or toehold any-where. Strange—unsettling strange—that a fortress guarding the frontier should be as well designed to keep men in as out. Of course, with a crack troupe of acrobats . . . but I tried not to think about that.

The slaves in the Keep seemed sullen and dour, as though the Count's venomous breath pervaded every man's blood. Sadly absent was the good-natured, late-evening slave chatter that relieves long hours of silent obedience. My few tentative attempts at conversation aroused only monosyllabic replies and curious stares. They wanted none of my acquaintance, and it was not until much later that I clearly realized why. One does not make a friend of a man whom one knows is doomed; rather one secretly is pleased that it is *he* who will take the brunt of the master's caprices instead of oneself. Count Lagos ruled with an iron grip and a cruel whim that lashed out without warning, wanting only a victim, and a hapless dwarf afforded a nicely expendable scapegoat.

None of the slaves were women. Indeed, there were no women at all in Lorrach Keep, and their absence I keenly felt, for women seem to gentle a place by their very presence. Still, if Lorrach boasted even one female slave it must needs have enough to go around, impractical to say the least in a frontier outpost. The troops took rotating jaunts down to Basilia and Vindonissa, where camp women and town whores were plentiful. Count Lagos himself sometimes brought in a female slave or two, but he never kept them long.

The common troops themselves were a variegation of uprooted and displaced men. None were of Gallic or Germanic blood, for the Roman army does not arm men on their home frontier. Gauls and Germanni in particular might not leap too eagerly to hold the Rhineland for Rome, so the soldiers stationed at Lorrach Keep came from diverse parts of the western Empire: Iberia, Italia, Illyricum, Africa. For twenty years the army must be their only loyalty, even above their own families, who sometimes follow them from outpost to outpost and settle in nearby camp-towns like Basilia on the Rhine. The sense of isolation only thickened the poisonous atmosphere within the ancient fortress.

The common soldiers had their comings and goings, drills and inspections, hunting and scouting parties to occupy the day, while at eventide, when they settled in their hall and the other slaves waited upon them, I must be in attendance in Lucifer's pit, as I thought of it, for the amusement of Count Lagos, his officers, and their cohort of horsemen.

I find it difficult to describe the wretchedness I suffered. If I wanted supper I snatched up the scraps thrown my way, and quickly, lest Caesar get his wolfish eye on them. Sometimes I felt the whip if I seemed not eager enough to please, yet Lagos truly took pleasure only in my humiliation. He delighted in showing me off to occasional officious guests and then berating me for clumsiness and a misshapen body.

"Monstrosito," he would point out gleefully, "is proof that the gods have a sense of humor. Why else create such a travesty of the human form, such a stunted and grotesque caricature of ourselves, why else but for the gods' amusement—and ours? Therefore, Monstrosito will now amuse us."

Whereupon he would have me released from the collar; the guests would stare and applaud as I did the few simple acrobatics I could do alone and under so much duress. Then they would laugh as the whipsman lashed me up the thirteen steps, forcing me to scramble on all fours up the steep stairs to escape the sharp, leaded sting.

Then, driven back to the slave quarters, I would be put to work by the hallmaster. For he had complained to the Count that I did no work to earn my keep, and it was a poor showing for the other slaves to see me lounging in a corner all day while they were laboring. *Lounging!* I suppose being chained to a post could be called lounging, but when the hallmaster removed the bolt from the collar, unbuckled it, and kicked me toward the common hall to scrub down tables, I was glad of it. But each evening after I returned from Lucifer's pit, exhausted and thirsty, then scrubbed every table, the hallmaster tightened the bolts again. He would never deign to give me the drink I so craved, but by now I had discovered, when all were asleep, how to swing the chain up over the ladle on the water-bucket, tip the bucket carefully, and aim a stream of cold water down over my face, into my dry mouth. Except once when the bucket was fuller than usual, I miscalculated and the chain slipped, overbalancing the bucket and dumping its entire contents over my head, causing much mirth in the slave quarters and a shivering wet night for me.

On a sunny, clear winter day, as I scraped and swept mud off the peristyle portico that perimetered the common hall, Count Lagos and his two hundred horsemen returned triumphantly from one of their patrols in the forested hills. I watched them clatter through the gates, Lagos's standard (a red wyvern on gold) and the Roman eagle (gold on red) held imperiously aloft. I saw they also carried other objects aloft, horrible objects: heads freshly cloven, faces contorted and drained, blond and bloody-bearded, impaled on the long lances and paraded about the courtyard to the whoops and cheers of the regulars. There must have been two dozen beheaded barbarians set upon the wall as prizes that day, and a half-dozen living prisoners bound and force-marched behind the horses. The beheaded proved to be the more fortunate.

Lagos had the six prisoners lined up before the citadel with all the Keep assembled. He accused the prisoners of encroaching upon the Empire's borderlands. He told them to have no illusions that they would not soon be telling him all they knew of Alamanni movements and plans. Some of the bedraggled barbarians looked defiant, others afraid. Lagos paced past them studiously, then he singled out the youngest, most terrified of the lot—a lad of maybe eighteen or so—and had him shoved forward. Two men turned a crank affixed to the citadel and, with a groan and creak, lowered that forgotten iron hook that had so shaken me when first I saw it. Now I learned why.

Two more men grasped the boy by his bound hands and shoulders and pinned his legs behind theirs. Quite casually, Count Lagos drew his hunting knife and sliced the boy's abdomen wide open. He then reached his gloved hand into the gaping cut and hauled out a handful of his screaming victim's intestines; he shoved the hook up under the bloody mass and signaled for the hook to be raised. The impaled boy, shrieking and writhing, was hauled off his feet and bright red blood splashed all over the ground.

Oh God oh God oh God oh God, I heard myself crying over and over, an unbelieving litany of horror.

It had happened so quickly. The stunned and horrified prisoners were still being held back by their bonds and the strong arms of the guards. Lagos was meticulously wiping his bloody gloves on a kerchief and watching the dangling, jerking, screaming boy.

Oh God oh God! Shaking, sickened, I shut my eyes against the sight, sweating, forcing trembling knees not to buckle. We stood there an eternity until the boy's death agonies were done and he hung silent and still. And there he stayed, while the red-brown splotch in the mud beneath him soaked up fresh blood, until dark. And the sound and sight of him haunted me unceasingly all that evening, all that sleepless night, all the next day, until next evening brought a new horror for me to contemplate.

Meanwhile, I heard some of the cavaliers boasting to the regular troops how they had massacred the Alamanni camp—a camp not of an army but of men, women, and children, with beasts and hovels—and what they had done to the fair-haired women before killing them. These were the men Lagos kept around him in the

Great Hall. If any of the regulars objected to rape, murder of children, and torture of prisoners, they kept quiet about it. And no word of this, it was understood, was to pass the gates of Lorrach Keep.

Evening next, Lagos feasted the five remaining prisoners in Lucifer's pit. None of them ate. Two of them could barely sit on the benches to which their ankles were bound. They showed signs of torture: ghastly burns, long furrows of peeled skin, fingers a joint shorter. Lagos looked pleased with himself.

After supper some of the men drunkenly banged cups on the tables and called for sport, *sport*, *SPORT!* until finally Lagos rose grinning amid cheers and salutes and gave them what they wanted. The Count chose a dozen officers, who took their long lances and ringed the circular ember pit in the center of the hall. A hapless prisoner was dragged forward and hands bound behind him. He fought in horror, knowing instinctively what was about to happen, but he was heaved unceremoniously into the center of the hot coal pit, while men roared with excitement and scrambled to tabletops to see the sport.

Screaming horribly, the man shot up and tried to come out of the burning coals, but he was shoved back relentlessly by a fence of lances. He staggered around the pit, emitting horrible sounds, flinging himself against the lances, which shoved him back into the fiery hell.

Oh God! I closed my eyes, covered my ears.

Suddenly a hand grasped my hair and snapped my head back. Lagos.

"Squeamish, Monstrosito?" He dragged me by the hair to the rim of the pit. "Watch—if you do not wish to join him."

Near enough to feel the heat, near enough to smell the scorching flesh, to hear the sizzle and crackle beneath the screams, I witnessed a death more hideous than I ever imagined possible. Lagos did not release me until all was done. That gruesome death haunted my waking and sleeping for weeks to follow.

Two other prisoners died in the kennels, pitted barehanded against the Count's wolfhounds. They were ripped to pieces by the crazed dogs, Caesar first among them.

I never knew how the fifth man died. It was done in the lower chambers of the Keep, somewhere in the dark bowels beneath the pit.

The sixth man had both his eyes seared out, both hands lopped

280

off, and was escorted to the nearest Alamanni stronghold to serve as warning and give witness to the fate of captives.

It was murmured among the slaves and regular troops that once Lorrach Keep was the citadel of a sorcerer of antiquity—a sorcerer a thousand years dead who upon his death became one of the demons he had consort with—and that even now he and his horde of demons haunted the Great Hall's depths.

As far as I was concerned, the demons in the Great Hall were of flesh and blood, and Count Lagos lord over them all. I had seen the men's faces and their mad delight in the prisoners' terror and agony. I could well believe the evil sorcerer had incarnated as Count of the Rhine Frontier and driven demons to possess his men.

I lived in terror of Count Lagos, for I knew not when he might decide to use me for sport. Then Lord Fairfax came to call. He was Provencial Governor of Maxima Sequanorum, brother-in-law to Count Lagos—and a toad. He reminded me of a gibbous, wrinkled toad with half-open eyes that blinked when he swallowed. With him came Lady Fairfax, the Count's sister. She displayed the same aristocratic Roman features as her brother, but her emaciated and skeletal figure gave her an air more cadaverous than elegant. I was reminded of a mummy I had seen on display in the Alexandrian Museum. Now, I know I am a fine one to speak on the appearance of any human being, but no jest was in my thoughts, for I do by my own experience attest that these people, too, were demons inside.

They lounged on three dining couches placed in the Great Hall for the occasion. I stood, collared and chained, hoping the Count would overlook me tonight, knowing he would not. As the first course was served by silent slaves, the Lady Fairfax studied me curiously over her winecup.

"Lagos, what is this hideous thing you have on a chain?"

"Ah." Lagos smiled at his sister. "So you notice my dwarf, Levinia? I call him Monstrosito."

The Lady laughed. "You've always been clever with words, Lagos. What do you keep him for?"

"For amusement. He does acrobatics—after a fashion. Monstrosito, where are your manners? Bid Lady Fairfax a proper welcome."

Carefully, fearfully, I bowed before the Count's sister, a deep, courtly bow—perfect, though my hands were trembling.

"Welcome, great Lady . . ." my voice wavered "to Lorrach Keep. We are honored." I looked up to meet her laughter.

"Wonderful! Why is he on a chain? He looks quite tame."

"Oh, he *is* quite tame," Lagos concurred. "The chain is for . . . effect. You'd be surprised how shocked some people are when they see I have a dwarf on a chain, though they attempt to pretend they're not. Many people are squeamish about such things, but they dare not admit it to *me*. I fancy they're afraid of me. Thus when I make jest of him and say 'he's a perfectly absurd mockery of humanity, don't you agree, lord so-and-so, lady so-and-so?' they force themselves to chime right in and humiliate poor little Monstrosito. I find it extremely amusing."

Lady Fairfax looked me over, drained her wine goblet, and held it out to be refilled, clicking her tongue in mock sympathy.

"Poor little Monstrosito," she repeated. "But we are not squeamish, are we, brother? My Lord Fairfax?"

Lord Fairfax was deep in his soup.

"*Fairfax!*"

Fairfax slurped, glanced at me, swallowed and blinked. "Quite, my dear. What else does one do with such a creature but chain it somewhere?" He resumed slurping.

Quite. What indeed? I tried to look disinterested.

Another course was served—some sort of galantine of chilled animal fat and meat. Lady Fairfax picked a little at hers, wiped her fingers daintily, and lifted her wine cup.

"I'm afraid I've filled up on soup. Can we not see some of the dwarf's tricks?"

Lagos nodded. "Monstrosito."

The whipsman unbuckled the collar, though I could have managed it myself. Silently I did flips, wheels, stands, and as many variations as I knew until finally Lagos called a halt and I was allowed to stand at rest, hot and dizzy and nearly breathless.

Lady Fairfax set her goblet down and applauded. "Very good, Monstrosito! Here, you may have my salad."

She took the plate of galantine and flung its contents to the floor. It slapped and slid across the flagstones and came to rest in a quivering, greasy mass.

I stared down at the lump of fat and felt suddenly sick. For once I wished Caesar was here.

"My sister offered you supper." I heard the hiss of warning in Lagos's voice.

Obediently, I scooped up a slippery glob in two hands. I tried, really tried, to swallow a mouthful, but I was overheated, exhausted, and . . . and *angry* . . . and my body betrayed me. The jiggling muck slid about halfway down before it came back up again. I gagged, and the slime went splat on the stone floor and wriggled there.

"Oh, *disgusting!*" exclaimed Lady Fairfax.

Lord Fairfax heaved in a fit of mirth somewhat between wheezing and croaking. "Huh, huh, huh, huh, huh! Your dwarf may have better taste than we do, Lagos!" He ignored his wife's livid glare.

Lagos's face blotched crimson and white.

"Eat it!" He pointed. "Get down and eat it!"

I stared at Lagos, then at the mess on the floor, and reluctantly got down on hands and knees. No doubt about it, I could not eat it; I was gagging already. I raised my eyes to the Count.

"Why, he looks positively sullen!" complained Lady Fairfax. "He certainly is due a lesson in manners."

I? I?

"Huh, huh, huh, huh, huh, huh, huh!"

Lagos held me in his cold stare for an interminable moment, then his eyes glittered, and a reptant smile curled his lips.

"Defiant, Monstrosito? I wondered how long before tame little Monstrosito turned defiant."

To my horror I realized the mirthless hiss behind his teeth was laughter.

"Get up." Lagos signaled the whipsman to replace the collar around my neck. "I suggest, Monstrosito, throughout the remainder of supper you contemplate possible means of correction I might employ this evening."

Whether I willed or no, I contemplated.

"By the way, Fairfax," Lagos remarked casually as more wine and sweetmeats were served, "you've never toured my dungeons, have you?"

"I've never had the pleasure," said Fairfax, tasting a sweetmeat. He gulped it down and rolled his eyes—just like a toad. "I hear you've quite an interrogation chamber down there."

Lagos gloated. "I have my little devices."

"And vices," quipped Lady Fairfax, tittering on the wine.

"Pity I haven't any prisoners at present, or I would stage a little demonstration."

Lady Fairfax tittered again. "Did you not say something, brother, about a lesson in manners this evening?" Her glance landed on me. She smiled the same reptant smile as her brother.

Did I once foolishly believe that a woman gentles a place? By now I was trembling and my heart pounding.

"So I did, Levinia. Monstrosito hasn't visited my secret little chamber yet, have you, Monstrosito? How have you escaped it so long?"

Oh God.

"We'll remedy that tonight."

I stared helplessly up at the Count. I felt a tug on the collar as the whipsman twisted the chain around an iron ring in the floor, as if I might stupidly try to run—as if I had any strength or will left me.

They leisurely finished the wine. Lagos dismissed the officers and cavaliers from the hall and gestured to the whipsman and another of his henchmen. The henchman fetched torches for himself and the whipsman and held aside a greasy tapestry. Behind it gaped a vorant black hole into which the whipsman dragged me on the chain.

Now I learned to my infinite terror that there was indeed a darker Hell below the floor of Lucifer's pit. Panic overwhelmed all reason and I pulled back in a useless attempt to resist. The whipsman jerked me forward, and I sprawled down the stone steps right into him. He gripped the collar with his huge hand, half choking me, and forced me before him down the dark, spiraling stairwell into restless shadows cast by torchlight.

Behind me I heard a hollow scuffing and Lady Fairfax's echoing giggle. "What fun!"

"Careful, my dear. It's slippery."

The remainder of the descent faded in a nightmarish swirl. Not until we had traversed a low, narrow corridor and I was flung roughly to the floor of a dank and sooty chamber could I cough and gulp for air. My vision cleared to see Count Lagos swing the heavy door shut with a sonorous clang and shove the high bolt home. The chamber sprang afire with light as torches were set to oil lamps. The instrumental purpose of the chamber leapt out in vivid detail. On my knees I looked up at the five figures towering over me, staring down with devouring interest. I bowed my head and shuddered.

"Get him ready."

A hand reached for the collar; I struck it away, not thinking, just reacting. My mind was numb, refusing to believe what my senses told it. I struck at the hand again; it struck back. Inexorably, regardless of my struggles, they stripped me bare and slung me onto the table of wood and iron in the chamber's center. They shackled my wrists and ankles and jerked the chains tight through iron rings set fast at each corner of the table.

I lay on my back, breathing hard, gasping, staring at Lagos, stunned, terrified.

"You see, Fairfax, my 'bed of intrigue' is large enough to hold the hugest of men, yet it perfectly accommodates Monstrosito, though he appears pitifully small stretched out upon it." He grinned viperously. "This may be to your benefit, Monstrosito. Perhaps we can add a few inches to your height, eh?" The black onyx on his finger made circular motions; the whipsman and henchman busied themselves on either side of the table. The chains on my arms pulled tighter. Then tighter.

"The wheels catch on each notch until the release is pulled."

"Ingenious."

"Tighter."

I whimpered.

"A large man's joints may be pulled from the sockets. Again."

My shoulders and arms burned as though they were ripping apart. I groaned. Groin muscles caught fire.

"I daresay this device could tear Monstrosito completely apart," Lagos remarked thoughtfully.

"Oh, Lagos, *disgusting!*"

"Quite. We certainly won't do it if it's going to disgust you, Levinia. How are the irons coming? Not hot enough yet? Here, Fairfax, let me show off my instruments. . . ." and he began to talk of horrible tortures as he might talk of stables or kennels.

My senses reeled beneath the smell of burning charcoal, the whoosh of bellows, the murmur of voices, the ache of muscles stretched taut—I could scarcely even turn my head. A shadow over me brought my eyes open with a start. Levinia, sipping from her goblet, regarded me at her leisure.

"Pay attention, Monstrosito," she admonished tipsily. "This lesson is for you."

"*Please* . . ." I whispered hopelessly, "*Lady. . . .*"

Her response was delirious laughter. Plunking the goblet down near my head, she moved away, and moments later returned to my sight bearing in a thick-gloved hand an iron brand, a fierce red rod of fire. I cried out involuntarily. She waved it crazily over me, a dancing ribbon of fire, and swept toward my groin.

Lagos caught her hand. "Now, now, Levinia. There's an art to inflicting pain. It must be done with deliberation, not carelessness, or you will lose your prisoner, and the sport will be over. And if you seek information . . . but, of course, poor Monstrosito doesn't have any information. . . ."

Now I was sobbing uncontrollably.

"Allow me to guide your hand. You choose your spot; I'll control the pressure. Not there . . . not yet . . . we do want him conscious. . . ."

And molten, searing fire burned into the inside of my thigh; a scream tore through my throat; my body strained against unrelenting chains. Thereafter was a hellish ordeal of smouldering irons that scorched my flesh again and again while I writhed in helpless torment. My pitiful sobs brought no release from the hot agony, the cruel shackles, the woman's scathing laughter, demon faces, my own maddened cries.

I was losing consciousness in a red haze when wine splattered over my face.

"Not yet, Monstrosito," hissed Lagos. "We're not finished yet."

"*Oh God!*" I wept.

"God doesn't hear you down here, Monstrosito."

XXXI

Fully laden tribute wagons creaked and groaned into the outpost yard, pulled by trudging oxen. Grain, salt, pork, wine, tools, goods of all kinds poured into the fortress storehouses. Then the empty wagons rattled out the gate, across the bridge, and down the mountain. I watched. I waited. Free of the collar, I was supposedly in the wellhouse, pumping water through the pipes into the common hall. But I had done that hastily and disappeared. Hunkered down amidst stacked barrels, intently following every wagon with my eyes, scrutinizing each one carefully, searching the undersides, I chose my wagon and waited. Finally it returned, clattering noisily toward the gate.

I rolled between the wheels and scrambled madly for the forward axle, grasping it with both hands and swinging my feet up to hook between axle and wagon-bottom. Now I held on for my life, hidden, I hoped, behind the solid wheels and beneath the low-riding wagon.

The wagon stopped before the gates to let another enter. I held, muscles aching, but I held. The wagon lurched forward; I fought to tighten my hold; we crossed the bridge and jounced over the split-log road. Still, I forced my limbs to hang on. When I knew I must drop, I waited for a sharp switch in the mountain road.

I let go, let the wagon rattle over me, and scrambled into the underbrush before the noses of the next oxen-team appeared around the bend. I was free! Loose in the Black Forest!

287

Melting into the hushed vault of dark evergreen, I came near to crying aloud. Since my cruel ordeal in the torture chamber, I had taken a full month to gain the strength, the will, the opportunity to escape. And now, joyously I filtered deeper into the hush of the wood. Where stray streaks of sunlight penetrated the trees and touched the mossy carpet, the forest floor seemed emblazoned with brilliant patches of green brightwork. My quiet footsteps left soggy prints in the soft mud on a zig-zag course behind me. No matter. I made my way deep into the vert; I would be far away before they missed me.

I had no plan but to put a thousand miles distance between myself and Lorrach Keep. If I would continue my journey home, then I must cross the River Rhine eventually, but not here—not so near Basilia. To be seen anywhere along the Rhine within the Count's suzerainity would mean the end. To enter into Maxima Sequanorum where that toad Fairfax governed would be insanity. A hunt would be on; word would go out. Lagos would not take lightly the escape of a "tame" dwarf from his inescapable Lorrach Keep. But I would be long gone—north—into the oak and pine wilderness of Germania.

Swiftly I traveled, until weariness slowed my course, and I stopped to catch my breath on a grassy knoll. Greeted with clear cobalt skies and a warm spring wind, I sat trembling. Lorrach Keep had taken its toll; I was a pale, thin waif weakened by confinement, fear, inability to eat or sleep. I had come there in winter; now the Earth was deep into spring.

Had I been there just one season?

Rested, I forced myself to push on through the forest where pines grew so high and thick that the forest floor was a brown carpet of pine needles and bright shoots of greenery. I had no food or water, no warm clothes, but I did not care. If I died in the wilds, so be it—at least I would die free and of natural causes.

A trickling, bubbling sound led me to a thin stream sliding over slick, mossy stones. I pushed through the bracken and ferns that crowded the rocky stream bed, fell upon my face, and drank and drank and drank. I bathed my face in the cold water and rolled onto my back to rest. The bent ferns made a soft cushion; sunlight and treetops made dancing patterns across my eyelids; the brook made soothing murmurs of liquid peace. I drifted.

No! I sat abruptly upright. Some inner instinct drove me to swiftly bathe my face again, drink my fill once more, gratefully, and move on.

Then I heard a sound that made my blood run cold.

The hounds!

Had they missed me so soon? Had they so soon guessed I had gotten past the gates?

I heard the cry that proclaimed the hounds were on the scent of their prey. I broke into a run. Then I caught the sound of hunting horns, beyond and above the deep-throated chorus of hounds. Panic overtook me. I burst through a wall of briars and thorns, heedless of scratches to my hands and face, tripped, and fell rolling into a damp creek-bed overhung with green. I fled along the umber tunnel, stumbling on stones, miring in mud, until I found a place to scramble up the other bank, mud and briars fighting my ascent. My hair tangled up in thorns; heedless, I tore away. I could hear the hounds closer now—and the horns.

I pounded through dapple-shaded woods; the needle-strewn earth muffled my footfalls, but not my thudding heart, nor my rasping breath. Unerringly the hounds came on. And when they closed in on me, would they tear me to pieces? Or would they surround me, fence me round with snapping fangs until the hunting party came for me?

Some instinct made me glance backward in my flight; the black wolfhound in the lead raced toward me at twice my own pace. I stumbled, staggered, fell against a tree-trunk, slipped to my knees and flung both arms over my face in futile defense.

The hound stopped inches away, hackles bristling, and worried around me with deep-throated snarls. Caesar. Now the other hounds caught up with him. I tried to shrink from them, shrink to somewhere within myself, for I was trapped between the tree trunk and a dozen massive jaws, savage fangs, predator cries, as the hounds danced around the tree where I huddled afraid to move, too exhausted to move, too defeated to move.

The hunting party rode up to take their quarry. Count Lagos reined his horse and smiled down at me dangerously.

"Shall I set the hounds loose on you, Monstrosito? Or will that be too quick, too easy?"

He called off the hounds and dismounted. Grumbling, the wolfhounds slunk away.

"Escape, my little imp? A foolish gesture. I shall have to teach you better."

I stared wretchedly at his approaching boots. The onyx ring clipped me under the chin and forced my head back sharply so that I gazed straight up into the harsh face gloating over me.

"So you feel like running, do you? Then run you will." Releasing me, he uncoiled a rope he was holding. "Show me those overgrown paws you call hands."

Fearfully, without will to resist, I held both hands before me. He bound them together excruciatingly tight. How far, I wondered dazedly, back to the Keep? Lagos tied the other end of the rope to a loop on his saddle. He mounted the horse and regarded me cooly.

"Now we shall see how you like running, Monstrosito. And never fear, I'll take care that you reach the Keep *alive*."

He kicked his steed; the horse lurched forward with a jerk on my wrists, and I ran. I ran interminably, followed by the great tongue-lolling hounds, encloaked in the dust of the hunting party's mounts. Whenever I fell I was dragged a distance over rough ground and then made to get up and run again. Again and again I fell; slower and slower I ran. The rags on my feet shredded on rocks and briars as I was pulled down the creek-bank and up the other slope at a treacherous crossing. We reached Lorrach Keep at a slow crawl, for I could manage no more; my vision blurred; my feet bled; my lungs burned with sobbing breaths. Finally, finally, the horse walking before me, tugging relentlessly at my wrists, stopped in the courtyard, and I collapsed on the hard-packed mud.

The gates resounded shut. Barely aware of the order to assemble and the sudden activity around me, I lay in deepest despair, prisoner of a never-ending nightmare.

I heard a squeaking, clanking noise overhead and an order to get up. In a terrible dream I struggled to knees and elbows, then onto raw, burning feet—a difficult task with bound hands. I no longer felt my fingers. Blood smeared my wrists and hands.

I looked up to see the iron hook lowering before my eyes. Sickening visions rioted in my head.

Oh God, oh God, I trembled, trying to back away. Hands grasped me, ripped away my tunic, forced me mercilessly forward.

"A lesson in running," proclaimed the Count. "And the next man careless enough to let Monstrosito past the gates will receive the same."

The Count's henchman set the hook between my bound wrists. I was not to be impaled after all. The hook jolted upward, and I cried out at the pain that stabbed down my arms. I dangled above the ground, a hand forced my head up, and I stared into the nightmare face of Lagos.

His eyes swept over me, calculating.

"Twelve lashes!"

He let my head drop.

The lead-tipped whip cut across my flesh like fire, and I cried out with each sharp lash. Like a searing blade the whip struck again and again. In a red cloud of agony I felt a monstrous scorpion slashing its fiery tail all around me, stinging me relentlessly, then pain overwhelmed my failing consciousness.

I awoke in a black pit of fire. The fire raged in my flesh; the blackness pressed in from all directions. I needed no sight to show me where I was; the stale, musty air and damp stone floor told me I lay in the dungeon below the citadel, deep in the bowels of Lorrach Keep.

I burned all over. Every movement set off a fresh streak of pain. And there I lay, in agony and darkness and silence.

Not quite silence. Occasionally I heard a scurry and squeak of rats in the dark. Something crawled over me and I brushed it away—a spider or something. Soon the cool, dank air made me shiver, then I was shaking all over with chills. For I know not how many hours I huddled on the stone floor, freezing and sweating and burning with thirst, before a silent guard flooded the cell with torchlight, dumped a pile of table-scraps on the floor, and poured a pitcherful of water into a dirty basin by the door. Then the light was gone, and I crawled in the dark toward the basin. I cared for nothing but the water; the scraps lay in a heap until a few rats grew bold enough to snatch the pieces away bit by bit.

I was too ill to care. Sickness, chills, and fevers made a battleground of my body. At long intervals sound and light invaded the timeless black in the form of a guard dumping food and water, and during those moments my half-blinded eyes caught odd glimpses of the tiny cell: a stone basin on the floor, piles of filth in the corners, rattails disappearing into chinks in the stone, iron rings devoid of chains along the walls, scorpions scrabbling for cover—and my own body laced with ugly welts swollen and scarlet with infection. No wonder I suffered burning deliriums in the dark, saw demonic faces and figures dancing and cavorting over me. I huddled in a black mire of feverish dreams.

Sometimes I heard voices in the dark. I felt Mother Hagia's cool, dry, wrinkled hand on my hot forehead and heard her crooning voice, "Dominico, sleep now, 'twill all be over soon," and I would be comforted. Then in odd moments of lucidity I would

291

remember she was dead and wonder if I was dying, too. I hoped so. How easy to slip into death and let Mother Hagia lead me away through this darkness.

But there were demons in the dark, too, and when they gibbered and leered around me I shrank in terror from death, for they waited greedily to drag me into Hell. Sometimes I believed I was dead already, and *this* was Hell: pain and fever, demons and horror. The worst was Lagos. Or was it Lucifer? He held me on a chain and pulled me relentlessly toward a pit of fire while I fought ceaselessly not to be dragged in, until I woke screaming and sent the rats scattering for their holes.

Other times I dreamed my mama rocked me gently in her arms and sang a Gallic lullaby. Or my papa laid his big hands over mine and rumbled quiet words. Or Ronaldo knelt beside me with his carefree vagabond grin. But when Felicia clasped my hand, her eyes brilliant with sorrow, I wept because she must be dead like the rest. Mikato, too, though his face was lost in shadows, and I could not see him.

Then the demons came again.

In a dark timelessness, the fever eased, leaving me cold and weak and uncomprehendingly alive. Mayhap I should have been grateful, but I was not. The loneliness of the lightless prison was harder to bear than the fevered dreams. Now I was unsure if the spirits of the dead had truly come to comfort me, yet the visions, the touch of familiar hands, had seemed so real. And now they were gone. No, I was not grateful to be alive.

Now I saw nothing. I heard the patter of rats and the scuttle of scorpions. At long whiles an unspeaking guard came with the table-scraps. I scooped aside a pile for myself and left the rest for the rats, else I would have to fend them off in the dark. I rarely noticed what I ate. More precious to me was the fresh water added to the basin. I sucked it up greedily, on hands and knees like an animal. And I lived in close confines with my own excrement, like a caged beast, except no one would leave a beast in such a dungeon for so long.

I tried telling myself tales to keep from going mad, but the sound of my own voice in the suffocating blackness was too pitiful, and my mind wandered distractedly so that the tales trailed off in bewilderment and tears. Waking and sleeping became confused. Nightmares crouched in dark corners waiting to creep up on me when I slipped into sleep.

Rarely, footfalls and a glimmer of light passed my cell door.

Twice, I heard screams of human agony so distant and tortured they could have come from the depths of Hell.

Then, instead of a guard with supper, the black silhouette in the blinding torch glare was Lagos. He inspected me perfunctorily. I must have healed well enough, for he had the guard haul me to the torture chamber, where my pleas were stiffled with a wadded rag while he calmly explained to a guest what he was about to do. And they branded me with red-hot iron at their pleasure until Lagos grew bored with the sport and had me thrust, sobbing and convulsing, back into the dark dungeon, which welcomed me like a cold, hard womb.

I woke pain-wracked and in deepest despair. I wanted nothing but to die, but some perverse thing inside me refused to let go. My life was torment and bleakest futility, and all I ever thought I knew or believed was useless. Illusion. In anguish and wretchedness I pleaded with the gods for mercy, for if there were gods surely they must have seen me suffer enough. I prayed for the angel of mercy or the angel of death—in my tormented mind they seemed one and the same. I begged and wept incoherently, for my thoughts were disordered and easily escaped my grasp, and I did not even know if any god heard or cared. Even the one I most hoped would take pity on me, the one who would understand suffering, the one who was mocked and whipped and nailed on a cross to die, even he remained silent. In my delirium I believed the promises of prayers answered, but no answer, no solace, no whisper came back to me—not even in dreams.

Now I had come to it. I had no place left to go. The black emptiness. It had been there waiting to swallow me whole all along, and there I drifted helplessly, a desolate soul in a mindless void, immured all around with a hard, unyielding wall of pain, like the cold dungeon walls that held me in darkness.

Then in the never-ending silence briefly sundered by light and food and water, a guard came empty-handed and spoke to me.

"Hie, up you! You're wanted"—he jerked his thumb—"up there."

I covered my eyes. The torch was too bright, and I could not remember what "up there" meant.

"Come on!" the guard snarled, grasping my arm and dragging me to my feet. "He's waiting!"

Blinking, stumbling, I had to be pulled along the narrow corridor and up the spiral steps. The guard pushed aside a heavy tapestry and thrust me into the light.

My eyes shut defensively against the alien glare of two dozen oil lamps, but I had seen enough to recognize Lucifer's pit. I heard a babble of noise fade to a hush, then a voice I recognized from nightmares.

"Monstrosito!"

Ah. I tried to place that word somewhere in the void that was my mind.

"Come forward, Monstrosito!"

I unscrewed my eyes and focused on an onyx-ringed finger. It tapped impatiently on a chair arm. I did not like that finger.

"Monstrosito!"

I knew I was expected to respond, but I could not think how.

"Come forward!" Lagos roared.

I took two unsteady steps and halted in confusion. Naked, filthy, and scarred, I was stunned to discover myself standing in the light before a hall full of staring people. I could not focus on the faces. They kept moving farther and farther away from me.

Lagos rapped out in anger, but I could not respond. I could answer, I reasoned, if he would just stop talking gibberish, but concentrate as I might I could find no words that made sense. He came swooping toward me across a vast distance, still spouting gibberish. I stared, uncomprehending. His words, the lights, the faces all drifted apart in disconnected fragments, and only I stood unmoving, unspeaking, unresponding, for how does one respond to senselessness?

Lagos's face bobbed before me, filling my vision. He appeared to be hissing—or laughing—and I could find no reasonable way to react to him, for what was laughable about the world breaking apart? I gazed through him into the only thing that was not disintegrating into chaos: the black void. And while the world fragmented into a jumble of nonsense all around me, I drifted unconcerned in the still ocean of solitude.

Something struck across my face and knocked me to the floor, but the solitude remained undisturbed. A foot kicked me over onto my back, and oil flames spun in crazy circles, but I was perfectly still, and none of this could possibly concern me.

Hands dragged me across the stones while fires and boots and faces floated dreamlike on waves of motion, and none of it was ever going to hold still and fit back together, so I was relieved when my heels bumped up the steps, and the noise and confusion sank slowly into a pit of oblivion and was swallowed up by a door in the dark.

Cold, sharp air rushed at me, fresh, night air, and, ah, now there were brilliant white stars, cold, remote, alien stars pretending not to be fragments of chaos, but I knew that was a lie. Once the stars had names and patterns and histories, but that was before the universe broke apart, and now I could connect none of them and why would I even try. Nothing in the universe was connected to anything anymore. Not that it mattered. It had been lies anyway—all lies—a universe of lies.

XXXII

Slowly, slowly, the universe pieced itself back together. In the slave quarters they cropped my sticky mass of hair, shaved my beard, plunged me into a tub of cold water and told me to wash. I sat in the water shivering, staring at the surface, and the light fragmented on the water like everything around me. I tried to hold very still so it would all come back together, until the hallmaster shoved my head under and held me down and I struggled to come up for air. Finally he pulled me up, coughing and choking and gasping.

"Wash, damn you! You stink like a sewer!"

I took the rough, wet cloth he slung in my face, and I tried carefully, meticulously to do as he said; but then he left, and the light was shattering wildly on the water so that I had to hold very still again and make it stop. If it stopped moving I could see if there was a pattern to it; if I knew the pattern the world would come back together. Aye, I could piece things together if I just had a sensible pattern, and there was one on the water if I could just get it to hold still long enough. . . .

A fist struck me alongside the head.

"Aahh!" spat the hallmaster in disgust. He called a slave over to scrub me, which he did roughly and thoroughly until my skin stung and burned raw, especially some wounds which had not quite healed.

The hallmaster was a relentless enforcer of reality—I *did* relearn to scrub tables and flagstones and jump to orders because he was expert at getting my attention with his fist. Thus the world forced itself back together blow by blow. The season was autumn. I had lost the fragment that was summer; instead I had imbedded in me a shard that was a cold, black dungeon of rats and nightmares and pain. Around it other fragments gathered: slave quarters, kitchen, common hall; kicks, cuffs, shoves; serving, fetching, scrubbing. Outside was mud, courtyard, walls. At the center stood the Great Hall, inside which awaited terrors and ordeals unthinkable.

Some things I could not fit into a pattern. The sky would not fit. It stretched above and beyond the walls and seemed to have no boundaries, and it pained and angered and bewildered me to think about the sky. The sky was a mocking fragment of the universe of lies; I had no use for it, could find no reason for it, must not think about it. Indeed, thinking was perilous. I dared look neither backward nor forward. The past tormented me with memories unreachable; the future promised agonies and horrors inescapable. And the present was relentless, miserable, and bleak. In the hierarchy of Lorrach Keep, I was the sole member of the lowest stratum; soldiers and slaves treated me with contempt. It was: "Fetch this or that, Monstrosito," from the slaves, but one would be sure to hold the object far above my reach and goad me with jeers to jump for it. Soldiers were not above tripping me up as I balanced a tray of full wine goblets, for which mishap the hallmaster would knock me about the head. The cavaliers practicing maneuvers on horse once caught me crossing the yard and began a game of catch the dwarf, which rapidly became a contest of opposing sides herding, grappling, or dragging me toward opposite goals—a Hunnish game usually played with a dead calf, and I had no doubt what killed the calf. I was saved when the horsemaster halted the game and ordered them back into formation, but not before I suffered painful bruises and cracked ribs.

I scarcely dared look outward, for I was surrounded by a universe of grim walls and brutal men who stood over me like giants and made my waking moments a hell. Nor dared I contemplate inward, for dreams and confusion and fear conspired to make my sleeping moments another hell. In truth, nightmares made sleep ofttimes more terrifying than waking. I spent many cold night hours in desperate concentration, fighting to remain suspended in the silent void, to hover just beyond the borders where lurked dreams. I fought to hold my heartbeat together, my breath together, my mind and body together, until dawn brought relief. Then I need think no further than the immediate cold, laying the next stick on the fire, carrying a platter of steamy breakfast bread to the next table, dodging the next boot, taking the next blow of the hallmaster's fist, scrubbing the next table, sweeping the next flagstone. Aye, to think beyond the immediate—therein lay peril.

I was plagued with bouts of trembling at unexpected moments, shaking and losing my grip on whatever I held in my hands, sensations of falling when I knew I was huddled against the wall; but the wall was falling, too, and fragmenting, and the universe breaking apart again and darkening, and if I could not pull myself back I fell over the brink into a howling black maelstrom, splinters of the universe whirling in chaos. Then I sank into dark oblivion for a long or a short time. Ofttimes the world rushed back together abruptly, like iron filings leaping to lodestone. But other times I had to piece the universe together bit by bit, as though it were a broken mosaic I must make into sense. And I would find I had lost fragments of time. Once, I discovered myself standing with forehead and fists pressed desperately against the gate of the Keep. Angry voices shouted around me. I had no memory of approaching the gate, no how or why, just the realization I was there and they were jerking me away. The hallmaster beat me fiercely for it.

In my most lucid moments I knew I was going mad, but knowing it did me no good. I could not tell at any given moment whether I was experiencing sanity or insanity.

The maelstrom was sometimes terrifying, a whirlwind descent into madness. Then I resisted, though usually it was the stronger and sucked me in. Yet, when the universe around me held a horror worse than madness, the maelstrom promised safety, my only refuge, and I welcomed it. The maelstrom's center was merely oblivion; the Keep's center was Lagos.

In my nightmares Lagos was sometimes a monstrous red-eyed serpent coiled in the Great Hall. I was trapped in the hall with it, and it sought me tirelessly, lunged from a great height to strike as I dodged behind the iron tripods. It meant to swallow me alive. Other dreams were worse. Lagos was a bloated, black spider crawling for me along vast cobwebs, and I balanced the strands and tried to escape, but the spider ran too swiftly and shook the web out from under me. Invariably I fell and became trapped in the web, my struggles entangling me further and the spider springing upon me.

Sometimes the nightmare was no dream. The whipsman would appear in the common hall and signal that I was wanted.

Overwhelmed with panic, I would be shoved into Lucifer's pit, my knees sometimes giving way on the descent. I never knew what awaited me. Ofttimes there were guests whom Lagos wished to entertain or shock, depending upon his mood. He would hold me up to ridicule and bid me do acrobatics. I tried, but my performances were painful and pathetic. I was neither limber nor strong enough; the strain on my muscles and joints was agonizing; terror of Lagos turned my limbs and heart to lead. If I was lucky I would at last be allowed to make the difficult climb up the thirteen steps, goaded by the whip and laughter, allowed to return to the common hall unscathed.

Usually the Count merely enjoyed toying with my terror; he savored watching me tremble in confusion and dread. But if he was sufficiently bored I would be dragged into the dark hell below the hall and stretched upon his altar of pain, where the Count's ministrations forced my reeling senses into sharp, hot focus on the merciless grin gloating over me.

Those interminable evenings of torment were rare—just often enough to make anxiety and dread follow me like shadows whether I be waking or sleeping—for Lagos had done what he set out to do—he had broken me. Now his interest in my fate waned, and he searched for new victims. His ready source lay in captured barbarians. After extracting all the information he desired, he delighted in torturing them to death.

I was unwilling witness to a few of his entertainments. I saw a man's skull slowly crushed in a screw device, squeezed like an olive in a press. Though I closed my eyes near the end, I heard it all. He took a long time to die. There were others, too. And I stumbled through each moment of horror, each hour of despair, like a weary dreamer who tries to outrun the nightmarish creature at his heels, but each desperate step is slower than the last. No escape, no defense, no hiding place.

Contempt had been my only mirror for so long, I stood in bemused shock when I came face to face with my own reflection in the sun-brightened curve of a bronze shield. The shield, unaccountably left propped against the portico on a clear winter day, held a sharp, vivid image on its polished surface.

I stared. At first I did not even recognize the image. The only reflection I was accustomed to seeing in the disdain-filled eyes which glanced down at me was of something less than human, a creature ungainly and deformed, a monstrous bug lucky not to get squashed underfoot. I had met that reflection in every face around me for so long, it was the only image I had, the only reality I knew, for I met it every day, whichever way I turned.

But now I stared.

I saw not a shriveled caricature of humanity nor a mockery nor abomination, as I mutely heard myself described time upon time.

I stared at a dwarf, a dwarf with a shock of red curls tumbling across wide, startled brown eyes. A little man, thinner, older, and wearier than I remembered him, with a look of apprehension in his face that surely was not there before—before—before—

Ah, before the world shattered into pieces and flew apart. Of course he was not real, not anymore. He was a fragment of that shattered universe, a fragment caught in bronze.

I stared. He wore a torn, stained tunic knotted about the middle with a strip of cloth. Beneath the frayed hem his calves and feet were rag-wrapped and bound, and he looked such a pathetic tatterdemalion I might have laughed or cried, but laughing and crying were two of those things that made universes crack and splinter and spin into maelstroms.

I stared.

In the shield's depths his hair glowed with a bronze flame, and his eyes were lit with amber. His cheeks were ruddy, and the sky behind him golden. I felt I gazed through a burnished window, a window that opened onto a brilliant, shining universe, and on the other side of the window gazing back at me was a lucent being who once must have been me, but now. . . .

The amber eyes tugged at me, wistful, compelling.

Ah, no, a trick of sunlight and bronze. It has to be. He cannot be real. He was of that other universe—the universe of lies. His universe is no more, forever gone, and this is but a stray fragment caught in bronze like a bee caught in amber.

I could neither move nor look away, nor could I shake the feeling that I stared not into a broken image of some fragmented mosaic, but that I looked through a luminous window into another universe altogether, a universe where a living dwarf stood beneath a vivid golden sky and bid me enter.

If I stepped through the window, which universe would be real? Would all be golden and small and precisely curved from the inside?

The dwarf slowly reached toward my outstretched hand, our

fingertips nearly touching, both trembling, and I met his anxious eyes and felt a sudden fear. Whatever he meant to tell me, I could not bear to know. His eyes widened, too, as if he realized suddenly that *my* universe held terror for *him*. If I touched the shining window his bright world might shatter like glass, and I remembered how implicitly he believed in that world. Oh, aye, though I could not quite remember what there was about that world to believe or disbelieve, I remembered he believed in it utterly. Yet here he was reaching out to me and I to him, and if our universes touched which would shatter and which would remain?

Be real, I pleaded with the glowing figure and warm, golden sky. *Let me in.*

Two fingers of mine met two fingers of his, and nothing happened. Three fingers—nothing. All ten fingers, then both palms flat. We touched—not flesh, but metal—an unyielding metal barrier between us. We could not reach each other.

I met puzzlement in his amber eyes, then disappointment, hurt, bitterness. Furious, I crashed a fist against the barrier.

"Ha!" burst a derisive voice from somewhere. "If I was that ugly, I'd smash meself, too."

I spun about to face two hall slaves lugging a heavy tub of water between them. Bemused, I blinked up at them as they passed, my eyes absorbing with difficulty a pale, all-encompassing version of the window-world.

"If I was that ugly," snorted the other as they staggered on around the corner of the portico, "I wouldn't go lookin' in no mirrors."

I stared until they were gone, then slowly returned my gaze to the bronze mirror. For a long, silent moment I stared. It had happened again. I had gone tripping along the fringes of madness, all unknowing, all unsuspecting. Of course no one stood before me, only my own reflection—a ragged dwarf, haggard and wounded beyond his years. (How many years? And where are they now?) But why would my own reflection be cause for such confusion and aching and loneliness? I felt utterly separate from the weary little man who looked back at me.

A trick of light and bronze.

Aye, a broken remnant of a shattered world, an image shimmering on an iron shield gilded bronze. And I was a bottomless well of pain, alone in a grey courtyard beneath a slate sky, and even if the light could reach me, I felt I would cast no reflection at all.

301

. . .

I stared across the frozen grounds at the open tower door. Someone had carelessly left it ajar. Count Lagos was still gone with his cavaliers to patrol the Germanni shore of the Rhine, and in his absence discipline in the Keep was lax.

I raised my eyes to the top of the tower. No guard stood visible on its rampart balcony. I thought of wending my way up one of those tall towers. I mentally gauged the drop to the cracked flag-stones below. The towers had been as shut to me as were the outer gates. Now someone had left a door half open.

Numbly, I crossed the muddy froth of snow, expecting a warn-ing shout from a watchful guard, but I only heard the flop and crunch of my clumsy rags on the uneven, frozen yard. No one stopped my approach to the door. I slipped through the opening and climbed the spiraling steps. As I passed beneath each high window on my resolute ascent, I caught glimpses of empty sky. Then I crept into the round tower room with shuttered windows obscuring all directions. The guard lay snoring near the cold bra-zier, an empty wine jug by his head. The morning watch would be coming up soon. With stealthy steps I crossed to a wooden door and slipped out onto the narrow balcony that encircled the tower.

I set my thoughts on nought but the balustrade, determined to take no pause, leave no space for reflection, grimly resolved to climb up and leap free without looking down, without thinking.

But as I laid hands on top of the balustrade, my gaze just clearing its height, I stopped cold in the frigid wind and caught my breath.

I could see over the walls. For the first time in over a year, I looked beyond the walls of Lorrach Keep. And I was totally un-prepared for the sight. I had forgotten the Earth—the dazzling, glittering Earth. A flock of high-flying feathery clouds raced above the snow-spired forests. Snow clouds gathered over the moun-taintop. Wind swept and rocked the trees from horizon to horizon.

Earth called me, held me, overcame me, and I could not breathe for yearning. The assault on my eyes and soul swept me into unbearable joy, unbearable longing. All the world, so close I felt I could touch it, so beautiful it made my heart ache, so far out of my reach, so impossibly denied me I could scarcely endure it.

Like the pale sun illuminating a haze from somewhere invisible, gradually it dawned on me that the world had not cracked and broken and shattered into irretrievable pieces at all. How long had I been wandering in a nightland of total madness? How deep in the darkness must I have stumbled if even at my most lucid all my perceptions were based on an insane premise? The universe had never been shattered and flung into a dark chaos of whirling fragments, but I had. And the terror of it was, the fragment I clung to for refuge was the most irrational, unbelievable . . .

No, the terror of it was, the reality of Lorrach Keep was so hellish I could only deal with it by retreating into insanity, and I was still here. Lagos would get his hands on me again, and what new sort of madness would I descend into?

Aye, the terror of it was, I was going to die a raving lunatic in this place that was madness itself, and death when it finally came would be a mercy. Why not jump from the tower while I had a chance? I imagined my body broken and splattered on the flagstones. And it seemed to me the Keep was waiting, just waiting to suck the life out of me. It seemed like an outpost of Hell where bodiless demons gorge on fear and pain and hideous deaths.

If I die here, what if my soul is trapped here forever?

Maybe I'm already trapped. Maybe this is what Hell really is —an endless cycle of fear, torture, madness, longing. Maybe I can't die. Or maybe I've died a hundred times over and don't remember. Maybe part of Hell is not really knowing.

My head was spinning, my forehead resting on the backs of my hands. I gripped the balustrade harder and forced my head up. The clouds and trees and sharp wind that made me shiver helped to clear my thoughts. Another crazy premise.

Please, I whispered soundlessly, as if the Earth were a living soul who could respond to me. *Please.*

Now I heard a clatter and shout coming up the spiral stairwell. At the same moment a flutter and flap of wings took to the air, and I raised my eyes to watch the flight of ravens disturbed from their tower nests. Raven wings carried them effortlessly over the walls, into the open sky. I watched two of them disappear eastward into the distant trees. An unkindness of ravens.

Hopelessness bowed my head. I waited in desolation on the cold, windy tower until guards seized me back from the balustrade.

XXXIII

The common hall rang and rustled with the chink and creak of armor. An oily odor hung in the stuffy air as six hundred men treated their leather and mail acruements with oil and polish. Midafternoon though it was, the shuttered hall seemed dim and chill. A blazing hearthfire and smokey lamps competed with a growing dark cloud-cover and ever-thickening deluge of snow. The same late winter storm that kept the regulars to the hall delayed Count Lagos on his return from patrolling the Rhine's northern bank.

The unexpected and unseasonal blizzard coupled with the Count's absence cast a strange mood over the hall. The troops were both restless and festive; they wanted something to fend off the cold and make them forget how sick they were of each other's company. Hot mulled wine was the order of the day, and I was kept hopping with the other slaves, balancing platters of steaming mugs between the crowded benches. As the troops were much more interested in their cups than their armor, they may as well have been polishing the tables. Or the floor. It was slippery going.

I crossed the far end of the hall, concentrating on delivering unspilled a half-dozen full mugs of hot brew to a table next to the entryway. The floor ascended in four stone steps to a wide landing just before the doors. As I passed the steps, both doors burst wide open. Freezing wind and swirling snow blasted the hall. All heads turned. All eyes raised. Framed in the white portal through which the blizzard raged stood a massive, shaggy snow creature.

I stared up at the fantastic apparition on the landing. It . . . he . . . stood blinking in surprise, arms half raised as if the doors had just blown from his grasp. He shrugged a bulky pack off his back, leaned a stout walking staff against the wall, stretched out long, furry arms, and pulled the doors shut to the howling wind.

Absolute silence held the hall, save the crackling of the hearth-fire. He peered along the rows of tables to the wide fireplace, then he sniffed the air and grimaced. I stood nearest him and likely was first to ascertain he was human, not some wild snow beast, though he half looked like one. The man was a giant—six and a half feet or more—for he had to duck his head under the portal, and the heavy bearskin greatcoat that covered everything from beard to boots added to his bulk. A fur cap shagged over his eyebrows and ears, giving him a glowering visage. Moreover, this entire mountainous person was coated with snow. Frost clung to his thick beard. He tugged off the furry cap and shook his head; wet, thick, straw-colored hair fell in long strands around his face. He started down the steps.

I stood directly in his path, and too late I realized he did not see me. He must have stared into a white wall of snow all day, and now his eyes were half blinded in the gloomy lamp-lit hall. Hastily I jumped to move out of his path, but between balancing a platter of mull and the slick oil soaked up by the rags on my feet, I lost my footing and went nowhere.

Off the bottom step his knee struck full force beneath the platter, slamming it flat into my nose. Mugs of hot mull went flying. He tripped straight over me, hit, and skidded on wet flagstone. I landed on my back, sticky honey-wine dripping in my hair and down my tunic, my nose throbbing.

For a second the only sound in the hall was the metallic roll of cups across the floor. Then the well-sotted regulars burst into hilarity, undone by the impressive sight of a colossal barbarian flipping heels over head off the steps.

I rolled over and felt gingerly for my nose. The barbarian was slowly sitting up, dazed, looking around to ascertain just what had befallen him. Then his gaze settled on me and he came swiftly to his feet. I felt the wisest course would be to make myself scarce, so I came to my feet, too. As his broad hand reached for me, I struck at it wildly and tried to back away. But the oily rags slid on the wet flagstone and I sat down sudden and hard on the bottom step.

"Ah, laddie, I never did see you!" the man exclaimed in a rustic

305

accent. "And if I hurt you . . ." He stopped short and stared, seeing me properly for the first time. An expression of unabashed astonishment transformed his face.

Frozen in shock, I found myself looking straight into barbaric blue eyes.

"*By Othinn's Beard!*" he swore softly.

Half-kneeling, he sat back on one heel, and his eyes took me in as though he had never seen my like before and was astounded beyond belief at the sight.

Trapped between his huge form and the steps, I looked up trembling, and he filled all my vision. I had never seen a Germanni barbarian this close before, and certainly not such a gigantic one. Nor had I ever seen eyes quite that color before—pure deepest blue, more intensely blue than the hottest part of flame—certainly never met such eyes locked straight into mine from just two feet away. And he was big enough to crush me under one boot. And I had just tripped him flat on his face. I could not still my trembling.

Slowly the amazed expression behind his beard melted into a wry smile.

"Do you generally greet folk by tripping them down the stairs, master dwarf?"

I managed a hesitant shake of my head. His smile widened a little.

"Nor do I generally greet folk by knocking them in the nose. Grant me pardon—I didn't see you. You know you ought not go hopping up invisible like that. 'Tis dangerous."

Incredulous at hearing an apology, relieved he was not going to stomp on me, I nodded shakily and dabbed my nose with a grubby sleeve, for by now it had started to bleed.

All this transpired in a space of seconds. The merriment in the hall fell to low murmurs, and the commander in charge came striding swiftly toward us. Tipsy or no, he knew his duty. The barbarian glanced in the approaching officer's direction, then returned his gaze to me, regarding me strangely for a moment as if trying to puzzle me out. Unenlightened, he rose to his extraordinary height and turned to face the commanding officer. If the captain was momentarily taken aback by the giant who suddenly towered over him, he recovered his composure quickly.

"Salute, Captain," grinned the yellow-maned barbarian, raising a casual fist to his shoulder. The officer did not return the salute.

"State your business. How did you get in here?" demanded

the captain stiffly. Well he might. No Germanni had ever walked into Lorrach Keep of his own will, and no Germanni should ever have been allowed past the gates.

"Well, now, there's a blizzard outside, Captain, and my business is a roof and fire and good company. Your lads at the gatehouse were kind enough to let me through." He spoke unhurriedly, a rich tone of far northern origins in his easy Latin, his voice resonant. He swept his gaze past the captain to the watchful faces of the soldiers, and he scarcely needed to raise his voice for his robust timbre to be heard the length of the hall.

"There's no place like a frontier post for hospitality, so I was right glad to stumble up against your gates. Lucky, too. You can't see a blasted thing out there."

"This is no inn! The guards were out of line. They should have put you in chains. You could be an Alamanni spy."

"Could be, Captain—but I'm not." He grinned. He did not look like a man who would be easily put in chains. "Saxonius— Romans call me Saxonius—and Saxons are at peace with Rome." He half chuckled. "For the winter, that is. I can't vouch for spring when the sailing's clear. But I'm no sailor, Captain; I'm a minstrel, and no stranger to Roman outposts, so don't go too hard on your gatesmen."

A minstrel? The captain looked doubtful. A minstrel was not to be dismissed lightly, not after an uncommonly long, dreary winter and no let up in sight. Already the regulars were stirring with new interest.

"Can you prove who you are?"

He raised an emphatic yellow eyebrow. "I can prove I'm a minstrel, right enough. The rest you'll have to take on my word, which stands good in garrisons all along the Saxon Shore and up the Rhine from Colonia to Mainz, and I expect it will stand good in Lorrach, too." He opened the bearskin greatcoat for inspection. "You see I am unarmed, Captain. What harm to trade a warm fire and supper for some lively tunes? Your men look in need of good cheer to go with that sweet wine, which I'm hoping they'll be saving a kettle or two for me."

The regulars chuckled; the captain made his decision.

"Saxonius, is it? You seem to be what you claim, so I'm willing to take you on your word. However, you'll not be allowed to leave the Keep until Count Lagos returns. He'll wish to interrogate you."

"Interrogate, is it? Fair enough," he nodded. As he turned to mount the steps and retrieve the pack and staff, he found me standing in his path again. He eyed me curiously as I hastily moved aside.

During the conversation between the captain and the minstrel I had been quietly gathering up the fallen platter and cups, taking my time, listening unheeded. But the sixth mug lay directly between the two men, at their feet, and I waited unnoticed, not wishing to get underfoot, especially under the captain's foot.

Now the captain noticed me. Deliberately he rested his boot on the cup and stared at me with displeasure.

"This one, Monstrosito. You forgot this one."

I hesitated when I saw the glitter in his eyes. I knew the captain. I knew a swift kick awaited me. I also knew I had no choice but to obey him.

"The cup, Monstrosito," he said harshly. "Come get it."

Reluctantly I set the platter down on the bottom step. I approached haltingly. Almost within kicking distance, I glanced up in apprehension.

"The cup," he repeated.

I took a cautious step forward, prepared to reach for the cup under the captain's boot, which would lash out at me as soon as I was close enough, and . . . a stout wooden staff struck pavement just in front of me, barring my next step. The minstrel leaned down casually and whisked the cup from beneath the captain's foot.

"Allow me, Captain," he said in his easy, pleasant manner. Rising like a giant from Germanni legends beside the Roman commander, he bounced the cup on his huge palm. "I've made a muck of your hall. I'll be playing all the livelier to atone for it, I ken."

The commander nodded curtly, not entirely certain whether the barbarian's interference was deliberate or not. But I was certain. When he turned about and tossed me the cup, no one saw him wink but me. I caught the cup gratefully.

"I could do with a dozen of these brimmed with hot mull— for starters, eh?"

With a quick nod I snatched up the platter and hurried past, well out of the captain's reach. Returning to the kitchen, I carefully ladled hot, honeyed wine from the kettle and filled six mugs. Before I reached the minstrel, however, from behind me the hallmaster lifted the platter from my hands and knocked me aside with his knee. I stumbled against a crowded bench, and one of its occupants shoved me away. I ended on the floor, staring after the hallmaster's heels. In disappointment I watched the hallmaster slide the mull before the minstrel. His bushy brows raised in momentary surprise at the hallmaster, then he glanced around the hall briefly before saying him thanks.

I had wanted to do that for him. Just that small thing to thank him . . . thank him for smiling at me . . . for speaking to me as one human being does to another . . . for being not of this place of nightmares.

He had shrugged out of the bear coat, but that did nothing to diminish his stature. His lion's share of yellow hair and beard, the shaggy goat-hair vest belted over his shirt, the equally shaggy goat-hair boots propped on the hearthstones as he leaned his long frame against the table and tasted the sweet wine with an appreciative smack, just made him seem all the more larger than life and out of place, surrounded by Roman soldiers in the dim, chill common hall. Yet he seemed not to feel out of place. His quick blue eyes flicked from face to face as he talked. He jested and laughed with the regulars, answering their questions, relating the gossip from northern posts, warming his feet and hands by the flames. And they crowded around him, fascinated.

I crept as close as I dared, climbing onto a bench at the side of the hall to see him. My fascination was of a more desperate sort. The minstrel's presence was real and solid. He was a tangible chunk of that outside world that so eluded my thoughts. My mind grasped at the fact that not only was the universe whole and unchanged, but that it could invade the Keep like sunlight invades a black room and makes darkness vanish. I had no illusions that the minstrel's presence could make Lorrach Keep vanish, but the simple, miraculous fact that he existed, not a fragment caught in bronze that I could never reach, but a vital being I could see and even touch if I were close enough, that irrefutable knowledge made much of my confusion vanish. Lorrach Keep was an inhuman prison, and the universe that lay outside could not be a shattered mirage of lies, not if he were of it. Here was the one real certainty I could cling to, and I tried to sear across my memory the sight of the golden-haired minstrel by firelight.

A hand hauled me off the bench. One of the other slaves marched me and a bucket of lye water to the back of the hall. I scrubbed sticky mull off the flagstones, then mounted the steps at the entryway and stood to watch, until cold wind blasting under the door chilled my wet feet. Then I lugged the heavy, sloshing bucket back to the kitchen.

Time came to ready the hall for supper. The captain gave orders to clear out the neglected armor. Grumbling, the men gathered pieces of leather and mail, wrapped themselves round in cloaks, and prepared to cross the fifty feet of snowy barrage between the common hall and the barracks. Cursing as they slipped on the wet stones at the end of the hall, they filed out.

The hallmaster called me back into the kitchen, brained me with a copper ladle for loitering at the door, and set me to splitting crusty round loaves and spreading the tough insides with olive oil. Then I tore the bread into chunks and dropped it into wire baskets, which were snatched up as soon as they were full and hung from the hearth to soften over steaming pots of pork and cabbage stew. I slipped one chunk of greasy, cold bread into my tunic, in case all the bread was eaten before I got my share of supper, which happened frequently.

The regulars returned. Bowls of steamed bread were passed down the tables. The cooks ladled mouth-watering stew onto plates, which the rest of us carried two at a time in a quick stream to the men. The hallmaster did the honors of serving the captain and the minstrel himself. They occupied the seats of rank, facing each other across the end of a table nearest the blazing hearthfire.

By the time all the men were served, it was almost time to start all over again and serve up seconds, so there was much coming and going. I passed nearby the yellow-bearded barbarian several times, and his blue eyes flicked briefly over me, curiously, though he kept his attention on the captain's conversation and the stew.

When the last of the plates had been sopped with the last of the bread, the men stacked the plates in our arms as we passed along the benches. I carried my last armload, a stack I could not see over but manuevered with peripheral vision toward the kitchen. Another slave passed close, Favius, and though I saw it coming, I could not avoid his deliberate bump against my arm. Every last plate slid and clattered to the floor. Wearily, I restacked them.

Now the men wanted mull, and we busied ourselves serving them. And now the minstrel rose, stretched contentedly, and allowed such a hearty meal was worth a whole night's luting. He strode to his pack, which rested with his staff near the hearth, and carefully took from it a long bundle of black cloth. He unwrapped the black woolen cloak (for I saw it had a hood) and revealed a magnificent lute, the like of which I had never seen. Of polished walnut, it had a long neck befitting the minstrel's reach. Its eight strings responded with clear, bell-like tones to the thumb he ran across them. Deftly he tuned each string to the other, then with a satisfied look he plucked the strings in a rapid waterfall of sound. The cascade of notes one after another became a lively tune, and the men took up their cups and shuffled closer. As the minstrel's rich, resonant voice rang the hall with a quick, silly soldiering ditty, I was pushed and crowded out of the way. I crept into the shadows at the side of the hall and listened. I had never heard music in Lorrach Keep. The music, like the minstrel, seemed strangely dreamlike in the grim Keep, as if both realities could not exist together at the same time. As if one of them had to give way.

He sang a festive drinking song followed by a favorite raunchy ballad with a lusty chorus. The men saluted their cups and chimed in merrily.

I could not recall ever seeing real merriment in the Keep before. I stood mesmerized against the cold wall until the hallmaster jerked me back to my reality, forcibly reminding me I was here to fetch mull, not be entertained.

The soldiers called for favorite tunes from across the western Empire, and the minstrel seemed to know them all.

"Sing me a chorus, man," he answered one, "and I'll play it whether I know it or no!" He tipped his cup and listened, then accompanied the drunken balladeer on the lute. Soon the whole hall rang in loud chorus. Then when he struck up a merry roundelay the regulars went to stomping and kicking and swinging each other about in such a drunken melee that I retreated hastily beneath a table, fearing I might be trampled. I hunkered down as they even shook the table above my head, dancing atop it so vigorously. When the roundelay ended they cheered and whistled and called for another.

I took the opportunity to slip through them while they were all standing fairly still. I made my way to the kitchen where the slaves were settling down to supper. Grabbing a greasy plate off a stack, I took my place, last in line to the pot. Two others came in late, took up plates, and glanced sharply down at me. I backed off and they moved into line in front of me. The first lesson I had learned in the slaves quarters was that in the supper line being smallest meant being last.

When my turn came the man doling the stew tipped the pot and dredged the bottom, ladling up a few shreds of cabbage floating in a greasy, watery stew. I looked up hopefully. He dredged again and plopped more of the same in my plate. Half-starved, I fished out the pieces of cabbage with my fingers and devoured them quickly before some mishap took my meal. Then I retreated to a far corner with the warm broth. Surreptitiously, I felt around my waist for the chunk of bread I had hidden. Locating it, I reached down the neck of my tunic and pulled out the morsel, a bit grimy and squashed, but a feast to me. I dunked it in the broth to soften it, brought it eagerly to my mouth, and had it snatched suddenly from my hand.

"Stolen bread, Monstrosito?" grinned Favius who held my supper. "I'll take this. How'd you like hallmaster finding out you been stealing bread, huh?"

I stared at him dismally. He prepared to eat my supper.

"Hallmaster just found out!" a harsh voice interrupted him. There stood the hallmaster, fists on his bulbous waist. "Give it back to him."

The bread plopped hastily back in my plate, and the man cautiously sidled away. I froze. The hallmaster leaned over me, steadying himself abruptly against the wall; he had been tippling the mull all evening. He wheezed at me.

"I feel real good tonight, heh, heh, real good. And right generous, too." His meaty hand patted me on the face clumsily as he leered over me. "You and me, tonight, we'll have a little chat about how generous I am, Monstrosito."

I knew what he meant. That was the second lesson I had learned. My dismay must have shown. He squeezed my face painfully, eyes glittering.

"You ought to be glad I feel so good. I'm giving you a chance to earn your supper." He let go and straightened up, his greedy grin swaying over me. "So enjoy it."

I watched him wobble away. My head bowed, eyes shut tight, and I felt the shaking start in the pit of my stomach.

No!

I could not let things shake apart; it would do me no good. I opened my eyes and stared at the chunk of bread. I would earn it whether I ate it or no, and some of the shaking might ease if I were not so hungry. Even soggy, each bite was harder to swallow than the last. I washed it down with broth, which felt warm in my stomach but gave me no comfort.

Now it was quieter out in the hall. I could hear the lute and the minstrel's voice crooning softly. Many of the slaves had been drawn to the doorway by the song. I had to get out of here, out of the kitchen, away from the hallmaster, away from my tumultous thoughts before they built into a tidal wave of madness. I squeezed by the wall and a forest of legs and out into the common hall. The regulars were settled down now, listening, swaying over their cups to a love song. I crept along the wall, found a space half in darkness beneath a burned-out oil lamp, and huddled out of the way, hugging my knees and listening. The minstrel finished his love song and began a heroic ballad. The firelight waned and the hall grew colder. Above the minstrel's warm voice the wind whistled high and keen at the shutters. Melancholy settled over my soul.

A plaintive wanderer's lament pierced my lonely vigil, half remembered—no, fully remembered, from my vagabonding years. The last person I had heard sing those words, that melody, had been Felicia. And the memories which arose with the notes of that song were near impossible to bear. I pulled myself into a little knot of pain and sank into a deep well of anguish. *That* universe had shattered, certainly. My vagabond world had been the first piece to go. Remember? Remember how the universe fell apart chunk by chunk underfoot until there was nothing left, no place left to stand? I stared dry-eyed into the maw of the maelstrom.

The last note of the haunting melody died away. For a moment the silence was almost peaceful, but then the stirrings and mutterings of the soldiers disrupted the moment, and I remembered where I was. Much stumbling and scraping and cursing and chorusing accompanied the regulars' reluctant exit for the barracks. A shock of cold wind swept the hall and chilled it utterly. Then silence hung in the hall like darkness, and I still huddled there against the wall, arms clasped around knees, forehead pressed down, shaking.

I was afraid—afraid to leave the cold, empty hall. The hallmaster was waiting for me, and I dreaded him. Sooner or later he would find me. I knew of no refuge, yet I sat shaking, afraid, in the silent hall.

And memory taunted me with the bitter knowledge that this hopeless waiting was all that was left of my life. I careened between fear and despair and found nowhere to turn. And the maelstrom spun below me like a bottomless black hole waiting to suck me into chaos.

Then I heard faintly the scrape of footsteps on flagstone. He had come for me. I gripped my knees harder and shuddered.

"Master dwarf," spoke a quiet voice that was not the hall-master's. "A word with you, master dwarf?"

Slowly I raised my eyes to take in the shaggy goat-hair boots. I tried to look further, but he was taller than I could manage. Half in weariness, half in relief, my head fell back to my knees.

I heard him move, and next his voice came so close I knew he knelt before me.

"I've been wanting all evening a chance to talk with you."

What for? My mind reeled, directionless.

"But dropping into a nest of Roman eagles isn't easy, especially this nest. I've had to bide my time." The minstrel paused, then spoke more softly. "Are you all right, master dwarf? Are you ill?"

I rocked my head side to side—*no, I'm drowning*—all the answer I could make.

A quietly jovial tone rippled the dark sea. "I hope 'twas not my tuning saddened you. 'Twas meant to gladden, not dishearten."

"I . . . I can't . . ." My whisper drifted off senselessly.

"Can't what, master dwarf?"

A whirlwind of things I could not do assailed my mind—carry on a conversation, stop shaking, face the hallmaster, pick up even one piece of my life, lift my head. . . .

"Leave me be . . . please. . . ." I scarcely knew if I spoke to the minstrel or the nightmare from which I could not escape. I heard him move again, but he did not leave.

"You *are* ill, master dwarf. You're shivering. You ought to come by the fire and . . ."

I somehow failed to associate the hand that touched my shoulder with the minstrel's voice. Frantically I jerked back, flush against the wall, eyes startled wide with fear. On one knee before me, leaning a thick forearm across the other knee, the lion-maned barbarian poised, his hand still half raised, and stared at me through troubled blue eyes. I stared back, stunned. Slowly he dropped his hand.

"Think you I would hurt you, master dwarf?" he said softly. "I would not."

Hesitantly I searched those clear eyes and found no harm in them. I found kindness instead, and assurance. The panic in my heart slowly stilled, and I met his steady gaze wonderingly.

"I never meant to startle you." He half smiled. "I took for granted that you knew I meant no harm."

"I don't know what you want of me," I whispered, almost pleading. He studied me thoughtfully.

"Ah, no, of course you don't. You've no way of knowing, have you? My fault, master dwarf. Let me make amends." Cautiously, as though not to frighten me with any sudden moves, he settled himself cross-legged on the cold floor. He leaned forward and clasped his hands together.

"Now, I want to tell you a tale. . . ."

A tale! He is full of surprises!

"A simple tale, but a true one. 'Tis about a boy—who is me, you'll soon figure out, so I'll tell you right out. This boy, me, grew up hearing tales and songs about gods and dragons and giants and such, and he also heard a good many tales about dwarves, and he believed them every one. He took it in his head that dwarves were all about, to be found in tree-stumps and caves and around any bend if he but knew where to look and could be quiet enough and quick enough. So he spent a good bit of his boyhood lying in wait in enchanted vales (never mind how he knew they were enchanted) and following mysterious footprints along boggy creeks, just knowing some unexpected moment he'd see one of Sindre's folk and politely make his acquaintance. Well, he never found one dwarf, you might guess, so as he grew to manhood he began to disbelieve. Sooth, he still sang the tales, but he forgot all about his childhood fancies, even in the most enchanted places.

"Now imagine that boy grown to manhood, imagine his surprise, *my* surprise, when I tumble down the stairs over a living, breathing dwarf—and in the most unlikely place, the *last* place I would ever look."

As the tale unwound, my head sank wearily to my knees. I guessed early where the tale was going. I knew what the minstrel thought. Once upon a time I could have risen to the occasion and made much of myself. But that time was long gone.

"Of course I want to keep an eye on him, this dwarf," the minstrel went on, "for fear he'll disappear as suddenly as he appeared. But I have to wonder why one of Sindre's folk would be in a Roman outpost? Not by his own choice, I'll warrant."

"Minstrel . . . I'm not what you think," I told him hoarsely, too dispirited to raise my head. "I'm not the stuff of tales and songs . . . I'm . . . I . . . ." My words trailed off into uncertainty.

"Very real," the minstrel finished for me. "Aye, and very much in trouble, I ken."

I looked up at him then, achingly.

"I'm not so blinded by tales that I cannot see when a little kit is ill-used and in need of a friend." Cautiously he offered me his open hand, as if I were a wild creature that might any moment startle away. "Will you come talk with me by the fire? 'Tis shivering cold back here."

I searched his face again. He half smiled from the corner of his beard and raised one brow inquiringly over an eye as blue and warm as a woad cloak that once was mine. I needed very much that outstretched hand, needed to touch the reality in that solid offer of friendship. I slid a trembling hand into his steady one, and unhurriedly his fingers closed warm and comforting over mine.

His smile and nod were reassuring. "Come with me, kit. I have a little something in my pack 'twill do us both good."

With an easy tug he helped me to my feet. The hall had grown darker and colder, the fire fallen to embers, and a few regulars who had never made it back to consciousness snorted and snored. Outside, the wind whistled mournfully. The minstrel piled more wood on the coals and poked the fire back to life.

"Now," he sighed, when flames hugged the wood, "we can warm our hands and better our acquaintance. Come on into the light, man, where I can see you."

I stepped up onto the hearth, into the warm glow of the fire, and faced him uncertainly. He studied me with lively interest from tangled curls to forworn rags. I studied him, too. He knelt before the fire, and the light crowned his yellow hair with a golden aura. A pleased smile began at the corners of his beard and spread in all directions until his whole face was alight. And the warmth of that smile drew a natural response from me, a bemused smile that was a shy reflection of his own. *What does he see?* I wondered. *What does he think?*

"Are you a drinking man, my friend? A certainty you are. Wait right here and I'll fetch something to take the chill off our bones. Minstreling is thirsty business, and barely time for a quick draught or two between tunes, like tonight. Anywise, that honeyed-down ration the army mislabels wine may suffice to warm a cold night, but *conversation* now, real conversation, calls for a more potent brew—something sharp and stout with a little bite. So happens I have the very thing."

As he spoke he had gone to his pack, rummaged out a three-quarters full wineskin, and collected two empty cups from the floor. He set the cups between us and filled them with rich, plum-purple liquid.

"I've saved this for just such an occasion. A drink worthy of Othinn himself. Guaranteed to warm the heart, loosen the tongue, and lift the spirits. Salute." He raised his cup to mine and clinked them together solemnly.

He spoke true. The wine was sharp and stout enough to wake the dead. I felt my spirits lift just tasting it. I savored the heady flavor, the crackling fire, the peaceful lull, the friendly company. Outside, a freezing wind howled and shook the shutters with cold fury. Inside, I sat with the minstrel within a cozy sphere of fire-light.

"*Monstrosito!*"

I jumped, nearly dropping the wine. I had forgotten the hall-master. He stood swaying at the kitchen door, a cold fury of his own distorting his plethoric face.

"*What are you doing there? Get up, you lazy-ass! Over here now!*"

I sat frozen, reality closing round my one peaceful illusion like an iron trap. The hallmaster came heaving and weaving across the hearth.

"When I say *come,* don't stare at me like a stump-brain!"

He came lurching toward me, too drunk to heed ought but his own compulsion. Instinctively I looked to the minstrel.

"Jump to it when I say jump, or I'll have your hide, you worthless . . ." He grabbed a fistful of hair to jerk me to my feet, his other fist raised to deal me a blow. But the minstrel moved just as swiftly, on his feet on the instant. The hallmaster found a brawny hand clamped around his wrist and a dangerously annoyed barbarian giant attached to it.

". . . maggot!" the hallmaster strangled off. He let go my hair but could not free his arm. The minstrel bared his teeth and twisted the arm unhurriedly.

"You do see that we're engaged in private conversation, master dwarf and I, do you not?" The further the minstrel twisted, the further the hallmaster's knees buckled. "It rankles me, sloth-brain, to be interrupted by the likes of you." Now the hallmaster cringed on his knees, forced forward as the minstrel exerted tighter pressure. "'Twould be wise of you not to show your pig face to me again. Understood?"

"Understood!" squawked the hallmaster.

"Ah." The minstrel released his hold and the hallmaster flopped forward, wincing as he dragged his strained arm around to its natural position. With a glare of hatred, the hallmaster staggered heavily to his feet and stumbled toward the kitchen. His face the color of stewed beets, he braced himself against the portal and spat.

"Count Lagos will hear of this!" He glared past the brawny barbarian who blocked his way. "And I'll collect, *bug,* with interest!"

Three massive strides and the minstrel grabbed the front of the hallmaster's tunic, hauled him more than a foot off the floor, and looked him eye to glinting eye. I would not have imagined anyone short of Hercules could lift the hallmaster.

"Should I see," gritted the minstrel, "aye, or even *hear* you've laid hands on him, you slimy maggot, I'll break your neck!" Then he heaved the hallmaster bodily into the dark recess of the kitchen. The minstrel stalked back and dropped against the hearthside. He quaffed a hearty swallow of wine. His anger cooling, he looked long at me. I bent my head over my cup, inhaling the potent fragrance. Both relief and a strange melancholy engulfed me.

"My thanks, minstrel," I mumbled, trying not to think about the price I would pay tomorrow.

"Master dwarf, what might be your name?"

"You heard, did you not?" I muttered bitterly, without looking up.

"I heard what *they* call you. 'Tis not your name."

I shook my head. "Does it matter?"

Now he sat forward abruptly, cross-legged, and leaned toward me, intent.

"Of course it matters, man! It *has* to matter!" I raised my head then and met his searching blue stare. His voice gentled. "It matters to *me*. Your true name? Have they taken that from you, too—along with all else?"

And I saw he tried to reach me, and I had to find a way to him, else I was lost.

"Dominic," I whispered. Then more surely, "Dominic is my name."

XXXIV

"Dominic." The minstrel smiled. "A bold and noble sounding name—Dominic. A name that rolls off the tongue like poetry. 'Tis one *befitting* tales and songs." I peered up at him sidewise.

"Ah, you smile. I'm glad to see it. Now I'll be telling you *my* name."

I stared at him in bafflement. "Is not Saxonius?"

He snorted. "No, is not. Saxonius is Roman, not my true name. I am Kevin Dunskaldir."

He half laughed as I strove to repeat the unfamiliar syllables. "Kevin, my given name, and Dunskaldir, which might mean something akin to Danesinger, but there's no Latin word that truly means skaldir. You might translate my name, 'maker of the Dane song.' "

"Then you're not Saxon at all? You're a Dane?"

"Half-half," he shrugged, making a side-side motion with his hand. "But Romans, they only know Saxons, so Saxonius I am. Why, the most of them wouldn't know Danes from Thuringians, and I'm mightily surprised you even ken I spoke of a people."

"I . . . I read of Danes somewhere, in a geography. A people of the far north, seafaring warriors in painted ships . . . 'tis all I know."

He raised both eyebrows, one after the other. "'Tis knowing more than any Roman I've met south of the Saxon Shore. Read it, did you? Where might you be from, master dwarf?"

"Gaul. Downriver. Near Terverorum."

He sipped his wine in silence awhile, and I sipped mine, feeling the warm glow of it touch my cheeks and lighten my head.

"How came you here, Dominic?" he asked suddenly.

How? I groped through the strange dark maze that was my memory, and I saw again the green forest and the gates shrieking together, shutting me away from the Earth forever. My eyes closed wearily.

"In a cage," I remembered.

He was silent a moment, then his voice came back low and grave.

"How long since then?"

"I don't know." My words quavered. "What month is this?"

"March, by now."

"A fourteen—no . . . a sixteen month." A tremor caught in my throat. "Sounds like not a very long time, doesn't it?"

"Sounds like an eternity," he said quietly. I nodded and stared into the dark winecup. "I've heard of this Count Lagos. Is he the devil they say he is?"

I trembled, gripping the cup so hard it shook. The minstrel's hands reached out and steadied mine.

"I need no answer to that," he murmured. We sat thusly, his huge hands encircling mine while my trembling ceased. The wind wailed a mournful warning, but the minstrel's presence made cold and fear seem far away.

"Dominic."

I looked up, so long unaccustomed to hearing my name, hearing it now so softly spoken.

"Know you what it means when a man swears his oathname to another, handfast over the cups?"

I shook my head, staring into those flame-blue eyes.

"Among my folk it means they are oathbound in friendship, and one will help the other in need. I would swear now . . ."

"*Minstrel!*" My urgent whisper shook with the terrible realization that had at last clawed its way to the fore of my thoughts. All else fled before visions of this gentle barbarian's fate at the cruel hands of Lagos.

"*Minstrel, you cannot stay here!* You must get out if you can— before Lagos returns—else 'twill be too late!"

"What are you saying, man?"

"I've seen what he does to the Alamanni—to *all* the captives. I . . . I don't want to see it done to *you!*"

320

He regarded me in thoughtful silence, then withdrew his hands and poured us both more wine. He took a long draught.

"I'm not Alamanni," he finally said. "Nor am I captive, nor am I an enemy of the Empire. What reason could he find?"

"I'm not sure it makes any difference to Lagos," I told him fearfully, "whether he finds reason or no. I have seen . . . gods, I have seen . . . he enjoys it . . . *they* enjoy it . . . the suffering. . . ." I choked on my knotted thoughts, took a long breath, and met the minstrel's sober gaze. "I know this, minstrel. No Germanni has ever left Lorrach Keep alive."

He looked troubled. "And you, Dominic? What are your chances of leaving here alive?"

I stared at him bleakly.

He shook his head, swallowed another mouthful of wine, and watched me sip mine. Now he caught my hand and carefully turned it palm upward. The ragged sleeve of my tunic fell back and exposed scars cut into my wrist by shackles and ropes, and above that, a long welt left by hot iron.

"Lagos did this?" His face was grim.

I met his look of anger with a bare nod.

He released my hand, stood with slow deliberation, and stepped to the fire; he leaned both hands against the hearth and stared into the crackling embers. Cold and darkness had gradually crept back into the hall, but the minstrel rammed more logs onto the embers and jabbed at them savagely with the poker until they took flame.

I gulped a mouthful of wine, set the cup aside, and cautiously rose to my feet, stretching legs cramped from sitting on hard stone. I halted where I stood; my head spun wildly, and I could not feel my feet. It seemed to me the room danced with fireflies flashing before my eyes. Then they darkened to black fireflies shrilling around my head. And the minstrel caught my sudden drop toward the floor, caught my arms and held me steady, walked me slowly to his pack, and sat me down to lean against it. Gradually the fireflies winked out and disappeared.

"Must be the wine," I muttered. Cautiously I sat up and focused on the minstrel's sober face.

"Dominic, on my oath, I will see to it we *both* get out of here alive."

Maybe it was the wine, but in that moment, seeing him, hearing him, I believed he could actually do it.

"You would help me?" I whispered wonderingly. "Why?"

"Why?" he echoed in disbelief. "How not, man? Think you I could abandon you here? What manner of man do you imagine I? . . ." He stopped at my stricken look, then went on more gently. "Are you not in need of a friend?"

I nodded faintly.

"Am I so difficult to trust, then?"

"No . . . I . . . 'tis *hard* . . ." I dropped my head into my hands. How could I explain that for me the whole universe had become impossible to trust? I tried. "I . . . I'd forgotten . . . kind people . . . good people . . . like you. . . ." I raised my eyes to his. "Minstrel, if ever I wanted to trust a man . . . 'tis you . . . and if ever I needed a friend . . ." My voice failed me.

"You have one," he rumbled quietly, laying a stout hand on my shoulder. "Kevin Dunskaldir swears oathbound on it."

I searched his face. His clear eyes mirrored the purity of twin mountain lakes, bottomless and still and blue to their depths. And I believed him. My heart ached with the need to reach out to him, to know what sort of soul dwelled within those strange eyes, but I was not sure I knew how to reach anymore.

"Minstrel . . ." I ventured, tentatively, "what means Kevin?"

His look was quizzical, his smile of understanding slow dawning.

"Gentle," he said. "It means gentle."

My quick smile was half relief, half surprise, hearing him so aptly named.

Again he offered me his hand. "Well met, Dominic."

I grasped it unhesitantly. "Well met . . . Kevin."

He nodded; his grin broadened; another blast of wind shook the shutters.

"'Tis certain we're going nowhere tonight." He delved into his pack. "We're both needing sleep." He tossed me the black wool cloak.

"Thanks, but you . . ."

"I have this." He shook the furry greatcoat flat. "'Tis dry by now." He buried the nearly empty wineskin somewhere in the pack, then he rose and turned his back and pissed in the embers. I did the same, and we stretched on the hearthstones, each parallel to the fireplace, our heads resting on either side of the pack. Within seconds, it seemed, I heard the minstrel's soft snores. Sleep had once come so easily for me, too, but no more. I stared into the embers and tried not to think about the morrow, tried not to think about the hallmaster, tried not to think how many ways I could watch a man die. The wine helped. I pulled the thick wool cloak snug and closed my eyes, drifting. *Kevin Dunskaldir,* I thought. *Gentle Danesinger.* I smiled into the darkness.

A stirring in the hall awakened me. Someone, Favius, was re-building the fire. Grey light seeped through cracks in the shutters. I struggled to my feet and promptly sat down on the pack, head in hands. The wine I had needed, the wine that comforted me the night before, now turned treachery on me, as always. I had not drunk so much that I was sick, but enough to make me queasy and weak and unsteady. The minstrel still slept, and now Favius hissed at me as he passed.

"You're wanted back there!" He disappeared into the kitchen. I stared after him. Nothing could induce me to go in there of my own will. The hallmaster appeared in the doorway and glared a warning at me, but he dared not approach the barbarian, even in sleep. I stared back at the hallmaster fearfully, but I stayed un-moving until he stepped back into the kitchen, snarling orders at the other slaves. I bit my lip. What a day this was going to be.

I watched the fire crackle. One of the regulars who never made it to the barracks last night stirred and staggered toward the fire. The minstrel woke with a start. He grinned and stretched and scratched, looking none the worse for the wine. He rattled one water bucket then another and sighed, finding them both empty. Then he turned the spigot on the huge water cistern in the corner. A thin trickle splattered into his hand and died. He sucked at his moist palm and muttered an expletive in a tongue unknown to me. Now he shrugged into his bearcoat and took up the two buckets.

"Where will I be finding the well?"

I led him outside and pointed across the courtyard of knee-deep snow to the wellhouse. He cursed and struggled through the drifts while I waited, shivering and stamping on the portico. The day was emerging leaden grey, overcast and skyless. The minstrel came trudging back with sloshing buckets.

"Wouldn't pump through the pipes," he muttered. The reg-ulars inside crowded up for a drink, but he passed the first ladleful to me. "'Tis haul it by hand or not at all. Any that want water after this lot can fetch it themselves."

We quenched our thirsts. The minstrel pulled up a bench and propped his shaggy boots on the hearth to dry. I stood near the fire, warming off the chill that had penetrated so quickly. The smell of barleycakes baking filled the hall. Bellies rumbled and mouths watered. More regulars began stamping in from the barracks. The unlucky man who drew the bottom of the bucket grumbled and cursed the pipes and made the trek to the wellhouse. The slaves appeared with the first platters piled high with smoking barleycakes. There was a general melee over the hot cakes. The minstrel's long reach snatched two off the top. He sat beside me and gave me a piping hot barleycake.

"This'll take the chitters out of your stomach, friend."

I bit into it gratefully. More men crowded the hall, and more barleycakes emerged from the kitchen. Then I saw the hallmaster talking to the captain and gesticulating angrily; both pairs of eyes were fixed on the minstrel and me. The captain made no response but to wave the hallmaster away and stare. I glanced at the minstrel; he was too intent on wolfing down breakfast to have noticed.

"Kevin," I said in a low voice so that none other could hear. "Meant you what you said last night? About helping me?"

"Sooth, I gave my oath on it," he said shortly. "Think you I lied?"

My voice wavered. "Could have been the wine talking."

"Could have been," he agreed, staring hard. Then he grinned. "But 'twas not."

"They were discussing us—the captain and the hallmaster."

"Were they, now? I can imagine what that craven had to say to the captain. I wonder what he'll be doing about it?"

"*Attention!*" the captain bellowed over the hubbub. Talk ceased down the tables. "Listen up. The Count is now three days overdue. I want details out clearing the road this morning—the rest of you, full dress and in the yard for inspection. None of us wants to be caught with our asses bare, do we?"

"*No, sir!*"

"Now, take a look at our guest of last evening."

All eyes turned to the minstrel, who regarded the captain impassively.

"Saxonius is not to roam freely through the Keep. In deference to his minstrelry, he is confined to the common hall until the Count arrives. If he steps outside the hall, raise the alarm. If he approaches the walls or the gates, cut him down. Understood?"

"*Aye, sir!*"

"Right. Move out!" The troops rose with scraping and shuffling to file out the doors.

The minstrel muttered under the noise, "I ken this may not be easy." Then he stood as the captain approached.

"Understood, Saxonius?" demanded the commander.

"Oh, aye, understood perfectly, Captain. I'm a prisoner, without good cause."

The captain looked up at the stout barbarian, easily a head taller than the Roman, and clenched determined jaws. "I have to confine you, Saxonius. You're Germanni; you could be a spy; you may have information vital to the Empire. The Count will be the judge of your loyalties. I'm carrying out my duty. Consider yourself fortunate that you're not confined to a cold dungeon instead of a warm hall."

"Well, I am grateful for that, Captain. I've no great longing to see the inside of a dungeon. Would you mind me asking why I'm put up here and not down there?"

The commander met the minstrel's probing gaze steadily. "Because I believe you are exactly what you seem to be. A minstrel, a damn good one, and damn well at home with the regulars. But the decision on that is not mine to make."

The minstrel nodded. "No hard feelings, then, Captain."

The captain glanced briefly at me and then back to the minstrel. "You'll cause no more trouble in the hall."

"Trouble? I'm not aware that I've caused any trouble."

"You know what I mean, Saxonius."

"Aye, I know what you mean. There'll be no trouble as long as that craven hallmaster minds his own business."

"Monstrosito *is* his business."

"And dwarf-folk are mine. 'Tis my intention he comes to no harm."

The captain stared at the barbarian as though at a madman. He barked out a short laugh. "Tell Lagos that!"

"I intend to."

The captain took the minstrel's measure for a long moment. "I did not take you for a fool, barbarian."

"Nor did I take you for a niddering, Captain."

"A what?"

"What cause has a little kit like this to fear a captain in the Roman army? I have to wonder—can it be you take advantage of your size and rank to ill-use him? An ignoble pastime, Captain."

The captain glared at the minstrel, then with sudden fury he drew his sword. The minstrel responded with a barely perceptible shift in balance. His gaze, steady and watchful, never wavered from the Roman commander's face as he waited, unarmed and unafraid. After a taut moment, the minstrel's mild voice belied the tension.

"Am I wrong, then? Do you challenge me over the truth or a lie?"

The Roman stared at the barbarian in silent rage, then abruptly he sheathed the sword, turned on his heel, and strode the length of the empty hall and away without looking back. The minstrel sighed and sat down on a bench.

"I thought he was about to kill you," I said, shaken.

"He thought about it."

"What changed his mind?" I climbed up the bench and sat on the table.

"He wasn't so sure he could. Besides, I expect the Count wouldn't like it. I gather he prefers to deal with his captives personally."

"Kevin, have you any idea what Lagos does to his prisoners?"

"I've heard rumors. This Count has a grim reputation along the Rhine frontier. Tortures captives for information, they say, and holds gruesome executions afterward. The Alamanni fear him like the devil."

"And still you come here? A Germanni? Did you not consider the danger?"

"Sooth, man, I meant to avoid the place at all costs! I crossed east over the Rhine below Argentoratum, having recently had, um, a middling falling out with the commander there, and traveled south through Burgundian wolds. 'Twas my intention to go quietly around Lorrach Keep and cross the Rhine unseen. But it seems the fates that weave our paths had something more in mind. Why, I wasn't even knowing which direction the Keep lay in the blizzard, yet snow and gusts and drifts conspired to force me right up against the gates. And here I am, willing or no. Some call it blind luck; I call it a weird. Nature put me here, I ken, because here she wants me."

"A *weird*—does it mean an ill fate?"

"It can, aye, but it can just as likely be a *good* fate."

"Seems to be an ill luck, if 'twould end you here."

A smile quirked a corner of his beard. "I'm not so sure of that, Dominic, not yet. And who says 'tis ended? There's no knowing

326

where a weird is going until it gets there. A man is wise to wend it carefully, 'tis certain, as he would an unknown path or a strong current, and he'll need his wits about him. But there's no sense in fearing a weird. 'Tis an intertwining of forces that, once bound, is too strong to break. 'Twill run its course like a powerful storm until the force is spent."

"Like being swept into a maelstrom," I whispered.

"We hope not," he declared stoutly. "We will try not."

Now slaves bustled into the hall, some gathering the scattered cups from the night before, a few carrying buckets and brushes. Favius came as near as he dared, plunked a bucket on the hearth, and plopped a brush into the oily water.

"Hallmaster said you're not on holiday," Favius told me brusquely, keeping a wary eye on the minstrel.

I glanced to the kitchen door where lurked the hallmaster, a glowering hatred leveled not at me, but at the minstrel for intimidating him out of his own hall. Though I figured I was already in as deep a trouble as I could be, I saw no sense in aggravating him further. With a sigh, I dropped from the table to the bench and then to the floor. Favius backed off hastily when the minstrel stood and stretched.

"And I'll have one of those brushes, too," Kevin told him. Favius was dumbfounded. He looked to the kitchen door, but the hallmaster was gone. Finally Favius relieved the nearest man of his brush and tossed it toward the bucket.

I was pleased, but nonplussed. "You've no need to scrub tables, minstrel."

He grinned. "If not, I'll be pacing with boredom erelong." He set the bucket on the nearest table and started on one side of it, while I climbed upon the bench to work the other side. The doors at the end of the hall opened and two armed regulars silently took up posts on the entryway.

The minstrel glanced at the guards and leaned toward me, speaking low. "'Tis said no one has ever escaped Lorrach Keep."

"I have," I said. "Once."

He raised an eyebrow. "How?"

"Under a wagon. But the hounds ran me down."

"Hounds? There are hounds?"

"Aye, wolfhounds."

"How many?"

"Twenty maybe."

"Sooth! So getting past the guards is not the sole problem."

327

He chewed his lip in consternation. "I thought I might get *you* over the walls at least."

I stopped scrubbing. "You said we'd *both* get out of here."

"I would prefer it that way, aye, no doubting."

"So would I. 'Twould not go easy on you if you stayed to answer for it."

He looked me square in the eye. "I've no liking for staying, of a certainty. But I'll tell you now, Dominic, if I find no other way and it can be done, then I will settle for you going free without me."

I stared at him, then attacked the tabletop with the brush. "No."

"Ah, kit. . . ."

"No, I *won't* settle for it."

He sighed, but said nothing, for we had moved along the tables and come abreast of the slaves cleaning the next row. We finished in silence, working our way to the end where the two guards stood at watch. Kevin grinned at them.

"Come on up and have a sit-down, mates, by the fire. I can be persuaded to tune the lute."

The men glanced at each other, tempted but undecided. Then one shook his head at the other, and they both gripped their lances doggedly.

"No, Saxon, we have our orders."

The minstrel shrugged. We retreated to the fire, where he took up the lute and strummed his fingers lightly over the strings.

"I need to think," he murmured. He leaned back, closed his eyes, and played a melody over and over, his fingers seeming to dance carelessly. As I listened and watched, the tune gradually changed, but the rhythm remained steadily soothing like flowing springs. My eyes closed and, dreamlike, I let all else vanish but the music. For a long while I drifted in the lutesong, but eventually I felt the rhythm slowing and coming softly to an end. I opened my eyes to meet the minstrel's thoughtful gaze, the brilliant blue of a brisk autumn sky. Astounding, I thought, that a mortal could carry the sky in his eyes.

He smiled and set the lute aside. "Dominic, seems to me there's more to know of you than 'Gaul—downriver.' I'm wondering where you've been and what you've seen."

"All of it?"

His delight showed. "Is there much?"

"I guess there is," I mused. "Sometimes it scarcely seems real, like I dreamed it or read it or like it . . . sort of . . . just came apart . . . and I can only hold on to . . . fragments. . . ." I stopped, abashed, seeing a troubled look furrow his brow. "I guess it never really happened," I amended in consternation "—everything breaking apart, I mean." Realizing how mad I sounded, I bit my lip anxiously. "Must have been a dream," I muttered, turning my eyes to the flickering embers to avoid his perplexed frown.

Kevin broke the silence. "We don't have to talk about it."

"I think I *need* to talk about it, or I may lose it all again. There's just so many pieces, and I can never seem to hold them together long enough."

"Suppose we take them one at a time. You told me you read something of Danes. Where did you read it?"

"On a scroll . . . in the library."

"Where, Dominic?"

"Alexandria."

". . . *Egypt?*"

"Aye, Egypt. The Alexandrian Library."

"Othinn's Eye! What was it you were doing in Alexandria, Egypt?"

"Copying maps," I answered promptly, my mind still in the library. "Well, I was *supposed* to be transcribing Pliny, but there were so many things to see, and I took to admiring the maps. One scroll described lands that lay beyond the Empire's boundaries. It told of Northmen on the far isle of Scandia, the Danes, but only mentioned their painted ships and fierce warriors." I grinned at the huge barbarian. "I never imagined I'd *meet* a Dane. I'd have been terrified at the very idea, be sure."

Kevin grinned. "And were you not?"

"Well, maybe one moment, only until I made certain you weren't about to stomp on me with those massive boots."

He snorted. "And no wonder! Blowing in like a frost-giant as I did, and tripping right over you. But go on—how did you ever get to Alexandria?"

"We put in to port there; we were sailing from Constantinople to Rome."

One bushy eyebrow shot up, but he nodded at me to continue. I described somewhat of the city, the buildings, the harbors, and the people. I told him of riding the rolling hump of a camel out to the pyramids and the Sphinx, and of sailing the Mediterranean, that vast expanse of sea and sky, all-encompassing and ever-changing. I recalled how I clung to the rail of the tiny pitching ship while a towering dark wave of stormclouds rushed to overtake us, and how the sailors followed the starry map of the heavens to find their way on the sea. And as I put these things into words, they crystalized in my mind as events distant, but real and true.

The minstrel expressed but the haziest notion of where Alexandria lay in respect to Rome. I took a half-charred stick from the fire and sketched on the hearthstones the boot shape of Italia, then I roughly outlined the Mediterranean Sea around it, naming the shores as I drew.

"Here, Athens"; I marked, "here, Constantinople; here Alexandria; here, Rome." I glanced up and caught Kevin watching me with lively fascination. "Minstrel, you're not even looking."

"Oh, aye, I am looking! Dominic, do you carry a map of the whole Roman Empire in your head?"

"Aye, I guess I do."

"And have you traveled all over it?"

"Oh, no, not all over. I've only been half way round the Mediterranean. The eastern half," I indicated.

"Only half?" he grinned. He looked back to the sketch. "And where are we from Rome?"

I pulled another charred stick from the fire and drew a jagged arc above Italia. "The Alps lie between here and Rome." Above that I drew the crook in the river. "This is the Rhine." I marked a point below the crook. "Basilia is here." I leapt the river. "And we are here." I stared at that black dot on the stone. "Here," I repeated, suddenly confronted with a different perspective. Lorrach Keep that had swallowed me whole and so utterly devoured me was but a tiny walled speck midst a magnitude of earth and sea and life.

"Here is the lie," I whispered. "A fortress of lies." I turned to Kevin, needing to voice it, needing confirmation. "The world is still there, isn't it; still the same—not like this."

"Aye, 'tis still there, and not like this, not most of it anywise. This place is evil, Dominic; it reeks of it." Then, in low tones, he outlined a tentative plan of escape. He hoped we might slip from the hall in the night and make our way to the stables where we would likely find rope. Then under cover of darkness he could push me to the top of the wall and hold the rope taut while I slid to the ground. I would secure the rope around a sturdy tree, give it a tug, and he would haul over the wall. It was a risky and precarious plan, but the only one that looked even remotely possible.

"Suppose there's no rope," I worried, "Or 'tis too short to reach the trees?"

"If we can reach the wall unseen, then you go over regardless and no argument!"

"But what about you?" I objected. "How will you get out?"

"I'll find a way. Mayhap I'll give you time to get well away, and I'll try the gates."

"The wheels that open the gates are guarded in the gatehouse, Kevin. You'd have to get in somehow, take the guards, open the gates yourself, and get out, all without raising an alarm."

He shrugged. "'Twould be worth a try."

"If it comes to that," I told him, "'twould be easier if I just go round the outside and knock at the gates. They'll have to open them to come after me. I'll lead them a merry chase, and you slip out behind."

Kevin arched a doubtful brow. "And that will not raise an alarm?" He thought a moment. "Aye, if the guards' attention is diverted outside, they'll be less likely to notice me inside; 'twould be easier to take them." He shook his head. "This whole thing would sound better to me if we had a horse. Think you there might be one or two left in the stables?"

"Sometimes there is; aye, could be."

"We'll try it," he affirmed. "We'll slip out tonight if we can and try it. 'Tis chancy, Dominic, but no more chancy than waiting on Lagos, I think."

The regulars tramped in disgruntled and cold for the midday meal, though one could scarcely prove midday under such a somber, dreary sky. Olives, cheese, and bread were carried from the kitchen, and well-watered wine brought out by the pitcherful. I did my share of fetching and carrying, but I would not venture into the kitchen for fear of the hallmaster. The minstrel and the captain faced each other over the table and spoke cautious words. The meal restored their humor, and afterward the minstrel tuned his lute around some lively songs. The captain called for more wine; someone thrust a full pitcher of watery wine into my hands; I trotted to the table. Just as I arrived the captain unexpectedly swung about to rise from the bench. I tried to dodge out of his way, but his knee struck the pitcher, and his elbow rammed my eye. Wine soaked his tunic and leggings, streamed into the ankle of his boot. I scurried backwards, but not quickly enough. The force of his fist against the side of my head spun me hard against the heartstep. Before I could move he dragged me to my feet and bashed me back against the stone wall, exploding the wind from my lungs. An iron hand clamped around my throat; half senseless, I could but strangle mutely and struggle to pry his fingers loose. Those black fireflies swarmed all over me, singing a shrill death chant, while I frantically fought the deadly grip.

Suddenly the terrible pressure let up as one of the captain's hands pulled away. I heard the minstrel's growl:

"Leave him be."

"Let go, Saxon!" the captain snapped. "You've interfered for the last time."

"No. Leave him be."

Through a flurry of retreating fireflies I dimly saw the huge barbarian, his hand clamped firmly around the captain's forearm. The Roman's free hand still pinioned me against the wall, but now all his attention, all his fury, focused on the minstrel.

"You dare challenge me in my own hall!" hissed the captain, reddening with rage. "Over a kitchen rat!"

"Anyone can spill a little wine, Captain." The minstrel appeared unruffled, but for a cold glint in his eyes and an unyielding grip on the captain's arm. "Had it been me who gave you the drenching, I wonder, would you be so swift to strike?"

The captain's hand came off my throat, and I slipped limp and gasping down the wall. He spun lividly on the barbarian, but he could not wrest free.

"You call me coward?" the commander hissed through clenched teeth. Every man in the hall was leaned forward, listening.

"I'm calling you nothing. But I'm telling you, if you would lay a hand on him again, you'll have to pass me first."

There was no question of the captain backing down. His own officers and men were all witness to the challenge this time. Now the minstrel moved so that he stood between me and the captain. He released his hold on the other's arm.

"Back away, Captain," he said levelly.

The captain backed away, but only so far as to be well out of the minstrel's reach. Then for the second time that day, he drew sword on the minstrel. The minstrel stepped toward him, circled him catlike, lionlike, and retreated, drawing the captain across the front of the hearth, further from me, but by now I was incidental to the Roman. The captain thrust his sword at the minstrel, but the massive barbarian was startlingly quick. He leapt aside. The captain feinted high and slashed low; the minstrel was ready for him. He avoided the slash and kicked his opponent's arm on the pass. While the captain danced aside to regain his balance, swinging the sword two-handedly to repel any forthcoming attack, the minstrel bounded to the other side of the hearth and snatched up the staff he had left leaning there. He faced the swordsman with the stout wood balanced adroitly in his hands.

"Now," grinned the minstrel in anticipation, "a fair test: your skill with the sword against my skill with the staff."

The Roman's reply was a sudden lunge. This time the barbarian held his ground and knocked the thrust aside with an end of his staff. The captain attacked again, but the minstrel was too quick for him, forcing the sword downward with one end of the staff then using the other end to strike him a hearty blow to the skull. The captain staggered momentarily, but advanced with fresh anger. He feinted and failed; the minstrel seemed to read his mind. The captain hobbled back with a blow to his knee. He could not even come within striking distance of the minstrel, so long was the staff and so formidably wielded. Still, he came on, and the staff cracked down and outward across his right wrist and flung the sword from his hand.

"Concede," said the minstrel. "You are weaponless."

Eyes fastened on the minstrel, the captain crossed slowly to his sword and, rousing no movement in his opponent, grabbed up the weapon in his left hand and attacked in one smooth motion. Now the minstrel stepped in to meet the attack and with lightning skill disarmed him again. A blow to the ribs and a strike to the back of the legs drove the captain down to his knees. Then the minstrel was behind him, his own knee jabbing sharp into the captain's spine, the staff lodged hard underneath the captain's chin, forcing his head back. Cords tightened on the captain's neck and arms as he arched his back and fought to pull the staff down and off his throat, but he might as well have tried to wrestle a great oak.

"Yield."

The captain glared up at the minstrel and strained harder. The minstrel increased the pressure.

"I've no great longing to break your neck, Captain. You've proved yourself no coward and fought valiantly, but I've won, and fairly. Yield."

A harsh strangling noise rattled in the captain's throat. His face turned alarmingly crimson. His lips moved stiffly. "Yield."

Immediately the minstrel released him to fall forward on his hands, then sink to his elbows, gasping for breath. The minstrel waited, leaning against the staff, hands resting over one end, chin resting on hands.

Silence held the hall while the Roman commander rose slowly to his feet and faced the barbarian grimly. Again he crossed to his fallen sword, eyes on the minstrel. He retrieved his weapon; the minstrel watched unmoving. With an abrupt motion, the captain sheathed the sword.

The collective sigh was audible throughout the hall. The captain glared stiffly at the man who had bested him. The minstrel grinned.

"There's nought like a rousing go-to to liven up a dull afternoon, eh, Captain?"

The captain grimaced, tight-lipped. "You've won the afternoon, Saxon. You're a fighter, as damn good a fighter as you are a minstrel. I concede the quarrel."

The minstrel nodded. Now the doors burst open at the end of the hall, and a gatehouse guard burst in.

"Lagos returns!"

The captain swung about. "How long?"

"Coming up the mountain. Ten or fifteen minutes."

"Look lively!" he barked to his men. "On the grounds in five minutes!" He chose a guard of four to keep a sharp eye on the minstrel. "You're still my prisoner, Saxonius. Now I've a report to make."

XXXV

Was it just yestereve that Kevin Dunskaldir appeared out of a snowstorm? Was it only last night I huddled in the hall, trembling in dread, and the minstrel approached me with warm words and kind eyes? And now I had a new dread to contemplate. Lagos had returned, and the Keep became for me a deadly web of terrors once again. Soon now, Lagos would sit in judgment of the Germanni minstrel's fate. He would know the minstrel fought his captain and why, for I had seen the hallmaster watching from the kitchen. I was certain the Count would hear of it.

I had approached the minstrel with gratitude, and he had divided the last of his good wine between us.

"This may be the last chance we have at it," he said, "and there's no other man I'd fain share it with. Salute, my friend, to tales well ended, and may this be one of them."

I saluted to that, and scrounged in my tunic for the fist-sized chunk of cheese, crust of bread, and handful of olives I had hidden there during the course of serving the meal. The wine was just enough to take the sharp edge off my fears, yet leave them intact.

"Kevin," I said gravely, "'twill go best with you if you do not anger Lagos. Take a care in there. 'Tis Lucifer's own pit when Lagos sits in the Hall."

"You don't hold out much hope, do you, Dominic? Mayhap I can charm our way out," he grinned.

"Not Orpheus himself could charm Lagos. But if you can

335

convince him you are no spy, mayhappen he'll set you free." I did not voice my thought that he would never charm *me* out of Lagos's web.

He read my mind. "But not you with me, eh?"

"Not likely," I said softly.

He looked grim. "What will it take to get you out of here, I wonder?"

I shook my head, thinking of death.

"This weird is not yet done, my friend," he rumbled deeply.

I half smiled, trying to feel hopeful, not succeeding.

Kevin took up his lute, and began absently picking out a tune. I folded my arms on the table and rested my chin upon them, watching him and listening. Presently he became absorbed in the tune, trying this and that note and humming to himself. Betimes the melody jaunted gaily along; betimes the notes lamented hauntingly. Now the tune took on a life of its own, now rollicking, now weeping, while he played it repeatedly. Then gradually the two tempos merged into a flowing rhythm and slowly faded. He laid his palm flat across the strings to still the final notes.

"What do you think, Dominic?"

"Beautiful! Did you just now compose it?"

"Aye. The words are still hazy, but 'tis already named. I'll call it *The Merry Dwarf*." He winked. "You'll be the stuff of songs yet, Dominic."

My smile quickly faded. "Merry? I . . . why . . . minstrel, my heart is so far from merry the very word makes it hurt. Call it *The Melancholy Dwarf*. 'Twould be more true."

"Ah, but beneath the melancholy I sense a merry heart. Before you came to this foul place, I think you brimmed over with merriment."

I buried my face in my arms. "That was before," I muttered. "I'm not the same. Nothing's the same."

He laid a hand on my shoulder. "No, you'd not be the same. Has been hard, kit, I know. . . ."

"You *don't* know!" My brusque reply came unbidden. I heard him sigh and felt his hand rest softly upon the nape of my neck, wanting to give me some small comfort. But the buried emotions his simple, kind touch stirred within me threatened to wrench my heart wide open, and I could not bear the deluge of anguish welling up, not now, not in this hopelessness, not with Lagos yet to face.

Abruptly I pulled away and swung off the bench. I sat huddled on the hearth and stared at the crumbling embers. To hold myself together, I could not think beyond the immediate: my tightly interlocked fingers, the fiery skeleton of a log slowly collapsing, the hard stone floor, my breath in and out without rest, silence behind me. I turned. The minstrel sat staring at his clenched fingers. Would I soon watch him die, I wondered? I swallowed, trying to find my voice, wondering what I could say, but he unclenched his hands, pushed to his feet, and came to sit beside me on the hearth.

Kevin, too, stared into the embers. "No, I don't know, do I?" he said quietly.

We sat together in silence. Now the four guards came to attention at the far end of the hall as the door swung open, admitting the captain. By the time he strode the length of the hall, the minstrel was standing to meet him. I scrambled to my feet.

"Saxonius," the captain said tersely, formally, "His Excellency commands your presence immediately."

"I expect he does. You didn't happen to be mentioning our little chance-medley, did you, Captain?"

"If you mean our contest, I had to include it in my report, Northman. He would hear of it by other means."

"Meaning that sneak the hallmaster."

The captain pressed his lips together distastefully and nodded. The minstrel shook the black wool cloak from his pack and threw it around his broad shoulders, fastening it on one shoulder with a bronze brooch of intertwining designs. The cloak fell to just below the tops of his shaggy boots. He set a tooled leather strap to his lute and slung the instrument across his back. Then he took up his staff and glanced to me.

"Don't cross him," I muttered.

He nodded.

"I think you've no cause for concern, Saxonius," said the captain. "The Count dines early tonight and entertains guests. I praised your minstreling, and he expressed an interest." He hesitated slightly. "The Count orders that Monstrosito also attend."

I know I paled considerably. I tried not to show the fear those words caused me. The minstrel nodded reassuringly at me.

"Ready, Captain," he said.

At the doors the four guards took up positions beside and behind us. We stepped onto the portico into an early dusk; the sky remained clouded and somber, the air still and cold and permeated with a fine mist. Before we stepped from the portico into the damp, the minstrel moved his lute protectively beneath his cloak. In silence we crossed the trampled snow; the courtyard was cast in shades of grey. For the first time the minstrel saw the Great Hall closely. He stared up briefly at the heavy iron hook, chain, and hoist beside the bronze doors. The telling brown bloodstain lay hidden beneath churned mud and snow, so he seemed not to guess the hook's purposes. I hoped he would never have occasion to find out.

Before the doors the captain turned.

"You may bear no weapons in the hall, Saxonius. Leave your staff outside."

The barbarian glared at the officer. "I'll leave it *inside*—out of the damp."

The heavy doors opened at the captain's angered rap, and we entered the hot glow within. Kevin leaned his staff against the inner wall. The captain left us to the Count's own entry guards.

Sick with fear as always, I made myself walk beside the minstrel into Lagos's pit. As we halted at the top of the thirteen steps I felt all the horrors of the place come rushing up to suffocate me. Fighting back a futile urge to run, I forced my lungs to breathe slow gulps of the venomous atmosphere, but my heart thudded in panic.

Kevin Dunskaldir stood at the top of the steps and unhurriedly swept his gaze about the Great Hall enchained within its circle of iron tripods, the oily flames casting an adumbral light. His eyes dropped past the dark tapestries that hung the walls to the two hundred faces staring up at him from the tables. Now he stared straight across the hissing bed of coals in the hall's center. His gaze narrowed upon the lean figure of Count Lagos seated high upon the dais. The Lord of Lorrach watched him complacently.

"Mother Life," I heard Kevin's low mutter, "a hall fit for demons." Glancing grimly at me, he began a measured descent. Somehow, I followed.

The benches were full, and drink flowed freely. Every man's eyes had fixed on the tall, yellow-maned barbarian. He took it all in as he passed the tables of cavaliers, and they looked him over, their attention riveted by his huge presence and sure bearing.

The smokey heat rising from the central fire formed a vaporous shroud across our view of the Count. An enormous hog roasted on an iron spit over the fiery embers. The minstrel paced steadily around the firepit and came to stand before the dais, his black cloak flung back over one shoulder, the lute tucked under one arm. The two men regarded each other levelly. I stood aside, gripped in paralyzing fear of this bleak place and its merciless lord.

Finally Count Lagos nodded formally. "Welcome to Lorrach Keep, Saxon. Not often does a minstrel guest in my post."

"My thanks, Excellence. I had been doubting my welcome. Are you always so cautious of your guests?"

Lagos smiled smoothly. "When the guest is Germanni and arrives uninvited, I take precaution. Particularly when he brawls with my captain. How is it you presume to challenge one of my officers, Saxon?"

"'Twas a mere chance-medley," Kevin told him evenly. "I misliked his manners."

The cold eyes flicked over me. "Toward Monstrosito? I find that highly amusing—and most thought provoking."

Kevin kept his thoughts to himself and his gaze on the Count.

"I see now why my captain lost the encounter. I thought he exaggerated in his description, but you are every bit the giant he described, which gives me hope that you're also every bit the minstrel he says you are." Now the Count leaned forward intently. "What is your business here?"

"As I'm sure your captain told you, I sought shelter from the blizzard, Excellence. I generally expect a welcome in Roman posts."

"You were traveling freely through Alamanni territory—a Germanni barbarian. Any yellow-hair can claim to be a Saxon, and even a Saxon may spy for the Alamanni."

"I am no spy," Kevin told him brusquely. "I earn my way with the lute. I travel unarmed."

"Unarmed? In your hands a simple staff is evidently a formidable weapon."

Kevin smiled grimly. "Even a minstrel has occasion to defend himself from ruffians."

"Ah, and I suppose that category includes my captain?"

A chorus of chuckles rose here and there in the hall. The minstrel made no comment.

Lagos stroked his trim black beard with an onyx-ringed forefinger. "If you are not a spy, barbarian, tell me why a Saxon is so cozy with Roman outposts."

The minstrel answered readily. "Sooth, I was an ambassador of good faith between my people and the Empire for no few years."

Lagos eyed him derisively. "A hostage?"

"Aye, they called it that," the barbarian grinned. A few more chuckles spattered the hall.

"The Empire does not loose military hostages to wander where they will. Explain what you're doing skulking along the borders."

Now the minstrel sounded annoyed. "I've been seven years a peacemaker along the Saxon Shore and the northern Rhine. My good faith is well proved. I was trusted to mediate a federati treaty at Colonia between Romans and Franks, a treaty still honored by both peoples. I was sent to Argentoratum to negotiate between the Empire and the Burgundians, and had the commander at Argentoratum not been a treacherous fool, Burgundians would now be allied to Rome. I'm now on my way to Mediolanum on business that is not yours. Do not accuse me of skulking, Count Lagos."

The deadly quiet fairly cracked across the suffocating atmosphere. The Count's eyes narrowed to hooded slits.

"Barbarian dog!" he spat. "You are a prisoner in my Keep, and I can have your guts spilled and your belly stuffed with live coals on any accusation I choose!"

Kevin's eyebrows shot up one after the other.

"Now, answer me! Precisely why are you *skulking* through Alamanni territory?"

The minstrel eyed Lagos narrowly.

"*Shortcut,* Excellence."

Lagos glared through slitted eyes. "Tell me what you know of the Alamanni!"

The minstrel contemplated him long but said nothing.

"I have devices, *barbarian,* with which to wrest the truth from you efficiently and unpleasantly. Or hasn't Monstrosito told you?" His smile was viperous.

"There was no need," Kevin answered him. "Count Lagos's reputation is well known along both shores of the Rhine."

"Indeed?" Lagos laughed, leaning smugly back in his chair, pleased. "And what do they say of me along the Rhine?"

"That you torture your captives long after they've told all they ever knew—that afterward you kill them gruesomely for sport."

Lagos's long, hissing laugh cut off abruptly, and he snapped forward in the chair. "Did your friends the Alamanni tell you that, eh, barbarian? They are a threat to the Empire's borders, and I am charged to keep them in their place. It is necessary that they fear me, else their rabble armies would overrun us!"

Now the minstrel's strong voice thundered out in anger. "The

Alamanni are no threat to the Empire, Lagos! 'Tis *you* who are a threat to *them!* 'Tis not the Alamanni who cross the Rhine to attack Roman posts and Roman towns. No, 'tis *you*, Lagos, who sits on Alamanni land and hunts *their* forests, ravages *their* villages! Of course the *rabble* armies fight back! They defend their homes, their children, and their lives—from *you*, Lagos!"

Lagos struck the chair arm with his fist. "*Lies!* Alamanni lies!" A low growl from behind the dais announced the awakening of the wolfhound Caesar. "You *have* been with them, and they send you to skulk around Lorrach Keep, undoubtedly to gather information so they may plan an attack. But you'll not leave this Keep, Saxonius, if that is indeed your name, which I doubt. Instead, you'll tell me the location and strength of every last Alamanni stronghold and be begging me to listen. Seize him!" Lagos ordered, jabbing the onyxed finger at Kevin.

The guards who accompanied us moved forward; the minstrel whirled to face them.

"*Hold!*" rasped a commanding voice behind me. "Hold this instant! Lagos, as an appointed agent of the Emperor I forbid you to take this man prisoner until *I* have questioned him!"

I turned toward the two guests I had scarcely noticed. The man who shouted was on his feet, hands flat on the table, glaring up at the Count. Now he straightened and hooked his thumbs on the bronze-linked belt at his waist, a gesture which flung wide his short, wine-colored cloak and effectively displayed the gold-cast imperial insignia which hung upon his chest from a heavy gold chain. His hair, a shiny blue-black, fell long and straight. Crag-faced, he met the Count's angry glare with hawk-browed eyes chiseled above a sharply hooked nose. He wore a bronze-sheathed sword at his side.

In the taut moment of eye-to-eye confrontation between the imperial agent and the Count, my gaze drifted to the second guest seated at that table—and froze there. I knew him. Still youthful and dashingly handsome, still cool, aloof, and aristocratically attired, not fifteen feet from me, sat the man responsible for the slaughter of my vagabond family. *Fabius Sividicus.*

For one stunned instant I feared a fragment of the past had unaccountably fallen into the present and now perhaps *time* was crumbling into chaos. But only for an instant. Rocked to the depths of my soul, I stared at Sividicus the murderer guesting in the hall of Lagos the demon.

Sividicus was engrossed in the confrontation, for by now the

Count, too, sprang to his feet, snarling at the imperial agent. The wolfhound hunched forward, chorusing his master's snarl. "You have no such authority in my hall, agent!"

"I have, *Count!* You know why I'm here. I shouldn't have to remind you I'm commissioned by Emperor Honorius to thoroughly investigate the situation along the Rhine, particularly in reference to the Alamanni. I have every authority to question this man."

Lagos's eyes glittered, but he allowed the agent a cold smile and resumed his seat, signalling the guards to fall back. Caesar lay down, hackles up, eyes watchful. "Then do so."

The minstrel relaxed his wary stance. The agent came around the table and halted a few feet away, his hawk-like stare returning the minstrel's assessing one. Tall and sinewy as the agent was, he made no match for the barbarian in size, but he was not intimidated. He hooked a thumb in his belt, poised on one leg in a casual manner meant to communicate neither fear nor threat.

"You are Saxonius?"

The minstrel nodded. "I am."

"And you have acted as mediator between the Empire and the Germanni?"

"I have."

"An unbelievable stroke of fortune! Then it is in your capacity as mediator that I would speak with you, Saxonius. I seek any knowledge you may have on the political status of the Alamanni tribes."

Kevin eyed him carefully. "And who might you be? And why should I be telling you?"

The crook-nosed man smiled. "Christus Valorian, Agent Imperius. My interest is on behalf of Emperor Honorius, who has commissioned me to determine the possibility of a treaty with the Alamanni. If you have indeed been among them, your knowledge may be invaluable to me."

The minstrel shifted his gaze from the agent to the Count, who leaned intently forward on one elbow. He looked back to the agent.

"Valorian, eh? If 'tis a treaty the Emperor is wanting, then, aye, I have knowledge. But the words I have to speak cannot be spoken here. I gave my oath on it."

"In private, then. . . ."

"*No!*" Lagos's voice snapped the air like a whip. "No words will be spoken in private! Do not imagine that I am deceived,

Valorian, either by you or the Emperor's nursemaids. Those fat, spineless milksops worm their way into his counsel, but they know nothing of who or what holds the Empire safe for their like. It is *I* who am under investigation here—an investigation prompted by incompetent fools who want their purses and lands protected from invaders, yet do not wish to dip into those precious purses to pay for it!"

The Count basked in the imperial agent's surprise. "Yes, I know the insipid sheep of this province petition the Emperor, crying that I overtax them, and the Consul at Vesontio bleats the loudest. I am fully informed as to your purpose here."

The agent Valorian glanced sharply at Sividicus, who returned him a mocking smile.

"Then of course you are aware, Count," the agent reiterated "that other city councils of Maxima Sequanorium also petitioned the Emperor, claiming that Lord Fairfax seizes exorbitant taxes on your behalf. The Emperor's advisory council worries about conspiracy, as Lord Fairfax is your brother-in-law."

"If it is conspiracy to agree on taxes necessary to strengthen the frontier, then we are guilty. Pathetic, is it not, Sividicus? Rather like sheep complaining to the estatemaster that the shepherd keeps them from the wolves."

Sividicus the murderer nodded. "Exactly like, Excellency. And I am here to make certain the wolves are not let loose into the fold."

Valorian swung on the man. "The consuls were assured anonymity, Sividicus. You knew that."

Sividicus the butcher came to his feet and clasped with one hand the crimson woolen toga that draped his breast. Beneath the toga his full-length white tunic, embroidered in a gold and crimson laurel-leaf design, covered a close-fitted red undergarment that protected him from wrists to ankles. High boots of white rabbit fur were laced snug beneath his leather sandals. He exuded luxury.

"As the Senate's appointed representative in this matter, I deemed it necessary to inform Count Lagos as to the nature of his enemies. A man on trial has a right to know the identity of those who accuse him."

"This is not a trial," the agent said tightly. "It is an investigation into the feasibility of a treaty for the security of the Empire."

Sividicus smiled loftily. "It is the *preservation* of the Empire which is my concern. The noble aristocracy which has been the cornerstone of Roman civilization for eleven centuries is determined that the Empire shall remain *Roman!* We would see to it that no more Roman lands are given over at the whim of sniveling cowards to Germanni rabble! Already portions of Gaul have been handed on a gold platter to the Franks. The same stupidity was barely aborted with the Burgundians."

Sividicus met the minstrel's gaze with undisguised triumph, and sudden comprehension dawned in Kevin's eyes—and anger.

"The commander at Argentoratum did not act entirely on his own, I ken. How much a bribe did it take to persuade him to set back treaty negotiations for a generation or more? How much to make him break *my* oath to the Burgundians?"

"Not as much as we anticipated, Saxon," smirked Sividicus. "He, too, saw the value of keeping Roman lands for Romans. He now owns a small section of fertile land in southern Gaul, awaiting only his early retirement, which is being discretely arranged."

"That is *treason!*" accused Valorian.

"As you see it. We call it patriotism."

"Is it patriotism, Sividicus," the agent countered, "that prompts our worthy senators who refuse to meet the army conscription levied on their estates?"

"We cannot afford to denude our lands of laborers. The vineyards and fields require constant care, else production will fail. The aristocracy *made* this Empire, made it fertile and wealthy. We do not shirk our duty, Valorian; we pay the army twenty-five solidi a head—a high ransom to keep men on our estates."

Valorian's hawk-eyes and voice sharpened. "And then the Senate turns Janus-about and subverts the Emperor's efforts to hire soldiers with the ransom. Do you think a handful of gold secures the borders?"

Lagos nodded. "I do agree with Valorian on this point, Sividicus. Solidi will not hold the borders. It requires men with weapons—well-paid men—well equipped and trained."

"But not Germanni!" protested Sividicus. "The Emperor hires the very barbarians who would invade, even supplies them with weapons."

Lagos nodded again. "On this we are of one mind, Senator. Barbarians must not be allowed to camp fully armed within our borders—or even outside our borders, like the Alamanni. The moment our vigil is relaxed, they will invade."

"Not so," retorted Kevin. "The Alamanni want no part of the Empire. They are wanting peace, but a Roman fortress and Roman troops on this side of the Rhine make peace impossible."

"This Keep is necessary to ensure that they do not band together and cross the river. My cavaliers can detain them at any point within hours, followed swiftly by my infantry, giving troops on the Empire's shores time to mobilize where they are most needed."

"I'll tell you where they are most needed, Lagos," Valorian countered. "They are needed to strengthen Italia against possible invasion from the Goths in Illyricum. This border here is the most costly in the western Empire and ties up thousands of troops needed elsewhere. We need this treaty. The Empire is too large, our boundaries too vast to hold with sword and spear. General Stilicho makes peace on as many borders as he can."

"Stilicho is half Vandal himself!" sputtered Sividicus. "His barbarian blood proves stronger than his honor. He sells us out to his Germanni cousins!"

Cousins! I saw them sprawled in blood, my vagabonds, my cousins. Again I was Dominico, standing on the edge of the bloody camp—Dominico, steeped in anguish and loss—Dominico, seeing his whole life shattered, slaughtered by this murderer spouting about *honor.* I fought the turmoil in my heart, in my head, as his words rushed on.

"But the Roman nobility will not stand idly aside while Stilicho and the Emperor give away Gaul at their whim. Gaul is by rights Roman!"

Kevin questioned his claim evenly. "And what rights would those be, I wonder?"

Sividicus turned on him. "What do you mean, barbarian?"

"Seems to me it belonged by rights to the Gauls until Caesar took it by force—stole it, you might say—and enslaved the Gauls for no other cause than his own personal glory."

"They were *savages!*" snarled Sividicus. "Rome *civilized* them!"

"They were people. Rome stole their land, enslaved their children, and made herself rich off their sweat. Therein is Rome's only 'right' to Gallic land, I ken."

"Ah," pounced Sividicus gleefully, "now I perceive your true interest in this matter. Take heed Valorian; your barbarian mediator is out to see Gaul wrested from the Empire and plunged back into savagery—into the arms of savages like himself, who will reward him with a share of the booty, no doubt."

The minstrel eyed him stonily.

"I, for one," Valorian maintained, "have a clear duty to weigh his words along with all else and report my findings to the Emperor. I urge you to speak, Saxonius. If you speak the truth, it will be confirmed, and I can assure that you'll go free."

Kevin shook his head. "My words are not for the Count's ears, but for the Emperor's. I would fain speak openly with you, Valorian, but not within these walls. I swore an oath to the Alamanni. First give me safe passage from Lorrach Keep."

"Done."

Kevin inclined his head toward me. "And safe passage for the little one."

The agent hesitated but a second. "Done."

Low, hissing laughter from the dais killed any hope that might have stirred in my heart. The sneer on the Count's face was arrogant and perilous.

"You have no authority to make bargains in my hall, Valorian. For one, the dwarf is my property; you cannot take him. For another, the Saxon is my prisoner, and in my judgment a dangerous one. He's been within this Keep but one day and already attacked—*unprovoked*—both my infantry captain and the common hallmaster. No, I'll not release him merely on your less-than-established authority."

Valorian stared, inflamed. "You would dare oppose an imperial commission, Lagos? A commissioned agent has full authority to enforce the Emperor's writ under any circumstances in which he perceives a clear necessity."

The Count's smile remained impervious. "The Emperor's writ is quite precise. It enjoins me to allow you a discrete investigation. It does not state that you may interfere in *my* authority nor take any action whatsoever."

"Count Lagos is correct, Valorian," added Sividicus. "He has only to adhere to the letter of the writ."

"The writ also states that the Count is to *cooperate* with my investigation, not subvert it."

"I feel I'm being extremely cooperative," Lagos said smoothly, "allowing you to interrogate my prisoner freely and openly in my hall. But in my judgment there is as much reason to suspect he is a spy as not, therefore I will not allow you to supersede my authority in this matter."

Sividicus concurred, "And I am witness to the fact that releasing this suspected spy would most probably pose a danger to the Empire's frontier. Count Lagos is within his rights, Valorian."

"Indeed," continued the Count. "We've not necessarily ascertained that this man is who he says he is—that he has ever been a mediator of treaty negotiations. But as a token of my utmost cooperation in this investigation, I'm willing to hold him here, Valorian, while you confirm his identity with the commander at Argentoratum. You may even find the commander has charges against him. Is that so, Saxonius? Another, ah, chance-medley, possibly?"

"We had our disagreements."

"You seem to stumble into those with undue frequency."

"He laid plans for treachery against the Burgundian chieftans; I fouled his plans."

"Ahh." Lagos grinned again. "Perhaps, Valorian, you'd prefer to try at Colonia where the report might appear more favorable."

The agent's eyes hardened. "You know I couldn't complete such a journey in less than a fortnight."

Lagos lifted his hands in a gesture of generosity. "The prisoner will be here when you return, my word on it."

"In what condition?"

The Count smiled, slit-eyed. "Alive."

Valorian had long since lost the argument. He squared his shoulders. "I won't chance him left alone in your hands, Lagos." His voice was harsh. "We'll settle it here."

"Good." Lagos slapped both palms on the armrests triumphantly. "You may question my prisoner all you wish, Valorian. And to prove my good faith and full cooperation in the Emperor's wishes, should your methods fail, I'll assist in the investigation myself using methods of my own. I promise you, he'll speak—and quickly. I hate to prolong these little altercations unnecessarily."

"No torture, Lagos," objected Valorian. "This is a diplomatic matter, not a game for your private amusement."

"You underestimate my methods, Valorian," Lagos said pleasantly. "There are more inventive means of persuasion than torture. I shall consider it a challenge. Now," he announced, rising smoothly from his chair, "the meat is ready for carving and the first course waiting to be served. Winter journeys brace the appetite, do they not? And since this is a *diplomatic* matter," he gestured indulgently toward first the imperial agent and then the minstrel, "I invite our guest of honor, the *reputed* Germanni ambassador, to be seated and to dine with us. Indeed, I insist," he amended when the minstrel, frowning, looked as if he would refuse. "I must consider it an affront to my hospitality if you decline, and I might begin to doubt the sincerity of your peaceful rhetoric. An amicable discussion over dinner will certainly make me more favorably disposed toward your cause."

His blond beard stiffly jutting with dislike, Kevin inclined his head curtly and replied with deliberate ambiguity, "I accept the hospitality of your hall, Count Lagos, with the selfsame sincerity in which it is offered."

Now the Count truly laughed, suddenly all mirth and congeniality. "Perhaps you *are* a diplomat, after all, Saxon." He waved the three men toward the table at the left of the dais, where stood a carved chair at the end.

"Be seated, gentlemen—we'll hold up supper no longer." As Sividicus cooly took the place of highest honor just to the right of the Count's chair, the imperial agent took the second seat. The arrangement placed Sividicus inside the octagon formed by the tables and placed the agent on the outside. Kevin's eyes flicked briefly to me before he strode around the table and stood beside the agent.

"You must excuse my precautions, Saxonius," said Lagos as he signaled the four guards to move into position against the dark tapestry at the barbarian's back, "but you are, as yet, an unknown element. I'm accustomed to absolute control in my hall."

The minstrel gave no response but a flat stare, then he swept aside his black cloak with stiff dignity and leaned his lute carefully against the bench between himself and the nearest officer. That officer wrinkled his nose and moved pointedly down the bench to allow the barbarian giant more than ample space. The minstrel bared his teeth at him amiably. Not until the Count seated himself in the carved chair at the head of the table was the first course laid before them. I remained unmoving, as if carved of stone, hoping the Count would forget me, knowing he would not.

"I apologize, Sividicus," the Count was saying, "for the Spartan fare. Out here on the fringes of the frontier we must make do without expensive niceties"—he smiled at the imperial agent— "despite what the taxpayers imagine."

"Quite all right," said Sividicus as a slave ladled from the tureen bowlfuls of garlicky soup. The murderer helped himself to a chunk of olive-oil-dripping army bread. "I suspect your simple fare is much better for the digestion than some of the elaborate delicacies to which I've been accustomed."

"It keeps my men hale and hearty."

"Ah, this tour is good for the spirit. Every man should taste the soldier's life at least once."

"But not for too long, eh, Sividicus?"

"We are not all cut from such sturdy cloth."

Lagos directed his attention to the minstrel, who had tasted nothing. "I would think a man of your size, Saxonius, would have the appetite of a Hercules. I'm certain to be offended if you sit at my table and insult my hospitality."

Kevin silently took a slab of bread, bit into it, and washed it down with wine.

"I propose," Lagos went on pleasantly, "that we call a truce for tonight. I see you brought your instrument. A lute is it called? Not Saxon, is it?"

"Arabian," the minstrel answered tersely.

"Indeed? Perhaps despite our opposing political philosophies, you'd favor us with some music this evening. But wait, before you refuse, let me elaborate. We so rarely have fresh entertainment in the Keep; I'm afraid we usually have to make do with Monstrosito." His cold gaze poised on me, and the look in those soulless eyes froze my heart. "No, I've not forgotten you, Monstrosito." His long forefinger coiled like a scorpion's tail. "Come here."

Dreadfully obedient, I came forward and stopped a few feet from his chair. Kevin's wary gaze leapt from me to the Count.

"I'll play the lute, Lagos," he muttered.

Count Lagos smiled. "Oh, I've no doubt of that. You'll play a good many tunes before this night is through. But first, indulge me while I show off my little oddity here. You've become quite acquainted with him, I understand, but my other guests have not had the opportunity."

I knew by heart the ordeal that was coming. That my new-found friend was there to hear it made me all the more wretched.

"Allow me to present one of nature's most peculiar jests, this droll travesty of the human form you see before you. It seems the gods *do* have a sense of humor, however perverted. Why else create such a crude caricature of man but for their amusement—and ours? I submit it to you, gentlemen. Have you ever seen a human creature as grotesque or ludicrous as Monstrosito?"

Sphinx. I am like the Sphinx—I am of stone—none of this touches me.

"I've seen your dwarf elsewhere, Excellency," Sividicus the murderer said smugly.

"Have you indeed? Are you certain it was this very one?"

"Quite. There can hardly be two such creatures in the Empire sprouting identical shocks of red hair. In fact, I've seen him many

349

times—in Rome. He belonged to a motley clan of vagrant Greeks—acrobats, dancers, and the like."

Dead—all dead because of you.

"Extraordinary coincidence. Monstrosito does perform a few rudimentary acrobatics. We'll have him show us momentarily."

The main course arrived: fresh pork steaks served with stewed vegetables. The smell would have made my mouth water if my gut not been in such a tempest. Churning with rage, humiliation, and dread, I felt a too-familiar quaking deep in my solar plexus. Teeth clenched, I strove to stop the tremors.

"And you, Valorian. You're unusually quiet. What do you think of my little pet?"

Valorian answered the Count with sullen silence.

"Let him be, Lagos," Kevin said between clenched teeth. "We've heard more than enough."

"Ah, a champion!" sneered Lagos. "What would you do, barbarian? Take your staff to me? I think not."

Four lances lowered at ready, prepared to skewer the minstrel's broad back. I met Kevin's gaze across the table, and he was the only thing not fading into a tunnel of darkness. A golden haze of fireglow around his yellow hair seemed the only light in the hall.

Lagos laughed sneeringly. "Look at the stump! He's half mad! What makes him worth saving, Saxon? Look at him—fit for the dung heap. Truthfully now, have you ever before seen such a misconceived abomination?"

The minstrel's blue-hot glare seared into the Count, hot enough to forge a sword in.

"I don't know that word—*abomination,*" Kevin's tone scathed, "but I mislike the sound of it. I so mislike it, I ken I am looking at one now." His expression left no doubt that had he a sword he would carve the Count's liver out.

The Count's eyes narrowed to cold slits. "You insult me at my table?" he hissed.

"You insult *him!* You hold one of the dwarf-folk captive, and he means less to you than that hound. His is an ancient and noble race, a race as old as the mountains, and these forests were the dwarves' domain long before men ever set one foot before the other. Nowdays there are precious few left, and I find an arrogant Roman holds one prisoner and insults and degrades him for perverse entertainment. You sicken me, Lagos—you and all your Keep."

Folly, I knew, to defend me before Count Lagos. Yet I was glad of his words.

The Count laughed again, his sharp croak sinking to a deadly hissing through his teeth. "*Noble race! Precious few!* I had no idea you northern barbarians held such malformities of nature in superstitious awe. I find your curious sentimentality toward Monstrosito quite novel, Saxon, and amusing. The possibilities of this situation grow more fascinating by the moment, do they not?"

I heard my doom in those words.

Lagos waved a languid hand to include the minstrel, the imperial agent, the murderer, and the full hall of cavaliers. "Look you, gentlemen, at this filthy, ragged lump of flesh! Pathetic little Monstrosito? See you anything noble about *him?*"

I saw my friend's anger and dismay. Only he and the agent did not join in the mirth. I felt anything but noble at that moment, only helplessly enraged that the Count could so easily use me to torment the minstrel. *One day of friendship. One day of trust. One day of feeling human.* Was it worth it? I careened madly between fury and despair.

Kevin's hands clenched on the table as he growled above the falling laughter. "Let him go, Lagos! You have *me.* Let the little one go free—let him walk out the gates—and I'll tell you what you want to know!"

Silence. The Lord of Lorrach and Kevin Dunskaldir locked stares. Then Lagos sneered. "Germanni barbarians do not make bargains in my hall, Saxon. Nor are you in a position to barter. You'll tell me all I want to know anyway . . . *eventually* . . . and you know precisely why." His cold, serpent stare pierced into the disturbed blue eyes of the minstrel.

Slowly, as though with all his will, Kevin unclenched his fists. His voice rasped with forced calm.

"I'll tell you *now.*"

"Not at all." Lagos was suddenly the smiling, gracious host. "I won't hear of it. We'll save such unpleasantries for later. For now you're my dinner guest—why, Saxonius, here's dessert and you haven't even touched your supper. And you, Valorian, have scarcely eaten either. Is something amiss? Something I said, perhaps?" At that Lagos laughed, in high form. Apple slices glazed in honey were placed on the tables along with fresh pitchers of wine. Lagos turned to Sividicus.

"I'm intrigued, Senator, by this amazing coincidence. I trust you've more to tell us of my *noble* dwarf's origins. These eastern acrobats you mentioned—what manner of nobility were they?"

"Nobility? They were a lot of indigent mountebanks, little better than beggars and thieves. They plied their crude arts in the streets for coppers, but for the most part they were beggars, thieves—and whores."

"*You lie!*"

Aye, those words burst from me—unbidden. A fragment from the past, a fragment I had believed long dead, exploded sharp and sudden from some deep cavern of my being, maddened with anger and grief.

They all stared, surprised by the furious outburst from the tattered dwarf-slave. Kevin gazed at me in amazement. Count Lagos curled his lip. Sividicus stiffened, white-lipped. I felt as in a mad dream, out of control, saying mad things, but what use was sanity in this. . . .

You're doomed anyhow, Dominico. You've nothing to lose.

"You lie!" I repeated. "We were the best! The *very best!* You hired us yourself!"

"You were *nothing* without me!" spat Sividicus. "My patronage put you in the theaters, and then you ingrateful scum betrayed me!" He was on his feet now.

"Betrayed! *You* talk of betrayal? You *murdered* them!"

"They cost me my high standing in the Senate!"

"They *earned* you that standing, and to you they were *dirt!* And you *butchered* them! Hacked them to pieces—the old women—the babes—!"

"I was the laughingstock of Rome!"

"*Baby-butcher!*"

"I bought your miserable troupe only because of that *bitch,* that fickle *whore!* She played me false! She *used* me, then when she had what she wanted—" Now his eyes narrowed. "How is it you still live, stump? The captain assured me he killed every last one of you maggots."

I gritted my teeth. "I expect he thought this maggot not worth the mention."

"He had orders to leave no one living but *her*—he was to bring the dancing girl to me."

"You coward," I hissed. "You sent armed troops against helpless folk because a woman wounded your pride."

"She had to pay for her perfidy."

"Oh, she paid." My voice grated hoarsely past the knot in my throat. "We all paid."

The butcher smirked and resumed his seat. "The captain swore she wasn't among the slain, that she was not in the camp when he attacked. Where was she?"

For a moment I was tempted to gloat, to taunt him with her escape, but it would be an empty triumph—he had destroyed all she loved, and that alone would feed his pride. And suppose I said she still lived? Would he search for her? My voice turned to iron.

"The captain lied. They killed her. I saw."

The smirk slipped, replaced by resentment. I had struck a nerve. A small victory for Dominico.

"She should have suffered as I did. I humbled myself for years to get back into Symmachus's good graces—but I accomplished it. *I* survived."

"Aye?" I said acridly. "Is that why you're out running errands on the frontier instead of resting your laurels on your Iberian estate?"

A low staccato laugh broke from Lagos. Sividicus shot him a rancorous glare. Reckless and heady, I pushed on.

"You were nobody until we made a name for you, Sividicus, and when we walked we pulled it all out from under you. The applause was for *us*—the toast of Rome."

Sibilant laughter continued from Lagos. "Even you, Monstrosito?"

I met cold derision in his eyes.

I was two people whirling in a tempest of emotion—the doomed, humiliated slave he named Monstrosito and the furious, grief-torn vagabond Dominico. Between us yawned a gulf of madness. We could not touch across it, but we knew each other well.

"Even me."

"Show us," sneered the Count. "Show us what tricks the 'toast of Rome' can do. Show your barbarian friend to what depths your *noble race* has fallen."

I looked to the minstrel. Fists clenched atop the table, he stared at Lagos with an intensity of hatred I had not imagined could come from those eyes. Four lances pressed against his tensed back. His gaze dropped to mine; I saw his grief, his agony that he could do nothing. *He is unaccustomed*, I thought, *to situations in which he is powerless. Lagos will use me*, I realized starkly, *to shred his heart to pieces, bit by bit.* And the fury that realization caused me was like a glowing, burning sun in the center of my being. I felt the heat explode in my solar plexus and streak up my spine, and suddenly I straightened my shoulders, lifted my chin, and raised blazing eyes to the tormentor's face. The crown of my head was on fire with rage. The game, then, was to shame me before the minstrel. But was I to be ashamed of the fine art Brossos taught me? Would I so insult my cousin, the master acrobat? I thought all pride had long ago been beaten out of me, but now it surged through my blood like strong wine.

Abruptly I spun full toward the minstrel and, with a flourish, bowed deeply, my best performing bow. I raised my head and met his bemused stare with a fierce grin. The bold ring in my voice surprised him.

"With pleasure! I would be doubly honored, minstrel, if you would accompany me on your lute."

For an instant Kevin looked unsure he heard aright, then, not taking his eyes from mine, he took up the lute. Lightly he thumbed the strings, and I felt a strange comfort in the sound, as though for the first time in ages I did not perform alone. Drawing on some deeply etched memory as surely as if years had never intervened, I fell into slow cartwheels around the firepit, and the sound of the lute followed me.

For a suspended moment in time, I was Dominico and none other. I was perfectly balanced, centered in the dance of the universe. I wheeled faster and switched to somersaults, and as my body responded anew to old commands I felt a rush of manic exhiliration, yet I remained keenly focused in balance and motion. The lute paced with me, tumbling beside me in perfect sync. With dreamlike clarity I felt the music follow my every move, merge in rhythm with my flips and spins. Yet the minstrel's tune simultaneously gave shape to my tumbling, created the rhythm my movements fell into. The lute-song and my tumbling seemed to arise from one source in spontaneous harmony. And the tune seemed eerily familiar until I realized in the midst of a handstand that it was the same tune the minstrel had been playing earlier— the one he called *The Merry Dwarf*. Only the rhythm was new.

I could not keep it up. Disused muscles quivered in pain; my breath gasped and burned. I let the music slow my pace, felt the tune wending to its end, gratefully flowing along the rippling, melodious stream toward the final note, the final bow.

"*Caesar!*" Lagos's voice shattered the melody. "Hold him! To bay!"

I tried to halt in mid-cartwheel. The lutestrings clamped silent. I stumbled, and when I caught myself I was down on one knee, staring up into the snarling muzzle of the great wolfhound. The room spun around me. Beyond the hound's bristling black hackles, I was dizzily aware of the minstrel coming to his feet. I gasped, trying to bate my breath, stop my tremoring limbs.

"Move and he's dead!" I heard Lagos snap. "Caesar will have his throat out before you're over the table, barbarian!"

All motion ceased in the hall except the whirling in my head. All sound ceased but my raspy fight for air and the pounding roar in my ears—that, and a low growl rumbling deep in the hound's throat. Caesar hunched stiff-legged, baleful, gleaming eyes fixed on me—daring me to move.

"Be seated, Saxon," the Count said casually. "Caesar won't attack if Monstrosito stays perfectly still—unless I give the command, and I assure you I would not hesitate to give it."

At the edge of my vision I saw the minstrel's huge form slowly sink toward the bench. My mouth and throat were dry, unbearably so; my tongue clung to the roof of my mouth. Cautiously I tried to lick my lips, but even that small movement evoked a warning growl from the wolfhound.

"Now, Saxonius," said Count Lagos, "*now* we will bargain— on *my* terms. Now we find out just how much the little goblin is worth to you."

XXXVI

Kevin Dunskaldir's reply was low and raw. "What is it you're wanting?"

Lagos laughed. "Better! Much better! You know what I want, barbarian. Information. I want to hear those words you refuse to speak before me, yet are so willing and eager to speak to the Emperor. What business are you on, Saxonius?"

The pause was agonizing. I could scarcely breathe. Maybe the minstrel's business was more important than me. *You swore an oath—handfast over the cups!* I cried silently to him, and felt cowardly and selfish for it. I knew he swore an oath on that business of his, too.

"You'll call off the hound?" I heard the minstrel say.

"I'll consider it—*if* your information is worth his life."

"I carry a petition from the Alamanni chieftans to Emperor Honorius."

"Ah," the Count smacked in satisfaction. "I will see this petition."

"I do not carry it written. I carry it here"—he touched his forehead—"in memory."

"Then *recite* it. My patience, and Caesar's, wears thin."

The minstrel sighed deeply, then began the recitation in an oratory tone. "Greetings and long health to the Augustus Emperor Honorius, Glorious Sovereign of the Roman Empire. The gathered clans and chieftans of the Alamanni in high council petition the Victorious and Just Honorius in hopes of peacebond between the Alamanni and Roman peoples. The Alamanni have long respected the Empire's border, being the River Rhine, and have neither the wish nor the might to encroach on Roman soil."

Lagos snorted. "Respect? Fear of Count Lagos and his cavaliers is the only respect they know."

Choruses of agreement clamored across the hall. The wolfhound growled excitedly in my face.

"Continue," ordered Lagos.

The minstrel continued, reluctance in his voice. "The Alamanni desire friendly relations and trade with the Roman Empire, but under present conditions they must doubt the Emperor's understanding of their good intentions." He hesitated slightly, then went resolutely on. "The Alamanni are unable to live in peace with the Empire while Roman cavalry posted northeast of the River Rhine at Lorrach Keep continually raid Alamanni villages, burn homes and crops, kill livestock, rape and murder the helpless and innocent. The Alamanni blame not the Wise and Just Emperor Honorius, but Lagos, Count of the Rhine Frontier, instigator of all manner of violence and atrocities against the Alamanni. The clans in high council have pledged their desire to make peacebond with the August and Victorious Emperor, to respect the Rhine border, to establish fair trade with the Empire, to allow no invading armies to cross Alamanni lands, and to take up arms in the cause of Rome. In return the clans request only that the Empire trade fairly with the Alamanni and that all Roman military be removed from Alamanni lands and hindered from crossing the Rhine. The clans also request that the accursed Lorrach Keep be destroyed and razed to the ground and that the Lord of Lorrach be tried for grievous crimes against the Alamanni. This Count's presence is a torment and an offense to the Alamanni . . . and an *abomination,* a canker on the noble countenance of Rome."

The minstrel's tone had turned acerbic. "The list grows, Lagos. The Alamanni wished to demand your execution at their hands—by their own methods—but I advised them to save it until negotiations were well underway—when the demand might be considered more seriously."

The taut silence was punctuated by a chilling sound from Lagos—laughter. Suddenly the sounds stopped and his palms slammed onto the armrests.

"*Fool!* You have just sealed your own doom!" Then his voice smirked in self-satisfaction. "See, Valorian, how easily that was

357

accomplished? Well, well, barbarian, it seems we have no further use for Monstrosito, have we—except for sport, perhaps?"

"You said you'd call off the hound," gritted Kevin.

"You're mistaken. I merely said I'd consider it."

"Aye, *if* my information was worthwhile. You know it was, Lagos."

Valorian added his voice to the minstrel's. "'Twould be a poor sport, Lagos. The dwarf is unarmed, and your hound clearly outweighs him."

I dreaded not death itself so much; I more feared those long, yellow fangs, bared and snarling. The wolfhound's hot breath was close and foul, and I felt I must turn my face away or gag, but I dared do neither.

Then I heard Kevin speak, low and strained. "Among my folk a minstrel may ask a boon of the lord of the hall in return for his tuning, and if that lord is pleased, he will grant it. I ask you Lagos, Count—call off the hound and let the little one go. I am begging you, forsooth."

Blood thundered in my ears.

"Ah. Now you play a tune more to my tastes, Saxonius. And to demonstrate my benevolence . . . *down*, Caesar. Come."

First Caesar crouched low, as if he might leap on me regardless, then he wheeled and clattered on hard claws across the flagstones to the dais. He lay by the Count's chair like the black guardian of Hades's gates, eyes unwaveringly fixed on me, awaiting the command to tear into my throat.

I sank my forehead to the flagstone, overcome with exhaustion and relief.

"Stand up, Monstrosito! You disgrace my hall with this unseemly display of cowardice!"

With difficulty I stood, knees trembling.

"I cannot understand your affinity for this deformed creature, barbarian, but I'm willing to consider the boon you beg of me— *if* I deem your luting warrants it. I trust you will make this your best performance."

The minstrel eyed the Count with distrust. The Count grinned viperously, his cold eyes hooded and cunning.

"As proof of my faith in your skills I'll dismiss Monstrosito from the hall beforehand—consider the boon granted. Besides, I've already arranged an interesting little performance from Monstrosito in your honor, Saxon."

The minstrel turned a questioning glance to me. And I looked at the Count with full understanding. Too long familiar with his cruel caprices, I read the insinuation in his eyes, expression, and voice, that told me I was not being let off easily. The onyx-ringed finger flicked toward the whipsman.

"Escort him to the common hall. See he arrives at his destination."

The minstrel frowned, misliking letting me out of his sight, but he was as tightly entangled in the Count's web of malice as was I. Briefly I met the minstrel's troubled gaze before turning resigned steps toward the stairs, the whipsman on my heels.

"Now, Saxon," I heard Lagos command behind me, "we'll hear some music. It's time you earned your stay *and* your boon."

I heard the tuning of lutestrings, the settling of the hall to listen. Impatient with my slow progress, the whipsman prodded me along with his knee. I stumbled forward and awkwardly scrambled up the steps ahead of the whipsman's heavy boots.

A weeping of melancholy notes flowed from the lute. As I reached the top step, I half turned for one last glimpse of Kevin Dunskaldir, his eyes following me, fingers strumming a lament. *Does he know he'll play his heart out for nought?* Then the whipsman blocked my view and forced me through the doors.

Outside a fine mist drizzled from the cold grey gloom that permeated everything. It penetrated my tunic, while a freezing slush on the ground soaked rapidly through my ragged foot-bindings. I shivered in the sudden shock of cold, too abruptly chilled, coming overheated and asweat with exertion and fear from the suffocating hall. The whipsman grasped me roughly by the collar and half dragged me across the dark yard, through the slave quarters and into the common kitchen, which ceased its bustle and fell into attentive silence. He flung me at the hallmaster's feet.

"He's yours."

The hallmaster bent over me, twisted thick fingers in my damp hair, and hauled me to my feet. He wrenched my head back. The beady eyes glittered.

"I told you you'd pay, stump."

Then his fist struck my midriff a brutal blow that left me gasping on the floor.

Half-senseless with pain, I scarcely knew when he cast aside the rod with which he beat me. Dragging me into the storeroom he stripped off my tunic and slung me helpless over the grain sacks.

A whimper of hurt and dispair escaped my bloodied lips, and he chortled raspily at the sound.

"Now I collect my interest."

"None of that," snapped the whipsman's voice behind him.

"There's time," growled the hallmaster.

"Lagos's orders are explicit. They don't include pandering to your vices."

"The bug's got it coming to him."

"*You'll* have worse coming if the Count's game is mucked. Your fun can wait."

Through wracking pain I felt a pathetic relief. Dimly aware that someone bound my hands before me, I could barely open my battered eyes to make out the whipsman lashing my wrists together with leather cord. He unwound and tugged off my leg wrappings, then dragged me to my feet. I stumbled blindly between the two of them out into the night and gasped in shock. Sudden cold assaulted my senses; freezing drizzle pelted my bare skin. They forced me naked and barefoot across the frozen yard. Struggle was beyond me. Dazed, I staggered in their grasp. Then the dragging stopped. I would have fallen, but the hallmaster held me upright and cursed the rain. A clanking noise made me force open my eyes, and hazily I made out the ugly shape of an iron hook suspended just inches from my face. The hallmaster slipped the hook between my bound wrists.

"Crank him up. This blasted rain's freezing as hell."

The hook and chain jolted me off the ground. I hung, shaking now, shivering, bared to an icy wind that whipped the rain into a punishing frenzy.

"Hurry," whined the hallmaster. "It's getting worse."

"Go, then," the whipsman snapped. "I'll give Lagos the nod. This one won't last long out here."

Then they were gone.

Cold. Unendurable cold. Inescapable.

Pelting sleet like a million ice needles pierced my bruised flesh. I shuddered convulsively in the relentless, burning cold.

I could neither cry out nor resist when, at last, icy black waves surged over my consciousness, mercifully numbing everything until all I knew was the pain in my wrists and the cold maw of the maelstrom swirling up to drown me in darkness.

. . .

Something dragged me back from the blackness, pulled me back from dark oblivion, into the chaos of consciousness. Hands grasping me, a voice whose words I could not understand, abrupt motion—all tugged at my awareness when all I wanted was to drift in the dark night. But, ah, no, the darkness surrounding me must be the cold cell where they cast me after the tortures. Had I dreamed Hagia cradled me in her arms, rocked me gently in a boat upon a dark sea, and crooned in a far northern tongue? But now they laid hands on me to pull me back into the nightmare, back into the torture chamber. I made a futile attempt to struggle, a pitiful attempt to cry out, but I found no strength or voice.

"No more. . . ." I pleaded, but the words came out a faint whimper.

"Shhh . . . easy, Dominic . . . I've got you."

The voice was the minstrel's. I tried to focus on the face above me and failed. How could he be here in the dungeon? *Please—no—not another dream.*

"Kevin?" I whispered.

"Aye, little one, 'tis me." His voice sounded strange and thick.

Now I knew he was no dream. We were not in the dungeon, but outside in cold rain. Kevin knelt in the mud and, cradling me next to him, sheltered me within his cloak. With unspeakable relief I sighed and closed my eyes, rested my leaden head on his breast, and he lifted me up and carried me as easily as he would a child.

I drifted upon the cold, black ocean, half aware that he carried me beneath his cloak, carried me across the sleeted yard and into the silent hall. He dragged something bulky onto the hearth—his pack—and laid me carefully on it near the low embers, then he wrapped the wool cloak around me. I caught the faint flash of a blade.

I had been insensible to my bound hands until then. Now I saw them—swollen and ghastly blue—alien things. The minstrel painstakingly cut the leather thong and unwound it from deep, bloodied grooves embedding my wrists. Mercifully I felt nothing, but seeing the leather peel out of blue flesh made my head spin. I sought the minstrel's face, found it white and grim, and sank dizzily down the well of the black maelstrom.

Pain pulled me back. My flesh burned as though I had plunged in scalding water. The hearthfire now blazed high. The minstrel's head bowed over me, both my hands encircled within his own.

At first I thought he prayed, then I realized he breathed into the cocoon formed by his palms, breathed warmth into the lifeless hands he clasped. Those hands began to tremble. Suddenly my whole body shook, seized with violent shivers that set my teeth chattering. Convulsed by chills, I curled into a ball of pain, driven by cold and wretchedness to the only refuge I knew. I retreated far into an inner darkness and huddled in deepest despair—cast out by life, cast out by death, and below me spun the maelstrom.

The minstrel's hand lightly brushed my hair. I shuddered at the touch.

"Ah, no, kit . . . let me help . . . come to me."

I could not. The maelstrom became a whirlwind, sucking me into its mad emptiness. I could not bear being swallowed up in that awful aloneness, but as I fought to cling to consciousness my will, the universe, even the maelstrom, all began breaking apart around me, and I felt my whole being shattering into a million tiny pieces.

Kevin drew the wool cloak around me and, with infinite tenderness, gathered me close in his arms as though he might hold me together within his huge embrace.

"I'm here, Dominic. Hold to me."

He hugged me to him then and stroked my damp hair as lovingly as a father cradles and caresses a frightened child. The maelstrom howled around me, but it could not pull me from his strong grasp. And my forlorn heart, wearied with battling lonely terrors, desperately grateful for the warmth, the gentleness, the caring the minstrel wrapped around me—my heart *needed* this. I lay my head on his shaggy vest and huddled trembling in his arms, shaking with cold and misery. Tears flooded my battered face. Unashamed, I wept as I had not done since the endless horrors began. Terrors and humiliations and tortures spilled from me in shuddering sobs, and I gave myself up to grief.

And Kevin held me to his heart, and murmured softly the while in his own language. I need not understand the words; they came from his heart and spoke straight to mine. I could feel—or in delirium imagined I could feel—him sharing his own quiet strength with me as easily as he shared the warmth of his body. Gradually, responding to the kind voice and gentle hands, my aching muscles relaxed, and the trembling subsided and stilled. The violent sobs eased, my ragged gasps steadied and quieted. My head rested on the minstrel's dampened vest, and I felt the rise and fall of his breathing, felt his heartbeat strong and steady.

. . .

Reluctantly I awoke, disturbed by a familiar sound in the dark hall—one of the kitchen slaves stacking wood in the fireplace, cursing the cold, jabbing and blowing the coals to life. Something felt different, and I tried to ascertain what it was. For one, I hurt and ached and throbbed over every inch of my body. For another, I was warm—warmer than I had been in months. And I slept cozily beside one giant of a barbarian, my head nestled in the cradle of his arm. Aye, and I remembered why. I recalled the humiliating ordeal in Lagos's hall, the beating by the hallmaster, the torturous cold of wind and sleet, the warmth and gentleness of the minstrel. I knew why I was alive this morning.

Painfully, with hands stiff and uncooperative, I pushed back the heavy bearcoat, startled to see my wrists deeply gouged where leather bonds had cut into flesh. Aye, he had held my hands between his own and breathed life and warmth over them.

Through swollen eyes I focused on the minstrel's face, ruddy in the fireglow, the rugged features smooth and serene in sleep, and I realized how surprisingly young he really was beneath the lion's mane of hair and beard—scarcely older than myself, if at all. His gigantic stature, barbaric looks, confident bearing—all added deceptive years to his appearance. Even now, even in sleep, the arch of his brows was emphatic.

I felt I had known that face for a thousand years.

He stirred, his eyelids fluttered sleepily and blinked open. I stared into startling blue eyes, and I knew the soul that gazed back at me, knew it was kindred to mine.

He smiled. "Dominic—you live! You were near frozen—I feared—" The smile faded. Gingerly he smoothed back my tangled hair. "*Mother of Life*, look at you—your poor face." Quickly he drew my hands into his and looked at the mangled wrists. "Your hands are warm," he said with relief, "but what a wounding they've taken. Can you move your fingers?"

With difficulty I closed stiff fingers over his palm and met his anxious eyes. My heart overflowed; my eyes brimmed with thanks. I gripped his hand.

Kevin smiled, and I surprised my bruised lips with a smile of my own.

"*Verthandi*, 'tis good to see you alive this morn!"

I wanted to express my heart, to voice my gratitude for his presence and his kindness, but I could only press my brow to the

363

sturdy hand in silence. His other hand came to rest gently on the back of my hair, and I wished I could hold on to this moment, stop time forever, and never know anything but this comforting touch, this gentle friend.

Immediately the doors blasted open at the far end of the hall, startling both of us, admitting chill wind and bitter curses into our quiet solitude. The regulars stamped in for fire and breakfast.

I stared, distraught, into the minstrel's eyes. With much grumbling and shuffling, the troops came onward to the blazing hearth-fire. The minstrel halted my reluctant attempt to move.

"Stay here," he whispered quickly. He rolled out from under the bearcoat and let it fall over my head, leaving a warm hollow in the pack where he had slept. Gladly I stayed in the warmth and did not move, scarcely dared breathe until it became apparent from the muffled conversation in the hall that no one realized I lay hidden among the minstrel's belongings. The sound of his voice beside me, low and vibrant among the others, lulled me into sleep again. The last sounds I knew were benches scraping and the minstrel tuning his lutestrings.

"All right you muckabouts, get moving! Do you think you're the Praetorian Guard all of a sudden, that you can linger over breakfast and sweet songs all morning? Get off those elegant asses and look like the Rhine army, by Jupiter, or I'll find the stables need shoveling! Move out!"

Abruptly awake, I lay still and listened to the scrambling and grumbling. The captain's voice continued along the rows of tables.

"You think it's cold in here, grubber, wait 'til you get outside! This is the frontier—not Mediolanum! Out here you tough it! Count Lagos wants crisp, parade-ground manuevers this morning. We've a senator and an imperial agent come to inspect."

The stamp and clink of his boots and mail halted before the hearth. "Saxonius," the captain addressed the minstrel sharply, "my men are under orders to gut you wide open if you set foot outside this hall—you first, then the dwarf, if he's still alive. Where is he?"

"Alive."

The captain waited in silence for more, but the minstrel offered none.

"Fetch him!" clipped the commander.

"You fetch him, Captain. You might detain me, but you'll

not be forcing me to turn my friend over to you." I heard the minstrel stand and stretch. "I'm for more barleycakes. Care to linger with me over breakfast and sweet songs? Or staves, Captain?"

"Another point, Saxon, Count Lagos wanted made clear to you—should you attempt escape, or even *look* as if you might be attempting escape, Lagos will roast Monstrosito alive and serve him up to you for supper."

The minstrel's silence was so charged I could feel his fury. "What kind of man does the bidding of a fiend like Lagos? What kind of man, Captain?"

"Count Lagos is commander of the Rhine army," came the clipped reply, "and therefore my commander. My duty is to him."

"I thought mayhap I sensed more honor than that in you, Captain. I was mistaken, I ken."

More charged silence, then abruptly the captain's boots scraped the flagstone as he spun on his heel and strode the length of the hall. I heard him call sharply to the men outside. He summoned four of them back into the hall and in low tones gave his orders. Then I heard fists strike armor in salute. The doors slammed shut.

"Niddering brass."

Following the one terse comment, the minstrel stood silent for some moments. Whatever his thoughts, they expressed themselves in a burdensome sigh, and he strode across the hall toward the kitchen. I lay listening to the silence and absorbing a familiar, rich aroma that grew stouter. It was another long moment before I could stir my aching muscles into motion. I crept from under the bearskin, shivering as bare feet touched the cold stone floor, clutched the minstrel's woolen cloak around me with difficulty, my stiff fingers refusing to tighten without sharp pains streaking up my arms. Glancing toward the back of the hall I saw four guards with shields and lances standing before the doors. I trailed the long cloak across the hearth and stood pensively in the warm glow of the fire, irrationally glad to be alive. I pondered nothing more urgent than the small, black pot simmering on the flames and that redolent aroma—why, it was chickory! Ah, Mother Hagia had often brewed chickory tea, and the rich smell of it both saddened and comforted my heart this morning—and evoked a fleeting, half-glimpsed memory from the night. *Hagia.* Had I dreamed of her? Or had I suffered delirious visions while I hung from that hook, near freezing to death? Aye, they had been visions. I could not recapture them.

Kevin, with furrowed brow, reappeared from the kitchen carrying a stack of barleycakes. His glower vanished when he saw me standing before the fire.

"Morning, Dominic. Feeling well enough to be up, are you? Would you be feeling up to breakfast, too?"

He set the cakes on the hearth and found two empty winecups in which to pour the steaming tea.

"Have a sip of this, kit—'twill pert you up."

Cautiously, struggling under yards of cloak, I sat on the hearthstep. He settled beside me and laced the tea generously with honey from a jar.

"There's nothing like hot chickory tea of a winter morn to warm your blood," he smiled.

I took the warm cup he passed my way, but my hands shook and it would have slipped through my fingers had not his hands closed around mine and steadied them. The tea was too hot to drink, but the steamy chickory aroma invigorated my soul.

"Chickory. . . ." I whispered shakily. "I've not smelled chickory brewing since—since I don't know when. Wherever did you find it?"

"In my pack. You slept so soundly I took care not to wake you. You were needing the rest, I think."

I took a tentative sip from the cooling cup, savoring a strong, bitter-sweet flavor which warmed me with memories. Favoring my cut lip, I swallowed several hot mouthfuls and immediately felt better. In truth, I felt a wholeness and a clarity I had not known these many months imprisoned in Lorrach Keep. Somehow, through the night of cold misery and near death, through the warmth and safety in the minstrel's embrace, through the flood of grief and tears—somehow I emerged renewed.

As I sat drinking warm chickory tea this morning in the company of Kevin Dunskaldir, I felt no longer the divided and confused wretch who could not remember himself without his world shattering, to whom the universe was a treacherous nightmare with no waking. I felt whole again.

Yet I suffered no illusions that the horrors were over. The dark shadow of the Keep loomed over me, so relentless, so inescapably vile that this momentary peace seemed but cruel mockery. The nightmare crouched patiently, omnipotently, a staring cat over a trembling mouse. Aye, this prison of horrors made a mockery even of the bond that had grown between us, for I knew the Lord of Lorrach would use it against us. He would use me up, a piece at a time, to torment the minstrel. I shuddered, closed my eyes to shut out my friend's worried face, wishing I could close my heart to what was coming.

"What is it, Dominic? Are you hurting? Have you some injury within?"

I shook my head in quick denial. Slowly I set the near-empty cup on the flagstone beside me, reluctant to break the peaceful spell around us.

"Can you not guess what he means to do?" My voice sounded hoarse.

"I'm not sure I want to know," Kevin said grimly.

I raised my eyes abruptly to confront his. "You *will* know, sooner or later. Minstrel, he means to torture me and force you to watch." The clench of his jaw told me that the possibility had already crossed his mind. "Are you ready to face that?" My voice faltered to a whisper. "*I'm* not. I don't face torture very well. I . . . I cannot go through another . . . I *cannot*. . . ." I buried my face in my hands.

I felt him gingerly pry my hands down. He searched for words. "Mayhap . . . mayhap, kit, 'twill not come to that . . . mayhappen we will find a way to . . . to . . ."

"To *what?*" I retorted bitterly. I turned my face away, unable to look at him as my next words burst out. "Why could you not leave me hanging out there last night and leave well enough alone?"

"Dominic, what are you saying? Would you have me leave you to die?"

"Why not?"

Kevin spoke, his voice thick and raw behind me. "I could not. Understand . . . I could not just turn my back and walk away. Even when I feared you were dying . . . Dominic, I couldn't leave you dying alone and friendless."

"How do you imagine I will die now?" I said wretchedly, too weary to weigh the effects of my words. "I'd rather you ended my life this morning . . . with your own hands . . . before Lagos gets his chance at me—I swear I would. A quick death—I wouldn't mind it. Would you do that for me, Kevin?"

I turned when he did not speak and met a stricken look, his ruddy face gone ashen.

"Do not ask that of me, Dominic—to take your life! How can I?"

"Drowning might not be so bad. You could hold my head

down in the cistern until I finished struggling, for I'm not sure I wouldn't fight you whether I will it or no." I would not have thought he could turn any whiter, but he did. I regretted my blunt words and tried to soften them.

"There are worse fates, Kevin. I don't want to die Lagos's way, and you'll not want to see it."

He stared at me in disbelief, then stared at his own hands . . . imagining . . . considering . . . then suddenly recoiling in horror.

"*No! I cannot!*"

"Not even in mercy?" I asked tremulously.

He glared at me. "I'll not murder you, Dominic!"

"You may wish to God you had!"

"*No more!*" he growled.

I turned my face to the fire to hide the sudden tears. "Aye," I whispered. "No more. . . ."

Struggling to my feet under the weight of the thick cloak, I retreated across the hearth. Heavy silence hung between us. I blinked in the firelight, forced back the tears, and stared into the flames. The silence lengthened, then I heard his deep sigh and soft step, felt his hand fall lightly on my shoulder.

"Dominic. . . ."

I did not turn, not trusting my emotions if I looked at him.

"Dominic. . . ." His voice was deep and ragged. "I don't think . . . I do not *believe* 'twill come to that."

"You expecting a miracle, minstrel?" My muttered response was edged with despair.

"I don't know what I expect, but I cannot believe we've come this far . . . to meet in this place . . . only to have it end that way."

I gestured impatiently. "Why not? None of those others who've died here wanted to believe *their* lives could end that way, but they did! Believe it, minstrel. They all died the same way . . . *Lagos's* way. How can you believe this will end any differently?"

"Have you no faith, man?"

"*Faith?* In what?"

"In *life!* In nature herself."

"Oh, aye, aye." My voice cracked. "Look what nature has done for me."

"*Mother of Life!*" He gripped my shoulder hard. "Think you we meet here by accident? Think you 'twas happenchance I wandered snowblind into this nest of vultures and stumbled right over you? 'Twas my full intention to avoid this Keep, but the Earth forces drove me straight up against the gates with no choice but to freeze or come inside. 'Twas a weird brought us together, and we are still following it. In here, in my gut, I have a feeling—aye, something beyond feeling or kenning, something deeper—that tells me we should trust this weird and see it to the end."

I spun to face him now, knocking his hand off my shoulder.

"A *feeling?* Do you read the future? How? In stars? In chickory leaves? You *don't know* what's going to happen! You *can't know!* No one can! Think you this is some tale we are in? Think you we will come to the end of it, pay the storyteller, and go home? This is *real*, and you've no way of knowing 'twill not end in slow torment for both of us! You've no right raising useless hopes of some hypothetical supernatural force you expect to sweep over the walls and whisk us away!"

"Ah, no, you do not understand a weird, Dominic. . . ."

"No, *you* don't understand!" I was become distraught and knew I should shut up and let it lie, but fear and frustration overcame reason. "Are you *dense*, man? We're about to face Lucifer-knows-what sort of game in Lagos's pit, and you prattle on about mystical feelings and . . . and . . . *weirds!*"

I stepped away from him, toward the dying fire, and as I turned I half tripped on the unwieldy cloak. The minstrel reached to catch my fall but caught the cloak instead. The sudden tug stabbed like needles through my raw wrists. Pain shot up my arms, my fingers went suddenly limp, and the heavy cloak fell to the floor around my feet.

I stood naked on the hearth and wept, tears running silently, blurring my eyes. Angry at being left naked and vulnerable, I swept the tears aside and snatched up the cloak. Looking up, I caught sight of his face, the pain clear in his eyes as he read the grim tale of tortures seared into my flesh. But I was in no mood for sympathy or pity.

"Aye, look well, minstrel!" I cried bitterly. "Tonight you may see how 'tis done!"

And because I could not bear the anguish in his face, I looked away and pulled the heavy cloak around me. Shivering in the chill of the hall, I moved closer to the fire and stared dismally into the glowering embers.

A wall of silence stood between us, a wall of my own making, a wall I would tear down if I could, but I was hurting in body and soul and could find neither the words nor the strength to unmake it.

Now I heard his voice, soft and strained behind me. "You're right. I do not know the future; I cannot foresee the end of this. I never thought—I never imagined 'twould come to this. I . . . it seemed a simple thing . . . you needed help, and I wanted more than anything to help you . . . but if I am wrong . . ." His words broke off; he took a deep breath. "If I am wrong . . . 'twill be *you* who suffers for it. And if he tortures you because of my interference . . . then . . . can it be I do you no good at all—only more harm?"

I heard—*felt*—his words clear to my soul, and I stood ashamed, ashamed I had lashed out at him, lashed out at the one person who cared what happened to me, the one person who could be hurt by words of mine.

I spun to face Kevin. "*No good?* Minstrel, that's the maddest thing I've ever heard. Do you know what it has been like? Because of *you* . . . for the first time since . . . since *this* place . . . I feel . . . like a human being . . . like I'm *worth* something."

"You *are* worth something."

I smiled at his quick response. "Aye, I am. Has been hard to remember . . . until now. So end this mad talk about doing me harm. I'll not let you lay blame on yourself for *anything* that happens here. All goes to Count Lagos, where 'tis damn well deserved. He would've gotten around to me again anyway. Maybe the time comes a little sooner. . . ." I shrugged. "Maybe 'tis all the better. I'm sorry, Kevin . . . I didn't mean to lash out at you. 'Tis just that I'm not very brave when it comes to . . . I can be such a coward sometimes."

"Coward? You? I've seen what you bear in this place, what you've borne every moment for more than a year. I don't know how you hold heart and soul together. I don't know how you stand here and look at me with sanity in your eyes—yet you do."

Any sanity in my eyes, I thought, *is because of you—because you are the one thing I can look upon here and still remain sane.*

"These devils have done their worst," he went on intensely, "to make you feel you're *nothing*—lower than nothing—but 'tis *not* true. You spoke rightly yestereve, Dominic. 'Tis all *lies*. There's nothing of truth in this place."

"Except you," I said quietly.

He was surprised into a slight smile. "Aye. Except me. And you."

"I don't even feel *real* sometimes. . . ."

When I did not continue, he nodded. "I'll tell you something.

370

I've never met anyone more real, nor braver." He shook his head. "And so gentle a fellow, to be so ill used. Throughout everything that slimy spawn of Loki put you through last night, you stood before him nobly. Not even before the teeth of the hellhound did you falter."

"I was terrified, Kevin."

"Aye. And I. And in the face of terror you showed more heart and more courage than I've ever seen."

I shook my head with a wry smile. "'Twas not courage, my friend. 'Twas necessity."

"Sometimes, my friend, courage and necessity are one and the same." He paused and looked long at me, his serious eyes deep indigo in the gloomy light cast by waning embers.

"We will *need* courage to see this through. Do not lose all hope, kit, please. Hope and heart, and our wits, are all we have."

Wonderingly, I cocked my head and peered up at him. "You still believe we're going to get out of here, don't you."

He grinned. "*One* of us has to believe it."

I responded with a grin of my own. "What is it you think you're going to do, you great barbarian? Take on the whole Keep and storm the gates?"

"Maybe. I hope 'twill not be necessary. But whatever happens, we'll both be needing all our strength to see it through. And you'll be needing your breakfast." He passed me the forgotten barley-cakes.

The cakes were cold and greasy by now, but I was accustomed to cold, greasy fare. I devoured them with a heartier appetite than I expected, though my bruised jaws and mouth suffered through the chewing. And while I ate, he spoke.

"I'll tell you a thing that happened, a thing I'd not be telling if I didn't feel 'twas full of portent." The minstrel hesitated. "I'm not sure you'll not be thinking me mad . . . but something happened in a dream . . . 'twas east of here, the day before the snowstorm. I'd become uncertain how far east or west I'd strayed, and as I fell asleep the night before I wondered which way I should be going for a good river crossing—a safe and unseen one—when I had a dream. I dreamed I awoke to the sound of a flute playing deep in the forest. Aye, the flute played the most wonderful tune I had ever heard, and it seemed to me a tune I should know well, but just where and when I'd heard it before escaped my memory. I rose up from my sleep and wandered through the misted forest, following the flutesong. Soon, very soon, I found myself in a meadow open to the night sky. From there came the flute song, for the music shrilled through the clearing and danced around me like starry fireflies in that dark meadow. Then from the wood's shrouded edge appeared two shadowy figures, seeming more to emerge from the very mists than from the murky wood. And as they came nearer I knew these two beings.

"The first was a woman, lovely and seductive as the Earth beneath her bare feet. Night black hair tumbled around sea-green eyes and across shoulders gleaming white under starlight. Flung back from her shoulders hung a cloak of black feathers and around her neck draped a strand of bright gems that shone like the stars themselves, every gem sparkling on her breasts in rainbow colors pure as crystal. 'Twas the Brisengamen she wore, and no other, but I'd have known her without it. Freya the Lady, she was, Daughter of Earth and Sea, Mistress of all Life, Gatherer of Souls. And her companion, I knew, too. He, hobbling beside her, leaned upon a gnarled staff enspiraled with deep-carved runes. Beneath the blue cloak he stood taller than mortal men—except myself, of course—and a peaked hat made him seem taller still. The hat's floppy brim hooded the ancient face, shadowing one blue eye and a deep, empty hollow where another eye should be, and once was. Aye, I knew Old One-Eye, the Dread Wanderer, Reaper of the Slain. Othinn, he was, Lord of Winds and Fury.

"And in my dream Othinn spoke not, but fixed me with his wise eye and held me in a piercing gaze that read my thoughts, my heart, my soul. Slowly he nodded, and Freya stepped softly toward me, her dew-glistening gown and feather cloak soundless on the bowing grass.

" 'Raven,' she named me, her voice liquid and alive as a bubbling mountain stream, 'Raven, that which you seek is not far. Come, we will show you the way.'

"And with what swift silence they glided into the wood! Even lame Othinn melted through the mists ahead of me so quickly I could scarce keep his billowing cloak in sight.

" 'Follow, Raven, follow,' sang Freya's liquid voice, and even farther ahead beckoned that haunting flute.

"And I, thinking nothing strange at being named 'Raven' by a goddess in a wood, followed the two shimmery figures deep beneath the dark trees. Then we broke through to an open hill standing clear beneath the stars, and Freya and Othinn rose from the clinging mists and took to the winds, transforming into ravens before my eyes.

" 'Wait!' I cried, and the pair of ravens circled back, wheeled thrice above my head, calling the while, and flew straight into the west. And I, Raven, rose up and flew after them, a black feathered bird winging the night sky. 'Tis the last I remembered—skimming the winds toward Orwandil the Archer, those stars you call Orion. Come sunrise, upon awakening, I felt I had dreamed a dream of portent, yet I had no recollection of what I had dreamed."

I listened in fascination to his strange dream, and now I hastily swallowed the last bite of barleycake. "You must've remembered sometime, else you couldn't be telling it, could you now?"

"Aye," nodded the minstrel. "That's the queer part—how I remembered—the part that makes the portent a certainty. As I said, come morning I didn't remember—'twas early morning, just the day before I came here, and I stood upon a hillock reckoning which direction I should take. I could see a likely storm amassing up over the northern hills, so I thought I'd best cross the Rhine while the weather held. I reckoned on heading south, directly to the river, and then bearing east so that I might not venture too near Lorrach Keep—I'd been forewarned by the Alamanni—when out of the west flew two ravens, skimming the treetops. And, *Verthandi!* If they did not circle thrice above my head, cawing loudly, and streak away west again! *Now* I recalled the dream entire and stood thunderstruck on the mound, for I knew of a certainty if those two ravens were not Freya and Othinn them-selves, they were at least Huginn and Muninn—mind and memory of Othinn—eyes, ears, and messengers of Old One-Eye himself. Without hesitation, snowstorm or no, Lorrach Keep or no, I turned my steps westward and followed the flight of the ravens. You know the rest, my friend. I was overtaken by the storm and driven snowblind against the gates of this very Keep. Ah, and now you stare at me as if you be thinking you sit in company with either a lunatic or a fool. Do I sound that mad to you?"

Indeed I stared at him round-eyed and amazed, but not for the reason he imagined. For I had realized something that sent shivers up my spine and prickled the hairs up on my flesh.

"Did you say, Kevin, that you saw the ravens the day before you arrived here? Early in the morning?"

"Aye, sunrise. Why?"

" 'Twas that very morning, I climbed to the top of the tower, intending to leap to my death, but the sight of sunrise over the Earth held me fast. And the ravens—the ravens startled and flew from the tower over the trees—and two of them, *two* of them, minstrel, flew away *east*, beyond the horizon"—my voice shook—"*that very morning!*"

Kevin Dunskaldir's eyes glowed. "So the ravens came from here," he said softly.

"But . . . but 'tis not possible, is it?" I stammered, fearing my mind was wending paths of delusion, losing me again in a labyrinth of madness. "Two such events cannot be *connected* . . . except by coincidence, can they?"

"Three events, Dominic. Don't be forgetting my dream. Aye, 'tis the way of a weird, that events connect in inexplicable ways. Sooth, 'tis this upon which a weird depends, without which a weird could not exist—this intangible connection between *all* events—the life forces weaving together in harmony, resonating as one. 'Tis the Earthsong, the Lifesong, and nothing exists apart from it, for it is the instrument upon which all life is played."

I found I was shivering. Kevin stirred the embers and laid another log on the fire.

"This weird, I ken, is woven with deep design, so much is intertwining to meet here in this Keep. And in the Keep itself I sense a tight web of evil."

I shuddered and pressed my palms against the invisible wall of heat from the bright coals. I tried not to resurrect buried nightmares of Lagos, a bloated spider, chasing me along a shuddering, sticky web spanning the Great Hall.

"Who weaves the weird?" I heard myself whisper.

"Some say the Nornir, the three sisters, spin the threads of our lives, but—"

"You mean the Fates? I don't believe in the Fates, minstrel. Nor the gods. Not your raven gods, nor the Christian god, nor *any* gods! And if I did, I'd not trust them!"

Kevin's blue stare absorbed my bitter outburst with neither surprise nor recrimination.

"Aye," he said quietly. "I ken you've little reason for faith in gods of late. But, Dominic," a deep sorrow roughened his voice, "have you nothing left you to believe in? Is there *nothing* you trust?"

I stared back at him bleakly, then dropped my gaze to the hearthstones. Pale ghosts of gods and philosophies and faces whirled through me, as dry and dead as rattling leaves caught in a winter wind. Like dead leaves that crumbled in my hands and slipped through outstretched fingers, phantoms of all I thought I knew eluded me, cold and uncomforting. When I had lain most in need of help, in agony, alone and terrorized, no gods answered my feverish prayers, no philosophies answered my bewildered cries—only the dead had come in dreams, and even they drifted back to their own realms when the deliriums faded, leaving me more bereft and alone than before. No, none of them were real, none touched the emptiness that was me, none reached through the nightmare to hold me or comfort me—none but Kevin Dunskaldir.

Aye, *he* was real, *he* had reached me and placed his strong embrace between me and the nightmare, and *he* had not faded with the dawn. I raised my eyes to meet his expectant gaze.

"I trust *you*," I told him simply.

An inexplicable mingling of emotions played over his face—pleasure and warmth interwoven with uncertainty, worry, and resolve. He laid a light hand on my shoulder.

"Those are welcome words, my friend—and fearsome ones. I hope I am equal to them, but I'll not have your trust misplaced. Truth is, I cannot see the end of this any more certainly than you. Understand, I've no promises to offer you . . . only hope. . . ."

My smile was wistful. "I know. 'Twas not what I meant . . . I don't expect—Kevin, even if we never get out of here . . . even if the worst happens . . . I wish . . . oh, gods, I wish . . ." I bit my lip, striving for coherency.

"Aye," he said, "so do I wish. We should have met on a high mountain path, you and I, or a deep forest fen—not here, not like this. Still," he smiled encouragingly, "we are well met, my friend, and I for one am unwilling to believe this is the end of our meeting. When we are out of here and well away, 'twould do my heart good if we'd be taking the same road. What say you?"

I stared dumbstruck, swallowing against the dry silence in my throat. *What say I? Need he ask?*

"Do *your* heart good?" I murmured. "Minstrel, I'd like nothing more . . . I scarcely dare dream it, I want it so much . . . *if* we get out of here."

"Aye, *if*. My heart tells me we will, yet—ah, kit, I wish I could give you my oath on it, but 'twould be foolish to swear an oath on this. 'Tis beyond my kenning, and I'd not want to be dying on an oathbreaking. But I can swear this—we'll leave here together or die here together."

His talk of oath breaking recalled to me one of last night's events.

"You broke your oath to the Alamanni," I murmured. "You broke it for *me*."

"Aye. I'd sworn you an oath, too, Dominic. I could not keep one without breaking the other."

"So you chose mine."

"Thought you I wouldn't?"

"And if . . . if you *hadn't* sworn me an oath? . . ."

He looked at me for a long moment, unblinking and grave. "I'd have done the same. Nothing stood between you and the jaws of that hound except words of mine. I'd not let you die over words unspoken, oath or no."

I felt strangely comforted that my life had not hung on a chance oathgiving over a cup of strong wine. Emotionally I felt as if I tottered upon an unsteady pole. One misstep and I could plunge into chaos.

Kevin sighed. "I wish I could promise you 'twill all end well for us, but I cannot. I am no seer. And yet, my heart will not believe we meet for nought—to die in this foul place, at that madman's pleasure—*Mother of Life!*"

I might have argued that the fate he found so unthinkable I lived with hourly, burned deep into my mind and soul. I *knew* the madman's pleasure, and dying would be the least torturous part. *But what use saying it?* I thought. *What use anything?* Nothing I said or did could change what was coming. Lagos would likely soon be wrenching the life out of that giant heart of Kevin's by wrenching the life out of me before his eyes. I struggled to darken the windows of my mind, bury that knowledge alive in sealed catacombs. Best not to think . . . not to know . . . not to feel. . . .

"Kit?"

My eyes flew open. Awareness raced back from tombs where, unthinking, I had nearly buried it alive. I met Kevin's alarmed stare, his blue eyes darkened with concern. I swallowed hard. Every moment now was precious to me, every moment fragile; I must take care not to let any one of them shatter, for all the light I would ever know sat right here before me.

"Kit, are you all right?"

I nodded and attempted a smile. His concern remained undiminished.

"Let's have a look at your wrists."

I thrust both hands from the cloak and turned my wrists inner side up. They were laced with pus and bloody crusts.

"Aye. So I feared. We need to take care of these before you're in a fever. And you're needing clothes."

I looked toward the kitchen doorway, where the other slaves

were now coming and going, clearing the tables. "Mine are back there, I guess."

He rummaged in his pack. "You need better than those rags you were wearing. Ah, here it is." He pulled forth a white woolen shirt and held it aloft triumphantly. "'Twill make you a whole tunic and then some."

An ironic smile touched my lips. "Why? My rags aren't decent enough to die in?"

His expression sagged. "I wasn't meaning that. I was thinking if . . . *when* we are free of here, you'll be needing more protection from wind and cold than that worn tunic. This wool's thick and close-woven, and there's no holes in it. 'Twill be warmer."

"Oh."

I stared at his tired face. He was still thinking of escape, while I could only think of death.

"In that case," I said softly, "my thanks, Kevin. I'll be pleased to wear it."

With a quick grin he held up the shirt, and I stood so he could measure it against my height. Of course it fell in folds upon the floor; he gauged the length with his eye.

"More than enough left over for binding your wounds." He collared a reluctant slave by name of Quintus and sent him back to the kitchen for some strong vinegar wine, then he spread the shirt flat on the hearthstones, slipped a dagger from his boot, and cut about a foot of material from the bottom.

Unabashedly I shrugged out of the cumbersome cloak. Kevin dropped the woolen shirt over my head and it swallowed me like a tent. The length fell just below my knees, but both sleeves dragged the floor. I looked up and shrugged.

The minstrel laughed. "Woodenheaded, I am! I forgot the sleeves."

I grinned. "Be sure, you should stick to lute playing."

"Did *you* think of them, perchance?"

He cut the sleeves jaggedly. Garbed in thick, warm wool, *clean* wool, I hunkered down and watched him cut the leftover hem into strips. Quintus, surly and skittish, returned with a half-empty mug of sharp vinegar wine. He plopped it down and slunk away. The minstrel sniffed it suspiciously before he motioned me to hold out my hands.

"This will burn."

I nodded. And burn it did, as he poured the stinging liquid over the wounds, but I had known worse pain; I clenched my teeth and turned my wrists until they were drenched. The woolen strips with which he bound my wrists stung, too. I had to bite my lip as he tied them.

I knotted another long strip of cloth around my waist for a belt. The minstrel looked me over.

"Well, what do you think?"

I smoothed the folds of wool and grinned. "Not bad—for a lute-player."

"Now for your feet—you'll be needing boots."

"*Boots!* Ha! You've not enough binding."

"*Ha?* Ha, yourself. Put a foot out here."

I sat on the hearth and did as he asked, and he slipped the leftover end of a sleeve over my foot, making a boot that covered toes to knee. He bound the sleeve on snugly with one of the strips.

He grinned. "Not bad for a lute-player, eh? Other foot."

"Aye," I muttered, "if I can get it out of my mouth."

As he bent his head over the binding, I contemplated the yellow hair which wanted a washing and combing almost as badly as mine. I wondered at this great barbarian who cared so much that my feet be warm, that I be set free, that I not despair. How had we found each other, and how would this end for us?

He looked up. "Done," he smiled, and I felt drawn into those blue eyes, like gazing into a pure blue sky. His eyes seemed like that, boundless like the sky, but not so remote—oh, no, not re-mote at all, so close and all-absorbing that I imagined by just looking deep enough I might touch infinity there and disappear. What a blessed relief it would be, to leave everything behind and lose myself in those eyes, but I knew that was impossible.

I fingered the knotted binding at my knee.

"Thanks," I whispered. "I'll need them."

His broad hand covered mine. "Aye—I pray you will."

"Kevin? Will you play the lute? A little music? . . ."

"All the music you want."

I grinned shakily. "I could do with some of your stout wine just now."

"Aye, would that we had a drop." He got up to fetch his lute. "We'll have to make do with music; 'tis wine for the heart and soul. What would you hear, my friend?"

"I don't know. Whatever you like. Has been so long . . . I scarcely remember any tunes."

Kevin thumbed the lutestrings and settled back comfortably against his pack. "This damnable damp—'tis warping the wood," he grumbled. Deftly he tuned the eight strings and strummed them in harmony.

"Play one of your tunes," I said, "one *you* wrote."

"Ah, that I'm pleased to do anytime."

His fingers danced lightly across the strings. Head back, eyes closed, he seemed to search through a cascade of sounds, fading one rhythmic sequence into another until gradually he found a rhythm to his liking. As he played he seemed transformed. The long legs stretched comfortably, his body relaxed, lines of weariness and worry smoothed from his face, and I had a strange notion that he heard an inner music and that as he listened his hands danced upon the lutestrings of their own accord. A swift melody, soft and repetitive, ran beneath his fingers like water burbling over rocks—a sound that lulled and soothed and swept my mind along ever-deepening streams of vision. My eyes blinked to focus on the minstrel in the gloomy hall. The fireglow danced across his ruddy face and golden hair, and he was again the brightest thing in the hall, brighter even than the burning embers. Yet he seemed to be leaving the hall far behind, following the currents of his own melody, wending its rapid course even as he created it beneath his fingers.

I yearned to know his mind, his heart, yearned to follow him into realms unknown, for I knew instinctively that whatever country lay within him, it would be safe haven for a weary, frightened dwarf.

As mad as trying to walk into a golden reflection on a bronze shield. You cannot go anywhere, Dominic.

I closed my eyes, bowed a heavy head upon my knees, and let the music wash over me. Within my own mind were no realms of peace. I tried to drift in the stream of the lutesong, lose myself in the tumbling melody without being sucked into a howling maelstrom, but chaotic memories of the night's ordeal surged up to engulf me—unrelenting icy rain and bitter, biting cold, tortured wrists, freezing agony, terror and despair as icy blackness swallowed me.

And beyond the blackness—the visions. I remembered now. The music merged with the visions, and I remembered. On the other side of death—a silver crescent ship, and Isis, on a sea of stars, the Otherworld in her eyes.

XXXVII

Both doors burst open at the end of the hall and the regulars trooped and stamped in for a hot, midday meal, grumbling over suffering an inspection in damnable weather like this, cursing imperial agents and senators across the empire, but most particularly the two infesting Lorrach Keep.

I retreated out of their way and sat against the hearthstone wall. The hallmaster's rotund bulk filled the kitchen doorway. He gestured angrily for me to come; I looked away. It was then Kevin came to sit beside me, laying his staff across his knees. The hallmaster managed to glare and leer in one resentful expression, then he heaved himself into the recesses of the kitchen.

The troops stared at the huge barbarian sitting against the hearth, but his eyes were grim so they spoke no word to him. Even the captain, whose gaze the minstrel met with a face of stone, made no attempt upon his wall of silence. The barbarian giant's hard stare made clear that he had seen far too much and would bear no more of their company.

Thus in silence we sat, side by side, the minstrel and I, throughout the regulars' meal. I clasped my knees; he balanced his staff across his, and for the first time I studied the staff closely. The stout wood was carved all over with lines and spirals—not deeply, but artfully and precisely—and between the spiraling lines were carved angular symbols which I could not decipher. As my fascinated gaze followed the circular patterns, I noted the regularity with which the angular symbols were repeated. I decided they must be an alphabet of some kind, probably the minstrel's native language, and I wondered if he had carved the strange writing himself—and why—and what it meant.

Concealed here and there among the swirls of letters I discovered outlines of faces—fantastic beasts and birds. I might have imagined it some barbaric ceremonial staff, except that I had seen him wield it so effectively in battle, and the battered surface evidenced much hard use, so it was a practical tool, however fancifully carved.

And I wondered about Kevin Dunskaldir, about his folk, his language, and his island, all far removed from the Roman Empire. I wished there were time . . . yet even as I felt the afternoon slipping through my grasp, I realized how miraculous it was that we had even this little time.

At last the regulars finished their meal and left us in peace, left us free to speak our thoughts, or sit in silence worrying over thoughts unspoken. By late afternoon I had fallen to staring bleakly into the fire and shivering with something more numbing than cold. Fear closed an iron fist around my heart, leaving me fighting for breath, sick and trembling. It was not mere death I dreaded, for I had crossed the borders of death last night and learned it held no terror. But the unspeakable agonies which could accompany death in this place, the mind-rending horrors, were all too real for me.

I shuddered and tried to concentrate on the sound of the minstrel's lute; deep in thought he strummed his fingers over the strings. The melody sounded discordant, but familiar, and I gradually realized he played the tune he called *The Merry Dwarf,* but this time it was far from merry. The melancholy song seemed woven of sorrow, fear, and anger.

Aye, that was how I felt—sorrowful, fearful, and angry— and those feelings threatened to rush up in a maelstrom and drown me.

"Minstrel, stop!"

Abruptly he silenced the strings beneath his hands and stared at me.

"Please."

He put aside the lute and came to sit beside me. I stared into the fire, watching the flames dance lightly around a log in a deadly embrace. If wood could feel, I knew what agony it endured. I clasped my knees tightly.

"I'm *afraid*," I whispered.

"Aye, I know you are."

"I wish I wasn't. I wish I could be as brave as you."

"Truth, Dominic, I'm afraid, too." He hesitated. "I fear most for you."

I tore my gaze from the fire and looked up at him. "You ought to spare some fear for yourself, Kevin. Lagos doesn't mean to let you out of the Keep alive."

Kevin nodded. "I know that, too. But 'tis you this weird weaves around. Aye, a dire *thing* gathers here and you at its very center."

"A what?"

"A *thing*. A gathering. A drawing in of forces—forces of such a powerful nature that Othinn himself comes—is *bound* to come. Freya, too. Freya comes because I trust her and because"—he smiled mysteriously—"because dwarves have ever been favorites of hers, since the making of the Brisengamen. Even the gods have their weirds."

"But what have they to do with *me?*"

"'Tis clear as runes, man! *I* am here because of you, *Freya* is here because of you, and one other is here because of you."

I stared at him, uncomprehending. "Who?"

"*Who?* That senator. That pompous slime of a senator."

"*Sividicus?*"

"Aye, that Sividicus. Does it not strike you strangely, that *he* should arrive here just now? Strikes *me* strangely." His voice dropped. "Wasn't it he who murdered all your family, leaving you kinless? He has a weirgild to pay and I'm thinking 'twill be the ravens who collect."

One word echoed in my head, desolate and hollow. *Kinless.*

"No, not all of them. I let Sividicus believe so, but I was not the only one to survive that night. Three of us escaped—four counting the babe Felicia carried in her womb."

"Felicia?" In a leap of intuition the minstrel understood the unspoken. "She would be the dancer? The one Sividicus wanted?"

I nodded.

"What became of her? And the other one? Where are they?"

"*I don't know!*" My voice shook with anguish.

Out of the gathering silence came Kevin's low voice.

"Somehow you lost them, kit. What happened?"

What happened? My head whirled. *Ravenna. The tavern. Mikato.*

I felt like a rudderless ship tossed upon a raging sea. The eratic rise and fall of my emotions frightened me, and if I dwelled on *this* shred of the past, despair would splinter all that kept me afloat, would close over my head like dark waters. . . .

I pressed clenched fists to my head. "I . . . I *can't*. . . ."

"We needn't speak of it. We'll speak of other things."

Gratefully, I nodded. I knew I probably did need to speak of it, but not now, not here. Trembling, I clasped my hands together tightly.

"Kevin . . . I'm not the same person I was before . . . before I came *here*." My voice dropped near a whisper. "I wish you could know *that* Dominic—the one who never encountered a hell like this, couldn't even imagine . . ."

"I do know him."

I shook my head. "He shattered into a thousand bits, along with everything else."

"I'm looking at him and he looks all of one piece to me."

I looked away.

He touched my knee and spoke gently. "Forgive me. I do not take this so lightly as I sound."

"You think I'm mad as elf-fruit, don't you?"

"Not a bit, but *you* think you are, and making light of it doesn't help, I ken. Dominic, the universe did *not* come apart, but *your* universe did, so 'tis truth to you. but will you give a thought to believing me when I say *you* are still here, too? All you've ever been is still within you, whole and sound. These past two days I've watched you fighting your way back through this maelstrom you speak of. Mayhap I'll never know fully how hard it is, how much courage it is taking, but I know this—in the depths of your being you are more than you know, Dominic."

He laid a hand on my shoulder, shook me gently. "I'm counting on that, you know—your inner strength—to help us face what's ahead, to help us out of here."

I swallowed hard. "You're mad, you know that, minstrel? If I have any inner strength, I don't know how to find it." I shook my head wearily. "And even if I could, what good would it do?"

"What good giving up, man?" This time he shook me less gently. "I for one am not willing to meekly lay down my life— not to a mad dog like Lagos! Nor am I willing to watch you lose yours!"

I blinked up at him. *Nor I yours,* I thought. I took a deep, ragged breath.

"I'll try, Kevin, I will. Only . . . I don't know what strengths you mean . . . I don't know where to look. . . ."

Those calm blue eyes regarded me gravely for a long moment, then he nodded.

"I'm thinking we both could do with some counsel just now. Mayhap we'll find those strengths."

He reached into his goat-hair vest, fumbled at something near his belt, and pulled forth a smallish pouch of rabbit fur, just of a size to hold in one palm. Settling cross-legged before me, he lay the pouch on the flagstone between us.

"We'll read the runes."

I stared, uncomprehending, from the rabbit pouch to his serious face.

"I call three gods to this running—Othinn, Freya, and Verthandi. Have you gods of your own to call, Dominic?"

Emphatically I shook my head.

He gazed at me a moment, then closed his eyes. Face tilted slightly upward, he seemed to search an unseen world, a world within, until he found what, or who, he was looking for. In a voice so low it reminded me of distant rumbling thunder, the minstrel began a poetic invocation in his strange northern tongue. I listened, fascinated, then held my breath as he fell silent. Now he chanted the names of the three gods—*Freya, Othinn, Verthandi*—chanted the names thrice, then in all seriousness opened the blue sky of his eyes to me and added gruffly in Latin, "And on Dominic's behalf, any other interested parties."

I grinned crookedly.

He winked.

"Now my friend, we discover the powers we'll be needing to wend this weird." He took the rabbit pouch, opened the drawstring, and held the bag toward me.

"Choose one."

Curiously, with no guess as to what might be inside, I slipped a hand into the bag. My fingers touched stones—smooth stones. I closed my hand around one and drew it forth.

"Keep it hidden," he said, "until I've drawn."

I closed hand into a fist while he drew a stone.

"Let's read your rune first."

I opened my fingers, and on my palm lay a smooth white stone with sparkly flecks in it. Scratched straight and deep in the stone were two crossed lines that looked like a numeral: $\times$

"*Ten?*" I said, disappointed. "Is it a game piece?"

Kevin smiled at the stone in my hand. "No, not a game piece, nor ten, nor even Latin. 'Tis a rune—Gyfu is its name."

I touched the stone, turned it over, found it smooth and white on the other side; I turned the cross-mark up again.

"A rune? Is it writing?"

"Aye, it is writing, but 'tis much more, too. A rune isn't one of your puny Latin letters—a rune is a mystery, a personality, a *power*. And this rune,"—he touched the stone in my palm—"this is Gyfu. Here are the strengths you must draw on in this weird."

I looked at the lines crossed in stone, thinking that was impossible.

"What does it mean?"

"Gyfu means many things. For one, it means gift—often a gift of the goddess."

To me there was but one gift of a goddess, the Gift of Isis, a vale of blood-red mushrooms, a bitter taste on the tongue, and vision—vision of all things connected in luminous webs of moonlight, a vision of souls dancing in rainbow ribbons of light, a vision of severed rainbows on bloodied ground. I drew back from the vision and clenched my fist tight around the stone.

"Gyfu also means oaths given handfast—partnership and friendship."

I raised my eyes to his in wonder. The rune I had chosen meant the one thing I had any faith in—Kevin Dunskaldir's friendship, given handfast over the cups. I opened my hand and studied the rune anew.

"Some call it truce and say it is two crossed swords, but 'tis two crossed staves supporting each other, or crossbeams of a hall adding strength to strength. And 'tis friendship pledged handfast. See, the lines are four arms and the hands clasp in the center.

"The third meaning of Gyfu is balance."

I looked up. "Balance?"

"Aye, the balance of the forces, the life forces, the Earth forces."

"I don't understand . . . what does the rune *mean?*"

"It means all these things. Of a certainty the friendship pledged is ours, and that, I ken, is a strength you are needing just now. As for the gift of the goddess, I only know how that speaks to me. *You* are a gift of the goddess, my friend—Freya entrusts me with one of her own—but the rune may speak differently to you.

"As for balance. . . ." Kevin shrugged. "I've no kenning for it, not in this weird. 'Twill mean something, 'tis certain. This rune is yours, Dominic, so you'll do well to look within and find whatever meaning balance holds for you."

I stared at the stone, knowing precisely what balance meant to me and finding that knowledge useless.

"What says your rune, Kevin?"

"Oh, aye, mine." He opened his hand and revealed another smooth white stone, this one with an arrow carved into it.

"Tyr's rune." His great shaggy head nodded as if he half expected it. "Tiwaz the Warrior. Judgement by battle. We'll not be strolling out the gates peaceably. The spear," he said, tracing the lines ↑ , "is Tyr's spear of justice. The wind is its swift passing, and the lightning its striking, for Tyr is Skylord, wielder of winds and storm."

Kevin stared long at the rune. His jaw tightened in resolution.

"*What*, minstrel? What is it?"

"Tyr's rune bids me search deep within my soul for the warrior. I thought I'd done with him." He closed his fist on the stone. "If the gods require a warrior, so be it."

"Is it a bad omen?"

"Could be a warning of dire circumstances, kit."

I laughed sharply. "Think you that's *news?*"

He leveled blue-sky eyes at mine. "I thought I had quit the warrior. Aye, I quit Othinn and Mithra both in a night and swore oathbond to Freya. Now, by my oath, Freya will have me surrender again to the battle fury. That itself is a manner of madness, but I ken if I will drink Othinn's mead of poetry, I must also wear the warrior's cloak at his bidding. And this is Tyr's rune I draw—Tiwaz—the warrior's sacrifice."

"What mean you—*sacrifice?*" I breathed.

"Old One-Eye's battle madness is its own sacrifice. 'Tis a surrender to blind power, a surrender to the forces in motion, to necessity, to fate—'tis a sacrifice of the self, willfully done, to the fury of the storm. Aye, like your maelstrom—and make no mistake, 'tis *your* maelstrom, Dominic, not some strange sea you are sailing—'tis your own being. The warrior knows this and doesn't fear the storm. He is not torn asunder, but is wielded as a weapon—yet not like that either, for the warrior and the storm become one."

He stared into shadows as his words trailed off, but now his gaze came back to me. His face wore lines of worry, but then he met my glance and transformed the worry into a resolute expression. It seemed to me in the past two days he had grown older before my eyes.

"There's no knowing the way of a weird, but the gods are in it, Tyr's swift spear of judgment is in it, Othinn and Freya are in it, so we wend it in good company."

I sighed. I wasn't sure I believed in gods—dreams or no, coincidences or no—and if there *were* gods, I wasn't betting they could be counted on to help mere mortals. But Kevin Dunskaldir believed in them; mayhap the minstrel was on better terms with his gods than I was mine. I hoped so.

"What about that other one? The one you called to the runing?"

"Verthandi? She is one of the Three Sisters, the weavers of our Fates you don't believe in, remember?" His beard turned up in a half grin. "Oh, she's here, all right; her time is always now, the moment at hand. She weaves our destinies in each living moment, in every breath we take, every beat of our hearts." He juggled the runestone in his palm. "She speaks to us now—shows us our strengths. I trust she will speak to us tonight when the moment to use them comes."

He raised somber eyes to mine. "*Whatever* happens, Dominic, if the chance comes, seize your moment—*escape*—don't turn back for *anything!*"

"Don't talk like that."

"I mean it, kit. I don't know how much sacrifice Tyr's rune demands of me."

"*No!*" I cried. "It doesn't mean that! You swore we'd leave *together!* It doesn't mean *anything!* They're just *rocks!* Nothing but bloody *rocks!*" I shook the runestone in my fist and flung it wildly from me—straight into the hearth. It struck the bricks and ricochetted into the fire.

Kevin raised one surprised brow, then another.

I stared in dismay, realizing what I had done. "Oh, no, Kevin! I didn't mean it!" I leapt to retrieve the stone and came near burning my hand.

Kevin grabbed my shoulder, pulling me back. "Leave it, Dominic—it doesn't matter."

"Doesn't matter! Your rune, and I threw it in the fire—your rune of friendship!"

"Aye, but is just a *rock,* as you said, sure not worth burning yourself for. The life of the rune isn't in the stone." He tapped the shirt over my chest. "The life of the rune is here, written in your heart, within your deeper self." He smiled reassuringly. "So is our friendship written. You cannot throw it away so easily."

I swallowed hard. "Be sure, I never meant to."

Now the far doors of the hall banged open and through them strode the captain followed by a half dozen of his troops. The minstrel dropped the Tiwaz rune back into the pouch and stuffed it away in his vest. Our gazes held an instant, then he stood to face the advancing officer. I stood, too, slowly.

The captain came to a crisp halt.

"His Excellency Count Lagos commands your presence in his hall, Saxon."

The blue eyes narrowed. "What is it he's wanting, Captain?"

"Count Lagos considers negotiations."

Kevin grinned tightly. "I scarcely believe that. He made clear last night he feels no compunction to negotiate."

The captain studied the barbarian wordlessly before deigning to reply.

"This agent, this Valorian, has been at him; the man is saddled and ready to ride to the Imperial Post at Basilia. He means to send word to the Emperor and return on the morrow with a provencial agent and a restraint on any action the Count might take contrary to the interests of the Empire. I believe the Count's guest, Senator Sividicus, persuaded Lagos that a personal hand in the treaty negotiations would be the wiser course."

"You know much about your superior's business, Captain. I'm surprised."

"I am in the Count's confidence," snapped the officer, squaring his shoulders and glaring at the barbarian.

"Are you now?"

The minstrel's mistrust was not lost on the captain. His tone sharpened.

"Count Lagos commands your presence. I suggest you obey peacefully. His patience with both you and the agent wears thin."

Kevin donned his cloak and looked to me.

"Not the dwarf," said the captain. "Only you."

The blue eyes were icy. "Why? What game is Lagos playing?"

"A game you will lose if you cross him, barbarian. Monstrosito is an item in his negotiations. He considers how much you will concede for the dwarf's freedom."

Kevin looked to me and muttered, "I mislike this."

The Roman snarled. "You're a fool if you annoy him, Saxon. Lagos doesn't have to give you *any* concession if he so chooses."

"Aye," Kevin said tautly. "That's what I mislike about it."

Our eyes met, and I knew what he was thinking. The last time we were separated had been calculated to show the minstrel what Lagos was capable of doing. What about this time? And I—I was torn between my reluctance to be separated from my friend and my terror of facing Lagos.

I realized Kevin's eyes were full of indecision, questioning me. He would not leave me if I did not want him to.

I held my head high and sure, mouth dry, voice uneven.

"Go on. It could be that chance."

He hesitated a moment more. Reluctantly, he nodded.

"I want your word, Captain. No one here will do him harm."

"I'll see to it."

"Your *word*, Captain."

The captain looked annoyed. "You have my word, Saxon. No harm will be done him in my hall while you are gone."

The minstrel glanced to the kitchen door where hovered the hulking form of the hallmaster.

"Tell *that* one. He'll not lay a hand on him."

The captain looked to the kitchen and raised his voice. "*No* man will lay a hand on the dwarf! *My* command!" He turned to two of the guards. "See to it."

The hallmaster snorted and faded into the dim recesses of the kitchen. The captain spun to the barbarian.

"Satisfied?"

Kevin nodded briefly, far from satisfied, but it was the best he could hope for. He took up his staff from the hearthside.

"I'll be back."

I nodded, knowing he could not promise, only hope.

"Ready, Captain," he said and strode toward the end of the hall. The troops fell in on either side of him.

I watched him go, wondering if I would see him again, and if so, under what circumstances. At the top of the steps Kevin halted, turned, and peered back across the dim-lit hall, maybe wondering the same. Then he was gone, and I stood on the hearthstep staring at the dark doors. I never felt more alone.

XXXVIII

 I turned to the fire for solace, stared into the low-flickering flame. Was there truly a chance the minstrel could peacefully negotiate our way out of Lorrach? I doubted it would be so easy.

Now I remembered the rune Gyfu. It lay somewhere in the fire. I edged closer. The flames burned lower than before, and my eyes searched the embers and ashes until I found the runestone. It had fallen through the fire into a pocket of ash beneath the burning wood, the crossed lines facing upward.

I took the iron poker and, pretending to stir the fire, nudged the runestone across the embers and onto the hearth. The stone was blackened and hot to touch, but not cracked. I picked it up with the frayed end of my belt and rubbed the stone clean.

There I sat alone on the hearthstep, cradling the runestone Gyfu in my hand and trying not to succumb to despair. *Oaths, friendship, balance,* I chanted in my head, concentrating on the words so as not to slip into the terror gathering and swirling below me. The mindless litany did not help. I stared at the cross-mark in the stone as if I could read something more there. Kevin had said it represented the strengths I must draw on—but how? Would that I could draw on those strengths as easily as I had drawn the stone from the bag.

I closed my eyes and searched for strength beyond the maelstrom of fear growing in my gut. Striving to look into it, I felt despair and terror surge up to engulf my mind, overwhelming me with the most vivid knowledge that this Keep was indeed Hell-on-Earth and I was powerless to affect its inescapable procession of horror. That relentless knowledge wanted to rip my mind into a jumble of chaos. *'Tis your maelstrom, Dominic,* I recalled Kevin's words, but I knew I had not the strength to do battle with it. Not now.

Panic shook me. I forced my eyes open and met the face of the white stone, forced the vision of Kevin's blue eyes into mine—calm, steady, deep blue eyes drawing me into their sanity.

I clasped the runestone between my palms, pressed my forehead against interlocked fingers, and pleaded with the universe.

"Please!" I whispered desperately into the darkness. *"If there be gods—if there be power to help us—don't let it end here."* And silently I prayed for freedom, freedom from these walls, freedom to wander the limitless Earth with Kevin Dunskaldir, freedom to know his gentle companionship . . . but those images were so painful to contemplate, so real the possibility of those dreams being torn asunder in torment and death, that tears streamed from my closed eyelids, heedless of the noise and murmur growing in the hall.

Heedless, until I heard the dreadfully familiar guffaw of the hallmaster just above my head. My eyes jerked up in horror. His massive bulk stood over me. In shock, I scooted backwards, but he only continued to wheeze.

"My, my, Monstrosito! Crying and sniveling like a brat! Well, it won't do you any good, bug."

He stepped forward; I backed hard against the wall. He leaned over me, stinking drunk.

"What's this!" he snorted, fingering my shirt collar. "New clothes? Hoo-hah! The slug's got new clothes!"

He laughed, swaying and unsteady, and I tried to sidle out of his reach. Again he came toward me, nearly toppling over, but two of the regulars grabbed him roughly and shoved him away.

"Captain said leave him alone!" one of them growled.

Hallmaster whined, straining for balance and dignity, "I wasn't gonna *hurt* him, gents—just scare him some."

"Stay away or you'll feel the brunt of my lance."

Cheated of his fun, the hallmaster turned malevolent eyes on me. "I'll have you when Lagos is done with you anyway, rat." He leered drunkenly. "You can look forward to it."

"You won't have him!" interrupted a sharp voice. The captain strode the length of the hall. "Monstrosito won't be returning."

I tried to read his face, to fathom what he meant by that, but he was speaking to the hallmaster.

"Go and fetch me his collar and chain. *Now!*"

Blinking stupidly, the hallmaster careened toward the kitchen. I felt the runestone still clasped in my palm. Quickly I twisted it into the folds of my sash, snug against my side. I came to my feet, thinking not enough time had passed for negotiations to be closed; they must have just gotten underway. The captain's gaze fell on me and held there dispassionately. In that moment, I knew we were in the midst of one of Lagos's games.

The hallmaster lurched back with the hateful collar and chain, bringing it deferentially to the captain's hand and casting gleefully curious glances at me. A sickening, hot tremor of fear stirred in the pit of my stomach.

"Now get your stinking carcass back into the kitchen and see to my men's supper, which you should be doing instead of filling your fat belly with the wine stores. I'm taking an accounting of the wine when I return. *Move it!*"

The hallmaster jerked and staggered toward the kitchen, but his weight got the better of his balance. He keeled off the portal frame and landed flat on his back with a belch and a groan. The captain advanced on me with the collar and chain.

Now it begins.

I looked into the eyes of the captain as he knelt fastening the thick leather collar.

"You gave him your word," I accused abruptly.

He looked surprised that I had anything to say. "I spoke for my hall," he said without remorse. "I do not speak for Lagos. Move, dwarf. He's expecting us."

He tugged on the chain, and I moved whether I would or no, down the length of the hall, up the steps, and out into a chill, grey twilight. A sharp whinny and the stamping hoof of a horse somewhere echoed upon the still, cold air. My woolen boots slipped and slid in melted brown snow as he dragged me across the misted courtyard. Cold, wet slush soaked through the cloth to my feet by the time I was thrust, blinking, into the lighted dome of the Great Hall.

All was a blur; I had not time to get my bearings. The captain hustled me to the edge of the pit and, grasping the chain just at the collar, shoved me forward over the drop. I thought to hit flagstone, but he held me over the side, my feet still on the edge, my hands grasping at the choking collar.

I saw Kevin, on the far side of the hall, come to his feet. I gasped for air. A dozen lances ringed the minstrel.

"My captain will hang him, Saxon. He'll push him off and snap his neck like a chicken's."

Kevin froze. I struggled frantically, clawing at the collar, fighting for breath.

"On your knees to me, barbarian."

No! I wanted to shout to Kevin, but I could barely draw air. My efforts made a ghastly, desperate sound.

"He appears to be choking to death. It shouldn't take long. *On your knees.*"

I could not see, all fading into black fireflies as it was, the fight to breathe so all consuming as it was, but I knew he went down on his knees, because after an eternity of choking I was jerked back. I fell in a heap at the captain's feet, hacking and gasping.

Hauled to my feet again by the collar, I was forced down the steps into the stifling, crowded Great Hall. The captain turned me over to the whipsman and clattered back up the steps; I stumbled along behind the whipsman.

"This is treachery. 'Tis treason and deceit, Lagos!" I heard the imperial agent's outraged protest. "I never knew you capable of such dishonor!"

"Why, Valorian? I merely provide a little evening entertainment," Count Lagos said smoothly. "What matter to you how I use my own property?"

Now I could see the minstrel kneeling near the firepit. His arms were bound behind his back, his wrists lashed tight to an iron ring between his heels. The man securing the minstrel's hands slipped the rune-carved dagger from his boot and handed it to Lagos.

The Count smiled. "Nothing passes in my Keep without my knowing, barbarian."

I felt an upsurge of rage that Lagos had used me as bait in his entrapment. Kevin raised his head and met my eyes with wordless anguish, and I knew he thought he had failed me.

"We had an agreement," Valorian countered. "The dwarf is to accompany me with *your* treaty proposal to the Emperor while Saxonius waits here as hostage. When I return with Honorius's acceptance of your terms for the Alamanni treaty, signed and sealed, you will release the Saxon to me. Stand by your agreement, Lagos!"

I stared at Kevin, knowing he had been willing to trade his

freedom for mine. As the whipsman's tug on the chain abruptly stopped, I caught my balance and squared my shoulders. I wished I could cry to Kevin, *Don't blame yourself!* but I could only meet his stunned expression with my own.

"We merely proposed terms, Valorian. I had not yet agreed to them, as I recall. I have a better use for the dwarf. Come here!"

The last command he directed at me, gesturing imperiously with the onyx-ringed finger. I glanced again at Kevin and forced myself to come forward and stand on the spot Lagos indicated. I looked up into that viperous face; he saw my hate and fear, and he laughed.

"Feeling rebellious again, Monstrosito? Look at this! Grandly dressed for a stump-legged toad, wouldn't you say? But perhaps appropriate attire for your farewell performance." Lagos leaned forward, the tips of his fingers toying with the dagger point. "You've been holding out on me, my little anomaly. I understand you're a polewalker."

I shook my head dazedly.

"No? Esteemed Sividicus, whose word you surely don't dispute, tells me he's seen you walk a pole. In a theater, was it, Sividicus?"

"The Marcellus," Sividicus nodded smugly. "I distinctly remember. It was during practice. The dwarf and a boy were walking the pole while the dancers rehearsed below. The polemaster, I believe, stopped them—made quite a fuss, in fact."

I remembered. Brossos had caught Gorgi and me horsing around on the pole, which had that day been raised to performance height in the theater. Brossos had been angry with both of us— angry with me for risking my life at something I was not fully skilled to attempt, and angry at Gorgi for encouraging me. I would give much to hear that scolding voice now.

"Now, we've heard testimony from the honorable patrician. Do you yet deny you've ever polewalked?"

My voice, dry and cracked, was barely audible. "No."

"Speak up!"

"No, I don't deny it. Has been a long time. . . ." I looked from Lagos to Sividicus. *What use?* I gave it up with a shrug.

Lagos leaned back languidly. "I'm giving you the opportunity to favor us with a demonstration tonight. The glorious culmination of your pathetic engagement here. A grand finale, as it were."

I raised my eyes, half expecting to see a pole suspended over the Great Hall.

"We haven't a suitable pole to span the hall, so I've devised a little twist of my own." Lagos smiled grandly as he gestured to two waiting slaves. "Ready the pole for Monstrosito."

I thought I was numb to Lagos's perversities, but a cold shock ran through me as I watched them set up the manner of my death. They rolled forward the heavy iron pole used for spitting meat, but this time they laid it flush upon the firepit rim, spanning the glowing, crackling coalbed with the twenty-foot pole and securing each end in an iron ring.

"For God's pity! . . ."

"Lagos! He's no use to you dead!"

Lagos laughed through his teeth at the outbursts from Valorian and Kevin. "He's no use to me at all, barbarian. Except as entertainment for my men, and this is the sort of sport they like best."

I felt a strange mixture of terror and relief. The dreading and wondering were over, and this nightmare had an end at last—in the coalpit. The cavaliers cheered and called to be in on the sport. As the Count named the men who would ring the pit with lances, I turned to look at Kevin kneeling near the pit's rim, for this was goodbye, and the helpless anguish with which he met my eyes was like a knife in my heart. *He'll watch me die and blame himself.* I clenched my jaws and resolved to die with as much courage and nobility as I had. I could not make it easy for him, but I would not crawl and weep and make it worse.

The whipsman jerked the chain to get my attention and pulled me stumbling to my knees before him. Slowly I came to my feet. As the whipsman unfastened the heavy collar, I closed my eyes, gathering strength and courage.

"Praying, Monstrosito?" chided Lagos, now in high humor. "I doubt any gods want your shriveled little soul."

I looked straight into his eyes, eyes that had gloated over my agony innumerable times, and I knew whose soul was shriveled. And I knew of one goddess, at least, who would be awaiting me beyond that lake of fire. I did not deign to answer him.

"Now, show us how good you are at polewalking."

"For the love of God, Lagos!" The imperial agent stepped forward, horror and fury chiseled on his craggy face. "If you've a shred of human decency! . . ."

"You waste your breath, man," Kevin muttered harshly. His

eyes burned at Lagos. "Hell take you, son of Loki. If ever you loose me, I will kill you."

"I'm sure you would," chortled Lagos, then he leaned forward and hissed, "but I never *will* loose you, barbarian." At his gesture the whipsman shoved me toward the fire pit. I had no time to look back. The sizzling pit of bright-hot coals rippled with heat like a burning lake of fire, waiting to consume me in searing agony, and I could delay it only so long as I kept my balance over the fiery surface. . . .

Balance! My hand went to my side, where I felt the forgotten lump of the runestone sashed close to my ribs. So the rune's balance meant nothing more than this! Simple. I almost smiled at the simplicity of it. I heard Kevin groan; I turned to share the jest with him and met unspeakable grief in his eyes.

"You delay, Monstrosito?" taunted Lagos, enjoying my friend's grief and horror. "Your pole will become rather hot to walk upon soon. Surely you'd not want to leave us with too brief a performance."

Lagos gestured to the whipsman again, but I turned to the firepit on my own, Kevin's striken face rekindling my resolve to meet the end with courage. With slow, reluctant steps I approached the rim, approached the end of the iron pole, wondering if I could still do this at all.

You can do it, Dominico. 'Tis only a pole. The voice in my head was the voice of Brossos. Whether from realms of the dead or from my own memory made no difference; I answered.

Aye, but soon 'twill be a hot one!

Don't think of that. Take a deep breath and center. Steady, lad. You know how.

The familiar, rhythmic cadence of the voice calmed the racing panic in my heart and breath. I halted at the hot rim of the coal pit and closed my eyes. I breathed the stifling air, breathed deep and followed the breath inside, deep into myself where whirled the maelstrom. . . .

No time for that, cousin. Find your center . . . center of balance, center of being. . . .

The sharp tip of a lance nudged me unexpectedly just between the shoulder blades, nudged me forward. My eyes flew open, my foot shot out to catch my fall, and suddenly I was there—walking an iron pole inches above a sizzling orange bed of fiery coals.

No time to think of anything except the pole beneath my feet and centering every step, I focused on the other end and walked, slowly at first, then more quickly as my steps became more sure and the heat drove me onward. Even as I crossed the center of the fire pit, even then I knew I would reach the other side, realizing how well I knew how to do this. Yet even then, so centered and focused was I, so sharp and clear were my senses, that my awareness absorbed everything at once—the relentless wave of heat that engulfed my flesh, suffocated my lungs, burned my eyes, and with every step on the heating iron, steam rising off the damp cloth that bound my feet.

Reaching the other side, stepping off the pole onto the rim of the coal pit, was like stepping into a cool shade after trudging beneath a hot desert sun. Gratefully I drank in great gulps of air that was not searing. I turned to look back along the length of the pole and met the minstrel's ashen face across the rippling haze. Despite the circumstances, my smile and my bow were triumphant, and in that moment I felt like cocky, reckless, indestructable Dominico again.

Lagos was laughing with delight, and this whole performance was beginning to seem unreal, like a dream—before all dreams were nightmares—in which nothing matters because it *is* just a dream.

"Bravo, Monstrosito, bravo!" Lagos applauded. "I didn't think you had it in you. You'll do it for us again, of course."

Of course. This was no dream, and Lagos's delight was purely over his game being prolonged.

"No!" protested Kevin. "He's done what you wanted! He made it across! Let him go!"

"Aye, let him go, Lagos!" chorused the agent Valorian.

"My men are hungry for sport; winter has been long this year. However, to prove my magnanimity, I'll let my men decide." Lagos stood and raised one hand, holding the dagger straight above his head. "*Cavaliers!* What shall it be? Freedom? Or sport?"

The cry swelled quickly. "Sport! *Sport! SPORT!*"

The minstrel stared around at the shouting men in helpless disbelief, then his gaze met mine across the glowing pit. His head bowed in defeat.

The mad cry for sport was no surprise to me; I knew the cavaliers well. They had wrung all the amusement out of me they wanted; they used me up—stripped me of my dignity, my pride, my spirit, and my sanity—now they would use up my life for a moment's entertainment.

My head snapped up, eyes narrowed on the Lord of Lorrach

in helpless rage and hatred. He was going to use up Kevin, too, and this was just the beginning. Tonight he would use up his heart.

Indeed, Lagos raised his hand for silence and looked not at me but at the minstrel.

"The decision is made," he proclaimed, driving the dagger point emphatically into the armrest of his chair. "Monstrosito walks the pole."

I stared along the iron pole. It would be hotter now.

"Sport of this kind is criminal!" objected the imperial agent. "Both the laws of Rome and the laws of God forbid it!"

Ignoring him, Lagos gestured to me. "Monstrosito."

I felt another lance at my back. Indeed, ten or twelve men with lances ringed the firepit, awaiting the moment I would fall.

Don't think of it, Dominico. Think of reaching the other side.

I took a deep breath and stepped back onto the pole. The damp wool on my feet hissed and steamed against the hot iron, and as each precarious step carried me over the sparkling coals, I felt the heat rising against soles, flesh, eyes, and nostrils. I wondered madly how many crossings before I cooked to a turn.

"Besides," Lagos expounded as I balanced for my life, "we are not on Roman soil. Rome abandoned this land to barbarians; the only law here is mine."

I reached the pit's rim, expelled the breath I had been holding, and sucked in deep draughts of air. Now I stood nearer Kevin and could see the pain clearly etched upon his face, ruddy in the orange glow of the coalpit beside which he knelt. He pulled taut against the rope secured to the iron ring behind him, and his blue eyes spoke with wordless agony.

"The same for your God, Valorian," Lagos went on. "The Church has no bishop here; your God has no authority this side of the Rhine."

Valorian stood astounded. "Do you imagine God's authority stops at Roman borders?"

Lagos sneered. "Who speaks for him? *You*, agent? Who appointed you?"

"God's authority has nought to do with borders or bishops! God speaks where He wills! In the name of Christ, I demand you stop this atrocity!"

Count Lagos fired a glare of challenge at the imperial agent, then he grinned obscenely.

"Again, Monstrosito."

When I did not move immediately he signaled, and a lance tip prodded my shoulder. I turned back to the iron pole spanning the fiery coalbed, forcing deep draughts of stifling air past the fear in my throat.

"You presume to speak for your God, Valorian? We shall see who holds the authority here."

Another prod and I was out over the deadly brilliance, the consuming heat, with only a narrow path of hot iron and my own balance between me and burning death. Aye, and the iron was hotter still, scorching the wool on the soles of my feet, scorching through the cloth to remind me how perishable were both wool and flesh, but I held my breath and fixed my eyes on the far end of the pole. As I reached and crossed the center, the heat grew more and more unbearable; I dared not breathe the searing air. Eyes stinging and burning, I walked the last few feet nearly blind and stumbled with relief onto the rim of the pit. I sank to my knees, gasping, the bindings on my feet blackened and scorched.

Lagos laughed. "What think you of our little sport, barbarian? Pity, you don't seem to be enjoying this. After all, I've arranged this amusement solely for your benefit. *Up*, Monstrosito! Finish!"

Slowly I came to my feet, blinking to clear my eyes.

"You send him to his death!" Valorian cried out. "I'll have you up on charges of murder if you continue—both of you!"

Now Sividicus smirked. "For murdering a mad Pagan dwarf? I doubt Rome or the Church will be much interested. Come, Valorian, you take this all too seriously. Sit down and enjoy it."

"The two of you are *more* than mad," snapped the agent. "You're *rabid!* Maybe I can't prevent you, but neither can you force me to watch this man die for your entertainment. I'll take no more of it!"

Abruptly Valorian turned his back on the circle of fire. For an instant he paused as his eyes met those of the minstrel. Through the wavering heat it seemed to me Kevin's look was of desperation. Then the agent strode past him and toward the steps.

Catcalls from the men accompanied him. Now someone began the cry of *sport,* and within seconds the roomful of cavaliers took up the chant.

"*Sport! SPORT! SPORT!*"

They stood on tables and benches for a better view and stomped their feet.

"*Sport! SPORT! SPORT!*"

A lance tip pressed sharply against the nape of my neck, forcing me forward. I set my foot onto the hot iron for a fourth time, and I could feel the heat beneath my feet more intense than ever through the blackened bindings.

I walked the blistering iron pole over crackling, glittering coals, walked through a wave of heat that baked my skin, that felt as if it would singe every hair on my body, and I dared not breathe and I dared not stop or think. I forced my thoughts toward centering and balancing and reaching the far end of the pole. Halfway, and I felt as though my feet were on fire. More than halfway through the shimmering, suffocating heat and the clamorous demand of SPORT! SPORT! SPORT! and I knew I could make it to the pit rim and a moment's relief.

In front of me, suddenly, the man at the end of the pole lowered his lance, its sharp tip leveled at my throat. I stopped abruptly, just inches short of running upon the lance, and fought to regain my balance, struggled to keep from toppling into the bright death below.

I steadied myself on the pole, and above the excited cheers of the cavaliers and the Count's harsh laughter, I heard the minstrel's anguished, "NO-O-O!"

I felt a rush of terror, knowing I could go neither forward nor backward on the pole. The bindings on my feet were smouldering, the pain intense, and the heat of the coals stung and half blinded my eyes. In a moment I would faint from pain or heat and die in burning agony.

Or I could run my throat upon the lance and end it quickly. I tensed for it. My only moment was now! Yet I wanted life! Against my will it seemed, my lungs exhaled and tried to breathe the searing air. The hall throbbed and wavered, the edges of my vision shimmered into a dizzying, dazzling dance of brilliance, yet vividly I saw Kevin pulling like a madman against the rope that bound him, an animal cry tearing his throat. And I saw in dreamlike motion the imperial agent suddenly behind him, raising a sword behind the minstrel and sweeping the flashing blade downward.

Now!

I leapt forward, but not upon the lance. I ducked under it and ran the last few steps along the pole. Caught off guard, the lanceman tried to kick me backward into the coals, but I grappled onto his leg and clung for my life. With a panicked yell he flung himself back to keep from toppling into the coalpit. As we both hit the stone floor, I let go his leg and rolled away desperately, blindly. A cavalier's boot struck my ribs; I scrabbled on hands and knees across the flagstone, avoiding the boots and lances of shouting, laughing men. The sport was on.

Another kick sprawled me flat on my back. Surrounded, I looked up to see the man I had toppled standing over me, ready to skewer me on his lance. I tensed, ready to roll aside.

An animal bellow of rage made him look up—too late. Kevin pounced upon him like a maddened lion, wrenched the lance from his hands, cracked his skull with it, and swept clear a deadly circle around us—all within swift seconds. Now the cavaliers, whose full attention had been on me, circled the huge barbarian warily, forgetting their sport.

"*Kill him!*" shrieked Lagos furiously from the dais.

They came at him all at once; the long lance in his hands whooshed the air and collided with theirs. With superhuman strength he shoved them back, that enraged bellowing cry bursting from the center of his being, a giant warrior charging into them with the force of a rampaging bull. His blue eyes glittered wildly; fury bared his teeth in a grimace that was a terror to behold, and I, by now huddled on hands and knees, knew he was full in the battle madness.

"*Kill him!*" Lagos screamed, again, standing above the fray.

Those burning blue eyes turned on Lagos, and with a murderous cry he plunged through the circle of soldiers. In less time than I could draw breath, Lagos fell back in his chair before the unrestrainable onslaught, and the full weight of a battle-mad giant drove home the lance. It bored through the Count's shoulder, splattered flesh and bone, and thunked deep into the wood behind him, skewering the screaming Lord of Lorrach to his chair.

Kevin snatched his own dagger free of the chair arm and whirled to face the company of soldiers. Virtually forgotten, the imperial agent forced passage with his sword toward him. Suddenly a snarling black streak leapt straight up and sank savage fangs deep into the minstrel's wrist.

The dagger went flying and skittered across the flagstones. Kevin roared like a wounded beast and tried to shake loose the hound's ferocious hold while the hound tore at flesh and bone. Yelling furiously, Kevin flung out his arm, wolfhound clamped tight to the wrist, and slung the beast off him. The hound twisted in the air, struck the tapestried stone wall, and fell with a whimper to the floor.

I scrambled after the dagger, laid hands on it, lost it beneath the stampede of boots, and caught it again. Now the agent Valorian had reached the edge of the dais, holding men at bay with the slash of his long blade. A lance thrust at Kevin, but his broad hand shot out, caught the lance, and tugged. The surprised lance-man fell forward, and a shaggy boot met his face.

Armed again with a lance, Kevin yelled over the Count's tortured screams and the cavalier's shouts.

"DOMINIC!"

I staggered on pained feet, but I came dodging through a maze of men who spared me little thought, all their intent on the unassailable barbarian.

His eyes were still wild as I dived under the whirling lance and scrambled breathless to his side, dazed at the dizzying speed of events. Within the protective range of the agent's sword Kevin seized the moment and laid both hands on me, caught me up with a deft and sure motion, and as if an acrobat born, flung me up onto the high ledge that rimmed the Great Hall. Instinctively I dropped the dagger, tucked my head, and rolled as I struck the stone walkway precisely between two tall iron tripods.

Quickly I crawled to the ledge and, snatching up the fallen dagger, looked down.

"GO!" roared Kevin, beseiged by a hundred cavaliers and a hundred more between him and the steps.

Go? Where in hell does he think? . . .

Clutching the dagger, on hands and knees at the lip of the ledge, I stared down in dismay, and it was like looking into the deepest pit in Hell. The hound Caesar appeared directly below me, springing up and snapping great jaws at my face. I jerked back in panic, but large as the wolfhound was, he could not leap atop the pit wall. Still speared to his chair, Lagos screamed above the din while Sividicus retreated hastily from the thick of the melee. So many were the cavaliers, the barbarian and the agent were being separated in the mayhem. The agent's long sword fended off the soldiers' shorter blades, but he was forced to retreat further and further from the beseiged barbarian who, despite his bulk and the lance he wielded, was going down under the onslaught of men. Helplessly I watched my friend's colossal struggle to break free. The lance snapped in twain under the force of all the weight laid upon it. Kevin fell under the crush of bodies.

"No!" I cried.

Suddenly, with a wild cry of his own, Kevin rose up like a raging bear from its den—a table apart from his attackers; he had managed to wrench free and roll beneath it to the other side. With incredible strength he toppled the heavy table on its side and slowed their assault. The next weapon he laid hands to was the long bench. He swung the cumbersome bench, clearing a wide swath around him, then wielded it as a battering ram against the bottom of the overturned table, slamming a dozen men to the wall.

Now Kevin wedged the bench against the table, ran up it, and vaulted for the top of the wall, clawing at the stone with fingers and elbows. I hurried frantically to help him—as if I could pull him up—and the light of the oil lamps glowed off the wildness in his eyes, luminous as cat's eyes, blue as cobalt glass, and for that instant I looked full into the eyes of the Warrior of the Gods, uncanny, terrifying, yet I feared only for his life. Their hands were on him, held him back, and pulled him down amongst them again, he roaring like a lion in a pit of vipers. His fingers grasped the top of the tapestry; the musty cloth gave way to his weight, ripping from the wall. The tapestry became a weapon in his hands as he whipped it around and swirled it in the faces of his foes, blanketing them beneath the heavy cloth.

I could only watch helplessly. I searched for the imperial agent and found him backed to the wall far across the circular pit, unable to battle to the barbarian's aid.

Suddenly I realized Kevin had broken free! On top of the tables he bounded—his giant stride carrying him over hands, heads, and swords—making for the steps. A lance struck his side and fell away. He staggered momentarily, but it did not stop him.

I sprang to my feet, determined to reach the steps when he did, but I stumbled to my knees again as unexpected needles of fire razed my burned soles. I looked up in time to see the wolfhound Caesar taking the top of the steps. Hunched low, the blood-crazed hound streaked swiftly along the ledge toward me. *Damn!* I had no time for this! Gritting my teeth, I leapt to my feet and charged the hound at a dead run, lowering my head, throwing my weight forward. Mayhap the wolfhound expected no danger from the usually cowering dwarf, for when at the last instant I thrust the dagger straight out with both hands, Caesar ran full upon it, driving the blade deep into his throat.

The impact knocked me flat, and the gurgling hound collapsed on top of me, savage eyes still intent on my face, claws raking the stone floor beside my head. I heaved at the crushing weight and rolled the dying beast off the pit ledge. My hands and the dagger came away hot and wet with blood. Struggling to my feet

I looked up and saw Kevin take the steps in three gigantic bounds, black cloak flapping like the broken wing of a great wounded raven.

Kevin snatched up his staff from where it leaned by the door and wheeled to tumble three close pursuers back down the steps, where they tripped others up in a momentary jumble of men. Searching wildly, Kevin found me coming at a hobbling run, but I was too slow; I could not reach him before the cavaliers rallied, and he could not abandon the steps and our only chance of escape.

Had I not been delayed by the hound, had I been there at his side that very moment, events might have gone differently. How differently, I cannot know. I only know fate had its hand on us. Because I was not there, Kevin took desperate action to slow the pursuit and give me time. He braced his back against a wooden support post, set one great boot against the tripod lampstand lighting the steps, and shoved. Startled, he caught his balance, surprised at how easily the top-heavy stand went over. Hot, burning oil spilled from the hissing bowl, splashing across the steps and onto the heads of men trapped between the raining oil and the press below—

Screams arose together with a ringing clash of iron and stone as the heavy bowl struck the edge of the steps and glanced off, jerking the iron chain linked to the next lampstand—

The second tripod wobbled uncertainly for an instant, then slowly pitched downward into the pit, pouring more flaming oil upon heads below—

No steps to deflect its fall, the lamp jolted hard on its link with next tripod—

I flattened breathlessly against the outer wall as the third lampstand, just in front of me, rocked abruptly and crashed over the ledge, deluging the hall again with hot oil—

The chain tugged at the next tripod—

—which began to tip—

By the time I reached Kevin nearly a third of the circle of oil-laden tripods had toppled; soot-stained tapestries burst afire, while men rushed the steps and slipped back, burning—

Lagos aflame, spitted to his chair, shrieked wildly, writhing—

Men attempted to scale the walls, Sividicus among them; the tapestry tore away, covered them over, and caught fire under a deluge of burning oil—

The Great Hall erupted into a shrieking, leaping Hell.

Stunned, I took in the relentless momentum of the toppling lamps. Kevin, too, stood transfixed. The warrior spirit lifted, the wild look gone, leaving him awe-struck before the devastation he wrought. His face ashen, the blue eyes stunned, he stared at the swift-falling circle of fire—

I peered into the choking black smoke and caught sight of the agent, his short cloak afire, struggling madly through the few survivors. He ripped the flaming cloak from him, staggering toward us just a step ahead of the falling tripods—

"Kevin, *there!* The agent!" I cried, grasping his sleeve and pointing into the fiery maelstrom—

Now Kevin saw him. He dropped to the edge of the pit and extended a long arm. In a desperate sprint the agent reached the wall just ahead of the oily rain and leapt. Kevin caught the agent's hand and pulled him from the pit an instant before the last two lamps toppled and engulfed the remaining tapestries, tables, and men in flames—

Searing heat and smoke drove the three of us back from the inferno. We stumbled choking and blinded through the doors— the minstrel supporting the falling agent—stumbled out into the blessedly cool night air. Collapsing on cold muddy ground, we knelt and stared at the renewed burst of flame roaring up the chimney of the Great Hall.

No more than a minute had passed since Kevin pushed over that first tripod. Now we heard nothing over the roar of the fire—no more screams from within. Silently, tremblingly, Valorian crossed himself. Then he was toppling. Kevin caught his fall and helped him lower to his elbow where he half lay in the mud. Both hands were badly burned along with one side of his face—half the long black hair and an eyebrow singed off. He gasped and shuddered, in great pain.

I wanted to help him, wished I could do something about his pain. I put out a hand to him, but thought better of touching his burns.

"My thanks, friend," I murmured inadequately.

"Aye," added Kevin. "Had you not cut me loose. . . ."

Valorian was made of stern stuff; he waved away our thanks. "I wondered . . . if my God ever called me . . . if He called on me to make a stand for Him, no matter the odds . . . no matter the risk . . . would I have the courage?" He looked from the minstrel to me, more triumphant than anything. "I did not fail Him."

"No," Kevin reassured him gently. "You did not fail."

Valorian closed his eyes, satisfied.

Then the eyes popped open in the ravaged face. "You are not free yet," he gasped, struggling to sit up. The minstrel helped him. "I have no authority . . . not here . . . not over the Keep . . . the captain . . ."

Indeed, we had forgotten. Now men streamed gawking and cursing from the common hall. We heard shouts of dismay and confusion as they beheld the Great Hall behind us spouting fire and black smoke.

"Go!" Valorian urged. "My horse—at the stables—I left orders—he should still be ready to ride—" The agent sank back to the ground, resting on his unburned side. "Take him!" he whispered hoarsely. "Go!"

"And leave you here?" I protested. "To them? No, you come with us!"

Valorian half smiled, half grimaced. "I cannot ride, little one. Nor will they kill an imperial agent. But if you stay, I cannot guarantee your lives." He rolled his eyes up to the minstrel. "Besides, *one* of us must remain to carry the Alamanni petition to the Emperor. Now—go quickly! Before 'tis too late!"

He was right. Men were coming toward the Great Hall, staring up at the fiery chimney. None as yet noticed us huddled at its base. Kevin squinted across the courtyard.

"The gates," he murmured. "We'll have to take the gate-house."

"I'll clear the gatehouse," I told him, rising painfully to my feet and pressing the bloody dagger into his hand. "You fetch the horse."

"No," Kevin argued, "'tis dangerous. Stay with me."

"There's no time," I argued back. "We need the gatehouse free." I started for the gates at a fast limp.

"*Dominic!*"

"I can do it!" I assured him over my shoulder. When I looked back he stood staring after me in exasperation. Then he raced for the stables.

I ran for the gates, pumping all the urgency I felt into my voice.

"*Fire!*" I screamed at the gatehouse. "*Fire!* The Great Hall burns!"

As I thought, both towers were unmanned, and the gatesmen,

likely huddling around a warm brazier, knew nothing of the fire as yet.

Doors to the gatehouses flew open on either side of the gates. Heads poked out and stared. The great round structure of the hall now smoked like a giant charcoal kiln.

"Fire brigade!" I gasped, staggering. "Roust a brigade! Fire's spreading!" Now I fell and rolled to my back, groaning, sprawled so my blood-splattered tunic reflected in their torchlight.

"*Fire!* I gurgled a last time, obviously done for.

The gatesmen thudded over me, abandoning me to my death throes. Behind them I rolled to my feet, invaded the nearest gatehouse, and laid both hands on the spoked wheel that controlled one of the heavy iron gates. A harsh clanging bell from above told me one of the gatesmen had run up the tower and was sounding an alarm—belatedly. He might be down the steps any moment.

Urgently I grasped a spoke above my head and pulled. My fingers slipped; I wiped them on my leggings and tried again. My slight weight would not turn a gatewheel normally handled by two full-sized men. I could not budge it. Desperately I ducked under the wheel, grasped a low spoke from the other side, and tugged upward with every ounce of muscle and sinew I could muster. The wheel moved—barely—and slowly gave way, quarter inch by quarter inch, to my tugs. I had neither the strength nor the weight. . . .

A pair of burned, blackened hands laid hold of the upper spokes. Through the soot and singed hair, I met the fierce grin of Valorian. He pulled with me, grimacing from the pain to his burned palms, and the gatewheel turned, shrieking as it picked up speed.

Boots clattered on the tower steps. The guard descended into the gatehouse.

"Who opens the gate?" he demanded.

"Christus Valorian, Agent Imperius!" snapped Valorian, never ceasing the turn of the wheel.

The gatesman looked at me, then back to the agent.

"By whose order?"

"My own!"

The gatesman strode two uncertain steps toward us. "Only Lagos can give that order!"

"You do *not* refuse the gates to an agent in the Emperor's service, soldier!" The wheel turned faster under his anger.

"But Lagos. . . ."

"*Lagos is dead!* I will have the gate! Return to your post or I'll have your hide as well!"

A ghastly sight the agent looked—sooted and scorched and a wild, pain-crazed grimace distorting his features. The gatesman clattered a hasty retreat up the steps.

Lagos is dead! Hearing the words spoken made it seem suddenly real.

"I have it now," Valorian told me as the wheel gave further. "Go and find your barbarian."

I let go a spoke and started away, but at the gatehouse door I paused and looked back.

"My thanks again," I told him.

"Go on!"

"What about you? . . ."

"I've a job to do! Go while it's still in my hands!" More softly he added, "And God speed."

He was right; there was no time. I left him pulling the wheel. Racing toward the stables, I crossed a yard in an uproar—fire, smoke, shouting men, an excited baying from the kennels, the neighing and stall-banging of agitated horses.

Suddenly, between me and the stables, loomed the hallmaster.

He caught sight of me and yelled for two running slaves. "Favius! Quintus!" He pointed a stubby finger at me. "The bug! Get him!"

They fanned out on either side of the hallmaster, and all three came at me. I had no hope of outrunning them, not with my short steps and burned feet. Yet if I stood still they would surround me in a trap of hands and legs. I backed away, trying to evade them—backed over something sticking just above the mud—very nearly tripped over an old metal barrel stave.

Desperately I clawed at the curved stave, rusted and crusty with mud, ripped it from the ground, and whipped it around in the close space between myself and the three men. It whistled a warning in the cold air. The space widened; warily they circled me.

"Kitchen rat," wheezed the hallmaster, still drunk, "you've got nowhere to run. This time you're mine."

Not if I could help it. I went for the hallmaster, whirling the stave rapidly, and sliced him across the knees. He howled and hobbled in a little dance, but I could not pursue him, for I was engaged in fending off the other two. Still, there was his hateful, swinish face watching for his chance through malicious, sunken eyes. I lunged for him again, slapping the stave across his big belly and immediately spinning to catch Favius just below the knees.

There we danced in the red glare of the burning hall. I could not break free; the stave was neither sharp enough nor heavy enough to incapacitate them.

"Catch him, you slugs!" the hallmaster spat.

But instead of waiting for the other two, I leapt after the hallmaster again, striking higher; if he was going to take me, I wanted it to cost him. I caught him sharp across the cheek with a gratifying smack. He squealed. Then the dance was over; the other two jumped me. Kicking and twisting and hanging on to the stave in fury and panic, I fought them uselessly. The hallmaster ripped the stave from my hands and whipped it back and forth in the air, testing it. He licked his lips.

"I'm gonna slice you up like pork roast, bug."

The two slaves hastily grasped my wrists and stretched as far away as they could without letting go. Dizzy with pain and exhaustion, I could not break their hold. The hallmaster flung back his whipping arm; I flinched, about to get my own back with interest.

Out of the din thundered galloping hoofbeats.

"*Dominic!*"

The hallmaster turned his head and the minstrel's staff struck him flat across the nose with all the force of a charging horse behind it. He dropped like a stone, gurgling in his own blood, his neck broken. The other two let go my arms and ran for their lives. I sank to the ground, but staggered to my feet again as Kevin wheeled a huge grey steed around.

By now we were being converged upon by running soldiers. Kevin circled the horse close and thrust down a hand for me. He swung me up on the saddle before him, where my fingers closed upon the saddle's edge and clasped on for dear life, for the horse kicked off with a jolt.

Holding onto me with one arm and wielding his staff with the other, Kevin flailed through the thin line of men, and we cantered toward the gates.

The iron gate was closing. I caught sight of Valorian leaning wearily in the gatehouse doorway; someone had indeed taken it out of his hands. The captain stood resolutely before the fast closing gate, a long lance in his hands. He turned the sharp lance to meet our charge.

"*Down!*" hissed Kevin, yet he himself sat upright, a target impossible to miss. For a horrifying moment I thought he would be impaled on the lance, but in the last split-second he swerved the horse and swept his staff upward with a battle-cry and a force that struck the lance aside and knocked the captain off his feet.

We were through the gate an instant before it resounded shut at our heels. We rode hard down the freshly cleared road lit faintly by clouded moonlight. When we had gone a few turns down the forest road, the minstrel pranced the grey steed in a circle, and we looked up the slope in astounded silence. Red billowing fire and black smoke roiled out of the ancient citadel, a horned demon's head roasting in its own pit of hellfire. Wordlessly we galloped on, until Lorrach Keep was nought but a blood-red glow above the mountain.

PART V

XXXIX

Something woke me—either the minstrel's low snores, the pale rosy light growing in the east, or the insistent call of nature. Quietly I rolled from beneath the minstrel's arm and the woolen cloak. I bit my lip and inhaled sharply, shaken by the burning in my feet, but I limped stiff-jointed between the outcroppings of rock that sheltered us. I heard only the stamp and snort of the big grey horse tethered nearby, covered with his blanket—that and a dawn wind playing through the trees. I shivered in the morning chill, but more from excitement than cold.

Stepping gingerly around a jumble of rock to do my business with nature, I sorted in my head the jumbled pictures of the night before. We had ridden hard half the night, first on the shadowy road down-mountain, then along a forested horsetrack running east. We stopped at whiles to listen in the still air, hearing only the frosty breath of the horse and our own heartbeats. By then the moon shone bright through the clouds to help us pick our way, and we rode on into the night until exhaustion and lack of moonlight forced us to take refuge here a few hours before dawn. Having only the minstrel's wool cloak for cover, we huddled together near the rocks and dropped into numbed sleep.

Now as I limped back to the little hilltop meadow between the rocks, the jagged fringe of light between mountain and sky shone with brilliance—the hidden sun burnished the peaks from beyond. Seconds later the sun's rim crowned the Earth with fire.

I breathed deeply of clean, crisp air, breathed freely for the first time in many, many months. With the sun came the realization—*I am free!* All my terrors, all the nightmares, were fallen behind me, destroyed in flame, while before me lay the glorious, beckoning Earth, and I was free to wander her as I will. I absorbed the vision, the fiery orange orb rising over the peaks, awakening to a new day the boundless world, illuminating her paths, the Earth all around me, vast and embracing.

My heart leapt in pure exhultation. I spread my arms wide to the rising sun, felt the warmth in my open palms and on my upturned face. Resurrected from memories half forgotten, in my head sang the paean to Apollo.

> O Apollo
> O bright brother
> Earth's burning lover
> Flame of life
> Shine forth from heaven into my heart
> Illuminate my mind
> Light my path with wisdom
> O Apollo
> O bright brother
> Fiery charioteer
> Shine the light of truth over all who dwell
> On Earth!

I dropped my arms and turned. The sun's rays turned the moist earth a rich golden brown and cast my shadow long before me, across the rock-sheltered hollow to the minstrel. He sat cross-legged, wrapped in his cloak, watching me with a bemused smile of affection and wonder, blinking into the new-risen sun that crowned my head.

I spread my arms again and burst into a joyous smile.

"I'm *free!*" I cried. "*We're* free!"

He grinned. "Aye."

"If not for you, Kevin—there are not words—how will I ever thank you?"

"The look on your face this morn, Dominic, is thanks enough—all the thanks I'll ever need."

Then I remembered. I hobbled toward him, fumbling at the side of my sash. Ah, it was still there.

"I have something of yours, minstrel." I handed him the runestone of oaths, friendship, and balance. Amazed, he turned the glittering white stone in the sunlight.

"Gyfu! How? . . .You've carried it with you?" Then he looked at me, awed. "Balance! And you walked that pole over the coals as though you were born to it! And I so feared . . ."

I grinned.

He tried to give me back the stone. "This rune is rightly yours, my friend—the rune and all it stands for."

"Aye, 'tis mine," I agreed, "but I carry it *here*." I tapped the shirt over my heart. "Your stone belongs with the others."

He nodded and replaced the runestone in the rabbit pouch as he spoke. "Best not be lingering too long this morning, lest they be ranging the hounds after us, though I think likely they won't. But first, let's have a look at your feet. How badly are they burned?"

The minstrel unwound the scorched bindings, and the pain was like fire all over again. Fortunately, the soles of my feet were not burned nearly so badly as they felt, though they were a mass of blisters. Rebinding my feet in the unburned portions of the cloth, Kevin nodded, satisfied.

"Water's best for burns. We'll clean them in the first stream we meet."

He turned his attention to the horse, removing its blanket, speaking to it softly.

"Ah, a fine steed you are—as bold and strong as Sleipner the Eight-Legged, and of a color of him, too—grey as a raincloud." The minstrel ran his hands along the horse's back. "Such a prize we've been gifted with, Dominic—a stallion worthy of Othinn, and by a worthy man, Valorian."

"I hope he's all right. He was hurting. . . ."

"Aye, I hope he recovers well from this, but it is as it is. 'Twas his weird, too, I ken." He stroked the horse's nose. "What shall we call you, who stormed the gates of Hell and brought us forth? Greystormer? What think you, Dominic?"

"Aye, Greystormer. 'Tis as noble and barbaric a name as I've ever heard."

I turned my attention to the saddle and pack that lay on the ground. We breakfasted on strong wine, hard bread, and sausage I found there. Valorian had provision for a day's journey in his pack, plus flint and shaved tinder. He also carried bandaging for wounds and a sack of barley and oats. Kevin poured half the grain on the ground for the horse. Then he opened his own vest and carefully peeled back the shirt. The wound in his side was not deep, protected as he was by the thick, hairy goat-hide, and it had crusted over and stopped bleeding on its own. He decided to leave it alone.

But his wrist, torn by the wolfhound, I insisted needed tending. The hound's fangs had clamped deep and worried and mangled the flesh; the wound was red-swollen and white-flecked. Kevin let me pour a good portion of the wine over it and bandage the wrist. While I did so he half grimaced, half laughed.

"Now I've a wolf-wound akin to Tyr's, though mine's not so grave, to be sure." Then he told me how twice the northern gods tried to bind Loki's get, the wolf Fenrir, in mighty chains, but that the great beast broke the chains both times. "So Othinn sent a messenger on eight-legged Sleipner underground to the realms of the dwarves, begging them for help. And such were the dwarves' skills that they fashioned a cord as light and slender as silk, wrought and bound with runes and magic. But when the gods bade the Fenriswulf to test his great strength against the soft cord, the wolf became suspicious. Fenrir would agree to the challenge only if one of the gods would place a hand between his jaws. And Tyr, the bravest of warriors, consented, placing his wrist in the fangs of the wolf. Then the gods bound Fenrir in the dwarves' silken cord, and the wolf tried to break his bonds. In his fierce struggles the wolf clamped tighter and tighter on Tyr's wrist and gnawed deeper and deeper into the flesh until even the bravest of the warrior-gods howled in agony. And when Fenrir realized he could not break free of the magic cord, he snapped through the bone in his fury, thus the Fenriswulf was bound, but Tyr lost his hand."

The minstrel grinned and flexed his fingers. "'Twas lucky for me the hound of Lorrach was not Fenrir, eh? And strange now I think on it, *both* wolfhounds were outdone by dwarves. You killed that hound yourself."

I shuddered. "Let's be on our way, minstrel. I want to be as far away from that place as quickly as we can."

Kevin agreed and saddled the horse he named Greystormer; he lifted me onto the saddle, then swung up behind. We traveled east, for that was where the trail ran, and we cared only to stretch the distance between ourselves and Lorrach Keep.

As we rode I pondered on the tale he had just told.

"Know you much of dwarves, Kevin?"

"'Tis hard to say. I know many, many tales and songs of the olden dwarves, but I never heard tell of anyone who had the knowing of any dwarf. Sooth, when I stumbled over *you*, Dominic, face to face in a Roman fortress, why, I did wonder if the blizzard was not confounding my eyes and conjuring up dreams."

"Were you not disappointed, minstrel, to find me just an ordinary dwarf?"

"Ordinary?" Now he laughed deep in his chest. "You speak of an impossibility, or one of your paradoxes—an *ordinary dwarf.*"

I laughed with him, just because I felt so gloriously free this morning. "Not a magical dwarf, I mean—not as in your old tales."

"Truth, I was relieved, more like. If the tales be true, the olden dwarves were a grim and surly breed, full of trickery and not of a temper to befriend a man." Now I heard the grin in his voice. "But *ordinary* dwarves, I ken, are more agreeable folk."

"Aye," I nodded sagely. "A bit like ordinary *giants* from the northern wilds."

Eventually the trail we followed worked its way southeasterly so that we found ourselves on a ridge overlooking the Rhine. The path took us over rocky ground, the river to the south with distant alpine peaks beyond, the vast and mountainous Black Forest to the north. Just below us ran another horsetrack, likely Lorrach Keep's road for quick access to the bridges above Rauraci and Vindonissa—so we stood with garrisons to east and west, the wilds at our backs, the Empire before us. Between us and Roman soil, however, ran the Rhine, swift, deep, and icy cold.

"Which way, Dominic? We ought to be deciding where we're going."

"Are we not running to the wilds?"

"'Tis a possibility. We ought to be looking for a river crossing, though, if we need it."

"You thinking of going back into the *Empire?*"

He turned to look behind us where the clouds were greying up again over the northern hills. A cold, damp wind swept downmountain from the north.

"I'm not thinking of riding into *that,*" he said. "I've had enough cold and wet these last few weeks for a lifetime. Nor have we proper shelter or provision for it. 'Twill make a chilling, miserable journey. What of south?"

"Maxima Sequanorum. Fairfax is governor—Lagos's brother-in-law. 'Twould be risky."

"If you'd rather not . . ."

"If 'tis my *preference* you're wanting, minstrel, I'd *prefer* to be sailing the warm Aegean Sea, thank you, instead of freezing here on the northern borders. But if 'tis my *choice* I'd go south and west, where we might at least find shelter and a fire—though the roads could be dangerous."

Kevin snorted. "Roman roads have never been anything *but* dangerous. Has never worried me overmuch."

"I'll bet not," I grinned. "I've one question, though. I'm wondering just how you're expecting to cross the river. I'm not swimming it, you know." I gazed down to the swift, cold water; chunks of ice raced downstream.

"Nor I. We've only to follow the river east; eventually we'll strike a bridge the Alamanni spoke of."

"A *bridge!* Minstrel, you *are* mad. Think you the Roman army will let us trot across their bridge easy as you please?"

"Maybe," mused Kevin. "Maybe not." He urged Greystormer down toward the horsetrail. "We'll see."

The bridge lay further upriver than we imagined; we did not reach it that day. The horsetrail veered away from the river, and by nightfall rain was upon us, so we spent a chilling, miserable night anyway. The next day was no better, for our scant provisions were gone and we journeyed in a cold, grey drizzle most of the day, gloomily facing another night without dry wood for fire. But late afternoon, in pouring rain, we at last struck a ruined Roman highway laid down two centuries ago when these lands beyond the Rhine were part of the old Empire. We followed the road south, and at eventide, in a black thunderstorm, we approached a bridge guardhouse. We stopped well clear of the dim light from the guardhouse shutters and peered into the gloom, searching for a guard on the bridge. I sneezed, as I had taken to doing frequently as the day waned, but the steady torrent of rain drowned the sound.

"This isn't going to work, you know," I said, wrapping the cloak tighter in front of me. The both of us sheltered in the minstrel's black cloak, though neither we nor the horse under us saw any hope of ever being dry again.

"If you keep quiet, 'twill work," Kevin told me.

"Suppose they make us dismount, eh? Then they'll see 'tis a lie."

"Suppose they're already on the lookout for a dwarf?"

"Suppose they're not? If you tell them I'm a child and they see you've lied, why, you might as well announce we're on the run."

"But if 'tis a dwarf they're looking for—"

Kevin's words were lost in a staccato of brilliance as lightning etched the scene before us, followed immediately by crackling thunder. I blinked. The narrow bridge spanning the river gorge had appeared and disappeared quickly, but long enough to see it was deserted and that no guard stood under the bridge-house portal. They must all be inside, taking refuge from the worst of the storm.

Kevin urged Greystormer forward, and the skittish horse stepped carefully onto the barely distinguishable bridge. We reached about midway, and lightning flared suddenly all around us, casting the empty bridge, parapets, and sleeting rain in stark light. Greystormer neighed sharply and reared in fright, but deafening thunder swallowed the sound. Kevin brought the wild-eyed horse under control and encouraged him on with calm words.

"*Thor* and *Tyr*," I heard the minstrel swear. "Temper your help with a little *sense*."

Indeed, the gods of thunder and lightning were with us, for all guards at this end, too, had evidently taken refuge from the height of the storm. A series of flashes revealed a fortress up the hill, then abandoned it to the black night. We rode on in freezing rain and took shelter in the trees only when it thickened to hail; half an hour later we took the road again, for doomed as we were to wet and cold, we might just as well be getting somewhere.

And so it was we came late—drenched, chilled, weary, and hungry—to a lonely inn and post at a crossroads. We had come a good ten miles and then some, I reckoned, from the border to the highway crossing. The rain had let up some, and the homey smell of woodsmoke drew us in. Fearing word might have come this far of a barbarian giant and dwarf who burned down Lorrach Keep, first we sheltered beneath a tree where the minstrel doubled the length of his heavy, wet cloak over me and pinned the ends together with the brooch. I pulled the hood low over my face, and we approached the stables. Two coppers to the stableboy assured Greystormer of a rubdown and feed—the minstrel having some few coins in his belt—and we entered the inn.

I closed the cloak around me. Even doubled it dragged the floor, and I struggled under the weight of it. My heart racing, I tried to walk like a weary child instead of a weary dwarf and let Kevin's hand on my shoulder guide me to the fire, for I could see nought but the floor and my muddy toes. The inn seemed quiet and near deserted on this dreary night. As we stood before the welcome fire, I let the heat billow into the cloak and stealthily warmed my hands. Ah, it felt good.

"Something hot, I bid you," said Kevin, propping his staff against the hearth, "for two cold travelers."

I sneezed.

"There's stew and mull," answered a voice that must be the innkeeper's. "I can warm milk for the lad."

Kevin knelt beside me, warming his hands.

"Milk for the both of us—and stew. 'Tis damnable cold and wet out. Not seasonable for these parts is it?"

"Aye, for this time of year. Has been an uncommonly cold winter, but we get the spring rains."

The innkeeper called into the kitchen for hot stew and milk. He asked nothing of our business, asking not being considered polite, but he expected to hear it, I knew, not talking being considered equally impolite. The minstrel knew it, too. He stood, warming his backside, attempting to dry out.

"We've relations out east. Had to take the boy once anyway. You know how they love to see the grandchildren."

The innkeeper made a noncommittal sound. "That'll be twelve denarii."

"What? Twelve?"

"Eight for the meals—twelve if you're staying the night."

"Aye," grumbled the minstrel, "'tis stay or drown." He fumbled at his belt, examined his few coins, and passed one over.

"*Well! Argenti!*" the innkeeper exclaimed, suddenly cheery. "Breakfast in the morning. Have a seat, gents. The wife'll be right out with your supper." He bustled off to the kitchen.

One table near the fire was occupied by two guests—I could see their boots—so we took the other. I clambered onto the bench with Kevin's help, the cumbersome cloak being difficult to manuever, and sat with my back to the company.

Taking the bench across from me, Kevin muttered, "I'm accustomed to singing for my supper—not paying for it."

I sneezed in reply. The other two guests resumed talking, having taken the measure of us. Barbarian though he be, the minstrel came unarmed, spoke good Latin, paid in argenti—and he traveled with a child besides. That was civilized enough for anybody in these borderlands.

I looked at Kevin. Soaked, cold, and weary, he had come away from Lorrach with only his staff, a few coins, and another man's horse. Everything else—his pack, his bearcoat, and his lute—he left behind. Possibly we were hunted men, and here we sat in an imperial inn and post, yet Kevin grinned at me and winked. I drew a steadying breath, trying to absorb some of his confidence, and winked back.

Soon came the innkeeper's wife, her plump hands setting a platter on the table between us. The platter held two bowls of savory-smelling stew that made my mouth water and two generous chunks of hardbread.

"Here you are, gentlemen—hot stew to take the chill off. 'Tis a sorry night to be traveling, especially with a little one—my Helena has warm milk for you, lad." The goodwife chatted on, placing a bowl, spoon, and bread before each of us, while a girl plunked steaming mugs of milk at hand. "We so seldom have children at the post, why, my girl's grown half her life without another child, except—"

She broke off abruptly, then went on in a softer tone, "Except her brother. He died of a fever winter before last. Not much bigger than your own boy, my Timian was." She paused a moment, remembering. Then her voice was brisk.

"You ought to pull that wet cloak off the lad or he'll catch a fever himself. Here, I'll get it." Her busy hands came at the brooch and instinctively I pulled away.

The minstrel caught her wrist. "Leave him be," he said levelly. "He's fine."

"Fine?" The goodwife was indignant. "Maybe now! He won't be if you leave him in that wet cloak."

"I don't want him catching a chill, woman."

"That's just what I'm trying to prevent, you big, ignorant—"

"Leave him be!"

"Oh, very well! Do as you will!" She snatched her hand free. "Come, Helena, we'll leave the *gentleman* to his supper."

I had been working hard to suppress a sneeze; now it exploded loudly.

"Sounds to me he's caught a chill already, and no wonder, with you to take care of him. Where's his mother?"

The minstrel stared at her in exasperation. "*Home*, madam, which is where I'm taking him. Now if you'll kindly leave us in peace—"

We were saved by another patron arriving, wet and stamping, shaking the rain off his cloak. The man was greeted by one of the guests; they knew one another, and he joined them at table. While the innkeeper's and goodwife's attentions revolved around the newcomer, Kevin and I devoured our supper. But our interest soon shifted to their conversation.

"Aye, I'm not on the road in this weather for a lark. I've news all right—news to reach the border posts immediately."

"Give, man! What is it?"

"Lorrach Keep has fallen."

"What? Alamanni?"

"No, not them. There was no attack, but the Great Hall burned and collapsed into a smoking heap of rubble, Count Lagos and his two hundred equestrians inside it—roasted alive."

There passed a moment of stunned silence.

"Without an *attack?*"

"By *accident?*"

"'Twern't no mucking *accident*. The infantry captain swore it was done by a giant Saxon and a dwarf, who then stormed the gates and escaped."

One of the men broke into fits of laughter. "*One* Saxon," he wheezed, "and *one* dwarf, you say, burned down Lagos's Keep and breezed away. Ah, that's rich, that is!"

"Were I that captain," chimed the other, "I'd not admit it if it *were* true. I'd blame the Alamanni, I would."

"He should've," the messenger agreed. "He'll lose his post, likely. Anyway, there's word to be on the lookout for a barbarian and a dwarf, though I'd lay odds they're long gone into the wilds by now. Besides, the only survivor who was witness to what really happened is an imperial agent, and he swears 'twas no fault of those two the hall burned; he swears 'twas the left hand of God brought down Lorrach."

"Hoo! This is richer all the time. First a giant and a dwarf, and now Almighty God!"

The men's laughter was interrupted sharply by the goodwife. "And who's to say it wasn't Almighty God? I've heard evil doings of the Count of Lorrach—tortures and such."

The messenger answered her wryly. "Madam, if that's all it took to rouse God's ire, he'd have destroyed the Roman Empire long before now."

"This deals us a blow at that," said one of the others, "if the Alamanni get wind of this."

"*If?* They're bound to know already. The fire was seen clear down to Basilia and Rauraci. We saw the glow of it, red as blood, from Vindonissa. We didn't hear what happened until late today, and I'm up to the lines to alert the forts. There'll be a cohort behind me tomorrow to strengthen the frontier just in case the Alamanni move on this."

Kevin and I had bent to our meal and listened closely, exchanging glances at whiles. Valorian survived; we were glad to hear it and not surprised he took our part and put God's hand in it. Word was traveling up and down the highways to watch for a barbarian giant and a dwarf; I began to think we were fools for being here. The discussion of a possible Alamanni attack roused the minstrel's ire, I could tell, but he held his peace; it would be pure folly to draw their attention in our direction.

"Eh?" The minstrel looked up. The messenger had spoken to him.

"I asked which road were you traveling? Did you see signs of the fire night before last?"

Kevin looked blank and shook his head.

"Not him," interjected the innkeeper. "He came east. Where did you say your kin lived?"

Kevin looked even blanker. By now I knew my friend's knowledge of the Empire's geography was hazy at best. I sneezed loudly.

"Raetia," I whispered.

He bent to me. "Eh?"

"*Raetia.*"

"Ah, bless you," he said, patting my shoulder. He looked up and cupped a hand behind one ear. "What is it you're wanting?"

The innkeeper spoke louder. "*Where* out east did you say?. . .'"

"I didn't," Kevin said gruffly. "*Raetia,* if you're making it your business. What's this about a fire? Something burn?" He waited, hand poised behind his ear.

"Aahh!" the innkeeper rasped with impatience. "Never mind!"

Kevin shrugged and bent to his stew. I grinned beneath the hooded cloak, and the corners of his beard twitched.

Conversation at the table behind me resumed, but I was losing its drift. The warm milk, hot stew, and cozy fire were making me sleepy, and I began to realize how tired I really was, so tired it seemed all I could do to sit on the bench. Almost without my knowing, my head sank to my arms and I leaned upon the edge of the table. I never knew I slept until Kevin's voice startled me awake.

"Madam," he said, "if you've a bed for us, we'll take it now. My boy's asleep in his supper."

"And no wonder," the goodwife scolded, "keeping the little

mite late on the road on a night like this. You should've stopped at Turicum, or didn't you come that way?"

"Eh?"

"Oh, follow me! I'll take you up to the room." Then muttering, thinking the barbarian could not hear, she added, "Great ignorant lout that you are, you likely brought the lad along Brigantium way."

"Eh?"

"Come along!"

I had slid from the bench, dragging the doubled cloak, and navigated to the bottom of the stairs, but now I peered up at the goodwife's skirts disappearing up the steps. I despaired of ever reaching the landing, much less the top. Weariness, the weight of the cloak, and my blistered feet were going to betray me. I took the first step and nearly stumbled.

"Come on, kit," I heard Kevin's hearty voice behind me. "You're asleep on your feet. Up you go!" He swept me up, and before I could swallow my surprise we were halfway to the landing.

There were times in my life when I would have objected angrily, declaring I could climb stairs as well as anyone, thank you. But at this moment I was simply grateful. I sighed my relief and thankfully gave up the climb to my friend. He carried me to the top of the stairs and down a narrow hallway dimly lit by the goodwife's lamp. She stopped at a low doorway through which the minstrel had to stoop and carefully maneuver himself, his staff, and me. He set me on my feet in a tiny room containing one straw mattress with coarse wool blankets—army issue—and a chamber pot.

"I'll knock for breakfast in the morning." The goodwife raised her lamp to light another one attached to the wall. "Mind you don't leave the lamp burning all night."

"Thank you, madam, but no breakfast for us. If you'd pack us a day's provision instead, I can pay."

"Right." She paused, then her tone was sharp. "You're only deaf when you want to be, aren't you?"

"Ah, no, it comes and goes. Something with the pitch of voice, I expect."

"I expect. You'll get that damp cloak off the lad if you've a brain in that head. Goodnight."

She closed the door, but as I was working at the brooch on

424

the cloak, she opened it again and poked her round face into the room.

"And no fires in the room, mind you, or you're out."

This time we listened for her footsteps retreating down the hall.

"Do you think they guess?" I murmured, flinging off the heavy cloak.

"No, I think not. They see what they're accustomed to see. No good worrying over it anyway. I'm for bed, now we've a proper one."

"And *dry*," I agreed. I sneezed twice in rapid succession. Indeed, I was shivering; the room was cold and not about to improve without even a charcoal brazier for heat. We doubled the blankets and I collapsed into the prickly bed while the minstrel removed his damp vest and boots. Bolting the door, he then leaned the chamber pot precariously against the door.

"If anyone *does* try coming through that door," he growled, snuffing the lamp and crawling under the blankets, "they'll make a muck of a noise doing it."

Now we heard a clomping of several pairs of boots in the hall. The footsteps passed our door; we heard the innkeeper's voice and doors opening and closing. A lone set of steps passed back by our room toward the stairs. The inn gradually quietened as the other guests settled in, until the only sound a steady rain pelting the roof.

"That's it, then. If they were thinking of arresting us they wouldn't be waiting 'til morning." The minstrel sighed; his words drifted. "I'm for sleeping . . . while we've a chance."

"Aye." Sleep had not come easily to me for more than a year. Only when overwhelmed with exhaustion would I let go my vigilance and fall into nightmare, often awakening to an even worse horror than stalked my dreams. But now I found myself sinking easily into increasing depths of darkness, sinking past every thought of whether we would be found out in the morning, sinking beyond any fear of lurking dreams, sinking into peaceful childhood memories of a cheery inn, cozy hearthfire, and sleeping in my papa's arms as he carried me upstairs.

No one tried the door in the night, and we slept overlong; we did not awaken until startled by the goodwife's rap on the door and call to breakfast. Hastily we made ready to go downstairs, for she was calling the other guests, too, and we wished to be away before they came down for breakfast. The minstrel doubled his cloak over me in near darkness, for dawn was just beginning to lighten the shutters, and we hurried down the stairs. The goodwife met us at the bottom step with a large, bulging sack.

"Here's your provisions. There's plenty for two day's travel, and your breakfast is in there, too. See you feed the boy soon; he shouldn't go empty with a cold."

"I will, madam. How much for the victuals?"

"Not a copper. You paid plenty last night. Here, lad, your cloak's slipping; let me set it right." She was quick, kneeling before me, her cheery face on a level with mine. She tugged the cloak forward over my shoulders. "You haven't a fever have you this morning?" With a quick movement she whisked the hood back from my head.

She gasped, and for a moment the two of us stared eye to eye, one as stunned as the other.

"Why you're not—!" Her surprised exclamation broke off.

I stared, dismayed.

A sound on the stairs above broke our locked gazes. Three pairs of regulation boots descended toward the landing. I glanced at Kevin; his grip tightened on the staff. My eyes came back to the woman kneeling before me, and I saw it all come together in her expression: a child who was not a child, a barbarian, Lorrach Keep burned.

The goodwife moved first. Just as the three men reached the landing she pulled the hood up over my head and straightened it busily.

"Why, you're not . . . not fevered at all this morning, are you, lad?" I could feel her fingers trembling. "Now mind you keep your ears covered or the wind will give you another chill."

She looked up at the speechless barbarian. "Lucky for you, sir, taking a child out in that rain. He could've caught his death,"— she rose to her feet and added sadly—"like my own did. Well, that's neither here nor there. Today looks to be clearing already."

The three men reached the bottom step and passed us with little more than a glance.

"I could chat all morning, but I know you're itching to be off home. Goodbye, lad." She patted me on the shoulder and turned me firmly around, shooing us out the side door. She came out behind us, pulling the door shut.

"Look there." She pointed up mountain. "If you follow that path, you'll come to a grotto and a statue of the Holy Mother. East and west from that shrine runs another high path as far in either direction as you'll need—well past Vindonissa if you're going west. 'Twill be safer than the highway."

I pulled back the hood a little and peered up at her. "Our thanks, madam, for your help—for keeping our secret."

"Aye," added Kevin. "It could mean our lives."

"Shoo! Get on with you," she fussed, "before those in there think about it." She looked at me. "If they wonder, I'll tell them 'tis a bonnie lad you are, and 'tis no lie if I forget to mention how old a lad. Off with you now—God bless." With that she disappeared into the inn.

We collected Greystormer from the stables and climbed the path pointed out by the goodwife. It wound high up the mountain beneath rain-washed trees. The spring storm had passed, leaving the Earth fresh and redolent with that smell of Heaven—or what Heaven will smell like if *I* have any say in it—and the dripping evergreens aglow with the morning sun.

We entered a hushed grove, and in a rock cleft stood a statue of the Holy Mother, Mary with the infant Christ playing at her feet. I knew she was Mary because her robe was painted blue, and bronze halos had been added to the stone, crowning both mother and infant.

But I knew well that before the statue had become Mary and Jesus, it had represented Isis and the infant Horus, for I could see where the wheat-bud crown had been chipped off the goddess's head. Likewise, her right hand, raised in benediction, showed remnants of an object chipped away, likely the sistrum on which music sacred to Isis is played. In her left hand she still carried a pitcher of water, nature's milk, while at her feet the infant Horus played with a cornucopia, spilling forth the Earth's fruits in abundance for humankind. He pressed one finger to his lips, reminding worshippers of the secret of their true natures, symbol of his soul's innocence, forever pure and holy in this life and the next.

Behind me in the saddle, Kevin, too, gazed long at the statue, the slanting rays of the morning sun dancing upon the serene face and glancing off the bronze halo.

"*Mother of Life,*" I heard him whisper.

"Aye. Mother of Life. She has been with us."

427

And in the hush of that green grove I made my peace with Isis. A short while later the minstrel silently headed Greystormer onto the western path, and we climbed to the high meadows under sky of a blue to rival a barbarian's eyes.

The country crowds attending the spring festival attracted many a disreputable character to the provencial Alpine town of Lausanna and I'll not deny the minstrel and I looked to be two of the most disreputable characters of the lot. Fair-goers gave us a wide berth as they passed.

"Kevin, don't smile. They think you're snarling."

"I am snarling. You said I should look formidable, didn't you?"

"Formidable, yes—not like you are about to eat them alive. We want someone to hire you, not set the city guard on us."

Kevin sighed, shifted his feet, and leaned on his staff. "Truth be known, I'd as soon not be hired. Guarding goods is not my kind of work, and I like to pick my own scrapes, if I'm going to get into them."

I sighed, too, and leaned against the wall we rested beside. "What do you suggest, then?"

He shook his head. "I wish I had a lute—or a harp."

"Aye." I gazed across the colorful, noisy square, where the spring market was in full force. Luck had been with us so far. Two merchants had already paid Kevin in trades-goods to accompany them and their wagonload of wares through bandit-infested Alpine passes. They figured one look at the barbarian giant guarding their wagon would discourage anybody with half a brain, which it usually did, and those few foolish enough to tangle with the barbarian had their skulls cracked for their efforts.

Now we found ourselves in Lausanna with no coin and only a few trinkets in wages; we spent our last denarii to stable and feed Greystormer. Stabling and feeding ourselves was another problem.

"What we need is to look more respectable," I mused.

The minstrel toyed with a green glass-inlaid filagree necklace, one of the remaining pieces he had received for guarding the wares. He perched it atop his head, where it winked and glittered like a barbaric crown.

"'Tis royalty I'll be taken for, eh?"

"Not likely. Not without a bath, anyway."

"I was meaning *Dane* royalty. No bath needed for that."

"If that's the royal condition in Denmark, you look about as royal as a man can get."

Kevin sniffed speculatively at me. "You'd be a bit of high rank yourself, I expect."

I grinned. "Lord Duke at least. Let's put that necklace to good use."

We traded it for a bath, not in the public bath house, but in the back room of an inn where folk could buy a hot bath with peppermint oil for five coppers—or a green glass necklace. Ah, it was luxury to wash the grime out of my hair with vinegar and then rinse it in peppermint. I soaked in the tub and watched sunlight from the shutters dance on the water.

Later, with lazy interest, I watched the minstrel tangle with his thick mane of hair, which turned golden as it dried. He trimmed his beard, then braided the forward strands of his hair into two thick ropes that framed his face. Now he truly did look like barbarian royalty.

We traded a pair of tiny bronze earrings for two spicy meat pies at a market stall. Then we wandered the crowded squares and forums like sightseeing provencials, until the minstrel was drawn to a stall of rare musical instruments. He asked to see a long-necked lute of polished walnut and turned it lovingly in his hands under the vendor's watchful eye.

"Let's buy it," I said at his elbow.

He shook his head. "You know we haven't enough."

Reluctantly, gingerly, he returned the lute to the vendor and turned away, shrugging his broad shoulders resolutely. Watching him wander on down the stalls through the crowd, I toyed with the brooch I had thought to keep—a cast-bronze fox head with amber eyes—the finest piece of the lot. I unclasped it and, rising to tiptoe, plunked it on the counter.

"For the lute," I said.

The tradesman examined the brooch critically and set it on his scale. "Not enough."

"The eyes are amber," I pointed out.

"This is my rarest instrument."

"And my rarest brooch. Perfect down to the whiskers. You'll not find another like it."

"And you'll not find another lute, either. All the way from Arabia it comes." He passed back the brooch. "No."

"Now see here," I argued. "How many folk do you think you'll find who can play the damn thing, anyway?"

"Plenty. Music festival starts in a week. Musicians are pouring in already."

"Are they?" I mulled over this piece of information. "They'll be buying instruments, too, will they?"

"They will."

"I'll warrant not one of them can play the lute as rarely as my friend."

He shrugged. "I'm not a patron of the arts; I'm in trade—for profit. Now off with you if you've nothing better to offer."

I turned away. The vendor was right; the lute was worth more than ten brooches. I stared thoughtfully up and down the street, the morning throng humming and haggling, tradesmen hawking their wares. I turned back to the music stall.

"Hey!"

"*You* again?"

"I've a better offer."

The vendor sighed.

"Suppose, just suppose my friend—who plays the lute like Orpheus in a dream—suppose my friend were to set up in front of your stall every morning for, say, an hour, at peak market time, and play his best on that lute. You've plenty of competition in the music trade, I notice, but the crowd would be around *your* stall—I guarantee it. Suppose my friend did that for a week, and paid you half his take, too, in exchange for the lute?"

The vendor stared at me, considering.

"He's that good, is he?"

"He is."

"He'll have to prove it to me."

"He will."

"Make it *four* hours a morning for *three* weeks, from today through the end of festival, with half his take, and the lute's his."

"Throw in that vine-carved flute, and you've a bargain."

The vendor slapped his palm on the counter. "Done. Let's hear him."

I dashed through the crowd and grabbed a startled Kevin by the hand. "Kevin! Come on! Follow me!"

"What? Where?"

"Just come!"

I dragged him back to the stall, and the vendor handed the lute over the counter to me. I turned and thrust it into the minstrel's hands.

"Your lute, Kevin Dunskaldir."

He stared at the instrument in amazement, turning it over and over in his hands, then looked at me, dumbfounded.

"But . . . how? Dominic, how did you—?"

I grinned. "Just play it. 'Tis yours."

XL

 Kevin Dunskaldir and I tramped the mountains, the Alps in high summer, and if I loved their solitude before, I loved even better sharing them with my friend. In the beginning I rode Greystormer more than I walked, but quickly I regained the strength I had lost during my long imprisonment.

We occasionally dropped down to small villages and towns, but we spent our best times alone in the heights, stopping only by isolated huts or shepherds' camps. We were welcome most everywhere we went, bringing music and song, tales and conversation. Then the minstrel and I would jaunt back up the high paths with fresh provisions in Greystormer's packs.

The finest times were evenings the two of us spent near a campfire after a supper of hot wheatcakes, sausages, and wild mint brewed with cold stream water. I loved watching him play his lute in the ruddy glow of firelight, listening to his rich voice. Often I accompanied him on my vine-carved flute and we composed melodies together. We told each other innumerable tales; we talked much and laughed much and spent hours staring into the night sky, traversing the constellations, his and mine.

That summer, too, Kevin cut me a yew staff and spent a merry time teaching me the use of it, showing me how, with a stout staff and the proper skill, I could fell a man twice my height. He also taught me how to cut runes into the wood and stain them with my blood for added effect, but I put more faith in the practice than the runes and told him so.

Summer wheeled toward autumn, and we came down from the heights. A prize pair of ruffians, we looked, too, fit for nought but the wilds.

"Lake Brigantinus," I said as we overlooked the long, dazzling blue stretch of water set between snow-laced mountains like a rough jewel in a filligree brooch.

"There's Brigantium just below us." I nodded down-mountain to the town heaped at this end of the lake.

Kevin's eyes were drawn north. "Can't say I won't be relieved, somewhat, to be past the Empire's borders."

I looked past the lake to the northern ranges and wondered why I was quaking inside.

"I've never been anywhere outside the Empire," I murmured. "Never seriously thought of leaving it behind."

"Second thoughts, kit?"

"No. Of course not. I want to see your country. I *want* to see what lies outside the borders. 'Tis just a disconcerting feeling, leaving all I know of civilization behind."

The minstrel snorted. "Now 'tis different in my country, be sure, but I wouldn't go saying my folk aren't *civilized*."

I grinned. "You know what I mean, Kevin. Besides, if you're any indication, I have to wonder, don't I?"

He guffawed. "I hope you're not thinking my folk are as *Romanized* as I am! Rome to them, my friend, is a curious tale of misty lands best avoided. Why, these coins we carry are exotic jewelry where we're going, not currency of the realm."

That quaking inside was excitement, I realized.

"Let's go then, minstrel. I can hardly wait."

"We have to get through this lot first," he said, giving me a hand up on Greystormer's back and leading the horse over rocky ground. "There's more brigands, outlaws, and deserters in these parts than all the Empire combined, to hear folk talk. Be sharp on the lookout for me; your eyes are better than mine."

We followed on the high ridges above Brigantium, but eventually the trail dropped down into a long gorge and became a narrow, broken highway, the concrete crumbling, brush and bramble pushing up through jagged cracks, impassable for any but foot or horse. But the old road wound north and we were on our way to the wilds. The exhilarating late autumn nip in the air carried with it an excitement that added to my own. I pulled the hood of my green woolen cloak over my head and let Greystormer pick his way over the rubbled surface, following the minstrel, who jabbed his staff vigorously into the ground with each swing of his sturdy arm. Greystormer, not usually skittish, lifted his head, sniffed the air, and laid back his ears.

"What is it, Stormer?" I scarcely had time to wonder. The rock-strewn gorge on either side leapt out at us in the form of armed men. Ahead of us two mounted men appeared in the road. I spun Greystormer about; two more horses had closed behind us. One of the men on foot reached for the bridle, but I kept the grey turning and knocked the grasping hand away with a downward blow of my staff.

Kevin struggled toward me, but the brigands had conspired to cut us off from each other, for he was soon fending off two men on horse who circled him closely. Armed though they were with lances, they could not pass his whirring staff.

All this I saw in a blur. At least four brigands on foot tried to close in on Greystormer. It became obvious they wanted the horse. Two carried swords but seemed more intent on unseating me than running me through; perhaps with the hood concealing my face they thought I was a child, if a particularly dangerous one. I dealt one a blow aside the head and tried to ride another down.

If I could only reach Kevin, I thought desperately, he could possibly mount the big grey, and we could ride out of this. Kevin was holding his own but having to defend two sides at once as the horsed bandits encircled him. He forced a lance from one of the men's grasp and ducked under the horse's nose. At that moment a blade flashed at me. I struck at it, realizing too late it was a feint. A red cloak swirled up into Greystormer's eyes. The horse shied back and reared. I slid to the ground just aside the dancing hooves, rolled barely away with my life, but came up staff in hand, hood swept back, and charged the forelegs of a horse whose rider caught at Greystormer's reins. The horse danced out of the way, and someone kicked me hard in the ribs. I struck out wildly, but already Kevin had reached my side and dealt a return blow.

"*Hold!*" a voice rang off the walls of the gorge.

The band of rogues halted their circling attack. Kevin and I stood frozen, back to back, gripping our staves warily at ready. Then spoke a voice, husky with feeling—

"*Dominico?*"

Startled, I looked up at the dark-eyed brigand on the horse; he swept back his own hood, revealing raven-black hair.

"*Mikato!*"

The vagabond dismounted slowly, staring at me with dark pools of emotion.

"Sweet Isis!" he breathed. "Dominico!"

My heart stopped in my throat. Stunned, I stood unmoving as stone as he tentatively approached me. He never glanced at the barbarian giant at my side. His eyes held a haunted look—the look of a man in one instant facing the most yearned for moment of his life—and the most dreaded.

My heart started up again, pounding so hard my head spun. Mikato stopped five feet away from me and sank to his knees, never taking his eyes from my face. And I—I could not say what I felt beyond shock.

He wet his lips, and they trembled. "Dominico—'tis really you—you're really here—"

I found my voice, falling back into the familiar vagabond Greek. "Felicia," I said abruptly. "Is she all right?"

He smiled hesitantly, seeming relieved that I had words for him. "Aye, she is."

"And the babe?"

"He's a babe no longer. He's six years old."

I stared through him, whispering to ghosts in the past. "Then . . . 'twas not all for nought."

For a long space silence hung between us. Mikato swallowed; his voice was hoarse. "Dominico, I feared I would never see you again . . . I feared I would never have the chance to say to you how sorry I am . . . how terrible a thing I did. . . ."

"*Sorry?*" I was incredulous. "Do you know what you did to me?"

"Aye," he whispered. "I know."

"Do you?" I took a deep breath to steady my voice, but it did not help. "I *trusted* you, Mikato—I trusted you with my *life,* and you sold it out from under me!"

Tears glistened in the dark eyes. "*I know!*" he repeated, anguished.

My voice dropped to a whisper. "How could you do that to me?"

Now the tears ran down his face. "I didn't know what else to do! I had to do *something!*"

"I understand *why!* 'Twas the *way* you did it. I'd have done *anything* for Felicia—*anything!* You knew that. You didn't think enough of me to come to me and say, 'Dominico, I've found a solution—would you be willing?' No, you stooped to *treachery* and broke my heart in the bargain!"

Mikato stared at me, grey faced. "You would've done it? You would've been willing?"

"*Yes* . . . maybe . . . *I don't know!* I'll never know!" Now I was near tears. "You never gave me the chance to find out."

"Oh, gods," he said brokenly. "Don't you know—I'd give anything if I hadn't done it, Dominico?"

I smiled fleetingly. "So would I."

His head bowed.

"What in Isis's name did you tell Felicia? That I fell off the pier and drowned?"

He shook his head and looked at me with stricken eyes. "I told her you hired out with a professional troupe, and that they were set to sail for Greece that very day." His words became barely audible. "I said you took your pay in advance and sent it for her, along with your love."

I swallowed hard. "You *would* have to make me sound so noble. And when I never returned? *Shipwreck,* mayhap?"

"I told her the truth."

"So noble of *you,* too."

"She guessed something was wrong. . . . She heard me crying for you in my sleep."

My stare was unflinching. "No one was there to hear *me* cry."

He met my eyes, tears flowing freely. "No matter what you think of me, Dominico, my heart is overjoyed to see you. I've prayed a thousand times over that you would come to no harm and that I might one day see you again, if only to hear how much you hate me. Now I have heard." He bent his head in defeat. "I expected no more. There were times I prayed that you might even forgive me just a little. For a moment I hoped . . . a fool's hope. . . ."

I heard the despair in his voice. Looking at his bowed head, I knew, despite what I may have felt those many years ago, I did not hate him now. Truth be known, my heart was overjoyed to see him, too. I approached him softly.

"Mikato."

He shook his head.

"Cousin."

He responded to that, raising startled eyes to mine.

"How do you know I wouldn't forgive you? You never asked me."

The uncertainty in his eyes questioned mine.

I half smiled. "You know I couldn't stay angry with you forever."

Slowly he reached out and touched my face with trembling fingers.

"*Cousin*," he whispered. Then he flung his arms around me and held tight and we embraced as we had both wanted to do all along.

Moments later Mikato grasped my shoulders and held me at arm's length, his dark eyes drinking in the sight of me, looking me over wonderingly.

"No, I am not dreaming this time," he said. "'Tis you, all grown up now—and bearded! How wild you look, Dominico! Like a—" He stopped midthought and raised his eyes to the blond barbarian giant leaning on his tall staff and watching us with a broad grin on his face.

Indeed, the whole band of brigands watched, pleasure and curiosity in their faces. How many understood our conversation in vagabond Greek I could not guess. I knew Kevin did not, but I knew from the look on his face he had no need of words to understand what was happening.

I grinned. "Like a barbarian, you were going to say?" I spoke now in the Latin tongue so that the minstrel might understand. "This is my good friend Kevin Dunskaldir, lute player and rune reader, singer of songs and teller of tales."

Mikato came to his feet, staring up at the barbarian towering over him. "And fighter at staves," he smiled, rubbing his arm, "as I've just learned from experience."

"Kevin this is my cousin Mikato, as I know you've guessed—vagabond, acrobat, juggler, and now bandit, if *our* experience is any indication."

Kevin put out a hand gravely, but his lively eyes belied his serious face as he gripped the vagabond's smaller hand. "This means, I hope, you'll not be stealing our horse."

Mikato looked surprised, then indignant—then sheepish. "Oh, no, no, *no!* Had I known it was Dominico—!" He turned to me as if still not quite believing his eyes. "Felicia will be so happy—I cannot wait to see her face when she sees you, Dominico!" He waved his arms to encompass the bandits. "We will celebrate tonight, my friends! Dominico is home! Give them back their horse! Do we steal from family?"

An awed young bandit gave Greystormer's reins over to the minstrel, and Mikato introduced his motley band of brigands. There were eight of them, an odd mixture of every blood found in this part of the Empire; they acknowledged us warmly as Mikato spoke their names. Clearly he was their leader—I suppose he could be nothing else—pulling a scattered lot of outlaws and refugees into a close-knit clan and making them one people. He had grown to manhood and was now the image of Ronaldo.

We mounted up, only four of the bandits riding, the rest vanishing into the trees on foot. We followed single file, Kevin and I on Greystormer, Mikato's black horse ahead of us, and left the road for a brushy mountain trail.

I let Greystormer fall behind a little and leaned back, speaking quietly to the minstrel.

"Kevin, do me a favor, will you? If it should come up, say nothing of what 'twas really like at Lorrach."

"Be sure, I won't."

I nodded. "'Twould grieve Felicia."

"And Mikato, do I ken?"

"Aye," I smiled, "and Mikato."

"They will guess, kit."

"Ah, but their guesses will never come near the truth, imagine what they will. Mikato has suffered guilt enough, and Lorrach Keep was none of his doing."

Kevin leaned suddenly forward, ducking a low tree limb, swept his cloak around me and closed his large hands over mine at the reins.

"You've come home, Dominic," he murmured, "as you've always wanted."

"You don't think I'm going to stay, do you?"

"I'm wondering."

"*Mother Life!* And leave you to go off to the northlands without me, you great barbarian?"

His grip on my hands tightened. "I was hoping not. I've never imagined either one of us settling down to a life of banditry."

I laughed. "Too respectable for the likes of us, eh? We'll just stay a few days. We've time for that at least—has been so long since I've seen them."

"Time? Are we in a hurry, master dwarf?"

"We didn't want to be journeying north in the dead of winter, remember?"

"Denmark will be there when we get there, my friend. Spring's better traveling anywise, I'm thinking."

I grinned. "You do the thinking from now on, Kevin. I seem to be forgetting how."

Deep in the hills we approached a protected valley snuggled between rocky cliffs. At first glance the only hints that it was occupied were an empty corral, a cluster of goats, and some folk tending a large cookfire. A few children with armloads of wood scurried out of the trees to follow us; once-bright clothes fluttered on a line; now people seemed to be materializing out of the very hillside until I looked closer and spied a half-hidden cave entrance—and then another.

"Hie! Felicia!" cried Mikato, leading us up a sloping ledge above which was still another opening in the rock. "Felicia, come see our booty, woman! I've a surprise for you!"

She appeared suddenly, further up the ledge, her dark eyes blinking in the sunlight and alighting uncertainly on the barbarian astride the big grey.

"A friend, love," Mikato said gently.

Her eyes fastened on me. Grinning, I swung a leg over Greystormer's neck and dropped to the ground. Her hand leapt to her heart, and she uttered a small cry of near anguish. Then grabbing up her skirts, raven hair flying, Felicia came running.